As Passionate as the Burning Sands
He Ruled

THE SHEIKH
who Desired Her

Three exotic and thrilling books by
three terrific authors:

Abby Green
Jennifer Lewis
Tessa Radley

THE SHEIKH WHO… COLLECTION

On sale 5th July

On sale 2nd August

On sale 6th September

On sale 4th October

On sale 1st November

On sale 6th December

THE SHEIKH
who Desired Her

ABBY
GREEN

Jennifer
LEWIS

Tessa
RADLEY

MILLS
BOON

Mills & Boon, an imprint of Harlequin (UK) Limited, Eton House, 18-24 Paradise Road, Richmond, Surrey TW9 1SR

THE SHEIKH WHO DESIRED HER
© Harlequin Enterprises II B.V./S.à.r.l 2013

Secrets of the Oasis © Abby Green 2011
The Desert Prince © Jennifer Lewis 2010
Saved by the Sheikh! © Tessa Radley 2010

ISBN: 978 0 263 90738 4

026-1213

Harlequin (UK) policy is to use papers that are natural, renewable and recyclable products and made from wood grown in sustainable forests. The logging and manufacturing processes conform to the legal environmental regulations of the country of origin.

Printed and bound in Spain
by Blackprint CPI, Barcelona

SECRETS OF THE OASIS

ABBY GREEN

Abby Green deferred doing a social anthropology degree to work freelance as an assistant director in the film and TV industry—which is a social study in itself! Since then it's been early starts, long hours, mucky fields, ugly car parks and wet-weather gear—especially working in Ireland.

She has no bona fide qualifications, but could probably help negotiate a peace agreement between two warring countries after years of dealing with recalcitrant actors. She discovered a guide to writing romance one day, and decided to capitalise on her longtime love for Mills & Boon® romances and attempt to follow in the footsteps of such authors as Kate Walker and Penny Jordan. She's enjoying the excuse to be paid to sit inside, away from the elements. She lives in Dublin and hopes that you will enjoy her stories.

You can email her at abbygreen3@yahoo.co.uk.

PROLOGUE

A SIX-YEAR-OLD girl stands at a graveside, on her own. Her face is deathly pale, her blue eyes huge and shimmering with unshed tears, her hair a sleek waterfall of black down to her waist. A dark, handsome boy, Salman, detaches himself from the larger group and comes over to take her hand.

He looks at her solemnly, too solemn for his twelve years. 'Don't cry, Jamilah, you have to be strong now.'

She just looks at him. His parents died in the same plane crash as hers. If he can be strong, so can she. She blinks back the tears and nods briefly, once, and doesn't take her eyes off him even when he looks away to where his own parents have just been buried. Their hands stay tightly clasped together.

CHAPTER ONE

Six years ago, Paris.

JAMILAH MOREAU had to restrain herself from turning her walk into a light-hearted skip as she walked up the French boulevard with the Eiffel Tower in the distance. She grimaced at herself. It was such a cliché but it was Paris, it was springtime, and she was in love. She wanted to throw her bags of shopping in the air and laugh out loud, and turn her face up to the blossoms floating lazily to the ground from the trees.

She wanted to hug everyone. She forced back an irrepressible grin. She'd always thought people over-exaggerated Paris's romantic allure, but now she knew why. You had to be in love to get it. No wonder her French father and Merkazadi mother had fallen in love here—how could they not have?

She was unaware of the admiring looks her jet-black hair, exotic olive-skinned colouring and startlingly blue eyes drew from people passing by—both men and women. Her heart was beating so fast with excitement that she knew she had to calm herself. But all she felt like doing was shouting out to the world with arms wide: *I'm in love with Salman al Saqr and he loves me, too!*

At that thought, though, her step faltered slightly and

her conscience pricked. He hadn't actually *said* he loved her. Not even when she'd told him she loved him that morning, as they'd lain in bed, when Jamilah had felt as if she'd expire with happiness and sensual satedness. She couldn't have held it back any longer. The words had been trembling on her lips for days.

Three weeks. That was all it had been since she'd literally bumped into Salman in the street, when she'd emerged from the university where she'd just finished her final exams. She'd practically grown up with him, but hadn't seen him in a few years, and a seismic reaction had washed through her at seeing the object of her lifelong crush. As darkly handsome as he'd ever been, and even more so. Because now he was a man. Tall, broad, and powerful.

His hands had wrapped around her arms to steady her, and he'd been about to let her go, with a thrillingly appreciative gleam in his dark gaze, when suddenly those black brows had drawn together, his eyes had narrowed and he'd snapped out disbelievingly, *'Jamilah?'* She'd nodded, her heart thumping and a hot blush rising up through her body. She'd fantasised about him looking at her like that for so long...

They'd gone for a coffee. When they'd stood in the street afterwards she'd been about to walk away, feeling as though her heart was being torn from her chest, when Salman had stopped her and said quickly, 'Wait...have dinner with me tonight?'

And that had been the start of the most magical three weeks of her life. She'd said yes quickly. Too quickly. Jamilah grimaced again as a dose of reality hit. She should have been more cool, more sophisticated...but it would have been impossible after years of idolising him from afar—a childhood crush which had developed into teenage obsession and now adult longing.

That first weekend Salman had taken her back to his apartment and made love to her for the first time... and even now a deep flowing heat invaded her lower body, making her blush as X-rated images flooded her mind.

She shook her head to dispel the images, kept walking. She was on her way to his apartment now, to cook him dinner. Her conscience struck again. Salman hadn't actually invited her over this evening—in fact he'd been unusually quiet that morning. But Jamilah was confident that when he saw her, saw the delicious supplies she'd bought, he'd smile that sexy, crooked smile and open his door wide.

As she waited to cross the busy road across from his imposing eighteenth-century apartment building she thought of the instances when she'd seen an intense darkness pervade Salman—whenever she mentioned Merkazad, where they were both from, or his older brother Sheikh Nadim, ruler of Merkazad.

Salman had always had an innate darkness, but it had never intimidated Jamilah. From as far back as she could remember she'd felt an affinity with him, and had never questioned the fact that he was a loner and didn't seem to share the social ease of his older brother. But in the past few weeks Jamilah had quickly learnt to avoid talking of Nadim or Merkazad.

She was due to return to Merkazad in a week's time, but she was going to tell Salman tonight that if he wanted her to stay in Paris she would. It wasn't what she'd planned at all, but the anatomy of her world had changed utterly since she'd met him again.

She arrived at the ornate door of Salman's building,

where he lived on the top floor in a stunning open-plan apartment. The concierge started to greet her warmly when she came in, but then a look flashed over his face and he said, '*Excusez-moi, mademoiselle,* but is the Sheikh expecting you this evening?'

Hearing Salman being described as 'the Sheikh' gave Jamilah a little jolt; she'd almost forgotten about his status as next in line to be ruler of Merkazad after Nadim. Merkazad was a small independent sheikhdom within the bigger country of Al-Omar on the Arabian peninsula. It had been her mother's home and birthplace, where Jamilah had been brought up after her birth in Paris. Her French father had worked for Salman's father as an advisor.

Jamilah smiled widely and held up the bulging bags of shopping. 'I'm cooking dinner.'

The concierge smiled back, but he looked a little uncomfortable, and a shiver of unease went down Jamilah's spine for no good reason as the lift ascended. When it came to a smooth halt and the doors opened the trickle of unease got stronger. Salman's door was partially open, and she heard a deep-throated, very feminine chuckle just as she pushed it open fully.

It took a few seconds for the scene in front of her to register. Salman was standing with his head bent, about to kiss a very beautiful red-haired woman who was twined around him like a climbing vine. Jamilah suddenly felt stupidly self-conscious in her student uniform of jeans and T-shirt.

Their mouths met, and Salman's hands were on the woman's slender waist as he hauled her closer. Exactly the way he had done with Jamilah. She must have made a sound or something—it was only afterwards that she'd realised that was the moment she'd dropped the shopping.

Salman broke off the kiss and looked round. But, Jamilah noted, he didn't take his hands off the woman, who was now looking at her, too, her beautiful green eyes flashing at the interruption.

Jamilah barely registered Salman's thick dark unruly hair, which had always curled a touch too near his collar, or his intensely dark flashing eyes, which she'd always thought held a universe of shadows and secrets. The hard line of his jaw, and his exquisitely sculpted cheekbones which somehow didn't diminish the harsh masculinity of his face, were all peripheral to her shock.

Numb with that shock, and a million and one other things all at once, Jamilah just stood stupidly and watched Salman say something low and succinct to the woman, who gave a little moue of displeasure before she stepped back and picked up her bag and coat.

She brushed past Jamilah on her way out, trailing a noxious cloud of perfume behind her, and said huskily, *'Je te voir plus tard, cheri.'*

See you later, darling.

The door closed behind Jamilah and reaction started to set in. Salman faced her now, hands on narrow hips, dressed in a dark suit, crisp shirt and tie. It was the first time she'd seen him dressed so formally, and it made him look austere. She knew that he was an investment banker, but he'd never really discussed it. She realised now he'd never really discussed anything personal with her—just seduced her to within an inch of her life.

Jamilah could feel a trembling starting up in her legs, but before she could speak Salman said curtly, 'I didn't expect to see you this evening. We made no arrangement.'

They'd made no arrangement to turn her life upside down in the space of three weeks, either! Jamilah's numb brain was trying to equate this distant stranger with the man who had made love to her less than twelve hours before. The same man who had whispered words of endearment in her ears as he'd thrust so deeply inside her that she'd arched her back and gasped out loud, raking her nails down his back to his buttocks.

She fought to block the images and felt like crying. 'I... wanted to surprise you. I was going to cook dinner...'

Jamilah looked down then, to see carnage. Broken eggs seeped all over the parquet floor. A bottle of wine, which thankfully hadn't broken, lolled on its side. She looked up again jerkily when Salman said, 'You can't just wander in here when you feel like it, Jamilah.'

A muscle ticking in his jaw showed his displeasure. And, from a depth she'd not known she had, a self-preserving instinct kicked in. Jamilah hitched up her chin minutely, even as her world started to crumble around her.

'Of course I wouldn't have come if I'd known that you would be...*busy*.' And then she couldn't help asking. 'Were you...?' A poison-tipped arrow pierced her heart. 'Were you seeing *her* while you were seeing me?'

Salman shook his head briefly, abruptly. Impatiently. 'No.'

Jamilah said through numb lips, 'Clearly, though, you're seeing her *now*. Evidently you've already grown bored. Three weeks must be your limit.'

She was aware of the raw pain throbbing through her voice. She couldn't hold it back. Not for the life of her. All she could think of was how she'd bared her heart and soul to this man in the early dawn hours. She'd said hesitantly, huskily, '*I love you, Salman. I think I've always loved you.*'

He'd smiled his lopsided smile and said, 'Don't be ridiculous. You barely know me.'

Jamilah had been fierce. 'I've known you all my life, Salman…and I know that I love you.' And that was when he'd pulled back and become monosyllabic. She could see it now, clear as day.

Salman asked now, with fatal softness, 'Just what exactly were you expecting, Jamilah?'

Jamilah shut her emotions away. 'Nothing. It would have been stupid of me to expect anything, wouldn't it? You're already moving on. Were you even going to tell me?'

Salman's mouth thinned. 'What's to tell? We've had an enjoyable fling. In one week you're going back to Merkazad, and, yes, of course I'll be moving on.'

Jamilah felt herself recoil inwardly, as if from a blow. This man had been her first lover…to call what had happened between them a *fling* reduced every moment to a travesty. Reduced the gift of her innocence that she'd given him to nothing.

Salman frowned and took a step closer. 'You *are* going back to Merkazad, aren't you?' He cursed under his breath—an Arabic curse that Jamilah had only heard in the souks of Merkazad amongst men—and said harshly, 'You didn't seriously expect anything more, did you?'

Her face must have been giving her away spectacularly, despite her best efforts, because then he said, with chilling devastation, 'I never promised you anything. I never gave you any hint to expect anything more, did I?'

She shook her head on auto-pilot. No, he hadn't. The

utter devastation of his words sank in somewhere deep
and vulnerable. It took all of Jamilah's strength just to
stay standing. He couldn't know how much he was hurting her. She'd played with fire and she was getting burnt
by a master. Every day had been heady, magical, but at
no point had Salman made a plan anything more than
twenty-four hours in advance. Now she just wanted to
leave and curl up into a ball, far away, where she could
curse her own naivety. But she couldn't move.

Salman watched the woman before him. He'd cut
himself off from any kind of emotion so long ago that
he almost didn't recognise it now, as it struggled to break
through. An aching pain constricted his chest, but he
ruthlessly pushed it down. For the past three weeks
he'd indulged in a haze of unreality, in believing that
perhaps he wasn't as damned as he'd always believed.
Bumping into Jamilah, seeing her again—seeing how
utterly beautiful she'd become—had broken something
open inside him. He'd had the gall to think for a second
that some of her innately pure goodness could rub off
on him.

When he'd seen Jamilah cross the street minutes
before, a huge grin on her face, he'd realised that she'd
meant what she'd said that morning—she *was* in love
with him. He'd tried to block her words out all day,
tried to reassure himself that she hadn't meant it…
tried to ignore the uncomfortable feeling of guilt and
responsibility.

He'd felt in that moment as he'd watched her approach
his apartment as if he was holding a tiny, delicate butterfly in his hands, which he could not fail to crush—even
if he wanted to protect its fragile beauty.

Eloise, his colleague, who had followed him up to his
apartment on the flimsy pretext of getting a document,

had come on to him at that exact moment, her brash, over-confident sexuality in direct contrast to the subtle sensuality of the woman approaching his apartment. In that moment he'd known he had to let Jamilah go... so comprehensively that she would be left in no doubt that it was over. So when his concierge had confirmed that Jamilah was indeed coming up, he'd felt something shut down inside him. He would crush the butterfly to pieces. Because he had no choice—had nothing to offer other than a battered soul riven with dark secrets. He could not love.

For a long moment Salman said nothing, just looked at Jamilah until she felt dizzy. Perhaps she'd imagined the awful scene? His frosty manner? *That woman...* For a second she thought she saw something like regret in his eyes, but then Salman finally spoke, and he stuck the knife in so deep that Jamilah felt her heart slice in two.

'I knew you were coming up. The concierge warned me.' He shrugged, and she knew in that moment what real cruelty looked like. 'I could have stopped myself from kissing Eloise, but I figured what was the point? Better that you find out now the kind of person I am.'

He twisted the knife.

'This never should have happened. It was weak of me to seduce you.'

Immediately Jamilah read between those words: what he meant was it had been all too *easy* to seduce her.

'You should leave. I imagine you have plenty to prepare for going back to Merkazad.' His mouth was a thin line now. 'Believe me, Jamilah, I'm not the kind of man who can give you what you want. I'm dark and twisted inside—not a knight in shining armour who will whisk you away into a romantic dream. This is over. I'll be taking Eloise out tonight and getting on with my life. I suggest that you do the same.'

Numb all over, Jamilah said threadily, 'I thought we were friends... I thought...'

'What?' he said harshly. 'That just because we grew up in the same place and spent time together we would be friends for life?'

Something inside Jamilah wasn't obeying her mental command to just shut up. 'It was more than that... What we had was different. You spoke to me, spent time with me when you wouldn't with anyone else... This last three weeks...I thought what we'd always shared had grown into something...'

A look of forbidding cold bleakness crossed Salman's face, and finally Jamilah curbed her tongue, wondering why on earth she was laying herself bare like this.

'You followed me around like a besotted puppy dog for years and I never had the heart to tell you to leave me alone. This last three weeks was about lust, pure and simple. You've grown into a beautiful woman and I desired you. Nothing more, nothing less.'

That was it. Whatever feelings Jamilah might have harboured for Salman over the years froze and withered to dust inside her. He'd also destroyed any halcyon memories she'd had of a bond between them. She forced words out through the excruciating pain. 'You don't need to say any more. I get the message. Whatever heart you may have once had is clearly gone. You're nothing but a cold bastard.'

'Yes, I am,' Salman agreed, with an indefinable edge to his voice.

Jamilah finally managed to move, and turned round to go, stepping out of the destruction of the fallen

shopping around her. She couldn't even attempt to pick
it up.

At the door she heard Salman say, with cynicism
ringing in his voice, 'Say hello to my beloved brother
and Merkazad for me. I don't intend seeing either any
time soon.'

Or you. He didn't have to say the words. They hung
in the air. Jamilah opened the door and walked out, and
didn't look back once.

One year ago.

The Sultan of Al-Omar's birthday celebrations were as
lavish as ever. They were taking place in the stunning
Hussein Palace, which was in the heart of the glittering
metropolis of B'harani, right on the coast of the Arabian
peninsula, about two hours drive from mountainous
Merkazad.

One of the Sultan's aides had been pursuing Jamilah
on and off for years, and she'd finally relented and agreed
to come to the party as his date. Her belly clenched now,
because she had to acknowledge that the main motivation behind her decision to come was because Salman
was going to be there.

Each year the tabloids across the globe exulted in
reporting feverishly on which A-list beauty he'd decided
to take as his new mistress. He never came to the party
with anyone, but he always left with someone.

Her date had left her side for a moment in the thronged
ballroom. It was the first night of celebrations which
were meant to be for family and close friends only, but
approximately two hundred people milled about the
room.

Jamilah's skin prickled, and she cursed herself for

her rash decision. She'd taken it because in all the years since she'd last seen Salman in Paris she hadn't been able to get him out of her head, and she'd started having dreams again. Dreams of when she was six years old and standing at her parents' grave, when Salman had come to take her hand and infused her with a strength so palpable she'd never forgotten it.

She knew it was ridiculous, but she'd fallen in love with him at that moment. And even though she'd long since disabused herself of the notion that that childish love had grown and developed into something deeper, she couldn't help her heart clenching at the evocative memory.

She cringed inwardly now when she thought of how her teenage years had been lifted out of the doldrums every time Salman had made a visit home from school in the UK, and she, tongue-tied and blushing, had been reduced to a puddle of hormones. But then his visits had become more and more infrequent, until he'd stopping coming home at all, turning her world lacklustre and dull.

She didn't have to be reminded of how Salman had regarded her lovesick attentions. It was bad enough that her motivation for going to Paris to study had had as much to do with the fact that Salman lived there than because it had always been her father's wish that she study in his home city. And she'd paid heavily for that decision.

Bitterness flooded her.

The dreams were the last straw. She couldn't go on like this, so she'd hoped that if she came to the party, if she saw Salman living the debauched lifestyle of the notorious playboy Sheikh that he was, he'd disgust her and she'd be able to move on. At least enough to feel some measure of closure.

She'd imagined greeting Salman with a look of practised surprise, a tiny smile of recognition. Not a hint of the emotional turmoil she'd suffered these past years would show on her face or in her eyes. She'd ask him how he was, while affecting a look of mild boredom, and then, with a perfunctory platitude, she'd drift away and that would be it. She would be over him. And he would be left in no doubt that their brief affair meant nothing to her at all...

Except it hadn't happened like that. As she'd been leaving her room she'd looked up from her bag, distracted, to see a tall, dark, broad figure in a tuxedo ahead of her. She'd nearly called out, because she'd thought it was his brother, Nadim. They shared the same height and build. But then she'd realised her mistake and it had been too late as a sound emerged from her mouth.

She'd had a first fleeting impression of him, cutting a lonely, solitary figure, and then he'd turned round with a frown on his face which had only grown more marked as he'd registered who she was. Jamilah had been too shocked and stunned at being faced with him like that in an empty corridor to say anything.

He'd rocked back on his heels, hands in the pockets of his trousers, and whatever fleeting hint of vulnerability she might have sensed about him had been smashed to pieces as his gaze had dropped down her body with lazy, sensual appraisal. 'Jamilah...we finally meet again. I was wondering if you'd been avoiding me.'

His deep, drawling voice had impacted upon her somewhere deep and visceral, and for one awful moment Jamilah had been transported back in time to that devastating evening in Paris, in his apartment. She'd given up any hope of sticking to the script she'd perfected in her head. With an iron will, she'd struggled to regain composure and sent up silent thanks for the armour of a designer dress and make-up. She'd forced herself to move, stride forward, fully intending to walk past him, but he'd caught her arm and the feel of his hand on her bare skin had caused her to stumble.

She'd looked up at him, and her treacherous heart had beat fast—too fast. 'Don't be ridiculous, Salman. Why on earth would I be avoiding you?'

An inner voice answered: *Because he broke your heart into tiny pieces and you've never forgotten it.*

Jamilah noticed then that faint grooves were worn into the brackets of his mouth. His eyes were hard—far harder than she remembered them being.

'Because I've never seen you at the Sultan's party before.'

Jamilah wrenched her arm free. 'This isn't exactly my scene. And, not that it's any of your business, I decided to come tonight because I was invited by—'

'Ah, Jamilah, there you are. I was just coming to collect you.'

With a rolling wave of relief, Jamilah saw her date approach. She let him come and put a proprietorial arm around her shoulder, for once not minding the way men seemed to find it impossible not to stake their claim. And with a few words of muttered incoherency to Salman she let herself be led away, leaving Salman behind.

Now she stood amongst the throng that had gathered after the sumptuous dinner—a dinner Jamilah had had to force down her throat—horribly aware of Salman's intense and assessing gaze from across the table.

To her utter relief, at that moment she spotted Sheikh Nadim and his date, an Irish girl called Iseult, who had come to work in Nadim's stables after he'd bought out her family's stud farm in Ireland.

Jamilah went to join them, and she could see their concerned looks as they took in her pale features. She felt light-headed. And then Iseult confirmed it by asking, 'Jamilah, what is it?'

Jamilah smiled tightly. 'Nothing at all.'

But Jamilah could feel whatever blood was left in her face drain southward when she saw Salman approach with narrowed eyes. No escape. *How* had she ever thought this would be a good idea?

Muttering something about finding her date, Jamilah fled across the room and out to the patio through open doors, where thankfully few people milled about. She rested her hands on the stone balustrade and sucked in deep breaths, only to feel every cell in her body react when she sensed his presence behind her.

She turned slowly and saw that the patio was now empty, as if the sheer force of the tension between her and Salman had repelled everyone else.

Not caring how she might be giving herself away, Jamilah said unevenly, 'Leave me alone, Salman.'

His voice was harsh against the silence. 'If you'd wanted to be left alone you should have stayed in Merkazad.'

Jamilah's mouth twisted to acknowledge that uncomfortable truth. To think she'd ever thought that she could cope with this... 'Ah, yes, because you never come home.'

His eyes flashed but he didn't deny it. 'Exactly.'

For a long moment neither one said anything, and then Salman took a step forward. Jamilah's heart lurched, and she noticed that the patio doors had been closed.

He said, with a rough quality to his voice that

resonated deep inside her, 'You're even more beautiful than I remember.'

Jamilah forgot about escape and glared at Salman. His compliment fell on deaf ears. There was an unmistakably predatory gleam in his eyes and Jamilah railed against it. He had no right. His face was cast into shadow, so she couldn't make out his expression. 'The last time you saw me you told me I was beautiful, Salman—or don't you remember telling me why you took me to bed?'

'You were undeniably beautiful then, but now there's a maturity to your beauty…an edge.' There was something achingly wistful in his voice for a moment, which caught Jamilah off guard.

She forced a mocking smile to numb lips. 'You should be able to recognise cynicism when you see it, Salman. After all you're the King of the Cynics, aren't you? Always coming to the Sultan's party empty-handed and walking away with the most beautiful woman here. Do you still stick to your three-week rule, or was that privilege afforded just to me? Tell me, how long did the lovely Eloise last?'

'Stop it.'

'Why should I?'

Salman stepped closer then, out of the shadows, and when Jamilah saw the starkness of his beautiful features she nearly forgot everything. He blocked out the light behind him.

'I thought you would have got over that by now.'

Jamilah emitted a strangled laugh. 'Got *over* it?' She crossed her fingers behind her back. 'I got over you long ago. I don't have anything to discuss with you—so, if you don't mind, my date will be looking for me.'

'He's no man for you. He's a runt—an obsequious

yes-man to the Sultan. What are you doing with him?' Salman asked.

Jamilah was belligerent. 'What do you care? He's perfect. The alpha male lost any fascination for me a long time ago.'

She went to walk around Salman, but once again he caught her arm. 'Tell me, do you shout out his name in ecstasy?' he asked silkily. 'Do you rake his back with your nails, pleading with him never to stop?'

He didn't have to say it, but the words hung between them: *do you tell him you love him?* As if held back by the flimsiest of walls, images and sensations flooded Jamilah's body and mind. She was unaware of Salman putting his hands on her arms and drawing her back in front of him. Unaware of the intent in his dark gaze. Unaware of the way his eyes dropped down her body, and unaware of the guttural moan as he drew her into him and his head lowered to hers.

She only became aware when the hot brand of his mouth seared hers, plundering and demanding, forcing her soft lips apart so that his tongue could snake out between her small teeth and suck hers deep. Jamilah had no defence. Desire burned up through her like a living flame and hurled her into the fire.

It was shocking how well her body remembered his touch—and how hungry she was for it. His hands on her back felt so wonderful. Even more so when they went lower and cupped her buttocks through the fine silk of her dress. He pulled her up and into him, where she could feel the hardening ridge of his desire, and with a soft mewl of frustration she arched against him, wanting more. Burning up with it. It was as if no time had passed at all.

And all the while their mouths clung feverishly, as

if taking a first long drink of water from an oasis in the desert. It was only when Salman pulled her in even closer that an insidious image inserted itself—that of a red-haired woman being held in his arms, being made love to in exactly the same way.

Suddenly as cold as ice, Jamilah wrenched her head away and pulled free. She stood apart, aghast at how out of control she felt and how hard she was breathing.

'Stay away from me, Salman. There is nothing between us. *Nothing.* And there never was. You said it yourself. It was just a fling, and I'm not in the market for another one.'

She whirled around, her dark blue silk dress billowing about her as she stalked to the doors, praying he wouldn't stop her again. And then she turned back. 'You had your chance. You won't get another one. And for your information I've called out plenty of names in ecstasy since you, so don't think what happened just now was anything special.'

Salman watched Jamilah stalk back into the party and for a moment an almost unassailable wave of despair washed over him. Seeing her again had provoked a maelstrom of emotions within him—emotions he'd not felt since he'd last seen her. He sagged back against the wall, his legs suddenly weak as he registered how intoxicating it had been to kiss her, hold her in his arms.

How *familiar.* And how necessary it had been—as necessary as taking another breath. It was as if no time had passed. He wanted her with something close to desperation. On that thought he resolutely stood to his full height again. He'd already seduced her and then rejected her. He had no right to want her again. He never wanted women after he'd had them. So why should she be different?

His mouth was a grim line as he followed her back into the party. He hoped that she'd been telling the truth when she'd claimed those numerous lovers, because then it would mean that his impact on her had been minimal, and he could ignore the fact that he thought he'd seen vulnerability and hurt in those stunning blue eyes.

Jamilah knew her parting words to Salman had been a cheap shot, but they'd felt good for a moment—even if they weren't remotely true. Giving up any pretence of wanting to stay at the party, within an hour she had changed, her face scrubbed clean, and was in her Jeep and heading back to Merkazad.

Eventually she had to pull over on the hard shoulder of the motorway when tears blurred her vision too much. She rested her head on her hands on the steering wheel. She had to concede that she'd been hopelessly naïve in having thought she could remain unscathed after seeing Salman—and, worse, after *kissing* him, which she was sure had been nothing more than his cruel experiment to see how she still hungered for him.

On some level she'd never been able to believe how he'd turned into such a cruel and distant stranger that day.

She ruthlessly stopped her thoughts from deviating down a self-indulgent path where she'd try to find justification for Salman's behaviour. He was cold and heartless—he always had been. She'd just been too naïve to see it before.

She'd often speculated if the cataclysmic events that had once taken place in Merkazad had anything to do with Salman's insularity and darkness. Years before Merkazad had been invaded by an army from Al-Omar, which had been against its independence. Salman, his brother and their parents had been locked up in the bowels of the castle for three long months. It had been a difficult time for the whole country, and must have been traumatic for Nadim and Salman, but Jamilah had been just two at the time—far too young to remember the details.

Years after their liberation she'd always been the one allowed to spend time with Salman, when he hadn't even let his own brother or parents near. He'd never said much, but he'd listened to her inconsequential chatter—which had developed into tongue-tied embarrassment as she'd grown older. Yet he'd never made her feel uncomfortable. He'd even sought her out the day he left Merkazad for good. She'd been sixteen and hopelessly in love. He'd touched her cheek with a finger, such a wealth of bleakness in his eyes that she'd ached to comfort him, but he'd just said, 'See you around, kid.'

It was that bond that she believed had flared to life and blossomed over those three weeks in Paris. And yet if she believed what Salman had said to her there—and why wouldn't she?—it had all been a cruel illusion. She had to get it through her thick skull that there could be no justification for Salman's behaviour, and after tonight she *had* to draw a line under her obsession with him.

CHAPTER TWO

Present day.

SHEIKH SALMAN BIN KALID AL SAQR looked at the
shadows of the rotorblades of the helicopter as it flew
across the rocky expanse below him. They undulated
and snaked like dark ribbons over the mountaintops, and
when he looked further he could already see minarets
and the vague outlines of the buildings of Merkazad—
and the castle, where he was headed. His home and
birthplace. He was coming back for the first time in ten
years. Ten long years. And he felt numb inside.

He could remember the day he'd left, and the blistering argument he'd had with his older brother Nadim,
as if it had happened yesterday, despite every attempt
he'd made to block it out in the interim. They'd been
standing in Nadim's study, from where he'd been running the country since the tender age of twenty-one. His
older brother's responsibility had always struck fear into
Salman's heart because he'd known he would never have
been able to bear it.

Not because of a lack of ability, but because at the
age of eight he'd borne a horrific responsibility for his
own people that he'd never spoken about, and since that

time he'd cut Merkazad and everyone associated with it out of his heart.

As if to contradict him a memory rose up of Jamilah—the kinship he'd always felt with her, the way that for a long time she'd been the only person he could tolerate being near him and, in Paris, the ease with which he'd allowed her to seduce him to a softer place than he'd inhabited for as long as he could remember. *If ever.* And then the way he'd callously told her that it had been nothing, that she'd imagined them having some sort of bond. His skin prickled at being reminded of that now, and with ruthless efficiency he pushed it aside and focused on that moment with his brother again.

'This is your home, Salman!' his brother had shouted at him. 'I need you here with me. We need to rule together to be strong.'

Salman could remember how dead he'd felt inside, how removed from his brother's passion. He'd known that day would be his last in Merkazad. He was a free man. Since he'd been that eight-year-old boy, since the awful time of their incarceration, he'd felt aeons older than Nadim. 'Brother, this is your country now. Not mine. I will forge my own life. And I will not have you dictate to me. You have no right.'

He'd been able to see the struggle that had run through Nadim, and silently he'd sent out a dire warning: *don't even go there.* And as he'd watched he'd seen the fight leave Nadim. The weight of their history ran too deep between them. Salman felt bitter jealousy every time he looked at his brother and knew his integral goodness had never been compromised, or taken away, or violated. Salman's had when his childhood had been ripped away from him over a three-month period that had felt like three centuries.

Salman knew Nadim blamed himself for not protecting him all those years before. And even though Salman *knew* that it was irrational, because Nadim had been as helpless as he had, he still blamed Nadim for not saving him from the horrors he'd faced. In a way, he wanted his brother to feel that pain, and he inflicted it with impunity, knowing exactly what he was doing even while hating himself for it.

Blame, counter-blame and recrimination had festered between them for years, and it had only been last year, when Salman had seen Nadim at the Sultan of Al-Omar's birthday party, that he'd noticed a subtle change within himself. They'd spoken for mere tense moments, as was their custom when they met once or twice a year, but Salman had noticed a sense of weightlessness that he'd never felt before.

He grimaced, his eyes seeing but not seeing the vista of his own country unfold beneath him in all its rocky glory. The fact that he was flying over it right now, about to land in mere minutes, spoke volumes. A part of him still couldn't really believe that he was coming to Merkazad for a month in Nadim's stead, while he and his pregnant wife went to spend time in Ireland, where she came from, before they returned to have their first baby.

A ridiculous and archaic law said that if Merkazad was without its Sheikh for a month then a coup could be staged by the military to seat a new ruler. This law had been put in place at a time when they'd faced numerous and frequent attacks, to protect Merkazad from outside forces.

They'd been in this position only once before, when their parents had died and an interim governing body had been set up until Nadim had come of age. Luckily

the army had been steadfastly loyal to their deceased
father and to Nadim.

But Nadim had confided to Salman that since his
marriage to Iseult some people were proving hard to
win round, were disappointed that their Sheikh hadn't
picked a Merkazadi woman to be his wife. He'd been
concerned that until his heir was born their rule might
be vulnerable for the first time in years. But if Salman
was there in his place there would be no question of
dissent.

Salman had found himself saying yes, bizarrely over-
riding his conscious intent to say no. He'd known on
some deep level that one day he'd have to come home
to face his demons, and it appeared the time had come.
He'd put his completely incomprehensible decision down
to that, and not to a latent sense of duty, or to passing
time…or to the fact that since he'd seen Jamilah at that
party a year ago he'd felt restless.

Even now he could remember the visceral kick in his
chest when he'd turned in that corridor in the Hussein
Palace and seen her standing before him like a vision,
like something from a dream he'd never admitted
having.

He'd only realised in that moment, as a kind of sigh of
relief had gone through him, that in all the intervening
years since Paris he'd gone to the Sultan's party every
year hoping to see Jamilah…and he had not welcomed
that revelation.

Salman's face darkened. She should have always been
firmly off-limits—a woman he *should* have turned his
back on—but he hadn't been able to resist. Even though
he'd known that she'd been way, way too innocent for his
cold heart he'd still seduced her in Paris, taken her in-

nocence, proving to himself once again how debauched he really was.

And, not content with that, then he'd cruelly broken her heart. A bleakness filled his belly at remembering the pale set of her features that day. The incredible hurt in those beautiful eyes. He'd watched her innocence and joy turn into an adult's bitter disillusion right in front of him, even as he'd been telling himself that he was doing her a favour.

He reassured himself that he'd saved her—from him and other men like him. Because he himself was beyond saving. He'd seen the face of evil and that would taint him for ever, and anyone around him, which was why he never allowed anyone too close.

Yet all that knowledge hadn't stopped him from kissing Jamilah at the Sultan's party. He'd only had to imagine her with that ineffectual date of hers and he'd been overcome with a dark desire to stamp her, brand her as his. His body throbbed to life now, making him shift uncomfortably; she'd tasted as sweetly sensuous as she had when he'd first kissed her in Paris, when he'd known he was doing the wrong thing but had been overcome with a lust so intense it had made him dizzy.

With an effort he forced his mind away from the disturbing fact that in the past year no woman had managed to arouse his once insatiable libido. But merely thinking of Jamilah now was doing just that, as if to taunt him, because she was the last woman he could ever touch again. If he had any chance of redeeming a tiny morsel of his soul it would be in this.

Salman knew Nadim suspected something had happened between them, and of course he didn't approve. The protective warning had been implicit in Nadim's voice in their last conversation. 'You're unlikely to see much of Jamilah. She lives and works down at the stables, and is extremely busy with her work there.' And that, Salman told himself now, suited him just fine— because the mere thought of even seeing a horse or the stables sent clammy chills of dread across his skin. He wouldn't be making a visit there any time soon.

With that thought lingering as the helicopter started to descend over the lush watered Merkazadi castle grounds, reality hit Salman, and claustrophobia surged along with panic. He fought the urge to tell the pilot to turn around. He was strong enough to withstand a month in his own country. He had to be. He'd heard far worse stories than his; he'd been humbled over and over again. He owed it to those who had trusted him with their stories to face this.

Not for the first time in his life did he wish that he could resort to the easy way out of drugs and alcohol.

He sighed deeply as the distinctive white castle came into clear view, the ornate latticed walls and flat-roofed terraces all at once achingly familiar and rousing a veritable flood of memories, some terrifying. He would get through this as he'd got through his life up to this point—by distracting himself from the pain.

'Miss Jamilah—he stumbled out of the helicopter with his shirt half undone and torn jeans. He looked like a…a rock star, not the second in line to rule Merkazad.' The main housekeeper screwed up her wizened face and spat out disgustedly, 'He is nothing like his brother. He is a disgrace to—'

'Hana, that's enough.' They were in a meeting to discuss the domestic schedule of the castle while Nadim and Iseult were away, and Jamilah was having a hard enough time just functioning since she'd heard Salman's arrival in the helicopter the previous day.

The older woman flushed brick-red. 'I'm sorry, Miss Jamilah. I forgot myself for a moment…'

Jamilah smiled tightly. 'It's fine. Don't worry. Look, he's only here till Nadim and Iseult get back…and then everything will be back to normal.'

Yeah, right.

The housekeeper's face lit up. 'And next year we will have a new baby in the castle!'

Jamilah let her prattle on excitedly, and hoped the dart of hurt she felt lance her wasn't apparent on her face or in her eyes. She loved Nadim, and she loved Iseult, who had become a very close friend, but much to her ongoing shame she couldn't help but feel a little jealous of their exuberant happiness.

In truth, when Nadim had told her they would be going to Ireland to see Iseult's family while they still had time before the birth, Jamilah had felt a tinge of relief. To bear witness to their intense love and absorption every day was becoming more and more difficult. And it had only intensified with news of Iseult's pregnancy some six months previously. Nadim hardly let Iseult out of his sight, and cosseted her like a prize jewel. Jamilah knew it drove Iseult crazy, but then she was as bad he was—visibly pining for her husband if he was away from her side for more than an hour.

Jamilah's relief that she would have some respite had been spectacularly eclipsed when Nadim had casually mentioned over dinner that Salman would be taking over as acting ruler while they were gone.

She'd not missed the way Nadim and Iseult had looked at her intently for her reaction; they hadn't asked questions after her bizarre behaviour at the Sultan's party last year, but it had been obvious it had something to do with Salman.

She was proud of the way she'd absorbed the shock into her body and kept on sipping her wine, willing her hands not to show a tremor. She'd said nonchalantly, 'That's nice. It's been so long since he came home...'

Nadim had said gently, 'You could go to France, if you like. Check up on the stables there?'

Jamilah had tensed all over and sat up straight. 'No.' She was aghast that they might think she would crumble, or that she would let Salman's presence affect her work. She'd shaken her head and sealed her fate. 'Not at all. I won't be going anywhere. We're far too busy here...'

But now, when Hana stood up and asked, 'Will you come to the castle to talk to the staff?' Jamilah almost shouted out another visceral *no,* and had to calm herself.

She smiled and said, as breezily as she could, shamelessly playing to Hana's pride, 'Why would I need to come to the castle when you have it all in hand so beautifully? We're busy here at the stables with some new arrivals...you can call me if anything comes up.'

To her intense relief Hana didn't argue, and left. Jamilah sank back into her office chair, feeling as edgy as a new colt, her heart racing.

A month.

One whole month of avoiding going anywhere near the castle and Salman. At least here at the stables where she lived she was relatively safe. For as long as she'd known him he'd had an abhorrence of horses, so she knew he wouldn't come near them.

She was over him, so the fact that he was right now less than ten minutes away meant nothing to her. Nothing at all.

* * *

Jamilah's phone rang at five-thirty a.m.—just as she was about to go out and do her morning round of the stables to check everyone was where they should be. She was grouchy from lack of sleep and the constant feeling of being on edge. And for the past few days there had been the non-stop clatter of helicopter rotorblades, as numerous choppers took off and landed in the castle's grounds. Even though it was a fair distance to the stables, some had flown close enough to the horses to spook them for hours. Jamilah had heard through the robust grapevine that Salman was hosting an unending series of parties at the castle.

Now she gritted her teeth and answered the phone in the office, which was part of her private rooms. All she heard on the other end was hysterical sobbing, until finally she managed to calm Hana down enough to listen for a minute.

With an icy cold anger rising, she eventually bit out, through a break in the tirade, 'I'm on my way.'

Clinging on to that cold rage, to distract her from the prospect of seeing Salman again, Jamilah went outside and got into her Jeep, making the ten-minute journey to the castle courtyard in five minutes, where Hana was wringing her hands.

As soon as Jamilah stepped out of her Jeep Hana was babbling. *'All night, every night…such loud music—and the food! It's too much…couldn't keep up with the demands and then they started throwing things…in the ceremonial ballroom! If Nadim was here…'*

Gently but firmly Jamilah cut through Hana's hysterics. 'Get the staff organised for a clean-up, and get Sakmal here with a coach. I'll have all these guests out of here this morning.'

By the time Jamilah had reached the quarters Salman

had commandeered for his private use about an hour later her rage was no longer icy but boiling over. She'd just seen the devastation caused by what appeared to be half of Europe's Eurotrash party brigade, and she'd just supervised about fifty seriously disgruntled, still inebriated people onto a coach, from where they would be delivered into Al-Omar and back home.

She pushed open the door to Salman's suite and slammed it back against a wall. The immediate dart of hurt at what she saw nearly made her double over, and that made her rage burn even brighter. At the evidence that he was still affecting her.

Two bodies were sprawled on an ornately brocaded couch. An empty champagne bottle and glasses were strewn around them. The nubile blonde woman was caked in make-up, wearing a tiny sparkly, spangly dress. She looked up drunkenly from where she lay beside a sleeping Salman, one arm flung across his bare and tautly muscled chest. Thankfully he was at least wearing jeans.

'Excuse me,' she slurred in cut-glass tones, 'who do you think you are?'

Jamilah strode over, trying to block out the sensually indolent olive-skinned body of Salman, and took the woman's skinny arm, hauling her up.

'*Ow!*'

Jamilah was unrepentant as she marched the sluggish woman over to where two maids hovered anxiously at the door, clad head to toe in black, their huge brown eyes growing wider and wider. Jamilah said with icy disdain, 'Girls, please escort this guest to the coach, after she's picked up her things, and then tell Sakmal he can go. That should be everyone.'

Jamilah shut the door firmly on the woman's drunken

protestations and sighed deeply. She turned round and Salman hadn't budged an inch. Her heart clenched painfully; he'd always slept like the dead, and now that was obviously exacerbated by his alcohol intake. Her eyes roved over his hard-hewn muscle-packed form. She hated to admit it, but for an indolent, louche playboy he possessed the body of an athlete in his prime.

Dark stubble shadowed his firm jaw, and a lock of black hair had fallen over his forehead, making him look deceptively innocent. Long black lashes caressed those ridiculously sculpted cheekbones. He looked like a dark fallen angel who might have literally just dropped out of the sky.

But an angel, fallen or otherwise, he most certainly was *not*.

Jamilah clenched her jaw, as if that could counteract the treacherous rising of heat within her, and went to the bathroom where she found what she was looking for. Coming back into the main drawing room, she said a mental prayer for forgiveness to Nadim and Hana for the damage she was about to do to the soft furnishings, and then she threw the entire bucket of icy cold water over Salman.

Salman thought he was being attacked. Reflexes that had been honed long, long ago snapped into action, and he was on his feet and tense before he really knew what was happening.

In seconds, though, he had assessed the situation and forced locked muscles to relax. Jamilah was standing in front of him with an empty bucket and a belligerent look on her beautiful face, and something inside him rose up with an almost giddy surge. For the first time since he'd returned he felt centred—not rudderless and scarily close to the edge of his control.

With her hair tied back, no make-up, dressed in a white shirt, jeans and riding boots, she might have passed for eighteen. Her stunning blue eyes were glittering like bright sapphires, and a line of pink slashed each cheek with colour. She was a veritable jewel of beauty compared to the artificially enhanced women who'd been vying for his attention these last few days, and self-disgust curled inside him when he remembered the one who'd eventually fallen into a drunken slumber beside him earlier that morning.

He'd vowed to order his private jet and get rid of the horde of unwanted guests, realising what a mistake he'd made, but it would appear by the look on Jamilah's face that it had already been taken care of.

'How dare you?' Jamilah was saying now, in a suspiciously quivery voice which he guessed had more to do with anger than emotion. 'How *dare* you come back here and proceed to turn this castle into your personal playground? Poor Hana is distraught. She has quite enough to be doing without pandering to you and all the Little Lord Fauntleroys you invited to join in the fun. And apart from the chaos and destruction here, your *friends'* constant arrival by helicopter has been spooking the horses at the stables.'

Energy crackled between them.

Salman rocked back on his heels and surveyed Jamilah with a lazy sweep, up and down. He seemed to be oblivious to the fact that he was soaking wet, and with a gulp Jamilah could see that this was not proceeding the way she'd expected at all. Salman didn't look remotely contrite, or even drunk. His eyes were as sharp as ever. And on *her*. She had to consciously not let her gaze drop to where his jeans must be plastered against his crotch and thighs.

He crossed his arms nonchalantly across his chest, making his biceps bulge, and Jamilah had the very belated realisation that she'd just wakened a sleeping panther. He drawled, 'Not even a kiss hello to greet me? That's not very nice, now, is it?'

Jamilah put the bucket down because she was afraid she'd drop it. She stood up to see Salman staring at her with a disturbing glint in his eye. Feeling the sudden urge to escape, and fast, she said glacially, 'Clearly you feel that Merkazad is too boring to sustain your attention. I'd suggest that if you're looking for entertainment you should follow your friends to B'harani, where they're headed right now on a tour bus.'

For a second Jamilah could have sworn she saw the merest smile touch Salman's lips, but then it was gone. And the urge to escape grew more acute. She whirled round to leave the room, but before she could reach the door she was whirled back again by a strong hand gripping her arm and a guttural, 'Where do you think you're going?'

'What the—?' she spluttered ineffectually.

Salman knew he should be letting Jamilah go. He'd *told* himself that he would not pursue her. But faced with her now, her timeless beauty, that sleek curvaceous body, he knew it was too much for his battered soul to resist.

Salman arched one ebony brow. 'Like I said, can't you even greet me with a civil hello?'

Jamilah glared up at him, already cursing herself for having come here to deal with this. 'Why would I want to bother saying hello to someone who can't even treat his own home or staff with any respect?'

His eyes flashed blackly. 'Exactly. This is my home, and you would do well to remember that.'

Jamilah spat out, 'You mean remember my *place?* Is that it, Salman? It's been a long time since anyone had to remind me that I'm not part of your family.'

She tried to break free, but his grip was too strong, and then two hands drew her round in front of him, and his gaze fairly blistered down into her defiant one. Of course she wasn't a member of their family; for all of Nadim's care, inclusion and protection after her parents had died Jamilah had always known her place—so why was she provoking Salman like this now?

'That's not what I meant at all, and you know it. The fact is that this is my home and I shall do as I like here. As acting ruler I don't have to answer to anyone.'

Jamilah stuck her chin out pugnaciously, something deep and visceral goading her on. 'You'll answer to *me*. I may not be the ruler, but the staff here know who is in charge and it's not you. You need to earn their respect first. And I won't stand by and watch you come in here and desecrate Nadim and Iseult's home.'

Before Jamilah could even question where that urge to provoke had come from suddenly they were a lot closer, and her breath faltered as Salman's unique and intensely male scent washed over her. Dimly she recognised that she couldn't smell drink on his breath. He hadn't been drunk? That didn't fit with the scene she'd just witnessed.

'Like I said—' his voice was as glacial as hers '—this is my home as much as it is Nadim's, and I will invite whomever I want, whenever I want.'

Unable to articulate a response, and quickly becoming overwhelmed by Salman's intoxicating proximity,

Jamilah tried to break free of his hold again, twisting around in his hands.

All it did, though, was force her back into his hard chest—and then she heard a muttered curse. Suddenly strong arms were below her breasts, and she was being lifted clear off her feet and carried bodily towards the bathroom. She kicked out with her legs, but her struggles were futile and puny in the face of Salman's overpowering strength. She was plastered against a hard, *wet* body. And that was entirely her fault.

She couldn't even get a word out before they were in the bathroom, and Salman easily held her with one arm while he turned on the shower. Both her hands were trying to free herself, to no avail. His arm was like a steel bar. She could feel her hair loosening from its untidy ponytail.

The water was running, and steam had started to rise around them when she finally spluttered out, 'What the *hell* do you think you are doing? Let me down this instant!'

In that moment Salman walked them both under the warm spray of the huge shower, and she heard him say grimly over her head, 'Giving you a little taste of your own medicine, Miss High-and-mighty.'

CHAPTER THREE

THE inarticulate rage that had risen up within Salman seconds ago was already diminishing, and he knew it had had more to do with this woman's effect on him than her belligerence and anger. And now he couldn't see anything but Jamilah, her clothes already soaked through and sticking to that glorious body.

Jamilah was gasping in shock, her back against the wall of the shower. Water was streaming over her head, face, into her eyes, and Salman's hand was splayed across her abdomen, holding her in place. Through the steam she could see his glittering obsidian gaze, his hair plastered to his skull, and water sluicing down that powerful chest, through the dark smattering of hair, over his blunt nipples.

She tried to smack his hand away, but he merely put it back and said grimly, 'You're not going anywhere.'

Humiliation scorched up through Jamilah as she became very aware of how drenched she was, and how her clothes were plastered to her body. As if reading her thoughts, Salman dropped his eyes, and she could feel her breasts respond, growing heavy, her nipples peaking almost painfully against her wet bra and shirt. She could only imagine how see-through the flimsy material must be under the powerful spray. A flash of fire lit his eyes, and they went darker in an instant—and, *awfully*, she felt an answering rush of heat.

Once again she tried to get free, but Salman merely moved closer and took her hands, raising them above her head. She struggled in earnest now, feeling intensely vulnerable, but it was a struggle against the fire that was gathering pace inside her body, in her blood. She had to stop abruptly when her hips came into explosive contact with his.

'Let me go.'

She longed to go for his vulnerable area with a knee, but he quickly manoeuvred them so that he could thrust a thigh between her legs and shook his head, saying, 'Ah-ah…'

The shock of feeling that powerful thigh between hers rendered her mute. All too easily he held her two hands in one of his, like an iron manacle. His other hand drifted down to cup her jaw and turn her face up to his. The spray bounced off him, cocooning them in steam. She gritted her jaw and tried to turn away, but he ruthlessly turned her head back.

He smiled down at her, and it was the smile of a dangerous predator. 'Aren't you even a little bit glad to see me?'

A treacherous kick of her heart made Jamilah all but spit at him. 'You're the last person I'd be happy to see, Salman al Saqr.'

He shook his head mock-mournfully and tutted. 'All those strong feelings still under the surface, Jamilah?'

Cold horror snaked through her, despite the heat around them. She had to protect herself. She forced her body to relax and mirrored his own easy demeanour. She even smiled sweetly. 'On the contrary. I don't have feelings for you, Salman. I never did. Whatever you saw in Paris was a very transitory and misplaced affection for a first lover. That's all. You mean nothing to me. I am merely angry because you disrespect your brother and sister-in-law, who I care about greatly, and your home. You've caused chaos in the castle, and I refuse to stand by and watch it for a moment longer.'

Salman's gaze glittered down. His jaw clenched. It was getting harder to keep her body relaxed as he came even closer and she felt his hips grind into hers. And then it was all but impossible when she felt the thrillingly hard evidence of his arousal. Heat climbed upwards and she lashed out. 'You're an animal.'

Salman growled, 'I agree. I feel very animalistic at the moment.' His eyes had grown heavy and dangerously slumberous, but still with that provocative fire igniting in their depths.

He tightened his hold on her jaw and swooped down, his mouth a searing brand over hers before she could take another breath. Their bodies touched, chest to chest, hip to hip, and Jamilah felt an immediate wild excitement coursing through her blood.

She wanted to rip the wet clothes from her body and arch closer to Salman, to feel wet skin on wet skin. A vivid memory of another shower, another time, flared up. He had lifted her naked body against the wall and urged her to wrap her legs around his waist. He'd found the hot wet core of her and had surged up and into her, making everything blur into a heat haze of passion.

Anger at her reaction and at the vividness of the memory made her kiss him back, defiantly at first, and then she realised the folly of that when Salman pulled her in even closer. She had to battle harder than she'd ever done in her life not to respond, not to let him suck her under to a dark vortex where past and present might merge and make her forget where she was and what he had done to her.

She seized her opportunity when he lifted his head momentarily. With an abrupt move she snaked out from under him and out of the shower, dripping water everywhere and only then realising how much the wall had been supporting her when her legs felt like jelly.

Salman turned slowly under the spray of water and looked at her. She fought the wild clamour of her pulse. As she watched his hand snaked down to his jeans. He flipped open the top button and drawled, 'I'm going to make myself more comfortable, if you'd care to do the same and join me?'

Jamilah dragged her gaze back up and shook her head, feeling as if she were on fire inside. 'I wouldn't join you if we were the two last humans on earth and the future of civilisation depended on us procreating.'

Salman smiled and lazily pulled down his zip. Jamilah could see the whorls of dark hair which led to his sex in her peripheral vision. Heat threatened to engulf her completely. She wondered why she couldn't move.

And then Salman said, 'But wouldn't we make beautiful babies?'

Jamilah made a garbled sound. She was so mad she wanted to cry, or slap Salman's mocking face. And through that emotion, completely unbidden, came the sudden *awful* yearning to be heavy with this man's child. That brought with it the return of bitter reality and the sharpest pain of all—because she *knew* what it had felt like to carry this man's child for the briefest time, before nature had taken its tragic course. She could still feel that dragging pain, the wrenching sense of loss, and he would never know.

Even now he was still mocking, taunting, pulling his wet jeans down over lean hips and off, blissfully unaware of the nuclear implosion happening within Jamilah. Before he could see any of it she tore her gaze away and grabbed a towel hanging on a nearby rail. While she still could, she walked on wobbly legs out of the bathroom to the sound of a dark, mocking chuckle and a softly intoned, *'Coward.'*

Salman stood in the shower after Jamilah had walked out, his hands against the wall and his head downbent between them. Only minutes before he'd held her captive. Dripping wet and the sexiest thing he'd ever seen. He finally turned the water to cold as he faced the prospect that for the first time since his teens he might be forced to pleasure himself just to reclaim some sanity. But he had to acknowledge now that his sanity had fled along with Jamilah.

Her white shirt had turned see-through the minute the water had hit, clearly showing her white lace bra and the puckered tips of her berry-brown nipples. Her breasts were still beautifully round, firm and high. And he knew that they would fill his palms like succulent fruits.

He groaned softly when his wayward body persisted in responding, despite the stinging cold spray, and he valiantly resisted the urge to wrap his hand around himself and seek all too transitory relief. There was only one way to relief now. Past or no past, history be damned, one thing was clear: he *would* have Jamilah back in his bed until he'd sated himself—until he'd sated them both. Because their desire was mutual, explosive and unfinished. And there was no way he could survive a month here without taking her. He'd go crazy.

All concerns for Jamilah's emotional welfare and the state of his soul were dissolving in a wave of heat. He took some reassurance from the way she'd stood up to him. He could be in no doubt that she was no longer some shy, timid and idealistic virgin. *And you did that to her.* He blocked out the voice.

His mind stalled for a moment. *Dammit,* she had been a virgin. He'd assumed that she'd been at least a little bit experienced. He could still remember his shock when he'd thrust into that slick tightness and felt her momentary hesitation, seen the fleeting pain on her face. And then heard her husky moans and pleas for him to keep going. She'd just been too seductive. He was only human, and he hadn't been able to stop.

His mouth tightened. But hadn't she all but told him that she'd had plenty of other lovers, and that the turmoil he'd witnessed that day in Paris had merely been a passing crush on her first lover. He should feel comforted by that thought…yet he didn't.

With an abrupt move he switched off the shower and stepped out. Towelling himself dry roughly, he made a mental vow that if he was consigning himself to hell for ever by resolving to have Jamilah in his bed, then she was coming with him—all the way.

As he found and dragged on clean clothes he thrust thoughts of Jamilah aside with effort. He had some things to attend to—and one of them was making sure that his ill-advised party guests had indeed been shown the door. For the first time in years living vicariously through those around him, watching them lose all sense of self and envying them their opiate nirvana, hadn't worked to block out his own reality.

* * *

'I apologised to Hana, and to Hisham.'

Jamilah steeled herself before she turned from where she'd been unpacking her suitcase in one of the guest suites. She hadn't wanted Salman to know so soon that she'd given in to both Hana's, and Nadim's chief aide's pleas for her to move up to the castle. Taking a deep breath, she finally did turn round—to see Salman in dark trousers and a white shirt, leaning insouciantly against the open door.

'I know,' she said stiffly, trying to ignore the response in her body and treacherously wishing she wasn't wearing her habitual uniform of jeans and a shirt—albeit fresh ones. It had been a long day since that eventful morning, and she was exhausted.

She didn't need to be reminded of how he'd wound the intractable Hana around his little finger. She'd been all but blushing when she'd told Jamilah of his *apparent* heartfelt apology.

'So…' Salman quirked a brow. 'You've been sent to babysit me? Are you going to ground me for bad behaviour?'

Jamilah heard the edge to his voice and guessed that he didn't often find himself in the position of having to apologise for his actions. She didn't feel that he was in any way repentant, despite his apology.

She focused on his eyes, and then wished she could look anywhere else when she was sucked into the dark depths and butterflies erupted in her stomach. Salman had a unique ability to plug into her deepest emotions and stir them around. He'd *always* had that ability.

That realisation made her voice frigid. 'They asked me to come and stay here. That's all. With Nadim and Iseult away there's a lot to take care of, and clearly you're not interested in taking responsibility.'

She saw his eyes flash at that, but it was gone in an instant and Jamilah wondered why she should be feeling bad.

Salman's mouth twisted into a mocking smile. 'What? And not live up to my reputation as the prodigal bad-boy brother?'

Jamilah's own lush mouth firmed. 'Something like that.' And then, before she could stop herself, she asked curiously, 'Why *did* you come home?'

A dangerous glint came into Salman's eye. 'I'll tell you if you have dinner with me tonight.'

He was flirting with her.

Jamilah's belly tightened in rejection of that even as a rush of heat washed through her body. She firmed her jaw. 'Just because your odious friends have gone, I am not available to entertain you in their absence.'

She stalked over to the door and started to close it purposefully, uncaring of the fact that Salman was in the way. To her abject relief he stepped back. But just before she could close it he stopped it with a hand and said, 'I'm going to be here for a few weeks, Jamilah... you won't be able to avoid me for ever. Especially not now that we're going to be under the same roof.'

Jamilah snorted indelicately. 'This castle is big enough for an army. We won't have to make much of an effort to stay out of each other's way, Salman. And, believe me, I have no intention of seeking you out. Now, if you'll excuse me, I've had a long day, I'm tired, and I want to go to bed.'

Much to her chagrin, she still couldn't close the door. She glared up at Salman and tried not to notice that he'd shaved. His jaw was dark and smooth. His clean and intensely masculine scent teased her nostrils. He was one of the few men she knew who hadn't ever worn overpowering cologne.

'This isn't it, Jamilah, not by a long shot. We have unfinished business.'

Fear caught Jamilah's insides into a knot. She knew she simply would not be able to survive if Salman decided he wanted to seduce her again just because he was bored, or curious. 'We finished any business we had a long time ago, Salman, and the sooner you realise that the better. And, quite frankly, I don't care if this is your home and you're the acting ruler—just stay out of my way.'

When Salman stood on the balcony of his suite a short while later, he felt a hardness enter his belly. The view of Merkazad at night was spread below him. It was a small city but beautiful, full of soaring floodlit minarets and ancient buildings nestling alongside more modern architecture. When he'd been much younger, before the rebel invasion, he'd loved to watch it at night and dream of all sorts of fantastical tales, and the great wide world beyond…but then, during and after the incarceration, it had become a prison to be escaped at all costs…

He was waiting for the inevitable rise of emotion, for nausea to cripple him as it had done whenever he'd looked at this view before. But emotion wasn't rising in its usual unassailable wave. Instead he felt suspiciously calm. As if something had shifted and this view was no longer as malevolently threatening as it had been for years.

All he could think about was Jamilah and how beautiful she'd looked just now, with that fall of silky midnight-black hair in a curtain around her shoulders and down her back. His gut clenched. She had looked tired. Faint purple shadows under her huge blue eyes. And that vulnerability had made him want to gather her up into his arms and carry her somewhere far away, into the dark starlit night, and lay her down underneath him. He amended his impulse. He just *wanted* her. He didn't want to protect her.

But he had once… He'd been twelve and she'd been just six when she'd broken through the numbness encasing him to provoke a protective instinct. He could remember the moment by their parents' graves as clearly as if it were yesterday. She'd been so still, so stoic. He'd felt an affinity with her that he hadn't felt with anyone else.

The earth shifted ominously beneath his feet as he had to acknowledge that perhaps Jamilah could be the key to his unfamiliar feeling of equanimity. That thought disturbed him far more than any view could.

Two nights later, as Jamilah lay in bed unable to sleep, she had to admit to herself that she probably would be better off if she was seeing Salman every day. Perhaps it would inure her to his presence? A voice laughed mockingly in her head at that. But anything had to be better than this awful restless *hot* feeling. She was useless at work, jumping at the slightest sound. She was turning into a nervous wreck.

She'd heard people talking and speculating about him—especially the younger girls at the stables. *'Is it true he's more wealthy than even Sheikh Nadim?' 'He's the most handsome man I've ever seen, but why doesn't he come to the stables?'*

This last comment had been made dreamily by one of the girls who'd run an errand to the castle. Before Jamilah could say anything, her chief aide, a man called

Abdul, had said curtly, 'He is the Sheikh. And he can do as he wishes. Now get back to work.'

Jamilah had looked at him aghast. Abdul was the most mild-mannered man she'd ever known, and had worked at the stables for longer than anyone could remember. He rarely opened his mouth to anyone. The girls had scuttled off, and he'd immediately apologised to Jamilah red-faced, clearly mortified. She'd waved off his apology, not knowing where the sudden passion had blazed from, and with the curious feeling that he'd been defending Salman. But from what?

With a groan of frustration, mixed with anger at her obsessive thoughts about Salman, Jamilah threw back the covers and got out of bed. She stripped off and went straight to her shower, where she endured the icy spray until her teeth were chattering—as if she could numb all feeling.

'You will have dinner with me tonight.'

Salman's voice was an autocratic decree from the ruler of Merkazad. If it had been Nadim, Jamilah would have said yes immediately. But it was Salman, and as her suddenly sweaty hand gripped the handset of the phone in her office she said waspishly, 'Why should I?'

Salman sighed, and her skin prickled.

'Because we need to discuss some things…'

Her heart thumped. 'I have nothing to discuss with you.'

Salman said, with an edge to his voice, 'What you said to me the other day appears to be true. As much as I might be acting ruler, I'm being constantly diverted to you.'

Jamilah couldn't even feel a bit smug for a second.

She just said faintly, 'I told you you'd need to earn their respect.'

'And until that day dawns I'm afraid that I need you—'

Jamilah's mind blanked when he said those words, and she had to concentrate just to keep up.

'To have dinner with me and discuss official business. Or do you want me to bother Nadim and his pregnant wife while they are spending time with her family?'

Immediately Jamilah answered, because she knew Salman would have no compunction about disturbing them, 'No. Of course not.' She continued in a rush, before she could lose her nerve, 'I'm finished at work by seven. I'll see you at eight.'

Salman's voice was husky. 'Good. I'll be looking forward to it, Jamilah.'

Jamilah let the phone drop with a clatter and put hands to hot cheeks. Suddenly breathless, she had to consciously block out evocative images and memories of those weeks in Paris and tell herself that never again would she be so foolish as to let Salman anywhere near the vulnerable heart of her.

A few hours later, though, seated in Nadim's private formal suite, which Salman had moved into, at an intimate dining table, Jamilah was struggling hard to cling on to her sense of equilibrium. Salman sat opposite her in a black shirt. It made him look even darker, more dangerous. She took another sip of delicious red wine and cursed the impulse which had made her change into a black dress and high-heeled shoes. And leave her hair down. And put on the slightest touch of mascara. She told herself it was just armour. And she needed all the armour she could get.

Salman put down his knife and fork and sat back, wiping his mouth with a napkin. She'd once teased him about the single-minded way he ate. To block the insidious memory, she commented, 'You're not drinking...' And then she smiled sweetly. 'Still recovering from last week? They say it gets harder with age to cope with the after-effects.'

Almost curtly Salman said, 'I don't drink.'

Jamilah frowned, and Salman's whole body tightened. If she had any idea how aroused and hot he was for her right now she'd run a mile. Since Hisham had shown her in earlier he'd been in a state of heat and lust. He'd expected her to be in jeans and a shirt, and wouldn't have been surprised to see mucky riding boots.

But she was dressed in something floaty and black. And, while it revealed nothing overt, it clung to her soft bountiful curves with a loving touch. All he wanted to do was smash aside the table between them and rip it off her.

He forced an urbane smile and tried to clamp down on his recently dormant but now raging libido. 'And I don't do drugs, either.'

Jamilah was reminded of how he'd certainly appeared sober enough the morning she'd found him passed out. His admission made her feel funny...curious. She shook her head, not understanding. 'How could you bear to be around those people, then? How could you invite them here and let them run amok like that?'

Salman smiled, but it didn't reach his eyes. 'What can I say? I'm drawn to their instinctive hedonism. I find their lack of engagement with reality fascinating.'

Jamilah had the sudden inexplicable sense that he *envied* those people, and battled her growing curiosity. Her voice was scathing. 'I find that hard to believe. It would be impossible to stay in any kind of proximity to that kind of world without being out of your head.'

His eyes darkened to unreadable black. 'Believe it or not, I've been drunk once, and only once.'

At that admission, which Jamilah could see he didn't welcome, his face shut down, became impassive. Jamilah remembered then that Salman had never drunk to excess during the time she'd been with him.

And then he said, 'What about you, Jamilah? Are you such a paragon of virtue that you've never over-indulged?'

Jamilah's insides contracted. She could remember heady nights of wine and food when she'd been with Salman, the delicious tipsiness that had imbued her and Paris with a magical hue of romance. It certainly hadn't done the same for Salman. Almost unconsciously she pushed away her half-full glass and answered, 'I'm no paragon of virtue, Salman, but, no, I don't feel that I need to see life through a veil of inebriation and crippling hangovers.'

He smiled mockingly, and she couldn't fail to notice something unbearably bleak this time. 'Because you wake up each morning with a sense of optimism about your life and the future?'

Jamilah went still inside. Once she'd been like that. So long ago that she almost couldn't remember it. But she couldn't deny that now every day when she woke up there was a dull sense of loss…of emptiness. He didn't know that losing the baby had made her fearful that she might never get pregnant again. No one knew what she'd been through. And she wasn't about to bare her soul to Salman now.

Much as she hated to admit it, her sense of isolation

had been heightened recently by Nadim and Iseult's unabashed joy in finding each other.

She wiped at her mouth perfunctorily with a napkin and sat up straight, looking pointedly at her watch even if she didn't register the time. 'What did you want to discuss, Salman? I've got an early start in the morning. We've got three new colts that need to be broken in.'

She looked at him then, and was taken aback at the sudden ashen tinge to his skin. Instinctively she leant forward and said, 'Salman?'

But, as if she'd imagined it, he recovered. He stood up abruptly and walked over to a cabinet, where he took out some papers. Jamilah felt decidedly shaky, and tried not to let her eyes dwell on his tight buttocks encased in superbly cut black trousers. He turned and came back and her face flamed guiltily. She willed down the heat, hating feeling so out of control.

He put down the sheaf of documents and she picked up the top one, feeling at a serious disadvantage as he stood looming over her with hands in his pockets. She could see that it was a press communiqué about an important series of meetings of Middle Eastern heads of state to be held in Paris later that week, regarding the global financial crisis.

She looked up at him blankly. 'So? What am I supposed to be seeing here?'

'I have to go to Paris in Nadim's place.'

Feeling threatened, and not sure why, and also more than a little disturbed by the fact that she wasn't feeling relief at being informed of Salman's incipient departure, she stood up and said, 'Well, have a good trip. I'll try not to miss you too much.'

She realised then that Salman hadn't moved back, and now they were almost touching. With a spurt of panic

Jamilah moved, but her heel caught in the luxurious carpet and she felt herself pitching backwards. At her helpless cry, two big hands came around her waist and hauled her up again. Breathing heavily, from fright and unwanted sensation, Jamilah could only look up into the black pools of Salman's eyes.

His fingers tightened on her waist and he said ominously, 'You're coming to Paris with me.'

CHAPTER FOUR

It took a few seconds for his words to sink in, and then Jamilah started to struggle. Her hands were on his arms, and the feel of his bunched muscles was scrambling nearly every thought. Even so, she managed to get out, 'No way.'

The thought of going anywhere with this man, much less back to *Paris,* had cold, clammy horror sinking into her bones. He wasn't releasing her, and Jamilah stopped struggling. It was futile.

She asserted stiffly, 'I'm needed here.'

To her utter relief Salman released her then, and she took a hurried but careful step back. He lifted up another piece of paper and showed it to her. 'I think you'll find that a copy of this is probably in your office, too.'

Jamilah took it and read, the words swimming before her eyes. She saw that it was from Nadim.

Jamilah should go with you. There are going to be some important people there from the biggest stables in Dubai, and I've already set up some meetings. Unfortunately the meeting in Paris coincides with the annual yearling sales here in Ireland, otherwise I'd go myself...

She looked up, and dropped the piece of paper to the table before Salman could see her hand start to shake. How could Nadim do this to her? And then she answered herself bitterly—because she'd put on a great show of making them believe that she cared nothing for the fact that Salman was going to be in Merkazad. And this was no more of a request than Nadim had made of her in the past. It was quite usual for her to go to meetings like this if he was otherwise occupied. After all, she did run the Merkazad stables.

She looked at Salman in shock, something else occurring to her. 'But it'll be a disaster if you go. Are you planning on going to any of the meetings with the leaders?' Before he could answer she said, 'Do you know how much damage you could do to Merkazad and Nadim if you insult a leader at something like this?'

She saw something unfathomable cross Salman's face. For a moment it looked like *pride*. As if she'd injured his pride. His jaw clenched. He smiled, and it was hard, harder than she'd ever seen. 'Which is precisely why you should come with me. You don't want to have a loose cannon wrecking Merkazad's reputation, do you?'

He was mocking her. She knew that. And she knew she deserved it. Even though she didn't believe he could be trusted with such a responsibility. This, after all, was the man who had left the running of his country squarely on the shoulders of his brother for as long as she could remember. Even when they'd been teenagers, and they had been home for the holidays, Salman had regularly eschewed the lengthy lessons in Merkazadi rule and law that Nadim had had to endure in preparation for his role. And yet, for reasons unknown to her, Nadim had never called him on it.

The tension between the two brothers had always been palpable, and Jamilah was aware that this was the first time Salman appeared to be softening in some respect—taking an interest even if it was somewhat forced and clearly unwelcome. Did she want to be the person who sabotaged that?

If she was to make a fuss and insist on staying in Merkazad she'd merely be proving to Salman that to her the thought of returning to Paris with him equated to a minor mental breakdown. Her one saving grace at the moment was that he believed her to be over their brief liaison.

She came to a reluctant decision and told herself she was doing it for Nadim and for no other reason. 'Fine,' she said, as blasé as she could, as if it was costing her nothing. 'I'll go to Paris.'

His dark eyes bored into hers so intensely that she started to get hot and tingly. She wanted to ask him to stop looking at her like that, but that would only give away the fact that he had an effect on her. *As if he wouldn't know that already from the wanton way she'd reacted to him in the shower.* Her lower belly felt hot.

He smiled, and her world tilted crazily. 'Good. You can stay with me.'

Jamilah faltered as she turned to leave. She looked back at him. 'But…surely you'll stay in your apartment? I can stay in a hotel.'

Salman shook his head. 'I sold that apartment years ago. I've been living in a suite at the Ritz. I have a spare room. You can stay there.'

Panic setting in, Jamilah blustered, 'I can look after my own accommodation.'

Salman waved her suggestion away. 'Don't be silly.

The meetings are taking place at the Ritz conference centre so it's the most practical solution.'

Jamilah stepped out of the plane and breathed the cool November Paris air in deep. She felt stifled, having been cooped up on a small private jet with Salman for a few hours, even though he'd kept himself to himself—surprising Jamilah by immersing himself in documents. She'd seen the headed paper and known they had to do with the meetings and that had surprised her even more. She'd fully expected him to toy with her mercilessly during the flight, but she might as well have been invisible.

Much to her chagrin that hadn't made her feel relieved or...*good*.

She felt Salman nudge her back. 'Are you going to stand there all day?'

Quickly she hurried down the steps and into the waiting chauffeur-driven car. She heard Salman greet the driver by name, and had to assume the man was his personal driver. Within minutes they were joining the hectic stream of traffic, headed for the centre of Paris.

Emotion surged within Jamilah, despite her best attempts to keep it down. She hadn't been back to Paris once since that fateful time. She'd been to Nadim's stables, which were just outside Paris, but not to the city. And yet here she was, *with Salman*.

Salman was acutely aware of Jamilah, resolutely facing away from him, looking out of the other window. He could see the line of her exquisite profile. Those long dark lashes. She'd tied her hair back in a chignon, and in her long dark coat she could have been any of a number of stunningly beautiful women in this city. His chest tightened. She was so much more beautiful than any of those women.

He'd had to immerse himself in work on the plane just to stop himself from giving in to a primal impulse to drag her into the sleeping cabin at the back and ravish her. And then, to his surprise, as he'd read up on the topics for the meetings he'd found his interest being stirred and ignited. For the first time in his life he'd felt something proprietorial for Merkazad rear its head. That feeling of vulnerability made his skin prickle uncomfortably.

Jamilah turned and asked huskily, 'Why did you sell your apartment?'

The unbidden answer rose up inside him. *Because I couldn't stand to live there after that day...*

Jamilah watched as something enigmatic lit Salman's eyes, and felt something in her own chest contract. But then it passed, and he looked away, shrugging. 'I grew out of it. I wasn't sure what I wanted instead, so I moved into the Ritz and I've been there ever since.'

'It must be a bit...impersonal living in a hotel?'

Salman looked back and smiled devilishly, every inch of him the supremely successful businessman in his charcoal suit and black coat. 'It suits me perfectly. And my needs.'

At the way he said *needs* Jamilah could feel colour flaring into her cheeks and looked away again. She could well imagine that it *did* serve his feckless needs. No woman being brought into the suite of a hotel would be under any illusion that their relationship wasn't as transitory as his accommodation.

Suddenly angry, Jamilah looked back, to find Salman still watching her. She reacted to that as much as to his words. 'I feel sorry for you, you know. You've cut off all ties with your own home, you live out of a suite in a hotel, you don't even have a relationship with your brother—'

Her words were cut off brutally when the space between them was breached and Salman was suddenly there. Her head was in his hands, so close to his that she could breathe him in. She felt his powerful thighs right against hers. Her breath came short and jerkily. Her heart hammered.

Blisteringly he said, 'I don't need anyone's pity, Jamilah, and I certainly don't need yours. I've made my choices along the way, and if I had to choose again I wouldn't do anything differently.'

At that pain lanced her so acutely that Jamilah gasped—but it all got eclipsed when Salman's mouth covered hers and she was thrown into the fire. Full of emotion—anger mixed up with an awful treacherous yearning and, unbelievably, a helpless and inexplicable tenderness—Jamilah gripped the lapels of Salman's coat and held him to her, matching his kiss passion for passion. The fire was stoked higher and higher.

With a guttural groan that resonated within her, he put his arms around her back and arched her up and into him, so that her breasts were crushed against his hard chest. They ached for his touch. Mouths fused again. Jamilah's hands delved into Salman's silky hair, moulding his skull, holding him to her. In that moment she would have gladly given everything up just for this. This hot insanity and distraction from the pain. The ever-present pain. Caused by this man.

That thought sliced through the frantic desire and the pulse beating through her blood. She pulled back in the same moment that Salman did. She was practically supine on the back seat of the car, Salman crushing her to the seat. She could feel the hard ridge of his erection against her thigh and her lower body throbbed painfully. She felt dishevelled, undone, and utterly exposed.

Salman lifted his head. The dark colour slashing his cheekbones and his heavy breathing sent only a sliver of comfort through Jamilah. She couldn't speak. It was only then that she noticed the privacy partition had gone up, and mortification drenched her to think of the driver witnessing this.

Salman's voice grated across her exposed nerves. 'Like I said…I don't want your pity. But I do want you. And you want me, too, Jamilah. Nothing's changed. We want each other as much as if it were that first time all over again.'

She opened her mouth to deny it, ridiculously, and Salman ruthlessly cut her off.

'*Don't* even think of saying it. You're not a liar, Jamilah. One of the things I've always admired about you is your honesty.'

She shut her mouth, and with an effort slithered out from under him, pressing her legs together and pulling her coat around her. She could feel her hair falling out of its chignon, and with shaky hands attempted to repair the damage. Her mouth felt swollen; her cheeks burned. It was futile to deny it any longer. 'I may want you, Salman, but that doesn't mean I'll go there. You washed your hands of me once already, remember?'

Salman was back on the other side of the car, his long legs spread out. His voice was tight. 'I never intended to hurt you, Jamilah. I should never have seduced you.'

Utter shock had Jamilah turning to face Salman's rigid profile. Only a deep self-preserving instinct had her saying faintly, 'I've already told you that you didn't hurt me, Salman.' *Liar.* 'What exactly are you saying?'

He flashed her a look, and she saw something indefinable in his eyes. 'I wasn't ready to let you go. I still
wanted you. I've always wanted you. But I had to let you
go...' his mouth twisted '...when you said you were in
love with me.'

As she watched he seemed to compose himself,
and that smooth mask of urbanity came back. It was
as if she'd just imagined his slightly tortured look. He
turned to face her more fully and said, 'But now that
time has passed, and seeing as you've assured me that
you're unscathed are you *sure* you want to persist in
denying that this attraction is still there? After all, what
do either of us have to lose now? We're both adults,
experienced...'

Shock was rushing through Jamilah. She was trying
to make sense of his words and at the same time make
sure he couldn't see the turmoil she felt. He was saying
that he'd let her go just because she'd been in love with
him? That he hadn't *wanted* to let her go? It put such a
new spin on what had happened that she wanted to go to
a quiet place and assimilate the information... But even
as she wanted that, she was aware that really it didn't
change much. He'd still cast her out because he hadn't
welcomed her ardent affections...

He was waiting for her response—so impassive, so
implacable. Panic beat at her breast, and Jamilah cast
him as cool a look as she could muster. 'I'm not interested in pursuing this line of conversation, no matter
how *adult* we might be. Out of the myriad women you've
no doubt entertained in your suite, I'm sure one will be
available to meet your needs. Because I am not.'

Jamilah avoided Salman's eye as they drew closer
to the iconic Paris hotel, feeling acutely vulnerable. As
much as she might think she'd had the last word, she

felt uncomfortably as if Salman had taken no heed at all and was merely biding his time to pounce.

As the car pulled in to a halt at the kerb outside the entrance of the hotel she could see doormen rush to the doors. Salman took her hand in a merciless grip and said softly, 'There's a lot to be said for slaking this desire between us, Jamilah. Here in Paris. Be done with it for good. I won't be calling up any other women because that's not what I need.' His jaw clenched as if in anger for a second. 'What I need is you…and it's the same for you. I'll be here when you're ready to admit it to yourself—because your body has already spoken.'

And then her door was being opened and she had to get out. She ripped her hand free from Salman's, saying caustically as she did so, 'Dream on, Salman.'

A short while later Salman was looking at the ornately decorated door which had just been shut in his face. A key turned in the lock at that moment as a perfunctory accompaniment, and he smiled grimly before turning and walking into the main part of the huge suite. It consisted of two bedrooms, with their own sitting rooms and *en suite* bathrooms, a formal dining room and salon, and a state-of-the-art office complete with every kind of technology for the modern businessman.

Sexual frustration pounded through his body. He'd never felt it this badly before. He was used to having his needs met, and for the first time had to face the prospect that he might just be facing his match. Determination fired his blood. He'd seen through the icy veneer that Jamilah had projected all the way up to the suite. He'd seen the pulse beating hectically under the delicate skin of her neck. She'd admitted she wanted him. He was going to woo her as he'd never had to woo a woman in his life.

With that thought in mind, and quashing the prickling of his conscience because once again he was ignoring her vulnerability, he felt the burning desire finally abate to a more manageable level, and strode into the office to take care of some work.

The following morning Jamilah felt tired and gritty-eyed after a disturbed night. She'd tossed and turned for hours in the huge luxurious bed, and had finally had to resort to *another* cold shower in the early hours of the morning. The key she had turned to lock the door on Salman the previous night might as well have been made of air; he'd still managed to infiltrate her every sleepless thought.

Now she felt more weary and exhausted than any-thing else as she emerged into the opulent salon. She was dressed in a dark grey pencil skirt and matching jacket, white shirt, buttoned all the way up, and black high heels. Hair pulled back into a sleek ponytail.

But nothing could have prepared her for seeing Salman standing at the main window, decked from head to toe in traditional Merkazadi robes of cream and gold, complete with turbaned headdress. He was all at once devastating and intimidating. Her heart flip-flopped ominously.

He turned and quirked a brow, reading her look instantly. 'What? I can play the part when I want to, Jamilah.'

Jamilah struggled to find her composure. She couldn't believe that seeing Salman dressed like this for the first time in years was having such an effect on her, but it was. It was transporting her right back in time to when they'd been so much younger, and he and Nadim had looked like two men old before their time at their parents' funerals. A deep melancholy assailed her and she valiantly fought down the emotion, terrified he'd see something of it.

She hitched up her chin and said, 'It's amazing how regal a robe can make one look.'

'When one is not regal at all?' He put a hand to his chest, and a mocking smile curled his lip on one side. 'You wound me, Jamilah, with your condemnation. I'm not likely ever to redeem myself in your eyes, am I?'

'I'm not here to redeem you, Salman.'

Her words struck him somewhere vulnerable and deep. Salman had to school his expression and walk over to her. 'I'm not looking for redemption or absolution from anyone.' He was unaware of the bleakness that flashed through his eyes. 'I'm looking for something else much more…earthy and immediate.'

Jamilah took a step back, unable to stand so close to him, and said briskly, 'I'm going to have breakfast downstairs. I'll see you at the first of the meetings.'

She turned and all but fled, and heard from behind her, 'Run all you want, Jamilah. It'll make the final capitulation so much sweeter.'

The main door slammed behind her on the way out, and it was a hollow and empty sound.

After a morning of intense meetings, where Jamilah stayed largely in the background as she was really only there to discuss the stables, she was reeling slightly at seeing how Salman had been so authoritative and informed. And it would appear he'd taken others by surprise, too—people who had perhaps expected him to live up to his feckless playboy reputation.

She couldn't in all honesty say that Nadim would have contributed anything more, and in fact Salman had put forward some audacious suggestions that she knew for a fact the more inherently cautious Nadim would never have sanctioned.

Now everyone was breaking for lunch, and she was trying to make a discreet escape, fully intending to find a coffee shop nearby despite the fact that lunch was being provided.

Jamilah stifled a gasp when she felt her hand being taken in a much larger one which had familiar tingles racing her up arm and into her belly. *Salman*.

He was already tugging her along in his wake, and Jamilah whispered at him, mindful of the people around them. 'I'm going out for lunch. *Alone*.'

He cast a quick glance back, and Jamilah saw the dark intent in his eyes. '*We're* going for lunch.'

'But you have to eat with the other delegates.' Desperation mounted.

Salman faced forward again, pulling her along remorselessly. 'You should know by now that I generally do not take well to orders.'

Knowing that he would not budge, nor release her, Jamilah followed with a mutinous look on her face which turned to burning embarrassment as they passed people she knew. One of them was the aide to the Sultan of Al-Omar she had abandoned at that party a year ago. She smiled weakly at him as she passed.

She could see that they were approaching the gardens at the back of the hotel. A staff member bowed deferentially to Salman as he opened a door, and then they were out in the unusually mild November air. It was a beautiful clear day that held a last lingering hint of the summer just gone.

Salman led her down a path through immaculately manicured lawns until she saw a beautifully ornate gazebo, with a table set for two, with full silver service place settings. Her stomach rumbled and she blushed.

Inside the gazebo a waiter bowed and seated them both. Totally bemused, Jamilah let him spread a snowy-white napkin across her lap, and listened while he explained about the specials on offer.

In shock, Jamilah made her choice for lunch, barely aware of what she was doing. She heard Salman say, 'I'll have the same.'

The waiter poured vintage champagne for her and sparkling water for Salman before taking his leave. A bird called nearby. The faint sound of the rumble of traffic came through the dense foliage of the bushes that climbed huge walls nearby. The gazebo was covered in trailing sweet-smelling flowers, and it was utterly secluded and idyllic.

Finally sanity returned, and Jamilah put down her napkin and stood up. 'I don't know what you're up to, Salman, but as I told you on the way here yesterday, you really should be consulting your Rolodex of contacts for this kind of thing. It's wasted on me, and I'd hate to think of you running up your tab needlessly.'

Salman affected a look of mild boredom though he felt anything but. Panic had clutched his gut when Jamilah had stood up. He knew he had to get this right or she would keep running. 'This is just lunch. I thought it might be nice to take it outside...' He waved a hand. 'I had no idea that they would put on this spectacle.'

Jamilah hesitated. There was indeed an outdoor area for dining—perhaps Salman had expected it to be there? Insecurity pierced her. Perhaps she was crediting Salman with too much ingenuity. He'd never shown any inclination for grand showy gestures when she'd been with him before…

She looked at him suspiciously. 'You really expected this to be in the other place?'

He nodded, an artful look of innocence on his face. Still thoroughly suspicious, Jamilah nevertheless found herself sitting back down, clutching her napkin. It was lunch. Just lunch. Albeit in the most seductive surroundings she'd ever encountered. Perhaps she was overreacting a little. And if she overreacted then Salman would have her in the palm of his hand.

Now she affected a look of mild uninterest. 'Fine. We don't have long for lunch anyway.' She flicked a glance at her watch. 'We have to be back in forty-five minutes.' And she sat with legs crossed, facing away from the table, as if ready to bolt.

The waiter came back at that moment with their starters. She waited to eat, suddenly very self-conscious. It was only when Salman said, with a smile playing around his mouth, 'Well? Aren't you going to eat? You must be starving…' that Jamilah gave in. She'd barely picked at breakfast that morning and nerves had curtailed her usually healthy appetite for days now.

So now, in spite of Salman's presence, she found herself all but licking her plate clean of its white asparagus starter.

Salman was sitting back, watching her, and she felt heat climb into her cheeks which she tried to disguise by wiping her mouth with her napkin. The little champagne she'd drunk was fizzing gently along her nerve-endings, making her feel all too susceptible to this…idyll. And to Salman's devastatingly dark and gorgeous presence.

'So…you are now running the stables for Nadim? Not bad for the girl who used to muck out the stalls.'

Jamilah smiled minutely. 'I still muck out the stalls, Salman. We don't stand on ceremony at the stables.'

He inclined his head and said thoughtfully, 'I can see that you would be a good boss—tough, but fair. And clearly Nadim values your opinion enough to negotiate on his behalf.'

An infusing warmth spread through Jamilah. Ever since she'd completed her studies in veterinary science in Paris, her ambition had been to manage the world-famous Merkazad stables, and to be doing it at her relatively young age was no small feat.

She shrugged lightly and avoided Salman's intense gaze. 'You know I always loved animals, I dreamed of running the stables ever since I was tiny.'

Something hollow sounded in Salman's voice. 'I know. Which is why it was good that you went home and followed your path.'

She looked at him, but his face showed no discernible emotion. And then the waiter came with their main courses and their conversation was interrupted. She'd often told him of her dreams when they'd been younger, when he'd listen in silence as she prattled on. Now she had to recall that he'd never really shared anything personal of himself—just as he hadn't in Paris. There had just been this intangible quality between them. And it still hurt to think that he'd seen her as an encumbrance.

But was he saying now that on some level he'd been concerned that she'd sacrifice her dreams for what had essentially been a fling in Paris? Coupled with what he'd revealed in the car the day before, she had to acknowledge that his rejection of her had perhaps not been as arbitrarily cruel as she'd believed it to be.

That thought made her quiet as she ate. But finally

curiosity overcame her, and she asked Salman about his own work. He wiped at his mouth with a napkin before telling her that he'd graduated to the much more risky world of hedge fund management.

He grimaced slightly. 'I'm now a part of that most reviled breed of bankers, the scourge of the recent banking crisis, and yet...' something cynical crossed his face '...reviled as we may be, business has never been so good.' He smiled, but it was without warmth.

'You have your own company?'

He nodded and took a sip of water. 'Yes, it's called Al-Saqr Holdings.'

Jamilah's fingers plucked at her napkin. 'And you don't mind being thought of...badly?'

He shrugged, eyes glinting. 'I've developed a thick skin. If people still want me to invest their money for them, to take risks on their behalf, who am I to deny them?'

'It sounds so soulless.'

'Much like living out of a hotel and leading a disconnected existence? You should know by now, Jamilah, that my soul is lost. I told you a long time ago that I'm dark and twisted inside.'

Jamilah had the shocking realisation in that moment that he really meant what he said. Why would he think that? On some level he truly *did* believe he was lost, and her heart squeezed. She could still see the boy who had come to comfort her at her parents' grave, who had instilled within her a sense of strength she sometimes still drew on. Which was ironic, when *he* was largely the reason she needed strength.

But for those three weeks he'd been gentle and infinitely generous. He'd been as she had remembered him—affectionately indulgent to her, and tolerant of her constant chatter and exuberance. But when she'd trespassed too far she'd been subjected to his icy-cold front and dismissed like all the others—cast out to the periphery.

She couldn't and would never forget his cruelty to her, but it was already becoming a more ambiguous, multi-faceted thing. Why would he feel like that about himself? What had happened to him to make him believe that? She knew if she kept on this path it would be a very dangerous one. She shouldn't be curious. She shouldn't care.

Abruptly she put down her napkin and stood up, making a hasty excuse, hating herself for it. 'I need to get some papers from the suite for my own meeting this afternoon.'

With smooth grace Jamilah saw Salman make a discreet gesture to someone behind them, and he stood up, too, indicating for her to precede him out of the gazebo. She was surprised he wasn't pushing for them to stay for coffee and dessert. She walked out a little unsteadily. And then he took her arm to lead her back into the hotel through the gorgeous private gardens.

As they neared the doors, where staff waited, she cursed her gullibility. She stopped and turned to him, looked up. 'You knew very well what you were asking for when you requested a table outside, didn't you?'

Eyes as black as sin turned her insides molten. He smiled wickedly. 'It was a mere manipulation of the truth to get you to stay.'

Jamilah fought the lazy tendrils of desire unfurling inside her. 'I don't want you to seduce me, Salman. I won't be seduced.'

'It's too late, Jamilah. We're here now...for a reason.'

His mouth firmed, 'I don't believe in fate, but I believe in *this*.'

He pulled her into him and his mouth was on hers before she could even squeak in protest. One hand went to his chest, to push him away, but his steely strength called to her, making her legs weak. She emitted a groan of pure self-disgust mixed with the inevitable rise of wanton desire. Their mouths clung, tongues touching and tasting. It grew more heated, and Jamilah found that her arms and hands had climbed up to Salman's neck and she was straining on tiptoe to get even closer.

She pulled back, her heart racing, disgusted to find herself in this position—*again*.

He held her fast against his body, where she could feel the heat and strength of his burgeoning arousal. 'Tell me again you won't be seduced...' It wasn't even a question.

Jamilah wanted to deny him, but the way she kept falling into his arms and responding so forcibly mocked her. Her heart fell at the unmistakable light of triumph in his eyes.

'The problem is that we are dealing with a force greater than ourselves, and the fact that our desire never got a chance to burn itself out,' he said.

Jamilah finally managed to pull away. 'Unlike you, I have a healthy respect for things that aren't good for me. I can resist this, and I *will*. Find someone else, Salman, *please*.' And she hoped to God that he would listen to her plea.

CHAPTER FIVE

JAMILAH had only gone back downstairs when she was due to have her own meeting with the envoy from Dubai. To her abject relief she hadn't seen Salman again, but she steeled herself now for the evening ahead, when they were due to go to a black tie function.

When she heard Salman moving around in the main salon she took a deep and shaky breath in. She regarded herself in her bedroom mirror. Make-up covered most of the ravages of the last sleepless night, and the aftermath of that lunch and the kiss. There was an awful feeling of inevitability burning low in her belly, and she couldn't ignore it much as she wanted to.

Her dress was strapless silk and floor-length, midnight-blue in colour—almost black. It managed to be effortlessly chic even while the low back presented a much more daring view.

Her mother had been a famous fashion model—one of the first Arabic women to break into the international scene—which was how she'd met Jamilah's father in Paris. Before Jamilah's parents had died so tragically her mother had already instilled within her a love and appreciation for classic elegant clothes and jewellery. Jamilah didn't buy much, but when she did it was always quality pieces.

She'd twisted her hair up, and now added a pair of her mother's sapphire earrings to match the simple necklace that adorned her neck. With another shaky breath she picked up her short *faux* fur coat and evening bag and left her room.

Her hands clenched tight around her bag when she saw Salman, standing and flicking idly through a magazine on the table. He looked up, and for a moment Jamilah felt as if she was drowning. She'd seen Salman in a tuxedo before, but something about seeing him now, *tonight,* seemed to hit her right between the eyes. He was simply the most stupendously handsome man she'd ever seen.

Salman looked at Jamilah. She was a vision in dark silk which showed off every elegant curve of her body. Her breasts were soft pale swells above the bodice, and a gem hung with tantalising provocation just above the vee in her cleavage. Her eyes glittered a dazzling blue, and Salman knew that if they didn't get out of there right now he'd take her to his bed and she would hate him for ever. And then he had to concede bitterly that he'd already taken care of that when he'd rejected her so cruelly six years before.

Curtly, Salman said, dropping the magazine, 'We should get going, or we'll be late for the opening speech.'

Jamilah nearly reeled back on her heels. She felt as if she'd just hurtled through a time continuum, been burnt by the sun and then thrown out the other side. Had she just imagined that incendiary moment?

Standing in the lift moments later as they descended, she felt very shaky and vulnerable. Salman was stony-faced and taciturn, and it gave her a sickening sense of *déjà-vu* to when he'd changed so utterly on that fateful day six years before. She welcomed it, and hardened the tender inner part of herself that had felt an awful weakening as the day had progressed, as if on some level his relentless pursuit was starting to dissolve her own resolve to resist. She could resist. She had to resist.

Outside the hotel, in the cool night air, he helped her to put on her coat. Visibly flinching when his hand brushed the bare skin of her shoulder.

Jamilah tugged her coat from his hands and said curtly, 'It's fine. I've got it. I'm sorry you had to touch me.'

His car was just drawing up, and he turned her to face him with his hands on her shoulders. Jamilah hated that she was feeling so raw. But the stark hunger etched onto his face sent tremors of awareness through her. Along with confusion.

'You think that I don't *want* to touch you?'

Jamilah couldn't speak. In her peripheral vision she could see the driver standing and holding the door open, but they weren't moving. Salman spoke again in low husky tones.

'If I hadn't got you out of that suite as quickly as I had, I think it's safe to say that your dress would already be in ribbons and we'd be indulging in the most frantic and urgent coupling of our lives. All I can think about is how I want to pull you onto the back seat of that car, spread your legs around me and take you right now—because quite frankly the suite is too far away. I've never before contemplated stopping a lift to make love to a woman, but I just did. Don't you have any *idea* how much I want you?'

Jamilah's mouth opened and closed with shock. Any resolve that had recently fired through her was washed away by a rush of desire so intense that she literally ached for Salman to do exactly as he'd said. All she could see was their naked limbs entwined, dewed with sweat, hearts beating frantically as they came closer and closer to the explosive pinnacle.

Just then someone emerged from the hotel behind them, and Jamilah blinked as she saw Salman's urbane mask come back. It was the Sultan of Al-Omar, and she issued a garbled greeting to the tall, handsome ruler. She vaguely heard him ask if he could share their ride to the dinner, as he'd lent his car out for the evening to someone else.

Bodyguards belonging to the Sultan and to Salman hovered in the shadows, ready to jump into their accompanying vehicles. It served to bring Jamilah back to some kind of sanity, and a few seconds later she found herself pressed tight against Salman, who had negotiated it so that Jamilah was on his right, with Sultan Sadiq on his left. All Jamilah could feel was her thigh burning where Salman's pressed against her. Strong and powerfully muscular.

The men spoke of inanities and their meetings. Jamilah couldn't contribute a word, her head still whirling at Salman's intensity just now. How on earth was she going to cope if he directed that at her again? With an awful feeling of fatality she knew she wouldn't be able to.

A couple of hours later Jamilah's nerves were overwrought after an evening spent at Salman's side, trying to ignore the feelings running riot through her system. He'd barely touched her all evening, but she'd felt the burning intensity in his restraint.

Now they were back in their car—without the Sultan this time. He'd come up to Salman earlier, with a gorgeous statuesque brunette on his arm, and it had been obvious he had plans other than returning to the hotel. Sultan Sadiq had almost as notorious a reputation as Salman.

They glided through the moonlit streets of Paris now, with the Eiffel Tower appearing and disappearing intermittently, all lit up like a giant bauble. The tension was thick between them, and just when Jamilah was contemplating the uphill battle she faced if Salman tried to seduce her again she heard him ask the driver to slow down. She only noticed then that they were beside the Hôtel de Ville, where a fairground had been set up in the main square.

Salman looked at her. 'Do you mind if we get out for a minute?'

Jamilah shook her head with relief. She needed space and air in order to gather her defences again.

They got out, and when the cool air hit her she shivered. She felt Salman dropping his warm jacket around her shoulders. She looked up at him, heart tripping. 'I can get my coat. You'll freeze.'

He smiled his lopsided smile. 'I'll survive. It'll take more than the cold to do me in.'

He took her by the hand and reluctantly she gave in, knowing he wouldn't let her go anyway. They walked towards the tinkling music. Some couples were strolling around, like them, hand in hand, amongst groups of teenagers and even some harried-looking parents with small children, seemingly oblivious to the late hour.

Salman said then, so softly that she almost didn't hear him, 'I've always loved fairgrounds. There's something so escapist and other-worldly about them.'

Jamilah's mouth dropped open, and she closed it abruptly when Salman sent her an amused glance. 'Don't look so shocked.'

'When were you ever at a fairground growing up?' They had nothing like them in Merkazad.

He was leading her towards where a merry-go-round glistened under a blaze of lights. There was a melancholic quality to his voice. 'There used to be a fairground in Merkazad, but when the rebels invaded they smashed it to pieces.'

'Oh…' No wonder she hadn't ever seen one. It would have been long gone by the time she'd been old enough to visit it. 'Why wasn't another one built?'

Salman shrugged. 'I think people were having a hard enough time just rebuilding their lives and homes.'

'Perhaps someone should build one again…'

Salman looked at her with an enigmatic expression. 'Maybe one day someone will.'

The intensity of his gaze on hers made her look away and say a little breathlessly, 'You don't mind *these* horses…?'

He followed her gaze to the brightly coloured horses that went up and down and round and round. 'No,' he said tightly, 'I don't mind these horses.' He looked back at her. 'I don't mind any horses in general, Jamilah. I just choose not to go near them. I leave that up to people like you and Nadim.'

His tone brooked no further conversation, and she caught a glimpse of something suspiciously like fear in his eyes. That slightly ashen tinge again coloured his skin. She'd been around horses and people long enough to spot someone who had a pathological fear a mile away, and for the first time she guessed that Salman's antipathy to horses went far deeper than fear. It reminded her of a phobic reaction. Her curiosity was welling up again, and with it a sense of danger.

She took her hand out of his and stepped up to the

beautiful antique-looking carousel, holding her dress in one hand. She handed some money over to the man operating the controls, and when it had stopped she jumped up to sit side-saddle on one of the horses. With a burgeoning feeling of lightness in her chest she stuck her tongue out cheekily at Salman, and just as it was about to start off again he threw some money at the man and stepped up beside her, standing close enough that she could feel his hard chest against her thigh.

'Hey!' she said, breathless all over again. 'That's cheating. You're meant to sit on your own horse.'

He locked his hands around her waist and Jamilah had to hang onto his shoulders for dear life as the horse started to go up and down. They were moving. It was causing a delicious friction between his chest and her leg. He reached up and pulled her head down to his. She was powerless to resist. Their mouths met, the up and down motion of the horse forcing them close together and then apart in an intoxicating dance.

The music faded, and everything dissolved into the heat of the kiss and Salman's arms around her, holding her like an anchor. Neither one of them heard the crude wolf-whistle from a passing crowd of teens. They didn't come up for air until the man asked brusquely if they were prepared to pay for another go.

Cheeks scarlet with embarrassment, Jamilah slithered off the horse, legs wobbly, and was grateful for Salman's steadying hand on hers as he led her away. Her heart was pounding and her skin prickled with anticipation. She had no doubt that right at this moment Salman intended taking her back to the hotel and making love to her.

Maybe he was right? Maybe they *should* indulge in this madness in Paris and be purged of this crazy desire and obsession? Perhaps that was what it would take to get him out of her system for good?

Just then Salman got distracted by something. She heard the rat-tat-tat of rapid tinny gunfire coming from a shooting range, and saw where a small boy of about eight was in floods of tears because he'd obviously missed his target. His mother was trying to console him, telling him she had no more money, pleading with the owner of the stall of give him something, but the owner was sour-faced.

Before Jamilah knew what was happening Salman was striding over to the stall, dragging her along in his wake. When they reached it, he let Jamilah's hand go and bent down to talk to the little boy in perfect French. Jamilah smiled awkwardly at the beleaguered-looking mother, and wondered what Salman was up to.

After a few minutes of consulting with the now sniffling boy, who had pointed out the prize he wanted, Salman handed some money to the owner. Then he lifted up the boy and rested his feet on a rung of the fence around the stall. He helped him to aim—showing him how to balance the rifle on his shoulder, explaining how to keep a steady hand. With his arms around him, Salman encouraged the boy to take the shot. To his ecstatic surprise and the owner's evident disgruntlement he hit it first time. A perfect hit, right in the bullseye—and it was the hardest target to hit, as it was clearly the most coveted prize.

Amidst much effusive thanks, Salman finally took a bemused Jamilah's hand again, and with a wave they walked off, leaving the now chirpy boy with his grateful mum. But as they approached the car, she could sense his mood change as clearly as if a bell had gone off.

When they were in the car, Jamilah turned on a tensely silent Salman.

'Where did you learn to shoot like that?'

Salman didn't turn to face her, and just said quietly, almost as if to himself, 'I shouldn't have done that. I shouldn't have encouraged him to take the shot. It was good that he missed. Better that he be disappointed and not want to do it again than...' He trailed off.

Jamilah asked, 'Than what? Salman?'

Suddenly a chasm existed between them when minutes ago it had been all heat and urgent desire. Salman had withdrawn to somewhere impenetrable. He looked at her, but his eyes were opaque, unreadable. 'Than nothing. It doesn't matter.'

It did matter, though. She knew it with a grim certainty when she thought back to that little scene, and when she recalled the automatic way Salman had handled even a toy gun with such unerring dexterity. Like a true marksman.

Jamilah said now, 'He didn't take that shot. You did. You just made him think that he took it. It's no big deal. It's just a game.'

Salman smiled, but it was grim. 'It's never just a game.'

'How do you know this? And you didn't answer me— where did you learn to shoot?'

For such a long time he said nothing, and she almost thought he was going to ignore her, but then he said, in a scarily emotionless voice, 'It was just luck...pure fluke.'

He turned back to look out of his window, and Jamilah felt as if she'd been dismissed. The rest of the drive to the hotel was made in a silence which had thickened so much that by the time they got up to the suite Jamilah felt too intimidated to speak.

Salman just looked at her, and for a second she saw such a wealth of pain that she instinctively stepped forward with a hand outstretched. 'Salman, what is it?'

And then the enigmatic look was gone, and a stony-faced Salman said a curt, 'Nothing. Go to bed, Jamilah.'

He turned on his heel and walked into his own rooms. Thoroughly confused, Jamilah stared after him for a long moment. And then, galvanised by something she couldn't even understand, she strode forward and opened Salman's bedroom door without knocking. He was standing in the dark, looking out of the window, hands in his pockets.

He didn't turn around, just said, 'I thought I told you to go to bed.'

'You're not my father, Salman. I'll go to bed when I feel like it.'

She walked over to where he stood and looked up. When he didn't turn around exasperation made her take his arm to turn him. He looked down at her, face expressionless in the moonlight.

'What's going on, Salman? One minute you're kissing me, and the next you're treating me as if I've got leprosy.'

Salman smiled mockingly and Jamilah wanted to slap that look off his face. 'Are you saying you're ready to fall into bed with me?'

He cast a look at his watch and gave a low whistle. 'Not bad. It only took twenty-four hours. I was convinced it would take at least two days. Was it my concern for the boy's distress that melted your soft-hearted resistance, or was it the impressive way I wielded the gun?'

Jamilah's hand came up then, and she did slap him. Hard enough to make his head turn. Her hand tingled and burned. Shakily she said, 'You deserved that—and not for what you just said, but for what you did to me six years ago.'

She turned and walked to the door, and Salman said softly from behind her, 'Make no mistake, Jamilah, I do want you. But if we sleep together I won't and can't offer you anything more than I offered last time.' Bitterness rang in his voice. 'At least you can't say that I'm not warning you up-front.'

Jamilah turned back. 'Go to hell, Salman.'

As she turned again and walked away she heard him say quietly, 'I've already been there for a long time.'

Something stopped her in her tracks at that. She turned again, despite all the screaming voices and warning bells going off in her head. 'What's that supposed to mean?'

CHAPTER SIX

SALMAN heard Jamilah's words, and his whole body contracted as if from a physical blow. Damn the woman, why wouldn't she just leave? A voice mocked him. *Like the way you forced her to leave six years ago?*

A wave of weariness nearly knocked Salman sideways then. He'd been so rigid, so controlled, so angry for so long. And this woman was taking a sledgehammer to all of that and smashing it aside without even knowing what she was doing.

Grimly he turned to face her, his face still stinging from her slap. He welcomed it.

When Jamilah saw the lurid print of her hand on Salman's cheek in the shadows she felt huge remorse. She came forward on stiff legs, and in a rush made a stilted apology for hitting him. She'd never hit another human being in her life, and was genuinely mortified at her behaviour.

But he just said grimly, 'I'm not sorry you hit me. I deserved it. And I probably deserve more.'

Jamilah shook her head. 'I don't get it, Salman. It's almost as if you want to be punished.'

He cracked a tight smile. 'Don't I?'

Jamilah was silent. She suspected he wasn't referring to his behaviour six years ago with her—or he was, but it was only a small part of a much bigger thing. 'What really happened with that boy tonight? Why did it affect you like that?'

Salman looked at her for a long moment, his dark gaze blistering her for her question, but as he did so she felt more and more defiant. She wasn't going to back down.

And then he said tightly, 'I don't think you really want to know why.'

Sudden anger flared that he should shut her out like this. She sensed that this was at the very core of who he was. 'Don't patronise me, Salman. I'm sure there's nothing you could tell me that would unduly shock me.'

That bleakness flashed across his face again before it was masked. He smiled grimly. 'Nevertheless, it's not something I want to discuss right now.'

Without even really thinking about what she was saying Jamilah asked, 'When *will* it be the right time, Salman?'

His mouth tightened. 'For you? Never. I would never do that to you.'

'You already did, Salman.'

She knew they were talking about two different things now, and yet it was all inextricably bound up together— Salman's dark secrets and the way he'd treated her, the way he still didn't trust her enough to reveal himself. And never would.

A sense of futility made her turn as if to go, but to her shock and surprise Salman grabbed her wrist and said tightly, 'Are you sure you really want to know, Jamilah?'

She faced him slowly and could see the intense glitter of his eyes, the way a muscle pulsed in his jaw. The moment was huge, and she knew that much of their history and this present madness was bound up in it.

Slowly, as if she might scare him off, she nodded her head. 'Yes, I want to know, Salman.'

Salman looked into Jamilah's huge blue eyes. He had the most bizarre sensation of drowning while at the same time clinging onto a life-raft. He couldn't believe he'd stopped her from leaving—couldn't believe he'd just said what he had. Did he really think he was about to divulge to her what no one else knew? His deepest, darkest shame? And yet in that instant he knew an overwhelming need to unburden himself here, with *her*. It could never have been with anyone else. He saw that now, as clear as day.

That little boy had had a more profound effect on him than he'd expected. He'd acted completely on instinct to go and comfort him, and when he'd seen what he could do to make him feel better he'd done it. It had only been afterwards, walking away, when the full impact of taking that shot had hit him.

His past had rushed upwards to slap him in the face far harder than Jamilah ever could. For a few moments in that fairground with Jamilah he'd been seduced by her all over again. Seduced into a lighter way of being. Seduced into thinking that he *didn't* carry around an awful legacy and a dark secret which pervaded his being like a poison.

The bravery he'd witnessed from others mocked him now—was he afraid to do this? For the first time he knew he wasn't. What he *was* afraid of, right here and now, was how Jamilah would react to what he was about to tell her...for if anything could drive her away for good *this* could. Perhaps this was the sum total of his actions—to be brought to his knees by her only to watch her walk away for good.

Jamilah watched as Salman clearly struggled with something, but then his face became expressionless. The light spilling in from the sitting room illuminated its stark lines and he'd never looked so bleak. He dropped her wrist, and it tingled where he had held it. He walked over to a chair in the corner and sat down heavily, and Jamilah, not taking her eyes off him, perched on the end of the bed. Her throat had gone dry.

His head was downbent, and then he lifted it, that black gaze spearing her. 'What I said to you that day in Paris…about how there had never been anything between us, about you following me around like a puppy dog…it was a lie.'

For a second a buzzing sounded in Jamilah's ears. She thought she might faint. As much as she wanted to deny that she remembered his cruel words, she said instead, 'Why? Why did you say it?' Relief was a giddy surge through her body.

'I said it because you'd told me you loved me, and I knew that if I didn't make you hate me you might not stay away. You might hope you could change me.'

He smiled then, and it was grim. 'But then, as you've said yourself, what you felt was merely a crush, so perhaps I needn't have been so cruel.'

Jamilah would have laughed if she'd had the wherewithal at this understatement of the year. She hoped the pain she felt wasn't evident in her voice. 'You wanted me gone that badly?'

'Yes. Because I couldn't take the responsibility of your love. Because I couldn't return it. Because I *can't*.' He was warning her even now not to expect too much.

Suddenly Jamilah wanted them off this topic. 'Tell me what you're going to tell me, Salman.'

As bleak as she'd ever seen him, he said now, his eyes intent on her, 'I know that I have to tell you. I owe you that much now.'

Jamilah nodded, and wondered why on earth she felt an awful foreboding.

Salman looked down at his hands for a long moment, and then began to speak in an emotionless voice—as if to try and distance himself from what he said. 'The week after my eighth birthday Merkazad was invaded. We'd had no warning. We had no reason to believe that we were in any danger. But unbeknownst to us the Sultan of Al-Omar had long wanted to reclaim Merkazad as part of his country. He resented our independence.'

Jamilah knew all this—and about how the current Sultan's father had been the one to launch an invasion with his most ruthless men. She nodded, even though Salman wasn't looking at her.

'We were sent to the dungeons while they ransacked and looted all around the castle. It took time for the rest of their men to arrive, thanks to our belated Bedouin defence kicking in, which held them off, but we were effectively trapped in the castle with the soldiers and any kind of rules of war went out of the window. These were men hardened by their experiences—the elite soldiers of the army.'

He looked up and smiled at Jamilah, but it was so cold that she shivered.

'They got bored. And so they wanted to amuse themselves. They decided to take me on as a pet project of sorts. To see how long it would take to turn a pampered son of the Sheikh into something else…something more malleable.'

A slow trickling of horror started to snake through Jamilah. She went very still.

'Every day they would come…and take me out of the gaol they'd made out of our old dungeon. At first I bragged to Nadim. I told him that it was because they favoured me. He'd always been the strong one, the one everyone looked up to, and now *I* was the one being singled out. I couldn't understand my mother and father's terror, and if they spoke up too much they were beaten. For the first few days they let me be the cocky little spoilt boy I was—precocious and undoubtedly annoying. We played games…football. They fed me well, made sure I had enough to drink.'

Salman's mouth thinned, his jaw clenched.

'And then it started. The breaking down. The food and drinks were denied me. They started beating me with fists and feet, belts and whips, for the smallest thing. I was bewildered at first. I'd thought they'd been my friends and suddenly they weren't. When I was brought back to the gaol in the evenings I wasn't so cocky. I was confused. How could I explain to Nadim what was going on? I couldn't understand it myself. And yet I couldn't ask for his help. I was too proud, even then. But he suspected what they were doing, and he begged them to take him instead. They ignored him and took me. And they told me that if I didn't go with them every day they would kill Nadim and my parents.'

Jamilah already had a lump in her throat. She wanted to ask Salman to stop, but knew she couldn't. If there was ever to be any hope of closure between them then she had to endure this.

Salman shook his head as if to dislodge a memory. 'The days morphed into one long day… There's a lot I don't remember, but eventually the beatings stopped. By then I was no longer confident, cocky or spoilt. They'd broken me. I had become their tea boy—their servant. They made me polish their boots, make them their lunch.' He took a deep breath. 'But then they got bored again, and decided to train me to be just like them—ruthless soldiers. So they gave me a gun and took me down to the stables for some target practice.'

'Salman...' Jamilah let out a low, horrified breath, shaking her head in denial of what was to come.

He smiled grimly. 'After it was over—when we were free—the thing that upset my father the most was the fact that they'd shot all the horses. Except they hadn't...it was *me*. I was forced to use the horses as target practice, and I got very good very quickly once they told me I had only one shot per horse. If I didn't succeed first time they would let the horse die in agony.'

Jamilah closed her eyes. *That* was why he knew how to use a gun. And that was why he never went near horses or the stables. She opened her eyes. She felt as if a cold wind was blowing over her soul. She was numb, and knew it was the protection of shock. 'Abdul defended you one day at the stables...I couldn't understand why...'

A muscle clenched in his jaw. 'That first day Abdul tried to stop them, and they offered me a choice. Either start killing the horses or kill *him*. It wasn't a choice. Worse than anything, though, was that they made me into one of *them*. I had to start thinking like them just to survive. I had to become wily. The day the Bedouin came and rescued us they found me up on the roof of the castle with a gun. I'd somehow got away from the rebels and was going to try and shoot them...' His mouth twisted. 'I was wild, feral... I was about to kill another human being because they had desensitised me so much that I believed it not only possible but acceptable.'

She felt sick. 'How can you even bear to go to Al-Omar after that?'

Salman shook his head. 'Sultan Sadiq is not his father. He and Nadim made a peace agreement years ago. And he personally oversaw the arrest and imprisonment of all the rebel elements of his father's army.'

Without even thinking about what she was doing Jamilah kicked off her shoes and padded barefoot over to where Salman sat. She knelt at his feet, took one of his hands in hers, and looked up at him, an unbelievable ache in her chest. 'I had no idea that such terror was visited upon you. Why does no one know this?' She felt the tension in his frame.

'Because I blamed myself for a long time. I believed that I'd been responsible on some level—that I'd invited their attention. How could I tell my father what I'd done? He'd never forgive me…or at least that was what I thought. I had nightmares for years of being pursued by a herd of wild avenging horses until I was so exhausted that I would fall and they would trample me to death.'

Jamilah shook her head, gripping his hand. 'It wasn't your fault.'

Salman quirked a weary smile. 'It's one thing to know that on an intellectual level, and another entirely to believe it with all your being.'

Abruptly he stood up, forcing her to stand, too. He took his hand from hers and tipped his head back, his features suddenly stern. 'So now you know. I hope the lurid tale was worth the wait…'

Jamilah shook her head. 'Salman, don't…'

Salman was reacting to how exposed and naked he felt in that moment—alternately drawn to and wanting to escape from Jamilah's huge eyes, which swirled with emotions he couldn't bear to acknowledge. 'Salman, don't *what?* I told you I was twisted and dark inside, and now you know why. Nothing else has changed, Jamilah. I still want you.' His mouth thinned. 'But I won't be surprised if you find your desire suddenly diminished. Not many people relish a battle-scarred lover. Perhaps I *should* take your advice and go and slake my lust elsewhere.'

The stoic pride on his face, mixed with a vulnerability she'd never seen before, made her want to weep. Jamilah fought not to contradict him vociferously. How could he think that? She remained silent, stunned by his awful revelations. She was reeling, in shock and numb all over, but she finally managed to get out, 'What you've told me hasn't disgusted me at all…you were a victim, and shouldn't have had to go through that alone.'

Jamilah sensed Salman's volatility, sensed his anger that he'd revealed what he had. She knew it must have cost him, and he wouldn't welcome the fact that she'd all but bludgeoned him into it. She had to walk away now or he might see how badly she wanted to step up to him, pull his head down and comfort him. She tore her gaze from his and turned and walked away.

At the door she stopped, but didn't turn back. All she said was, 'I'm glad you told me, Salman.' And she left.

For long moments after Jamilah had left the room Salman just stood there, in shock at how easily he'd let his darkness spill out, and at Jamilah's sweetly accepting response. He'd seen pity, yes, but it hadn't made him feel as constricted as he might have imagined. He'd always dreaded the reaction he might get. That was why he found it so easy to listen to others tell their tales.

There was an intense battle raging within him: to take Jamilah and slake his lust, drown himself in the sanctuary that he suspected with grim certainty only she could give him, or to push her away so far and so fast that she would be protected from him. *Again.*

And yet just now she hadn't run from him in horrified terror at the images that had haunted him all his life. He'd seen the compassion in her eyes and had recoiled from it, even as he'd wanted to bury his head in her breast and beg her to never let him go. He who'd never sought comfort from anyone! Even in the darkest moments, when he'd felt he was going mad with all the nightmares and memories.

The parameters of their relationship had just shifted, and Salman wasn't sure where they stopped and started any more. All he knew was that he *wanted* her—now more than ever. Even while he felt that need he acknowledged that after tonight she would have to come to him, but the question was, would she?

Jamilah lay in bed, wide awake, her stomach roiling at the thought of what Salman had gone through. Her head was whirling with all the information. So much made sense now: that terrible darkness that was like a cloak around him, his frosty relationship with Nadim and Merkazad, his fear of horses... And yet he also seemed to be even more of an enigma. She now knew his inner demons, but she'd never felt further from knowing *him*.

Jamilah turned over onto her side and looked out onto the empty square that housed the iconic hotel. Moonlight lit up the monument in the middle, throwing it into stark relief. Despite everything Salman had told her, what was at the forefront of her mind was the

fact that he'd lied about their bond being non-existent.
That he'd said it purely to drive her away. And it had
worked—admirably.

She had to concede now that if he had been nicer
about rejecting her perhaps a doubt always would have
lingered, torturing her even more? Perhaps she wouldn't
have left and got on with her life and career?

Eventually she fell into an uneasy sleep, full of dark
dreams and scary faces with no features, and when she
woke in the morning, nearly late for her first meeting,
she was relieved to see that Salman had already left the
suite.

In the cold light of day what he'd endured seemed to
be so much starker and worse. She sensed that he was
waiting for her to make the next move, and in all honesty
she didn't know if she had the strength to resist him any
more…not with this new knowledge in her head and,
worse, this desire to comfort him, heal him in some
way. She was very much afraid that his cataclysmic
confession had torn what remained of her defences to
pieces, and now she'd have nothing to hide behind. Not
even anger.

That night, after another elaborate dinner, which had
been held in their own hotel this time, Jamilah accepted
an invitation from the Sultan of Al-Omar's aide to go
for a drink to the bar. She'd always felt guilty about how
she'd run out on him at the Sultan's party the previous
year, after that tense meeting with Salman.

At least that was the justification for her agreeing
to the drink. In truth she'd been avoiding Salman all
day, still too raw to be able to deal with him and that
penetrating dark gaze now that she knew the reason for
the shadows behind it. But she'd known where he was at

every moment, and she'd seen how his eyes had flashed when he'd noticed her leaving with Ahmed just minutes before.

Earlier that evening she'd been ready before Salman, and had gone down to dinner without him. She'd congratulated herself, having managed to successfully avoid him yet again. But when he'd arrived at dinner he'd raked her whole body across the room with a look so hot she'd been surprised little fires hadn't broken out over her skin. She'd thought her dress was modest enough— vee-necked silk, with a tight waist and full skirt to the knee—but one look from Salman and she'd feared he'd melted it right off her.

'Jamilah.'

Jamilah flinched and looked at Ahmed, and smiled apologetically.

'I'm sorry, my mind is miles away…' She put a hand on his arm. It wasn't fair of her to be here with him when she couldn't concentrate on their conversation. 'Look, I think we should take a raincheck. I'm not great company this evening.'

Ahmed smiled ruefully, and Jamilah wished that she found the perfectly nice-looking man half as attractive as she found Salman.

'This wouldn't have anything to do with Salman al Saqr, would it?'

Jamilah coloured as Ahmed stood up and waited for her to stand, too.

He said as they walked out, 'Don't worry, it's not that obvious, but I've been in close proximity to you two before, if you remember.'

Jamilah went hotter when she recalled Ahmed finding them in the corridor, with tension crackling between them. She couldn't lie as she followed him out of the bar and to the lifts. 'He's got a little to do with it, I guess.'

In the lift Ahmed turned to her and said, somewhat stuffily, 'I know you won't want to hear this, but he *has* got a reprehensible reputation with women.'

Jamilah just managed to stifle a hysterical laugh. Poor Ahmed didn't know the half of it. But she appreciated his concern. He walked her to the door of the suite and she smiled at him, feeling sad. And then something rose up within her—a sense of desperate futility as she thought of Salman and the impossibility of their relationship. Perhaps if she just gave someone else a chance…

She moved closer to Ahmed and asked, 'Can I kiss you?'

The other man looked comically shocked, and his glasses practically steamed up as he blustered, 'Yes… of course.'

He moved forward awkwardly, and in that moment Jamilah knew it was all wrong—she shouldn't have said anything. But it was too late. His hands were around her waist, gripping too tightly, and then he was bumping her nose, aiming for her mouth before planting a fleshy wet kiss on her lips.

In a move so fast that she didn't know which way was up Jamilah heard a door open and found herself being pulled back and out of Ahmed's hands. Her relief quickly disappeared when she realised that it was Salman who now gripped her waist. She could feel his tall, taut strength behind her and her body reacted accordingly. Poor Ahmed was clearly terrified.

He backed away and said a garbled goodnight, then fled. Salman whirled Jamilah around in his arms, and all she could do was open and close her mouth ineffectually.

The difference between this man and Ahmed was comical. Her body was rejoicing as if it had just found its long-lost mate. Her hands were fists on his chest. He was still in his ceremonial robes, no tuxedo tonight, and she was very aware of his body through the insubstantial flimsiness of her silk cocktail dress.

He tugged her into the room with him, and her back thudded against the door when Salman slammed it shut. He crowded her, his hands by her head, eyes blistering down into hers. 'What the hell was that about?' He mocked her voice. *"Can I kiss you?"'*

Jamilah welcomed the surge of anger at his arrogant behaviour. It helped to distract her from dealing with the fact that facing this man made her feel so exposed and raw and *emotional.* 'It's rude to listen at doors and spy through peepholes. And who gave you the God-given right to order Ahmed off like that?'

Salman grimaced. 'I didn't say a word. He knew he wasn't wanted—just as he wasn't wanted last year. He looked like he was about to drown you in drool.'

Jamilah shuddered at the memory, even though she tried to hide it.

Salman went very still. 'I disgust you now. That's it, isn't it? Your head is full of awful images and I put them there.'

To Jamilah's surprise, Salman released her from the cage of his arms and swung away, energy blistering from him. Instinctively Jamilah reached out and took Salman's arm. 'No—*no,* Salman. Of course you don't disgust me.'

He wouldn't turn round, and said tautly, 'I felt your reaction just now. You'd prefer to be kissed by that toad than me.'

Jamilah's brain was blank for a moment, and then she

remembered her reaction to the thought of being kissed by Ahmed, the violent shudder that had run through her. She came and stood in front of Salman. He looked so proud and handsome. How could he possibly think...?

Salman still battled the jealousy that had ripped through him like corrosive acid when he'd watched Jamilah walk out of the ballroom with that man. He shook with it. And when he'd seen them kiss just now he'd gone blind with rage. He couldn't even look at Jamilah as she stood in front of him now. He'd never felt so exposed and weak in front of anyone. Not even those soldiers had reduced him to this.

Jamilah burned as she looked up and saw the intensity on Salman's face, the way he avoided her eye. Anger had turned into something much more ambiguous and explosive within her. A treacherous tenderness was rushing through her—exactly what she'd been afraid of all day. She would have to make the first move, to show him, prove to him, that she wanted him, and she could no more deny him that than stop breathing.

This was their moment of reckoning. She knew that much. A reckless exhilaration was thrumming through her blood now—and it had been from the moment he'd replaced Ahmed's hands with his own. In her head she finally capitulated to her most base desires and threw caution to the wind, saying, 'If you can't see that my reaction was for Ahmed, and not you, then you're losing your touch, Salman. You don't disgust me. Quite the opposite, in fact. So why don't you just shut up and kiss me?'

She'd shocked him as much as herself. She could feel it in the sudden tension in his body. He looked down at her and she wound her arms around his neck, for the first time feeling a little in control of the situation. She went up on tiptoe and pressed her mouth to Salman's. And then, when he didn't move, she pulled back and said, 'What's the matter, Salman? Can't you handle a woman taking the initiative?'

His hands went to her waist and burned through her clothes. 'Oh, I can handle it, all right, but I just want to know this: are you *sure* you know what you're doing?'

Jamilah shut out the cacophony of warning voices in her head and pressed even closer to Salman, exulting in the feel of his hard erection between them. 'I know exactly what I'm doing. I can take care of myself. I have been for a long time now.'

CHAPTER SEVEN

SALMAN smiled, and it was feral, and it made something deep inside Jamilah shiver with anticipation. 'I think I like you even more when you're dominant and bossy.'

Before she could make a retort Salman was walking her back until she felt herself thud against the door again. His head descended, and nothing but delicious heat and sensation concerned Jamilah any more. She held him close, fingers tangling in his hair. Their tongues duelled fiercely, as if they couldn't get enough of one another.

She'd hungered for him for too long. Desire was overflowing and all-encompassing, and she didn't have a hope of resisting—not that she could have after her provocative little speech. Jamilah had no idea where that confidence had come from, but knew she'd gone that route in a bid to feel as if she was the one in control.

But that and every other coherent thought fled when she felt Salman's hands on her back, pulling down the zip of her dress. His mouth left hers and followed the line of her jaw down to her shoulder, where she could feel him pulling down the strap of her dress. Her breath came jerkily, her hands dropped, and she sagged back against the door, her legs trembling. They'd gone from zero to a thousand in thirty seconds on the arousal scale.

Salman pulled the strap down her arm and she could feel her dress gaping open at the back. Nothing could stop it from falling down now, and exposing one bare breast. In the dim light he pulled back for a moment and looked his fill. All Jamilah could do was concentrate on not passing out with the intensity of the desire pulsing through her. She felt her breast grow heavy, and its peak tightened unbearably. She bit her lip to stop herself from begging Salman to touch her there.

She felt so wanton, and almost cried out when Salman cupped the fleshy weight and said throatily, 'So beautiful…I've dreamed of this, Jamilah. I've dreamed of *you*.'

His thumb passed back and forth over the throbbing peak, and when he bent his head and licked around it before sucking it into his mouth she did cry out, holding his head with her hands.

Desperation mounted through her as the memory of the bliss only he could evoke was awoken within her core. 'You…' she said breathily. 'I want to see you.'

Salman stopped his luxurious lavishing of attention on her breast and stood up. With sheer sensual grace and ease of confidence he tugged off his outer robe, and then the thinner under-robe. He kicked off his shoes, his eyes never leaving Jamilah's even though she couldn't help but look down and take her fill of his magnificent broad chest. He'd changed since she'd last seen him naked. He'd filled out even more and was truly *a man*. Broad-shouldered and leanly muscular.

The loose pants barely clung to his narrow hips, and his hands went there to undo the tie. Within seconds they'd fallen to the floor and he stood before her naked and proud, his erection making her eyes go wide. She'd forgotten how big he was.

He came close again, and tipped up her chin with a finger. Then he slid the other strap of her dress down the other arm until her dress fell to her waist. With a gentle tug from his hands it joined his clothes on the floor. Now all she wore were black lace panties and her high heels. Salman looked down her body. Jamilah could feel little fire trails wherever his eyes rested, and between her legs she was aching for his touch.

He reached and took the pin out of her hair, letting it fall around her shoulders, and then he said huskily, 'Are you wet for me, Jamilah?'

Jamilah groaned softly in eloquent answer as Salman trailed his index finger down and through the valley of her cleavage. She'd been wet for him since the moment she'd heard the helicopter bring him back to Merkazad.

And then she groaned even louder as Salman dropped to his knees before her and slipped one shoe off and then the other, looking up at her, black eyes glittering wickedly. 'I want to taste you.'

He pulled her panties down over her hips, down her legs and off. Then he gently pushed her legs apart before taking her right leg and hooking it over his shoulder, opening her up to him.

Jamilah was gone beyond any point of return, and had to put a fist to her mouth when she felt his breath feather through her dark curls. His tongue lashed out and laved her secret inner folds, finding where her clitoris throbbed for attention. She was a helpless captive to this sensual onslaught. She bit her hand, her body spiralling towards the most intense orgasm she'd ever had as Salman licked without mercy until everything exploded around her and went black for a second, her whole body throbbing in the aftermath.

He held her legs when she would have collapsed in a heap, their support completely gone. When she'd recovered enough to focus again, he rose up in a smooth move and lifted her into his arms. Jamilah was boneless. But being held in Salman's arms with her naked breasts against his chest was making little tremors of arousal start up all over again.

This was how it had been between them—intense and furious. Every time. Salman laid her down gently on his bed and stood up to look at her for a long moment. His intent gaze made her feel sensual and womanly. His obvious arousal made a heady pleasure wash through her in waves. But then she couldn't stand it any longer. She held out a hand. 'Salman...I want you.'

To her relief he came down on two hands over her and said gruffly, 'I want you, too. So much it hurts.'

She twined her hands around his neck and pulled him down on top of her, relishing his heavy weight and that potent hardness between her legs. She spread her legs wide and said huskily, 'Show me where it hurts and I'll kiss it better.' She wasn't unaware of the symbolism of her kissing away his hurts, of wanting to *heal* him, and emotion made her chest full.

He touched a finger to his mouth. 'Here...'

Jamilah reached up and pressed her mouth to his, her tongue darting out to lick and taste, teeth nipping gently at his lower lip.

She pulled back and Salman's eyes glittered. He pointed to his chest, 'Here, too...'

Jamilah ran her hands down the sides of his powerful torso, feeling a shudder run through him, and pressed her open mouth to his chest, moving down to find a blunt nipple and licking him there before tugging gently on the hard nub.

He shifted back and his erection slid tantalisingly along the moist folds of her sex. Jamilah's hips lifted towards him instinctively. She ached for him so badly that she moaned in despair when he moved away for a moment to don protection.

But then he was back, pressing down on top of her, kissing her hungrily. With a powerful move he thrust into her, making her gasp at the sensation. It had been so long for her that she was tight, and she shifted to accommodate Salman's length.

As Salman started to move, though, the tightness eased, and she could feel that delicious tension building and building. A light sweat broke out on her skin. She wrapped her legs around Salman's back, causing him to slide even deeper, and she felt his chest move against her breasts with his indrawn breath. With ruthless and relentless precision he brought them higher and higher, until there was nowhere else to go. For a second Jamilah felt a moment of fear at the intensity of the climax about to hit, and when it did all she could do was cling on to Salman until she felt him tense, and then the powerful contractions of her orgasm sent him over the edge, too.

For a long moment there was nothing but the sound of their ragged breathing and the pounding of their hearts. Salman eased his weight off her and she felt suddenly bereft, and hated herself for feeling like that. She remembered from before that Salman had never really indulged in post-coital tenderness, so she was shocked when he reached for her and pulled her into him, wrapping his arms around her, cradling her bottom with his thighs. She could feel him, still semi-hard, and blushed.

She lay there for a long time, listening to Salman's

breaths deepen and even out. She couldn't sleep. She was too wound up in the aftermath. She recalled her blatant provocation of Salman and winced. He might have shown her a more vulnerable side of himself than she'd ever seen, and he might have revealed that he hadn't intended to be so cruel in his rejection of her, but she knew that he would not welcome recognising that. He was too proud, had been invulnerable for too long. And he would lash out.

Wanting to be gone when he woke, dreading seeing his mocking visage at her easy capitulation, she carefully extricated herself from his arms and reached for a robe that was at the end of the bed. She pulled it on and tied it with shaking hands. She looked at Salman, lying sprawled on the bed like a marauding king or a pirate, and before he could wake walked out of the room and straight to her own, where she went into the bathroom, dropped the robe, and stepped into a hot shower.

She willed the tears not to come, hating herself for her weakness. Suddenly all her recent bravado was gone and she was the same soft-hearted naïve Jamilah, who hadn't learnt a thing about self-protection. Suddenly she heard a sound, and whirled around to see a naked Salman standing at the door of her shower. Ridiculously she covered her breasts and spluttered, 'What the—?'

He was grim. 'I'd bet money right now that you haven't slept with anyone in a long time. You were almost as tight as the first time we slept together.'

Water was getting into Jamilah's eyes, and humiliation nearly made her feel nauseous. She spluttered again. 'That is none of your business.'

'Well, if it's any consolation, I haven't been able to sleep with anyone since I kissed you at the Sultan's party last year.'

Salman stepped into the steam of water and it sluiced down his olive-skinned body. His admission took the sting out of Jamilah's humiliation. 'You haven't?'

He shook his head. 'No. Not until I saw you again have I wanted to touch anyone.'

'But…the blonde woman in the castle that morning?'

He grimaced and said curtly, 'She followed me and wouldn't get out of my room. I hadn't slept in nights, and I was too exhausted to carry her out.'

He hadn't touched her yet, and Jamilah's hands were still over her breasts. Salman reached out and took them down. His eyes turned sultry and dark, and all Jamilah's recent feelings of recrimination dissolved like ice on a hot coal. She was mesmerised by his statement and by him.

He took some soap and started to lather it up, and then his hands smoothed over every part of her body, soaping and washing. She leant back against the wall, her eyelids heavy, and could only watch as Salman became more and more visibly aroused. He turned her round and came up behind her, snaking arms around her to cup her soapy breasts in his hands, his fingers trapping her nipples until she squirmed against him, his erection sliding tantalisingly between the globes of her bottom.

She felt him reach down over her belly and lower, between her legs, to where she was hot and slippery with renewed arousal. He muttered roughly, 'I can't wait… put your hands on the wall…'

She obeyed him wordlessly, and felt him pull her back more, then spread her legs. With a keening cry of frustration she felt him guide himself between her legs, until he could surge up and into her heat.

One hand touched her, flicking her clitoris, his other

hand was on her breast, kneading and moulding the weighty flesh. Jamilah gasped for breath, struggling to retain some sanity as the water sluiced over them, heightening everything.

The climax came swiftly, rolling over them like a huge wave and throwing them high. Jamilah gasped, head flung back, as Salman pounded into her, every powerful thrust of his body sending her hurtling into another climax. With one final thrust he stilled, and she felt his release spill deep inside her. Only the faintest of alarm bells went off. She was too stunned, trembling all over in the aftermath.

Salman gently turned her around and gathered her close, settling his mouth over hers in a brief kiss. 'Are you okay?'

Jamilah could only nod. She was speechless, and just let Salman lift her out of the shower and wrap her in a huge towel. She'd been wrong. It had never been like this before. It had been amazing, yes. But this...this transcended everything that she had experienced with this man before. It was as if she'd had an extra layer of skin before, but now it was gone. And in a way it was; she was no longer an idealistic virginal innocent...

He dried her, before drying himself, and wrapped her hair in a towel. He hitched another towel around his waist and led her out to the bedroom, to sit beside her on the end of the bed.

Jamilah's brain was still numb from an excess of sensation and pleasure. Slowly reality trickled back, and Jamilah saw that Salman had his arms resting on his legs, head downbent. As if he could feel the weight of her gaze, he looked up. She saw that there was a grim set to his face.

'I didn't use protection.'

An old pain made Jamilah feel weak inside. She hadn't even noticed that they hadn't used protection. She forced out through numb lips, 'It should be fine. I'm at a safe stage of my cycle…'

She looked away, to a spot on the floor, and knew in that moment that she had to tell him what had happened. She didn't know if it was out of a desire to inflict pain because he'd made her feel so vulnerable, or out of a genuine necessity to let him know that for a brief moment he'd been a father.

She said quietly, 'Anyway, I'd know if I was pregnant after a couple of weeks.'

She could feel his look, his frown. 'What do you mean? How would you know?'

She took a shaky breath. 'Because I was pregnant before and the symptoms hit me almost immediately. But about a month after I fell pregnant I lost the baby.'

He turned her to face him, but instead of seeing the dawning of understanding all she saw was compassion. 'Is that why it's been so long since you were with anyone?'

It took a long second for her to realise that he wasn't putting two and two together. Could he really be so obtuse? Jamilah wanted to laugh and cry at the same time. And suddenly her desire to tell him the truth faded. What purpose would it serve when he clearly couldn't believe for a second that she spoke about *him?* And after everything he'd told her last night? Treacherously, she didn't want to give him something else to feel guilty about, and she hated herself for that weakness because it meant she was just as lost to him all over again.

She brushed his hand aside and said, 'Something like that… Look, I'm really quite tired. I'd like to go to sleep now. *Alone.*'

To her intense relief, after a long moment when he clearly didn't know what to do with the information she'd just given him, he said, 'Are you sure you want to be alone?'

Jamilah nodded, and with a last look Salman got up and left the room. Jamilah got into the bed with the towels still wrapped around her hair and her body. She curled up in a ball as silent tears trickled down her cheeks and she grieved for the baby who'd never had a chance.

Salman lay awake for a long time, thinking about what Jamilah had revealed. Hearing that she'd been pregnant with another man's child sent all sorts of ambiguous emotions to his gut. One in particular felt very similar to the jealousy he'd felt earlier.

He'd always vowed to himself that he wouldn't bring a child into this overpopulated world. The main reason being that he was quite simply terrified that he wouldn't be able to protect it from the terrors that were out there. From the terrors that he himself had witnessed, which he felt were indelibly marked in his blood and might possibly be passed down to a son or daughter. That was why he'd taken the drastic decision to have a vasectomy nearly ten years previously.

He'd mentioned his lapse about protection more out of a concern to keep them both safe from disease or infection. But Jamilah, understandably enough, had assumed he'd been concerned about pregnancy. He hadn't corrected her as he'd never told anyone about the vasectomy. But just thinking of it brought his mind back to how it had felt to take Jamilah like that, skin on skin, and arousal flared all over again.

He grimaced and rolled over, punching a pillow

before settling his head on it. He could see now what had added shadow and depth to Jamilah in the intervening years, and curiously Salman had to battle down an urge to find out more...to protect.

The following day Jamilah felt paranoid—as if everyone was looking at her. Could they see where it felt as if a layer of skin had been stripped off her body? Thankfully she was caught up in meetings for most of the day, so she didn't have to cope with facing Salman. Eventually she went to the bathroom to see if there *was* something on her face, and grimaced at her reflection. Despite the fact that she'd not had a good night's sleep her skin glowed, and her eyes were so bright they looked almost feverish.

Her lips seemed to be swollen, and they tingled at the memory of Salman's kisses. As if on cue she felt her breasts tighten and her nipples harden against the lace of her bra. She wanted him even now. She stifled a groan of despair.

Just then an acquaintance came out of a cubicle.

Jamilah composed herself and smiled at the woman, and washed her hands. The other woman smiled back, and was about to go, but then she turned and said hesitantly, 'I know it's not my place, but I feel you should know that Ahmed, Sultan Sadiq's aide, has been spreading rumours about you and Salman al Saqr...'

Jamilah flushed, mortification rising upwards. Stiffly she said, 'Thank you for letting me know.'

The woman walked out and Jamilah faced the mirror again. She sighed. No wonder people had been looking. She couldn't really blame the other man; that was effectively twice that Salman had upstaged him. But as of now her reputation was muck. Not that she was really worried about that; she wasn't bound by the same strictures as a lot of women from her part of the world. She had no family, and one of her parents had been European, so she'd always been something of an anomaly.

But it would be all over the place by the end of the day that she was sleeping with Salman, and he would have another very public notch to his bedpost.

She stood tall and smoothed her hair, before leaving the bathroom with her head held high. She had nothing to feel ashamed about except for her own very personal regret that she'd let herself be seduced by Salman all over again, despite all her lofty protestations.

'I have to go to a charity function tonight. I'd like you to come with me.'

Jamilah looked at Salman. He was dressed in a tuxedo again, and he'd been waiting for her when she got back to the suite. She was trying not to succumb to his intensely masculine pull—especially when she remembered the previous night. She was about to say no—she *wanted* to say no—and yet she hesitated. There was a quality to Salman's wide-legged stance which should have suggested power and authority, but which actually made Jamilah think of him as being vulnerable.

'What charity?'

Salman's face was unreadable. 'It's a charity I founded some years ago.'

Jamilah knew she couldn't stop the shock from registering on her face, and she saw Salman note it and smile cynically. 'You didn't have me down for a philanthropist, I see.'

Jamilah blanched at the fact that Salman was constantly surprising her with his multi-faceted personality, and got out something garbled, her curiosity well and truly ignited now, despite her best intentions.

'The charity is in someone else's name. They head it up publicly, and lobby for funding, but essentially it's my project.'

A thousand questions begged to be answered, but Jamilah held back. She couldn't not go now. 'Give me fifteen minutes and I'll be ready.'

Salman inclined his head and watched as Jamilah went to her bedroom. He'd actually been afraid she'd say no, and that realisation sent a feeling of nausea to his gut. He released a long breath, his heart hammering against his chest. He had no idea why he'd felt compelled to ask her. But some force had made him wait for her, and as soon as he'd seen her the words had spilled out. Frustration had been gnawing at his insides all day at being apart from Jamilah, and he didn't like it. Yet here he was, ensuring she be at his side for the whole evening and, more than that, witnessing him in a milieu that he'd never shared with anyone else. But then, he thought angrily, he'd spilled his guts to her only the other night, so why stop there?

The earth was shifting beneath his feet and he couldn't stop it. His desire for her burned even more fiercely now that it had been re-ignited, and in all honesty any woman he'd been with in the intervening six years was fading into an inconsequential haze.

He paced impatiently while he waited, and then he heard her. He turned around, already steeling himself against her effect, but it was no good. She was like a punch to his gut. A vision in a long swirling strapless dress of deep purple, which made her smokily made-up eyes pop out. Her hair was down around her shoulders.

Unable to stop himself, he walked over to her and cupped her jaw and cheek in one hand. He felt a delicate tremor run through her body, the hitch in her breath, and saw how her stunning eyes flared and darkened. Something exultant moved through him.

Words came up from somewhere deep inside him, and he had no more hope of holding them back than he would have of stopping an avalanche. 'You're mine, Jamilah.'

Her eyes narrowed, became mysterious. She was shutting herself off and he railed against it. 'And everyone knows it, Salman.' She smiled cynically. 'After your little theatrics last night we're the hot topic of the moment.'

Salman felt fire flare in his belly at the thought of that man touching Jamilah. He growled out now, 'Good. Because we're not finished yet, you and I.'

He bent his head and unerringly found her mouth. She resisted at first, but Salman used every sensual weapon in his arsenal until he could feel her curve softly towards him and her mouth opened on a delicious sigh. He plundered her sweet depths until she was clinging to him, and he was rock-hard and aching all over.

He pulled back and for a few seconds her eyes stayed closed, long lashes on flushed cheeks. He bit back a groan. But then her eyes flicked open and spat blue sparks at him. She trembled in his arms even as she said huskily, 'One more night, Salman. That's it. We go back to Merkazad tomorrow, and what we've had here is finished.'

Jamilah knew that after hearing the revelation of what Salman had endured as a child she wouldn't be able to keep up a façade of being unmoved while they made love for long. She longed to take him in her arms and comfort him, soothe his wounds, but he couldn't be making it any clearer that that was the last thing he needed or wanted.

Everything within Salman automatically rejected Jamilah's ultimatum, and yet he felt the desire to protect himself, feeling vulnerable for the second time in the space of mere minutes. First when he'd asked her to the function, and now this... Her ultimatum shouldn't be affecting him. He should be welcoming the prospect of his freedom. Hadn't he told her what to expect? Why shouldn't she want this to end? Any sane woman would...

He shrugged nonchalantly. 'If that's what you want...'

Her jaw tightened, and Salman longed to make it relax again, but Jamilah bit out, 'Yes, that's what I want. This ends here in Paris, for good.'

Anger and something much more ambiguous rose up around them as Salman reached for Jamilah's hand and took it. 'Fine. Well, let's get going, then. We don't want to miss a moment of our last night together.'

Our last night together. Even now, minutes later in the car, Jamilah had to struggle to beat back the prickle of tears. The realisation that she was still desperately in love with Salman was not so much a realisation as more a kind of resignation to her fate. How could she have thought for a second that she wasn't still in love with him? And, worse, falling even deeper all over again...

Her brave words that this would be finished in Paris still rang hollow in her head, because she knew it was just her pathetic attempt to make Salman think she was immune to him. She knew damn well that when they got back to Merkazad if he so much as touched her she'd be in his bed in a heartbeat. The only protection she

could hope for was that if she went back to the stables
and stayed there she'd be safe. Pathetic. She'd hide from
him amongst the horses and take advantage of his fear,
because she knew she wouldn't be able to trust herself
to be near him. When she thought of that, she automatically wanted to help him get over his fear. *Pathetic.*

At that moment he took her hand and urged her towards him along the back seat of the car. His face was
in shadow, all dark planes and sculpted lines, and she
couldn't resist. When he bent his head and took her
mouth in a soul-stealing kiss she gave herself up to the
madness.

She was dizzy after Salman's thorough kisses by
the time they reached a glittering hotel at the foot of
the Champs-Elysées, and it was only when they were
walking in that Jamilah realised Salman was nervous.
He was gripping her hand. She looked up at him but his
face was impassive.

An attractive middle-aged brunette was waiting to
greet them in an immaculate dark suit. Salman introduced her to Jamilah as the co-ordinator of the charity.
Their French was rapid, but Jamilah could keep up as
she was fluent, too. The woman was explaining that
everyone had just finished dinner and were ready to start
listening to the speeches, and then an auction would take
place. Salman nodded, and they followed the woman in
through a side door and took a seat at a table near the
front of the thronged ballroom.

Jamilah was aware of the way the energy in the room
had zinged up a notch when people noted Salman's arrival, and of the intensely appreciative regard from
women.

It was only when the speeches started that Jamilah
realised which charity it was, and a jolt of recognition

went through her. She'd read about it only recently when it had won a prestigious award. It was in aid of children who had suffered as a result of being drawn into conflict, and most especially for the notorious child soldiers of war-torn African countries. The charity was renowned for blazing a trail in setting up schools and psychological centres for those children, where they could go and be safe and get counselling to deal with their horrific experiences, with the view of either rehabilitating them with their families, if it was appropriate, or taking care of them till they could be independent.

Very few other charities offered such comprehensive, all-encompassing long-term care. No wonder Salman had set it up; he'd never had a chance of that kind of care to get over *his* wounds.

She watched dumbly as a young African man of about eighteen took to the podium. With heartbreaking eloquence he spoke of his experiences as a child soldier and how the charity had offered him life-saving solace. He was now living in Paris and attending the Sorbonne, having begun a law degree. By the time he'd finished talking Jamilah and many more in the auditorium had tears in their eyes. He got a standing ovation.

As he came off the podium he came straight over to Salman, who gave him a huge hug. He introduced the boy to Jamilah, who was too humbled to say anything more than a simple greeting. And then the crowd surrounded him and Salman sent him off with a wink. Jamilah could see how moved Salman was, too, with a curious light that she'd never seen before in his eyes.

He looked at her and she opened her mouth, questions and emotions roiling in her belly and her head. Still with that serious light in his eyes, he put a finger to her mouth and said enigmatically, while shaking his head,

'I don't want to talk about it—not tonight. But perhaps you can understand why I set it up...'

She could see the way his jaw had firmed, the determined glint in his dark eyes. She recognised his intractability. Eventually she nodded. And the obvious relief in his expression made her heart flip over in her chest. She'd just fallen a fathom deeper in love with Salman.

CHAPTER EIGHT

THEY stayed for the auction. Salman raised the bidding stakes by offering up a kiss from a well-known Hollywood heart-throb who was in the audience, and he bounded onto the stage, clearly loving the attention.

When it was over Salman tugged her up out of her seat and back through the side door. She looked at him as she tried to keep up, and asked a little breathlessly, 'Don't you have to…mingle or something?'

He looked back, eyes glittering. 'I employ people to do that for me. I extract the money, I run the charity anonymously, and I show my face every now and then.' He stopped in his tracks and turned so that Jamilah all but tumbled into his arms. 'Anyway,' he said throatily, 'I have a much more pressing engagement tonight.' With a subtle movement of his hips against hers she could feel exactly how *pressing* that engagement was.

She blushed, but forced herself to say, 'This is more important, though. I don't want to be responsible for taking you away…'

He silenced her words with a kiss, drawing her into a secluded alcove. People passed them by, but they were oblivious to everything but the heat between them. They finally came up for air and Jamilah groaned softly, resting her forehead on Salman's chest. Would she ever be free of this insanity?

When he took her hand again and led her out she was silent. Back in the car, she noticed that they weren't heading towards their hotel, and finally they pulled up at a small, slightly battered-looking restaurant boat that was moored near the Île de la Cité on the Seine. Lightbulbs were strung around the perimeter, bathing it in a golden glow. Her heart lurched. This had always been one of her favourite parts of Paris.

Salman led her down rickety steps and said, 'I thought you might be hungry...'

Jamilah's stomach growled, and she smiled. 'You seem to be more in tune with my eating habits than I am.'

He smiled, too, and for a second looked years younger—as if some of his dark intensity was lifting. She had to stem the rising tide of tenderness. Just then a rotund man came to the door and exclaimed over Salman effusively. Clearly he was a well-liked visitor. They were soon seated in a quiet corner, overlooking the slightly choppy river. The glowing lights of hundreds of apartments shone down on them, and on the water. Jamilah could see a couple on the path by the Seine stop and share a passionate kiss—it might have been her and Salman, six years ago. She sighed.

Salman took her hand and said lightly, 'You don't like this place?'

She shook her head and said quietly, avoiding his eye, 'It's perfect. I love it.' *And I love you. Still.* She curbed her words.

The waiter came then, to take their order, and Jamilah forced herself to relax. Salman ordered champagne and oysters, and they spoke of inconsequential things in an easy conversation that didn't stray anywhere near difficult topics. Jamilah could almost imagine for a second that she'd dreamt up Salman's horrific revelations...but then she only had to think of the charity and the work he was doing and remember.

By the time they had gorged on the succulent morsels, and after Salman had kissed and licked away the droplets that clung to her mouth, she was trembling with desire. When he stood up and took her hand to leave she didn't hesitate.

There was an ethereal quality to the silence between them as they travelled back to the hotel in the car, hand in hand. It lasted all the way up to their suite, and made Jamilah feel as if they were the only two people in the world.

Once they were in Salman's room, he took off his clothes with efficient gracefulness. Only once he was naked did he peel her dress down to expose her breasts and say throatily, 'I've been waiting to do this all night.'

With his hands on her waist he drew her into him, bent his head, and his hot mouth and tongue paid sensual homage to her breasts until she was gasping for air and her hips were squirming for more intimate contact.

When he had her naked on the bed, underneath him, he took her hands and lifted them over her head, capturing them there with one of his. He said, as he ran one hand down the side of her body, before his fingers sought the hot wet ache between her legs, 'I'm going to take this slowly...until you're begging for mercy...'

Jamilah whimpered as his fingers explored her moist heat and her hips bucked. She already felt like begging for mercy, but could only succumb to Salman's masterful seduction as he did exactly as he'd promised...

* * *

Jamilah had fallen into a sated drowsy slumber, but woke in an instant when she felt Salman brush her hair over one shoulder. He whispered in her ear. 'If you think this finishes here then you're very much mistaken, Jamilah Moreau.'

She said nothing—just felt a lump come into her throat. Salman settled himself around her, and eventually his breaths evened out. She knew he was right. She could no more resist him now than she could stop breathing and survive.

The only way she could make him reject her for sure would be to tell him how she felt. But the awful excoriating memory of that day six years before and the cruel rejection she'd suffered made her loath to reveal herself ever again. Even though she knew now that he hadn't *wanted* to hurt her.

Jamilah bit her lip. She had to batten down the fragile and fledgling flame of hope that rose up like a persistent desert flower in the face of certain demise once the rains had gone. She *had* to learn from the past. She would be the biggest fool on earth if she walked willingly back into Salman's arms once they returned to Merkazad. He'd only be there for another couple of weeks, and if she could just survive that long…

Next day, Salman cast a suspicious glance across the aisle of the private plane to Jamilah. Her chair was reclined and she was asleep—or she was pretending to be. Her face was turned away, and even that hint of obliviousness to his presence angered him. The minute they'd taken off she'd turned down the offer of lunch and yawned loudly. In all fairness he couldn't blame her. They hadn't got much sleep last night.

He tried to make sense of the tangled knot in his

head. He couldn't feel regret for having seduced Jamilah again—because it had felt too *right*. And now, as they flew back to the home he'd rejected a long time ago Merkazad was the last thing on his mind. To his surprise, he'd found himself enjoying the past few days, standing in for Nadim. They'd even managed to have a near-friendly conversation the previous evening, when Salman had filled him in on developments. And that was something that hadn't happened in a long time.

The woman sleeping so peacefully just a few feet away, *or not,* was the catalyst for these changes. Salman knew it, and it sent warning bells to every part of his body and brain. And yet he didn't regret telling her. If anything he felt guilty for burdening her with the images that had tortured his days and nights for years... He frowned; the images were already beginning to dissipate like wisps of cloud.

His mouth firmed and he turned away from the provocative sight of her tempting body. Resting his head back on the headrest, he closed his eyes. Things were different now from six years ago. Jamilah had matured and lived, had experienced things. He grimaced. She knew everything about him. But, despite that, he would be walking away and leaving her behind in Merkazad some day soon—and this time it really would be over. There simply was no other option.

'Stop the Jeep, Salman.'

When he didn't automatically obey, Jamilah was about to speak again, but then he did pull in. They were in the main courtyard of the Al-Saqr Castle. To the left the road led up to the castle, and to the right to the stables complex and training grounds.

Salman looked at Jamilah as she got out. 'Where do you think you're going?'

As nonchalantly as she could, while her heart was beating a rapid tattoo and every beat screamed to her, *coward, coward,* Jamilah said, 'Back to the stables, Salman. I'm going to be busy for the next few days, catching up.'

Salman jumped out of the Jeep so fast Jamilah's head swam. She instinctively moved away, but Salman cornered her at the back of the Jeep and caged her in with his hands by her head.

Dark eyes blistered down into hers, and she was instantly breathless. He ground his hips against hers and she could feel his arousal through his jeans, pressing her. 'So this is how it's to be? You run and hide at the stables?'

Jamilah tried to push him back, but he was immovable. She gritted out, trying to resist his magnetic pull, 'There's nothing stopping you coming with *me*—I have work to do, remember?'

Immediately he tensed, and Jamilah automatically wanted to say sorry when she saw the abject terror in the depths of his dark eyes. He pulled back and said coolly, 'Have it your way, then…we'll see how long you can last.'

He didn't have to say it. He wasn't prepared to deal with those demons. And, in all honesty, could she blame him? Even she felt sick when she thought of what he'd had to do. No wonder he'd escaped from here as soon as he'd had the chance.

Silently Jamilah told herself that she'd last until Salman was safely back in France and there were thousands of miles between them again. But as she watched him get back into the Jeep and drive away she had to fight back the treacherous feeling of disappointment that he hadn't tried harder to persuade her to go with him.

She turned and made the five-minute walk to the stables. When she arrived in the yard, which was normally her favourite place in the world, it suddenly felt cold and desolate and laden with malevolent images.

For the first day back in Merkazad at the stables Jamilah heard nothing from or about Salman—except the over-excited chatter of the girls who'd caught a glimpse of him that morning while they'd been exercising the horses. Jamilah wondered grumpily to herself where Abdul was when she needed him to nip that ardent gossiping in the bud.

By the time she fell into bed that evening, exhausted, she felt treacherously dissatisfied, wondering if Salman had lost interest after all. Perhaps he was going to import some of his hedonistic friends again to keep him amused?

Her dreams that night were hot and tangled, and she woke aching, and with an even bigger feeling of dissatisfaction.

Jamilah groaned as she got up for work. This was after only one day? She was a lost cause.

Around mid-morning, one of the castle maids appeared, and handed Jamilah a note in a blank envelope. With her heart skittering ominously, she turned away to read it. The slashing confident scrawl was instantly familiar.

Was yesterday as hard for you as it was for me?
I want you, Jamilah…

Jamilah dismissed the girl, who'd obviously been waiting to see if she wanted to send a reply, and it took her a couple of hours to get over the note and its sheer audacity. It also took her that long to quiet down the tumult of emotions the note had provoked: relief that Salman hadn't forgotten about her, anger at herself for feeling like a lovestruck teenager, anger that he was intent on pursuing the affair despite her declaration in Paris, and anger at her body's clamour to give in.

Just as she was thinking that, her mobile phone beeped. Jamilah opened the text. *Did you get my note?* it read. After a moment of deliberation Jamilah replied. *Yes. Not interested in pursuing this topic of conversation. I am very busy.*

She got another one back almost instantly. *I'm busy, too. In case it's escaped your attention I'm the acting ruler of Merkazad. Yet I can't seem to concentrate.*

Jamilah found she was smiling, and had to stop and rearrange her facial muscles. She resolutely turned her phone off and got back to work. But as the day progressed a flurry of envelopes kept arriving via staff from the castle. And they all contained increasingly explicit notes about Salman's varying states of arousal, what he imagined she might be wearing, how he wanted to remove it, and what he wanted to do to her once he had removed it.

By the end of the day Jamilah was over-hot and overwrought, but refused to give in to the pull to go and confront Salman directly and tell him to lay off. That was no doubt exactly what he wanted, and in the semiaroused state she was in there was no way she'd be able to resist him if he tried to seduce her.

The stables were her only hope of sanctuary, and she hated that she was using them as protection.

The following day the same pattern emerged. Note after note. Her phone beeping constantly even though she deleted his messages now, without reading them. He was driving her insane. She amended that. She was driving herself insane. But only because she couldn't stop thinking about what he was saying and reacting to it.

Are you hot right now? Are you thinking of that shower we had together in Paris? Where do you ache most?

It was a sensual attack for which Jamilah was woefully unprepared. And that night, when her phone rang by her bed, she snatched it up and said irritably, 'Yes?'

She heard a dark chuckle. 'Why so grumpy? Can't you sleep? Too hot?'

Jamilah gripped the phone hard in a suddenly sweaty palm, acutely aware of how hot she did feel in her small T-shirt and panties. She forced herself to sound as cool as she could. 'Not at all. Unlike you, I've been extremely busy.'

Another chuckle floated down the line, and Salman said with a mock self-effacing tone, 'Luckily I possess above average intelligence, so I find multi-tasking very easy. Although writing those notes *was* having an adverse affect on me while I conducted a public meeting in Merkazad.'

Jamilah had to stifle a giggle at the thought of Salman becoming aroused and trying to hide it, and then the giggle died when she realised that the thought was making her aroused. She couldn't believe it; they were no better than teenagers. She squirmed and pressed her legs together, aghast that he could have this effect on her down a phone line.

'Are you in bed now?'

'No.' Jamilah immediately lied.

'Liar,' Salman chided huskily. 'What are you wearing?'

'Seeing as how I'm not in bed, I'm wearing jeans and a shirt.'

'Like I said: liar. Let me guess. You're a small T-shirt and panties girl? That is when you're not naked with me.'

Jamilah squirmed again. 'No, actually. I wear pyjamas buttoned from top to toe.'

He made a tsk-tsk sound. 'At this rate you'll be going straight to hell, Jamilah Moreau.'

Quickly she quipped, 'Sounds like it'll be a bit overcrowded, with you there, too.'

'Touché.' That hint of bleakness in his voice sounded down the line, and Jamilah instantly felt chastened. But she didn't have time to think about it because he was saying, 'Do you know what I'm thinking of right now?'

More huskily than she wanted, she said, 'I don't think I really want to know, Salman. In fact I'm quite tired—'

He cut her off. 'I'm thinking about you lying there with your hair spread out, in a T-shirt which reveals your midriff and exquisitely shaped waist and hips. I'm thinking of how it's stretched tight across your breasts, and how your pants cling to your hips. I'm thinking of how I'd like to pull your T-shirt up so that I can bare your breasts to my gaze, see how your nipples harden and pout for my touch, for my tongue...'

'Salman...' Jamilah said weakly, as a liquid heat invaded her veins. Her hand was on her belly, and of its own volition was sliding down towards her pants.

'Salman, what?' he asked huskily. 'Stop? You don't want me to stop. You want me there, to suckle on your breasts until your back is arched, while my hand descends to spread your thighs apart, before coming back up to slide aside your pants and explore, to find where you're so wet and aching...'

It was Jamilah's own hand almost touching the spot he spoke of that brought her back to cold reality. She jackknifed off the bed and slammed the phone down into its cradle. When it rang again almost immediately she yanked the cord out of the wall.

And only when the waves of heat began to subside did she manage to fall into a fitful sleep.

The following day Jamilah was clinging onto her resolve, which felt like a flimsy life raft in a choppy sea. More notes had arrived that morning, but Jamilah couldn't even look at them now. She sent them back unopened to Salman, with the bemused maids.

So later that day, when she heard the arrival of a Jeep in the main stable courtyard, she whirled around, heart thudding ominously. *He'd come—he wanted her so badly that he'd come to get her.* And treacherously her resolve was already dissolving fast.

Salman stepped out of the Jeep and she felt weak with longing. He was tall and dark and she felt as if she hadn't seen him in months. And the look on his face was so determined it made her tremble all over.

But she couldn't give in. She couldn't.

He just stood there for a long moment. An unspoken dialogue hummed between them. Finally he articulated it. 'Come up to the castle with me, Jamilah.'

She shook her head and backed away, even as every cell in her body was urging her to go with him. At that moment one of the stablehands led a horse out of a stall just a few feet away. She saw how Salman's eyes veered wildly to the horse and then back to her.

He'd gone deathly pale in the space of a heartbeat, and he gritted out, 'Damn you, Jamilah. I'm not ready for this.'

And then he was back in his Jeep and screeching out of the stableyard, and she felt as if she'd just done something unutterably cruel. For the first time since she'd seen him again she got a sense that she had the power to hurt him, and it made her reel.

She was still standing there, slightly stunned, when she noticed Abdul by one of the stables. He just looked at her, and then shook his head slowly, and Jamilah felt even worse.

She barely slept a wink that night; not surprisingly there had been no more notes or phone calls from Salman after he'd left. Her head was whirling with guilt and her resolve not to give in to the almost overpowering pull to go to Salman.

She started work in a daze the next day, and was exhausted by four p.m., when the phone rang in her office.

It was a call that made her want to weep with weariness, for it meant that she had to take the chopper to a remote Bedouin oasis village, deep in a mountainous valley. Considering the time of day it was, and the way Bedouin hospitality worked, she'd more than likely have to stay overnight.

Apparently a horse was having trouble foaling, and its owner feared for its life and that of the foal. The stables' resident vet was away for a few days, and Jamilah had studied veterinary science, so she had the necessary expertise when things like this cropped up from time to time. She gathered her things and called the chopper pilot, then made her way to the launching pad behind the castle. As she drove by the castle she resolutely veered her mind away from the man inside…*somewhere.*

They flew over mountainous and rocky terrain, and Jamilah's heart clenched with emotion for this some- times inhospitable country. It was these local Bedouin people who had risen up and fought back against the in- vaders all those years before, who had saved the Sheikh and his family from their incarceration. *Who had saved Salman.*

Jamilah could see the village now, down far below in the crevasse of a deep valley. Mountain springs kept it verdant and lush, and it was like a tiny green pocket of paradise within a lunar landscape. It was only as they got closer that Jamilah saw a Jeep waiting and felt the first prickle of suspicion, but she told herself she was being ridiculous.

When she got out a driver was waiting, and he helped her into the Jeep. They were heading for the village, but she couldn't see any villagers, or any children waiting for their treats which she always brought. She reassured herself that it was late, dusk was closing in. These valley people were traditional and had probably retired for the night.

But before they got to the village itself Jamilah saw a tent set up by a palm tree and a picturesque pool, set back in its own enclosure. It was the kind of tent that was set up for Nadim whenever he travelled into the country. Her skin prickled ominously when the driver stopped the Jeep outside it. She got out, and at that moment heard the helicopter taking off into the distance.

Before she had a chance to register the significance of

that, someone stepped out of the tent. Someone tall and
dark and imposing, dressed in ceremonial Merkazadi
robes. As if she didn't already know...*Salman.*

CHAPTER NINE

THE jeep was already turning around and heading away. Jamilah stared at Salman, and an awful yearning rushed through her. Even though she'd seen him just the day before, she'd *missed* him. And a wild excitement was making the blood rush through her veins. She wanted to walk up to Salman and hit him and kiss him all at the same time. The sheer gall of his gesture made her breathless, but its sheer romanticism made her weak with longing.

Damned if she was going to let him know. She had to resist him—*had* to. For, as surely as night followed day, he intended to walk away from her again and she would never get over him. Not now. How could she when she now knew the secret behind his dark essence? His vulnerability?

She hitched her bag on her shoulder, eyes spitting blue sparks at him, and Salman felt curiously weak for a moment. Jamilah had never looked so beautiful. In worn jeans, a shirt and boots, no make-up, and her hair slipping out of its ponytail to curl in long dark silky tendrils around her face. Since he'd seen her last it had felt like a century.

She hitched up her chin and said frostily, 'I presume that there is no horse in labour?'

He shook his head, jaw clenched, and folded his arms.

'So you're kidnapping people now? Pretty inventive for a hedge fund manager. But really you should save your ingenuity for someone who wants to be kidnapped by you.'

Salman's insides clenched at her blistering tone, her obvious reluctance to be here, but he couldn't let her walk away. He needed her too badly.

Jamilah turned and started to walk away, into the village. 'I'm going to get a horse and ride back to Merkazad if I have to. It'll only take a day or two.'

She was grabbed from behind, her bag falling to the ground, and before she could emit a squeak of protest Salman had carried her bodily into the tent, which was lit with a hundred small lamps, imbuing the luxuriously furnished surroundings with a decadent feel. And right in the middle of the tent stood a low divan, covered in satins and silken throws. It was a seduction scene straight out of a movie.

He put her down and she whirled around, feeling her hair come undone completely. '*Will* you stop doing that!'

Her heart was careening wildly against her breastbone, but Salman just said calmly, 'The chopper will come back in three days. As will the Jeep. And you won't attempt to get a horse from any of the locals as they've been instructed not to let you have one.'

Three days!

Shock and something much more like panic made Jamilah say shakily, 'Why on earth would you want to isolate us here for three days?'

Salman's jaw clenched. 'Because you've denied us

three days by your theatrics, refusing to come back to the castle.'

Guilt lanced her at her own cowardly behaviour even as she said cuttingly, 'I run the stables, Salman. It's hardly *theatrics* to want to be near to where I work. That's where I live.' Sheer panic that he could wield such control over her and her emotions made her lash out unthinkingly, 'And could you *be* any further from the stables here?'

Salman paled in an instant, and immediately the words were out Jamilah felt contrite. He stepped back and she put out a hand. 'Salman, I'm sorry. I shouldn't have said that.'

He backed away, and conversely Jamilah wanted to pull him to her. He ran a hand through his hair and laughed curtly, harshly. 'You're right, though. It's pathetic. I couldn't even last a minute in that place.'

Jamilah walked up to Salman and took his hand. She said softly, all rancour gone, 'No one could blame you—not after what you were forced to do there.'

He looked down at her, his eyes two pools of dark shadows. 'I don't know if I prefer you spitting and hissing and resisting me or like this, full of pity.'

Jamilah shook her head, her hair slipping over one shoulder. 'I don't pity you, Salman. It's not pity…it's empathy.'

He lowered his head and pressed his lips to hers. Feeling completely exposed, Jamilah couldn't help but respond, and flames of passion were not far behind. When the kiss was fast developing into something much more urgent and carnal Jamilah somehow found the strength to pull away. Breathing harshly, she put her hands on Salman's chest and leaned back. 'I won't do this, Salman. I told you in Paris that it was over. I won't be your convenient plaything just because I'm here and it's easy.'

In two seconds he had taken Jamilah's face in his hands. His mouth swooped down on hers again, all softness gone, hard and hot and demanding. She could feel his straining body move sinuously against hers and had to lock her hips to stop herself from responding. Damn him—and her immediate response. She finally wrenched her mouth away. Her hands were still fists on his chest between them.

'Does that feel easy to you?' he demanded throatily.

'You can't use sex to avoid questions, Salman al Saqr, and I will not stay here with you for three days.'

'Believe me, if you showed no signs of wanting me then I would have no problem leaving you alone. Women who don't find me desirable have never turned me on.'

Jamilah could have laughed—as if such a woman existed!

'So…what? You've put a time limit on this desire? Is that it? Three days and we will have exhausted ourselves and burnt it out?' Even the thought of three days indulging in such a thing made her quiver inside.

Salman smiled and it was wolfish, sending skitters of anticipation down Jamilah's spine. 'In three days I'm hoping that we will be exhausted, yes. And perhaps some semblance of sanity will be restored—because one thing is certain: I haven't felt sane where you're concerned for a long time.'

It was suddenly important for her to know something. 'That night…the night in Paris six years ago…did you go out with that woman as you said you were going to?' Even now the poisonous image of the red-headed siren inserted itself with savage vividness into Jamilah's brain.

Salman slowly shook his head, and his hands relaxed a little on her face. She could feel him brush a lock of hair away from her cheek. His body was still welded to hers and his arousal was insistent. 'No...I never saw her again—except through work. And, believe me, she didn't take kindly to being let down.' His mouth thinned, as if it pained him to be admitting this. 'I actually went out that night and got blind drunk. The one and only time in my life.'

Jamilah pushed herself free of his hold and stepped away, turning around so he couldn't see her face. Emotions erupted in her chest. She knew he wouldn't just say this, knew that he would not lie—why would he need to? He'd been crueller than anyone she'd ever known, so why wouldn't he hesitate to give her the truth if he *had* slept with her? This revelation was inserting itself into a very vulnerable part of her, smashing aside another piece of the wall she'd erected around herself to keep out all hurt and feeling. He kept doing this—kept turning her memories of what had happened in Paris on their head, telling her that there had been so much more to it than the banal yet cruel rejection that had fed her anger for so long.

And she hated him for it, because she was sure that it cost him nothing to admit this. That he was completely unaware how seismic this admission was to her. She whirled back around to face him, willing herself to be strong.

'I won't give you three days, Salman. I feel sane enough for the both of us, believe me. This is pure indulgence on your part. You're bored and frustrated because for once in your life you're not getting what you want and you simply can't handle it.'

He moved towards her, and with big hands closing around her waist he pulled her to him. She could see anger flare in his eyes at her defiance. 'Your refusal to see me as anything but a feckless, petulant playboy is growing wearisome, Jamilah. This goes far deeper than such superficial emotions, believe me.'

She stood stiff in his embrace. But her conscience struck her. She knew well that she could no longer label him as such. He was far from the shallow playboy everyone believed him to be. She threw her head back, determined not to let herself succumb to the three days of bliss she knew only he could promise. It would be all too easy for her to hope for more, to believe that perhaps things were different this time round.

She ignored the provocative sight of the luxurious bed nearby. 'Well, what else am I supposed to think when you use your powerful position to get what you want?'

Her words struck Salman somewhere deep inside, and he fought not to let the emotion she aroused to show on his face. But the fact was this: he'd never had to go to so much trouble to get a woman into his bed before. He'd never been so consumed by a woman. His heart beat hard; that wasn't true. He had once before, and it had been *this* woman.

There'd never been a moment when she hadn't occupied some corner of his mind, when he hadn't been aware of her. He could see that now. Growing up, he'd felt guilty as a young man, being so aware of how her young, firm body had been developing and maturing. The day he'd left Merkazad she'd been sixteen years old and he'd touched her cheek, when in actual fact he'd had to battle a desire to kiss her.

'I want you, Jamilah. That's all that matters here. We're alone. Miles away from civilisation.'

He couldn't know how seductive those words were—how many times she'd woken from hot and tangled dreams in which he'd come back to Merkazad and whisked her away for exactly such illicit pleasure.

Suddenly sounding eminently reasonable, and not at all passionate, Salman stepped away and said, 'Night has fallen outside.'

Jamilah blinked stupidly, and could see through the gap in the lavish drapes that night had indeed fallen. Stars twinkled in a clear sky and a half moon glistened. Night creatures filled the air with their chirrups and sounds. And she hadn't even noticed.

'You must be tired and hungry. Why don't you wash and we'll eat?'

He said this as if he hadn't all but kidnapped her—as if they were not in some remote and magical part of Merkazad—but as if this were entirely normal. She watched as he walked over to the far side of the tent and picked up a gold-embossed box. He put it on the bed and turned to her, saying with a rough quality to his voice, 'I brought you some things to wear.'

The audacity of his statement made her melt inside while it also stiffened her resolve not to give in to this arrogant and autocratic game of his. 'I won't be wearing any clothes other than my own, Salman. This is ridiculous. I'm not your mistress.'

Her mouth thinned. 'But I am hungry, and I am tired. And clearly I'm stuck here for the night now. I'll wash and eat, and then I'm going to bed—*alone*. In my own clothes.' Belligerently she said, as she got her bag and made for the curtained-off washing area, 'I don't know where *you're* going to sleep tonight, but the least you can do is let me have the tent.'

Salman's eyes flashed, and she thought she saw his mouth quirk as if she amused him, but before she could respond to the fresh anger mixed with panic spiking within her he said smoothly, 'I'll arrange for one of the girls to come and help you, and for dinner to be served.'

Jamilah shut her mouth and all but fled to the washing area, which was lit with the light of a hundred gently flickering candles. Her heart ached in her chest as she was momentarily transfixed by the scene. In any other circumstance she would long for just this scenario. It came fully formed out of her fantasies. But not now, and not like this, with *this* man. And yet…her heart ached even harder…with *who else?*

He might want three more days with her, but what else might he demand? He wasn't done with her. And she certainly wasn't done with him. And yet all this fighting her response to him was exhausting. His notes and that incendiary phone call had taken a lot more out of her than she wanted to admit to.

Just then she heard a sound, and a young, shy Bedouin girl came in, dressed from head to toe in black. She started filling the ornate bath and gave Jamilah a robe to change into. Jamilah was aware of the feminine ritual even though she'd never been indulged like this before. This kind of thing was usually reserved for members of the ruling family—the Sheikha and the Sheikh's mistresses.

Her blood ran cold. *Was* she Salman's mistress now?

For this was exactly how a mistress was treated, wasn't it? Flown in to meet him, bought clothes, wined and dined, washed and readied for his pleasure. Disgust curled low in her belly even as something much more treacherous made her blood grow hot. There was something so inherently decadent and sexy about this ritual, and it called to a deeply secret feminine part of herself that she'd never acknowledged before. She hated to admit that.

The girl had prepared the bath, and the scent of exotic oils rose to make Jamilah's skin tingle all over. She stripped and put on the robe, barely noticing when the girl took her bundle of clothes away and said she'd be back presently. Too seduced not to be able to respond, Jamilah groaned softly as she slid into the perfumed satiny water. She never indulged herself like this. For such a long time she'd subjugated any kind of feminine luxury. For a second she forgot her tangled emotions and her anger at Salman: this was pure bliss…

Salman had come back into the tent momentarily, to see that the dinner preparations were being made to his specifications. He'd been pacing while staff scurried in and out. Now they were gone while they prepared the hot food. He heard the gentle movement of the bath water in the curtained-off corner of the dimly lit tent, and to imagine Jamilah there now, naked, was almost more than he could bear.

Knowing he shouldn't, but unable to help himself, he walked over to the screen. He could hear her soft moan of pleasure, the splash of water, and his body tightened unbearably. Through a chink in the screen he became transfixed when he saw slivers of Jamilah's body—the swell of her pale olive-skinned breasts with those dusky nipples. Her elegant shoulders. A tendril of wet hair sloping down to one bountiful curve.

Jamilah stilled in the water for a moment, soap between her hands. Someone was watching her. She could feel it. But she couldn't call out. She felt a kind of paralysis grip her, and suddenly didn't want to break the spell that seemed to be weaving itself around her. She knew it was Salman. She could sense his presence a mile away. And to know that he was watching her through the screen, illicitly, was the most erotic thing she'd ever felt.

Suddenly she had power in her hands. She had *him* at a disadvantage. She knew there was no way he'd come to her like this, while they might be caught, but still she could sense his eyes on her in this secret and brief moment. With a hitherto non-existent feminine pride and confidence she soaped her body, trailing her hands up each arm luxuriously, before soaping her shoulders.

With her eyes half closed she washed her breasts, and imagining Salman watching sent her arousal into orbit. Her nipples were already tight and hard, and when she ran her hands over them she couldn't stop the faintest mewling sound coming from her throat. She was meant to be teasing *him,* not herself, and yet…she couldn't stop.

His provocative notes from the past few days came back to her: *Do you touch yourself when you think about me? Are you hot now? Are you wet and aching for me? I dreamt of you last night and woke up hard, wanting you…*

Unaware of the spell she was binding around herself, Jamilah let her fingers trap one nipple, squeezing the hard peak so that a flame burst to life in her belly. Her other hand drifted down over her belly, under the water, to between her legs. To where the water lapped against her hot and slippery flesh.

It was only when she heard something that sounded like a strangled moan and then more noises that she came out of her sensual reverie, shooting up to sit in the bath, suddenly mortified and burning up all over. What had just happened to her? She'd been as good as starring in her own X-rated video! And all because she'd thought Salman had been watching. He probably hadn't been—it could have been anyone! *Oh, God,* Jamilah thought, what had she turned into?

Just then she heard the girl return, and Jamilah practically jumped out of the bath, grabbing the towel out of the girl's hands. Too mortified to look the young girl in the eye, she hunted around for her clothes, but they and her bag were gone. She asked the girl where they were and she blushed prettily, saying that the Sheikh had told her to wash Jamilah's clothes and to give *him* her bag. She said, 'The Sheikh has left some clothes for you…' Immediately Jamilah thought of that glossy box and its connotations.

When the maid indicated to Jamilah where there was an array of scents and body lotions, Jamilah said, more curtly than she'd intended, 'I don't need any of that. I just want my own clothes.'

A tortured expression crossed the girl's face, and immediately Jamilah felt contrite. She was only following orders, and in this rural milieu you absolutely did not question the demands of the Sheikh. Jamilah apologised and gave in, knowing she couldn't do anything else for the moment, 'Thank you for the bath, and the lotions… but I can do that myself. Why don't you bring the clothes you've been left in here, so I can get changed?'

While the relieved girl was gone, Jamilah picked up the nearest lotion and smoothed it on as perfunctorily as she could, trying to ignore its heady musky scent and the way her skin tingled to her touch. When the girl came back, looking much happier, Jamilah didn't have the heart to say anything more about her own things. She would work on getting them back some other way.

But when the girl opened up the big glossy box with unmistakable reverence, and pulled out a long kaftan-style dress which seemed to be made entirely out of spun silver, Jamilah gasped, transfixed.

The girl said in awe, 'It is beautiful, is it not?'

Jamilah touched it. 'Yes, very.' It looked as if it had been made by fairies—a human hand too clumsy for something so ethereal. When it moved, glints of dark blue thread shone like bursts of sapphire.

And with it came underwear made of lace so delicate it looked as if it would fall apart at a mere touch. The royal blue colour made the pale olive of her skin stand out, and to Jamilah's constant embarrassment her nipples stiffened against the delicate lace, as if it were a lover's touch. She hated that she was getting dressed to Salman's specifications. She hated that she was falling in with his plans. Even as a secret part of her felt the insidious slow curling, burning of desire which, once started, would not rest until it had been sated.

Once Jamilah was dressed, with the kaftan lovingly clinging to her every curve, the maid brushed her hair until it too shone like spun black silk. Eventually, when her nerves were screaming with tension, the girl was finished, and with downbent gaze she left.

Taking a deep breath, Jamilah emerged from behind the screen to see Salman's broad-shouldered powerful physique dominating the doorway of the tent. Instantly her insides contracted with a pulsing of pleasure she couldn't stop. She gritted her jaw and her hands went to fists by her sides.

She couldn't make out Salman's expression; he was too far away and in the shadows, and all she could think about was how she'd felt him watching her and how she'd touched herself so wantonly. If it even *had* been him! Liquid heat moistened her still sensitive sex.

And then abruptly, breaking the moment of tension, Salman strode in. The curtains closed heavily behind him and they were cocooned in this lavish tent, in a remote oasis in the far eastern reaches of Merkazad.

He stood tall and resplendent in Merkazadi robes by a table which had been laid and was now heaving with succulent-looking food. The smells alone were more enticing than anything she'd ever experienced before, and Jamilah firmly pushed aside the implication that it was because it was *here,* with *him.* Because he had done this for her.

On shaky legs she walked over, her stomach growling with hunger all of a sudden. She refused to meet Salman's eyes as she approached the table, acutely self-aware in the dress, and she would have kept avoiding his eye if he hadn't caught her arm in a burning grip and with his other hand tipped her chin up so that she had to look at him.

Roughly he said, 'You are more beautiful tonight than I've ever seen you.'

Jamilah bristled when heady pleasure suffused her body at his statement. She tried to block out how gorgeous *he* was, with a faint line of stubble accentuating his hard jaw, the robes making him look so effortlessly regal and powerful. 'Well, I hope it's worth it, after all the trouble and expense you've gone to, to get me out here.'

'It'll be worth it, Jamilah,' he promised. 'And the pleasure won't be mine alone. I'll make sure of that.'

Reacting to that promise, and feeling shrewish, she said, 'Well, you can save me the sordid details of whose pleasure it will be, because you won't be sharing *my* bed tonight, Salman.'

He chuckled softly and let her go, indicating for her to sit down. His easy laughter made her want to bounce something off his head, but Jamilah clenched her jaw and sat down, feeling very huffy and petulant. Alien moods for her—she was usually so calm and controlled.

It was a struggle for Salman to appear urbane as Jamilah sat down opposite him, refusing to meet his eye. He was harder than he'd ever been in his life, thanks to that little X-rated water show she'd put on. Only the return of the staff to prepare for dinner had stopped him from smashing aside the screen so that he could strip and lower himself into that bath, embed himself between her glorious legs and take her so hard and fast their heads would have been spinning for a week.

And that dress… It covered her almost as comprehensively as the ubiquitous shirts and jeans she wore, but it shimmered and clung to dips and hollows with a sensuality that made him grit his jaw and curl his hands into fists to stop himself from reaching out to touch her.

She sent him a skittish little glance, and he saw a pulse beat hectically at the base of her neck. Dark triumph filled him. She could fight this—*him*—until she was blue in the face, but ultimately she wouldn't be able to deny her own desire. But for now he forced himself to take control of his libido, and put a plate of different morsels of food together for her.

Jamilah took the plate Salman handed her, seeing that he had automatically picked all of her favourite foods. Her heart clenched. And then she saw him pour them *both* some champagne. She quirked a brow in his direction, striving not to remember how it had felt to learn that she'd been the cause of his one lapse of control with alcohol. That he hadn't been unmoved by his actions after all...

He smiled and held up his glass, 'To us, Jamilah.'

She smiled back sweetly and clinked her glass with his. 'To *me,* and the good night's sleep I'm going to have in this lovely tent, all on my own.'

He chuckled again and drank from his glass, and Jamilah's eyes were momentarily transfixed by the powerful bronzed column of his throat. Tearing her gaze away, hating the flush of awareness climbing up her body, she ate—and nearly choked on a plump, succulent prawn when Salman said lazily, 'I enjoyed our correspondence over the last few days—even if it was a little one-sided, and did leave me somewhat...unsatisfied.'

Jamilah wiped at her mouth with a napkin. She might have thrown the notes away in disgust, but not until after she'd read most of them with a guilty pleasure. Which Salman had honed in on as soon as they'd spoken on the phone. And she might have slammed the phone down on him, but she hadn't been able to get him out of her head. She hadn't been far off touching herself, just as she had in the bath earlier, and she squirmed to remember that now.

Salman caught her hand across the table, and her gaze skittered to his guiltily.

'Were you thinking of me just now…in the bath? You must have known I was watching…'

Enthralled and mesmerised, Jamilah could say or do nothing. To agree would mean that she couldn't turn back from him tonight, because he'd know that he'd turned her on with little more than the thought that he'd been there. In a strangled voice she said shakily, 'I don't know what you're talking about.'

He quirked a hard smile. 'I told you once before I admired your honesty. Lying doesn't suit you.'

Jamilah pulled her hand free and continued eating, even though her appetite had spectacularly fled. She was burning up from the inside out. Very aware of Salman lazily feeding himself, imagining his tongue snaking out to catch the juices from his morsels of food, just as hers had to do.

But, save running out of the tent and causing a furore by seeking sanctuary with one of the village folk, she was stuck. She didn't know or care where Salman would go tonight, as long as he wasn't here, but she had a sinking feeling that he'd made no such alternative preparation, despite her assertion.

She put down her napkin and finished the last droplets of sparkling liquid in her heavy glass. The sheer opulence of this whole scene stunned her anew, and she wondered how Salman had got everything here and prepared. She quashed her curiosity, affected a yawn, and stood up, ready to restate her intention to sleep alone.

Salman stood smoothly on the other side of the table and held out a hand, which Jamilah predictably ignored. Salman quashed the dart of anger and frustration. 'You know I'm not going anywhere, Jamilah.'

She looked at him, and underneath the defiance he saw something else—something infinitely more vulnerable that he hardened his heart to. He didn't want to deal with that. He just wanted Jamilah. And she wanted him. That was all he needed to know.

He walked over to the sumptuous bed and started to disrobe.

'What are you doing?' Jamilah's voice came out as a panicked squeak, and she cursed herself for not sounding more in control.

Salman turned around, supremely confident. 'I'm getting ready for bed.'

'But where will *I* go?'

He indicated with a hand. 'There's a perfectly good bed right here.'

'Yes,' Jamilah hissed, 'but not while you're in it.'

Salman ignored her, and turned away to continue disrobing. In the light of the hundreds of small glowing lamps, bit by bit his impressive body was revealed. And Jamilah could only stand and watch, until he stood there with his back to her, long, lean and powerful. And gorgeous enough to make her throat dry. His back was impossibly broad, and led down to the taut muscular globes of his bottom, and heavily muscled powerful legs.

It felt like the hardest equation in the world to work out why she had to get out of there so badly. And then he slowly turned around, and her world contracted to this tiny spot on the planet and this tent. And this man and this desire thrumming between them. The air seemed to be hotter, redolent with scents and whispered desires.

'Jamilah…'

Jamilah was finding it hard to raise her gaze from where it had dropped to take in his impressive erection. A pulse beat through her blood with gathering force.

And as she watched, and faintly heard Salman groan, he wrapped a hand around himself, as if unable *not* to.

Her legs nearly buckled at the sight of his hand moving back and forth slowly, how the silky skin slipped up and down over the strong shaft and, worse, she could imagine how it felt and was jealous.

'*Jamilah*…you're torturing me. I need you.'

Her gaze lifted with an effort. She felt all at once heady, languorous and energised. It was a combination that had her insides fizzing. But even as she felt her traitorous feet move towards Salman she shook her head, struggling to make a stand, not to give in.

'I…I can't. I won't do this. I can't do this again with you, Salman.'

On a broken sob which was torn from deep in her chest she turned around to block out the provocative view, to block out temptation. She was shaking all over with reaction, and just knew that if Salman succeeded she would never have a chance to get over him.

Big hands settled on her shaking shoulders with surprising gentleness and turned her around. To her chagrin she could feel tears prick her eyes, threatening to overflow.

Salman sounded tortured. 'Please, Jamilah, don't cry…'

A vivid memory of that day by their parents' graves struck Jamilah then. How Salman had told her not to cry, to be strong. She looked up at him, past and present morphing into one. Her heart beat fast. She loved him. She loved this man with an intensity that eclipsed anything she might have felt before. And it was already way too late to be saved or helped.

As the tears overflowed and slid down her cheeks at the acknowledgement of that truth, she felt something give way inside herself. How could she walk away from this now? When perhaps this was all she would have to remember? This oasis in the rocky desert, this moment in time…

Salman's face looked tortured, his eyes dark with some emotion that made her head reel; it was an emotion he hadn't revealed before. He said gutturally, 'I won't make you do this if it's going to upset you so much. I never wanted to upset you. I just thought you wanted me as much as I want you…but were fighting it to pay me back…because you know how much I need you.'

His tenderness undid her completely, and the fact that he wasn't being autocratic, wasn't forcing her, made her even weaker against his pull. She trusted him. She trusted that he actually meant what he said—that if she were to ask him to leave her alone he would. He'd walk out of there and let her have the tent to herself. Suddenly it was the last thing she wanted.

This was what she'd been afraid of—that it would be impossible to resist him now that she knew his deepest darkest self, because she ached so much to take that pain away. Jamilah shook her head on a reflex. He believed that she'd been trying to get some sort of revenge on him? That *that* had been behind her reluctance to continue the affair? She shook her head again, and put her hands up to Salman's face and jaw, caressing him. His breath hitched and his body tensed.

'No. That's not what I was doing, Salman. But I don't care about that any more. I don't care about anything but right here and now, and I can't keep resisting.'

She pressed close, so that she could feel his erection hard between them. 'Make love to me, Salman. I need you so much.'

He waited for a long moment, as if expecting her to

laugh in his face, tell him she hadn't meant it, and then with a growl of triumph his head swooped down and his mouth burnt hers in a searing brand. His arms wrapped tight around her and triumph coursed through Jamilah too, as if the two warring sides of her psyche had battled it out and the stronger side had finally won. She knew in some dim place that she would have to deal with the fallout of this decision, but not right now.

Right now she needed Salman with a pulsing intensity she'd never felt before. And the vulnerable chink he'd just shown her was the most powerful aphrodisiac in the world.

With one swoop he smashed aside all her resistance, lifted her up and carried her over to the bed, where he laid her down as if she was the most infinitely delicate and precious thing in the world...

A couple of hours later Salman was lying on the silken sheets, wide awake, with Jamilah's hair in a silken caress over his chest and her breasts pressing into his side. One arm was wrapped around her, holding her to him, his fingers near the enticing swell of her breast. Even though he'd never felt more sated in his life, his body was already responding with predictable force. He sighed deeply.

Jamilah had capitulated, but it didn't make him feel triumphant or complacent. He'd never known such an unremitting hunger for one woman. The more he got of Jamilah, the more he wanted. And it sent tentacles of faint panic through him. Because how could he leave and get on with his life when Jamilah's life was here? Seeing her tears earlier had been like a punch in the gut. He knew he shouldn't have pushed her—knew he shouldn't have brought her here. But he was weak, and he needed her, and the depth of that need stunned him.

He refused to believe that his need had grown more acute since the night he'd spilled his guts in Paris, but he was very much afraid that was the case. She was the only person he'd ever told about what had happened to him, and yet his fear of how she might have used that knowledge was eclipsed by this insatiable desire. And of *course* she hadn't used the knowledge.

Jamilah was a slice of sun he was indulging in, and he knew he was on a finite time with her—because she would want a *normal* life. With someone who didn't harbour the worst images of degradation and pain. How could she not? His heart clenched ominously when he thought of the children she would have with someone else, and he quashed the scary yearning feeling that rose up.

When he felt a telling change in Jamilah's breathing across his skin, he shifted her subtly so that she lay heavily over him, her legs spread on either side of his hips, just above where his arousal ached for more intimate contact.

The hitch in her breathing grew more pronounced as he drew her legs up. Reaching down, he found the sweet moist apex of her thighs, and her chest expanded deliciously against his when he explored her desire.

'*Salman…*' she shuddered out on a low, sleepy, husky moan, and that alone nearly drove him over the edge. He found her mouth and plundered the sweet depths, revelling in her sleepily sexy response.

With a subtle movement he replaced his fingers with his erection and, holding her hips fast, rocked up and into her, thrusting in and out with ruthless precision until her stunning eyes were open, looking into his. After long minutes of stringing out the torture for as long as she could last, Jamilah bit her lip and with her head thrown back splintered around him, sending him careening into an explosion so intense it took long minutes to float back down.

Sex. He could deal with this. Not the other. He just had to keep it all about sex.

CHAPTER TEN

Two evenings later Salman looked at Jamilah across the table, and she flashed him a teasing glance. He felt something intensely light bubble up in his chest, even as that ever-present desire pounded through him in waves.

He cursed himself for the clothes he'd brought for her. She was dressed tonight in a softly ruched silk dress, with thin spaghetti straps and a low neckline. It clung to her curves and fell in folds to her knees, revealing her shapely calves and slender bare feet. She was all the sexier for not wearing shoes. Her hair was piled untidily on top of her head and she wore not a scrap of make-up.

Only that afternoon, as they'd lain in a secret glade by a nearby pool, naked after a swim, she'd leant over him and taken him into her mouth, sending his mind into orbit even as he'd tried to stamp a control on his body that he'd never had to enforce before. But despite his ragged entreaties she hadn't stopped until he had lost all control and had been at her mercy completely. He'd never forget that self-satisfied sexy grin on her face. As if it was her mission to punish him for bringing her here in the first place.

Jamilah looked at Salman with wry impatience now,

bringing him back to the present with a jolt. 'Every time I talk about anything remotely personal you clam up.'

Salman sent her a warning look from across the lavishly decorated and heaving dinner table. 'I think I've already spoken far too much.'

'Yes,' Jamilah persisted with a gentle voice, 'about something that happened to you when you were a child… But what about everything else? Nadim? Your life so far?'

Salman found himself constricting inwardly. He knew he'd been avoiding talking about anything too personal—he already felt as if Jamilah knew far too much. His voice was brisk. 'There's nothing to tell. It's quite mundane and boring. I wanted to get out of Merkazad since I was eight years old, I've blamed Nadim on some level my whole life for what happened, which I know is irrational, and I've made a disgusting amount of money.'

He smiled then, and Jamilah shivered slightly.

'Don't try and psychoanalyse me. My life so far is exactly as you once said: *soulless*. And that's the way I like it.'

Jamilah knew she should stop and take the hint, but she couldn't. 'So, what? You won't be hurt again? That's impossible, Salman. We open ourselves to hurt every minute we're alive, but also to incredible joy.'

Salman was stuck for words for a moment. The concept of incredible joy was an alien one to him, and yet hadn't he caught a glimpse of it here with Jamilah? He shook his head mentally. Joy was not for him. He didn't deserve it. He was determined to wrest back some of his sorely lacking control. She was pushing him too close to an edge where his whole world threatened to drop away into an abyss.

Salman came out of his chair, and in a smooth move

Jamilah never saw coming plucked her effortlessly out of her chair, into his arms, and over to the bath behind the screen which had been prepared while they'd been eating.

Jamilah blushed to imagine what the villagers must think of them. Even though she knew she was putting on a good show of confident bravado to Salman, she was still quaking inside—sure he'd seen through her gauche attempts to make it appear as if she was in control of what was happening.

The past two days had slipped by with such deceptive ease that it scared her. They truly were cocooned in a tiny bubble of sensuality. The outside world could be going up in flames for all they knew or cared. And did Jamilah regret giving into Salman for one moment? As he undressed her now, with delicious intent, she felt some dim and distant regret, but told herself once again that she would think of it when this was over and she was back in Merkazad, in the real world, getting on with her life. She would have the rest of her life to regret.

Salman instructed her to get into the bath with a note of steel in his voice, and Jamilah responded with a delicious shiver of anticipation.

She watched as he too disrobed and stood there, powerful and intimidating. 'I want you to touch yourself like you did the other night,' he said.

Jamilah groaned softly. He was going to make her pay for what she had done to him earlier, in the glade. She'd noted the glint of determination in his eyes at the time, and now it was payback. She found the soap and let the magic of this moment out of time suck her under again, giving in to the heady pleasure and telling herself weakly that she'd let the questions go unanswered for now.

* * *

The following morning, early, Jamilah sat on a bench outside the tent and saw some of the local boys tending to the horses in nearby enclosures. She quirked a wry smile at the memory that she'd threatened to escape on one the other evening, when she'd arrived, and how Salman had autocratically declared that he'd forbidden anyone to let her take one.

Her smile faded, though, when she went inwards to the thoughts that had been plaguing her ever since Salman had fallen into a deep slumber beside her. She'd envied him his ease of sleep. It was day three. They were due to go back to Merkazad. And Jamilah knew she had two options open to her: she could avoid Salman again, for all the good it would do for her mental health, or she could try and take things further, but in the process risk much much more. She risked everything with that option—risked being hurt all over again.

She knew that if she insisted on pressing him to open up even more, he'd push her away for good. At least that was the gamble. Even as she accepted the futility of wanting that, a small, ever-persistent and ever-optimistic voice pointed out that things were different this time. This Salman was a different Salman from the one she'd known in Paris.

She sighed deeply. She couldn't stop the hopes and dreams. Was she on some level hoping for him to be cruel again? To reject her brutally? Wishing for a sort of punishment for having allowed herself to be so stupid as to believe that he might have changed? Her mouth tightened. She certainly deserved it, if that was the case.

She heard a movement come from inside the tent and resolutely stood up, mentally steeling herself for the exchange to come.

Salman had woken up to find Jamilah gone. He was

pulling on a pair of discarded jeans when she appeared in the doorway, dressed in her own jeans and a shirt. The village girl had returned them yesterday, washed and ironed. A frisson of unease went down his spine when he saw the familiar tilt to her chin and the crossed arms.

'Good morning.' His voice was still husky from sleep, and he could see how Jamilah's arms tightened fractionally, as if it had affected her. Immediately blood thickened and rushed to a strategic part of his anatomy. Pushing aside any niggles of inexplicable apprehension, Salman strode over to where Jamilah still stood, just inside the entrance, as if she were about to bolt.

He caught her face in his hands and pressed a kiss to her mouth, willing her to soften and relax into him. But she was rigid. He pressed a hand down her back to her bottom and pulled her into him, but to his chagrin she fought and pulled back, out of his arms.

'*No*, Salman. We're done with this. We're done here. Three days—that was it. We go home today, and I'm not going to go through this again with you. This time it is over. Really over.'

Salman looked at her and tried not to let those huge pools of blue affect him. He felt tight inside. 'Why does it have to end, Jamilah? I fail to see why when we're so good together. Why would you want to do that to yourself?'

'Because I'm trying my best not to be a complete masochist, Salman. You hurt me badly once before, and I'm not going down that route again.'

Salman felt sick inside. 'But it's not the same this time. We're different—*you're* different. You know why—'

'Why *what,* Salman? Why you rejected me in Paris

even though you didn't want to? Well, you did...and I have a confession now, too.' Her heart thumped ominously. 'I *was* in love with you. And it hurt me more than I can tell you. I'm not a robot, Salman. Perhaps it's easy for you to keep your feelings on ice and locked away, but I can't promise that...'

Salman felt anything but cold at that moment. He felt heat rising, because Jamilah had just told him she *had* loved him. He ran a hand through his hair impatiently, loath to keep on this track, afraid of what she might say...

Feeling desperate, as if something precious was slipping out of his grasp, and not liking it, he said, 'Stay here with me for another few days...until Nadim comes home. We don't have to deal with anything till then.'

Jamilah shook her head, her eyes huge and boring all the way to his soul. 'No. We have to deal with this now. All you're asking for is a stay of execution. I'm not interested in prolonging an affair that's just about sex. We have a relationship, whether you want to admit it or not, and relationships are about intimacy. Telling each other things, opening up. Nothing has really changed from six years ago, and when you walk away again, back to your life and your other women, I'll be right back to square one.'

Anger was like a tight knot deep inside Salman—anger at himself, for having indulged his weakness for Jamilah again. 'What do you want, Jamilah? More sordid tales of what happened to me? Like the fact that one day the soldiers brought out one of the maids from the castle and *used* her to give me a demonstration of what a man did with a woman? Is that what you want? Is that what will allow us to continue this affair?'

Salman saw how Jamilah paled, and immediately he

cursed and wanted to claw the words back. He'd had no right to tell her that. He'd already burdened her with too much. But even as he watched she composed herself and stood up tall, colour slashing her cheeks.

Jamilah shook her head sadly. His words *this affair* were lancing her inside. She was doing the right thing. That was all it was to him—all it ever would be. 'I'm sorry, Salman, truly sorry that you had to see that. But I'm not talking about that kind of intimacy. I'm talking about something that grows between two people in a relationship who…who care for one another, and you just won't admit that we have that. I'm talking about the banal details of our lives, our hopes and dreams.'

She had no idea how monumental what she asked was. Salman reached out to take Jamilah's shoulders in his hands, barely aware of what he was doing. 'You ask too much. It's an intimacy I'm not prepared to indulge in with anyone. I *can't*.'

Shock and renewed pain cut through Jamilah like a serrated knife-edge. She wrenched free of Salman, tears blurring her vision and slipping down her hot cheeks. 'I know the horrors you faced, Salman, and I can imagine how they made your belief in the fundamental goodness of man disappear. But it doesn't have to be like that again. What happened to you doesn't happen to everyone, and it's not to be expected.'

Salman's face was stark. He sneered, 'How can you possibly know what it's like?'

Jamilah put out a hand. 'Exactly—how *can* I know, unless you tell me?'

Unconsciously she put a hand to her belly.

'It's not that you can't indulge in that kind of intimacy, Salman, it's that you just *won't*. And all the sex in the world can't disguise that. I don't know why I let you believe that my baby wasn't yours, Salman, when you need a good dose of reality. *But it was!*'

She tried to dash tears away ineffectually, not even noticing the way Salman had paled. 'I know that must be hard to take—a man of your supreme control failing in one crucial aspect. But the fact is that it *was* your baby, and mine, and it died before it had a chance to live.'

The awful remembered pain nearly crippled her. She was livid with herself for being so stupid all over again. She was so angry she lashed out with words designed purely to wound and hurt as *she* hurt. 'Do you know what? I'm *glad* that baby didn't live, because you would have made a terrible father, Salman. You're an emotional wasteland, clinging onto your past like a shield, and you don't even deserve to be loved.'

Salman watched, stunned and in shock, as Jamilah fled outside. Her words had fallen like little arrow tips all over his skin. A baby. *His* baby. It wasn't possible. Medically, it wasn't possible. If it was any other woman he would automatically negate what she'd said, but it was Jamilah. She wasn't like that. She wouldn't lie. And, as if to compound the suspicion that she could be right, the doctor's words came back to him as if it were yesterday.

'You'll need to come for regular check-ups to make sure the operation has been successful. There shouldn't be a problem, but as with anything else there's a small failure rate.'

Recrimination burnt through him. Salman had naturally gone to the doctor with the highest success rate in his field. Once he'd had the operation he'd been supremely confident, and he'd been supremely busy. Of *course* he hadn't gone for any follow-up appointments… so it was very possible that the operation might indeed have failed. He had a sick feeling that if he went to get checked out that was exactly what he would find.

His head bursting and reeling with this knowledge, Salman remembered the hurt look in Jamilah's eyes the night she'd told him of the miscarriage. He'd thought it had been for the loss of the child, not because he hadn't recognised that it had been his. He cursed himself. Blindly, he went outside to follow her, but couldn't see her anywhere. He cursed again, and then heard a thunderous sound. Jamilah appeared from one of the enclosures on the back of a horse, hair streaming out behind her.

'Jamilah!' Salman shouted, furious with the fear that rose up even now to strangle him. He couldn't move, and could only watch as Jamilah cantered towards him, bringing the horse to a dramatic stop just feet away. Salman could feel clammy sweat break out on his brow. He'd never felt so weak in his life, and he detested that weakness.

A wealth of sadness rang in Jamilah's voice. 'At least I know you won't follow me, Salman. I'll come back when I hear the helicopter, and not before.' She whirled the horse around on the spot with an expert precision that even Salman could appreciate, and in a flurry of dust she was gone. Far away from him.

For hours Salman paced up and down outside the tent, his face as black as thunder. He'd issued orders and now waited for them to materialise. No one came near him, and there was no sign of Jamilah.

When the helicopter finally arrived he breathed a sigh of relief. Now she would come back, and he would talk to her. He knew now that he had to at least give her some kind of explanation.

The chopper pilot checked in with Salman. Time

went past with no sign of Jamilah. Salman felt rage building upwards, and wondered if she'd been stupid enough to try and ride all the way home. Then he reassured himself. She wouldn't have—not without provisions. Jamilah had local knowledge, and while their country might not consist of the more traditional desert, its rocky and mountainous topography held just as many dangers as an undulating sea of sands.

Just then Salman saw a young boy, leading a horse by the reins. It was the horse Jamilah had been on. With a different kind of fear constricting his insides into a knot, he strode over, learning that the boy had found it wandering in the village shortly before. Salman's insides curdled. It had come back without Jamilah.

Shouting orders—and an urgent one for someone to find the local doctor—and ruing the decision he'd made to bring Jamilah out here in the first place, Salman gritted his jaw against the onset of panic at what he was about to do. He swung himself onto the horse's back. He knew the chopper was nearby, but the horse itself would be the quickest way back to Jamilah's exact location. He would call the pilot and navigate him in if he needed to.

He hadn't been on a horse since the age of eight, but up until that time he'd been a more proficient horseman than even his own brother. Now he depended on knowledge he'd long since buried, nudging the horse in the direction it had taken with Jamilah and praying that it would take him back to her. If anything had happened to her— He blanked his mind. He couldn't go there.

The horse only started slowing down when it had cantered for about half an hour on the other side of the village. Miles from any habitation. This area was far from the lush oasis he'd left behind, and was as arid and rocky as the moon.

'*Jamilah!*' Salman's voice was hoarse from roaring her name.

He stopped the horse and turned it round and round, despair starting to snake into his veins even as he denied it. There was nothing remotely human as far as the eye could see. He knew the search party he'd commandeered wouldn't be far behind him, and they would have supplies, but there were treacherous rocks everywhere. A sudden mental image of Jamilah lying unconscious and bleeding made him squeeze the horse into a trot again as he called out her name for the umpteenth time.

And then he heard it—faint but distinct. '*Go away!*'

Salman's head went back. He closed his eyes for a moment, and the relief that went through him was nothing short of monumental.

He nudged the horse in the direction of her voice. 'Jamilah, *habiba,* where are you?'

'I'm *not* your *habiba.* Leave me alone. I'm fine.'

Salman followed the voice easily enough, and jumped off the horse when he saw a familiar, albeit dusty figure sitting on a rock, long tendrils of black hair loose over her shoulders. He made sure to tie the recalcitrant horse to a lone tree before walking over to her. She was looking resolutely away from him with arms crossed, and he sucked in a breath when he saw blood and a nasty bump on her forehead.

'You're bleeding.'

Salman's voice was like a balm to Jamilah's ravaged emotions, but at the same time she wanted to stand up and rant and rail and beat her fists on his chest until he might feel even a smidgen of the pain she felt. She sniffed, finally allowing that she'd been far more scared than she was letting on. 'The horse got spooked by an eagle and threw me. It was gone before I could get up.'

Salman was in front of her now, and to her chagrin all Jamilah could think about was how wrecked she must look. She still wouldn't look at him. His big hands were gentle, probing and touching her, smoothing back her hair to see the bump. She uncrossed her arms and slapped his hands away ineffectually, but she might as well have been swatting a fly. She heard the ripping of material and felt him press something damp to her sore head. She sucked in a breath.

Feeling very thirsty, but loath to admit it after doing something as immature and foolish as haring off on horse into the unknown with no supplies whatsoever, she gasped with relief when she felt an open water bottle being pressed to her mouth, a hand on the back of her head.

For the first time she let her eyes meet Salman's. She choked on the water; he looked wild. His eyes were very dark and his face was pale. He was covered in dust. He was encouraging her to take more water, and as she did so he said throatily, 'I'll save the lecture on running off so irresponsibly on a stupid horse for later. How sore is your head? Do you hurt anywhere else?'

Jamilah said meekly, 'I glanced my head off a rock. It's just a bump.' She saw how Salman's face paled even more. And then she said hurriedly, when that set off butterflies in her belly, 'I think my right ankle is sprained.'

He crouched down at her feet and peeled up her jean-leg. Her foot was indeed swollen above her sneaker and he gently took it off—and the sock. Jamilah winced with the pain as her ankle seemed to balloon before their very eyes.

Salman looked up at her and the set of his face was grim. 'We need to get you back to Merkazad.'

He lifted her up into his arms, and it was only then that Jamilah saw how he'd got there. She'd been too intent on ignoring him before.

'You came on the horse,' she said stupidly, her arm tightening fractionally around his neck.

She felt Salman's chest move. 'Don't remind me.'

With infinite gentleness and awesome strength he placed her in the saddle, and then with seemingly effort-less grace he smoothly vaulted on himself, behind her. The horse was skittish, and pranced, but Salman took the reins and brought him back under control swiftly. Jamilah was too stunned by this side of Salman she'd never seen before to say a word, but clearly he was an innately talented horseman.

The revelation almost, but not quite, distracted her from the sensation of Salman's rock-hard chest behind her, his powerful thighs cupping hers, and his arms en-casing her within their embrace. She felt safe, protected and cosseted, and yet again she was proving to herself that she'd learnt nothing.

They encountered the search party along with the local doctor not far from the village, and Salman di-rected the doctor and the girl who'd tended Jamilah that first night to follow them, thanking everyone else for coming to their aide, and telling them they could now relax. He sent one of the boys to tell the chopper pilot to get ready for take-off.

Jamilah's heart turned over as she heard how innately regal Salman sounded. He seemed to be morphing in front of her eyes into the man he was always born to be.

Within minutes Jamilah was being tended to by the shy girl and the local doctor, whom she would have trusted any day over the hospital in Merkazad. He pronounced to Salman that she should have X-rays just in case, but that he didn't think her injuries were more than a sprain and a bump.

With her jeans cut to above the knee on her injured leg, her ankle bandaged and a plaster on her head, Salman carried Jamilah out to the Jeep which was waiting. Despite everything that had happened, as they took off in the helicopter a short while later she felt an awful welling of emotion at leaving the little oasis, her eyes smarting with tears. She turned her face from Salman, terrified he might see her emotion.

Salman was grimmer than he'd ever been in his life. Jamilah had nearly killed herself in her attempt to get away from him, and he'd just found out that he'd been a father for the shortest amount of time—and the knowledge wasn't sending the sickening rejection to his gut that he might have expected. On the contrary, he felt a sense of *loss*. He glanced at the woman to his left. She was looking away from him, with her body angled away as far as possible.

He sighed. If there had been a moment in the past few weeks when Jamilah might not have hated him quite as intensely as she had since Paris, he'd well and truly quashed it.

'Salman, go away. You don't need to be here.'

He was implacable. 'Well, tough. I'm not going anywhere. And I *do* need to be here—you could have concussion.'

Jamilah sighed and wished her pulse would calm down. 'One of the girls can watch me.'

'*I'm* watching you. If it hadn't been for me you never would have gone off on that hare-brained horse.'

Jamilah sighed again, recognising Salman's immovability. He was sitting on a chair by her bed, arms on his knees, hands linked, watching her intently. She lay back and closed her eyes, hoping that if she feigned sleep he might leave. But knowing he wouldn't.

They'd gone straight to the hospital in Merkazad that afternoon, where Jamilah had been probed and X-rayed to within an inch of her life, all while Salman had issued autocratic orders and insisted on lifting Jamilah from place to place as if she were a complete invalid.

And now she was ensconced in the royal suite at the castle, having been bathed as well as she could be with her ankle bandaged, and fed a delicious dinner. All under Salman's watchful supervision. Only the shocked look from Lina, Iseult's personal maid, had stopped Salman from coming into the bathroom while she'd been washed.

For a long moment nothing was said, and tension escalated in Jamilah's body. When Salman spoke it was almost a relief—until she registered what he'd said.

'There's a good reason why I didn't think your baby was mine.'

Jamilah replied testily, 'Yes, because you arrogantly believe yourself to be infallible, and couldn't conceive for a second that something so human could happen to you.'

Jamilah heard him emit a short, curt laugh, but it came from the end of the bed where he now stood. Her eyes flicked open and her heart spasmed when she saw the pained look on his face.

'You're not far wrong in your analysis…but there was a bit more to it than that.'

Jamilah frowned, fingers unconsciously plucking at the ornately decorated coverlet on the bed. 'What do you mean?'

Salman ran a hand through his hair. 'The fact is that I made sure never to be susceptible to such a human failing. I made a decision a long time ago never to have children.' He sighed heavily. 'To that end I had a vasectomy when I was twenty-two. I spoke with the doctor who performed the operation today, while you were having your X-rays, and he informed me that there was every possibility it could have failed—and I wouldn't know as I've never been for follow-up checks.' He quirked a smile, but it was hard. 'Thanks to that arrogance you mentioned. I'll have to have tests to make sure, but after what you've told me, I think I know what they'll find...'

Shock coursed through Jamilah. No wonder he'd not believed it could have been his baby. This turned everything she'd thought she knew on its head, and threw up a whole slew of other implications that she didn't want to think about now.

She watched as he came back around the bed and sat down again heavily in the chair. An air of defeat clung to him, and he looked tired. A million miles from the cool arrogance he portrayed so well. 'Why did you do that?'

He looked down for a long moment before looking up, and the darkness in her eyes nearly made her want to say, Don't tell me if you don't want to. But she didn't. She was too weak—she wanted to know.

'Because,' he began, 'I never wanted any child of mine to go through what I'd gone through, and I believed that somehow the horrors I'd witnessed might be passed down, like some form of osmosis, in my DNA. I feared that I might not be able to protect my own child from evil, as my own father had failed to protect me.'

For a long moment neither one said anything, and then Jamilah said quietly, 'You must know now that that won't happen.'

The bleakness in his eyes reached out to envelop her. 'That's just it. I don't know. How can I know? How can anyone know? And I'm not prepared to risk such a thing. Not for anyone.'

Pain lanced Jamilah inside—so acute she almost called out. Because right now she harboured a secret. She held within her the living proof that Salman's seed lived and was healthy. She'd found out in the hospital earlier, when the nurse had done a routine pregnancy test as a precaution before the X-rays.

But how could she tell him? How could she be the one to stop him doing what he felt was right? After the horrors he'd seen, she couldn't blame him. With her heart breaking into pieces inside her, she asked fatefully, 'Even now you can't trust for a moment?'

He shook his head. 'I won't put anyone through living with me only to hope for more...' His voice was fierce. 'I won't do that to you, Jamilah. You deserve better than me. You deserve someone who can love you.'

Tears clogged her throat and burned behind her eyes. She turned her head away and choked out, 'Leave me alone, Salman. I don't want to see you any more.'

After a long moment of silence, she heard him get up and say heavily, 'Nadim and Iseult are coming home tomorrow.'

Jamilah was silent. She couldn't speak.

'I'll be leaving tomorrow evening...I have business to attend to.'

Emotion was rising within Jamilah, and she was afraid she'd crumble completely. '*Go,* Salman—just go.'

A deep sigh came, and then he said, 'I'm sorry, Jamilah. For everything. I'll have Lina come in to watch you…'

CHAPTER ELEVEN

SALMAN stood on Nadim's terrace and looked down over Merkazad. This view didn't threaten him any more. The emotions roused by the woman sleeping just a few suites away did.

He slammed a fist down on the stone balcony. He was a coward. He'd never felt more like a coward in his life. He wanted to go back into that room and seduce Jamilah until she was weak and pliant in his arms, until she admitted that she wanted him to stay, or until she said she'd go back to France with him.

But that was the one thing he couldn't and shouldn't do. He'd had countless moments to redeem what was left of his soul, and this was his last chance. He *had* to let Jamilah go, and never, ever pursue her again.

Even the thought of never seeing her again made him weak. But he stood tall and forced ice into his veins. Forced out all emotion. It was hard. It had been easy for so long to be unemotional, and now it was hard. He felt a flash of anger for the woman who had precipitated that painful thaw. But the anger dissolved just as quickly and was replaced by something much more poignant.

'Are you sure you're okay? Something about you is definitely different.'

Jamilah looked at her friend, and cursed the

Irishwoman's intuition. She felt herself grow hot under the narrowed amber gaze. Nadim and his wife Iseult had returned the previous day from their trip to Ireland. With their return, and the reality of a new royal baby arriving soon, the people who had been voicing discontent about Nadim's foreign wife seemed to have put aside their concerns.

Jamilah muttered something incoherent, and felt awful that she couldn't confide her secret. But at this stage—only scant days into her pregnancy—she was too superstitious after the last time. She felt vulnerable in the bed that she was still consigned to, wanting to escape Iseult's probing, and then it got worse.

She heard her say casually, 'Salman went home last night.'

'Yes?' Jamilah tried to sound as non-committal as possible. She'd feigned sleep when he'd come into her room late yesterday afternoon, but she'd felt the merest hint of a touch against her cheek, as if he'd trailed a finger down it, and it had taken all her resolve not to reach out and grab his hand and beg him not to go.

Iseult continued. 'He's been talking to Nadim about what happened to him as a child…I think they're finally going to be okay. And Salman seems to be interested in helping him run things here on a more regular basis.'

Jamilah's heart spasmed in her chest. If Salman was going to be a more regular visitor then surely that would have to be *good* news for his son or daughter? But the bittersweet prospect of it nearly made her want to double over with pain.

She forced a bright smile to her face. 'I'm really glad for them. It was time Salman shared what happened. It was too big a burden.'

Iseult's eyes narrowed even more. 'So you knew, then?'

Jamilah flushed, and cursed her big mouth. 'Yes… I… He told me.'

Iseult put out a hand. 'Jamilah—'

Jamilah took it and squeezed, barely able to cling onto control. 'Please, Iseult…not now. I'll talk to you about it again. I'm quite tired, actually…'

Iseult just looked at her and finally nodded, hauling herself up with an effort out of the chair. 'Okay. You know where I am.' She smiled ruefully, then said with a pointed look to her belly, 'I won't be going anywhere fast.'

Jamilah appreciated the attempt at humour, and gave her friend a quick tight smile. She watched as she left the room and then lay back, staring at the ceiling, wondering if she'd ever feel whole again.

A week later it was early evening, and Jamilah was back at the stables and hobbling around with a crutch to aid her. She didn't hear the Jeep come to a halt behind her, but she happened to look up and see Abdul's face in the far corner of the stableyard. His eyes had grown huge.

Jamilah frowned. 'Abdul…?' She turned to follow his gaze. When she did, she had to hang onto her crutch with two hands.

Salman was emerging from the Jeep, white-faced and with a grim expression. Just then a stablehand led a horse into the yard, just feet away from Salman, and she could see how he tensed and went even whiter.

But he stood firm, didn't move. Jamilah turned to face him fully, barely aware that Abdul had started to clear people and horses from the yard around them.

'Salman…'

He shut the door of the Jeep, and Jamilah only took in then that he was dressed in jeans and a loose shirt. He looked unkempt and tired, dark stubble lining his jaw. And her heart lurched.

He walked towards her, and Jamilah scrabbled back inelegantly, terrified that her composure would break. 'What...what do you want?'

Salman stopped a few feet away and quirked a brow. He looked weary, and a little sad. 'Somehow you never look pleased to see me, Jamilah.'

Her mouth twisted. 'Can you blame me?'

He shook his head. 'No, I guess I can't.'

'What are you doing here, Salman?'

'You could call it an intensive course in getting over my phobias—in getting over *myself*.'

Jamilah fought for equilibrium. She hitched up her chin. 'Well, good luck with that. But, if you'll excuse me, I have work to attend to.'

She turned and tried to walk away, but forgot for a moment that she couldn't walk. When she put weight on her sore ankle she yelped in pain and lurched helplessly into thin air, despite the crutch.

She was caught around the waist and hauled back against a hard, taut body. She felt Salman's arms tighten and his head came down, his mouth finding that spot between her shoulder and neck and pressing a kiss there. She moaned in despair at the inevitable rise of desire. And then with a struggle she fought to get free, twisting in his arms.

Salman eventually let her go, but she had to hang onto him, much to her chagrin, as the crutch had fallen. Her two hands were on his forearms, and she looked up at him, shaking her head. 'Why have you come back, Salman? What do you want?'

Sudden tears blurred her vision, emotion erupted, and she couldn't hold it back. 'Damn you, Salman, why can't you just leave me *be?* I don't want to be just your lover, or your mistress. I can't—'

Her words were stopped when he pulled her into him and his mouth covered hers in a searing brand. On a traitorous reflex Jamilah twined her hands around his neck and stretched up. This was both heaven and hell. She could taste the salty tang of her tears as they touched her lips.

Eventually Salman pulled back and looked down, smoothing a piece of hair from one hot cheek. 'Please... can we go somewhere to talk?'

Jamilah finally nodded. She couldn't deny this man anything when he stood so close and looked at her like that.

He lifted her up into his arms and asked gruffly, 'Where is your apartment?'

She directed him to the open door to her office, and then, once inside, through to the back, where her private sitting room and bedroom were. Carefully he sat her down on the couch, and then stood back.

Salman saw the wary look on Jamilah's tear-stained face, and felt pain lance his chest. And he welcomed it—even as he wanted to rip out his own heart for putting that wary look there. He took a breath. This would be hard, and he deserved for it to be as hard as possible—because he'd nearly thrown it all away.

'Will you just...hear me out?'

Jamilah muttered caustically, some of her fire returning, 'I don't have much choice. I'm a captive audience.'

Salman frowned. 'How is your ankle?'

'Fine...although I'm sure you didn't come all this way just to enquire after my ankle.'

'No.' Salman sighed heavily. 'No, I didn't.' He drove a hand through his hair, and then paced back and forth. Finally he stopped and looked at Jamilah. 'I didn't go home to France immediately. I went to Africa first—to the charity headquarters.' He grimaced. 'I thought I might distract myself there…but all it did was show me how lucky I am. What I could have if I only allowed myself to believe for a moment…to be brave enough.' He shook his head. 'Those kids…they have nothing. And no one. Very little chance to ever reclaim a normal existence.'

'Salman…?' Jamilah was confused.

He came and sat down—too close. But Jamilah had nowhere to go. He took her hand in both of his and she was shocked to feel a tremor.

'You broke something apart inside of me six years ago, Jamilah, and I wasn't ready to deal with it. But I've always known that some day I'd come back to you. It's as if I've always known you have that power. Ever since you were small…ever since that day at our parents' gravesides, when you were so silent and stoic…I felt then as if you could see right into me—and yet you weren't horrified by what you saw…'

A lump tightened Jamilah's throat again. 'I can't believe you remember that moment.'

He looked at her and her heart beat unevenly. 'I've never forgotten it. And the truth is, despite my stubbornness, even if I hadn't seen you again at the Sultan's party I would have found some way back to you…don't you see? I've been making my way back to you all along…'

Jamilah felt fresh tears welling. 'Don't, Salman— please don't say these things…if you're just saying this to persuade me back into your bed…'

He gripped her hand. 'I want so much more than that, Jamilah...I don't have any defences left where you're concerned. I flew to France from Africa, and a doctor confirmed that the vasectomy didn't work...he asked me if I wanted to do it again.'

Jamilah held her breath, her tears clearing. 'What did you say?'

He looked at her so intently she felt dizzy.

'I told him I'd have to think about it, and discuss it with someone.'

'Who?'

'You.'

Jamilah shook her head, and tried to stifle the flame of hope burning in her heart. 'But what do I have to do with it?'

Salman quirked a smile. 'Everything. Because there's no other woman on the planet I would contemplate having children with—only you.'

'What are you saying?' Jamilah wasn't even sure she'd got the words out, and somehow Salman was even closer, both her hands in his now.

'I'm saying that I've finally got it through my thick skull that I love you. I think I've always loved you. I can't live without you.' His smile faded then, and he looked more serious than she'd ever seen him. 'But with everything that's happened between us I won't be surprised if you don't want anything to do with me.' He took a breath. *'But*...if you could give me a second chance...I vow to spend my life making you happy, showing you how much I love you and need you... You're the only one who can possibly redeem my soul...'

Salman let her go and reached down to take something out of his jeans pocket. It was a small velvet box, and he brought it up and opened it. Jamilah looked down to see a gloriously simple sapphire ring twinkling up at her.

'Jamilah, you would do me the greatest honour in the world if you would be my wife.'

For a second she couldn't breathe. She looked at Salman, and then reached out to touch his face with a shaking hand.

'This is a dream. You're not real.'

He grimaced slightly. 'I am real, and very flawed—as you well know… But you're the only one who has the power to make me even half-human again. Even though I know that I don't deserve this…*you*.'

Jamilah finally took a chance that this was real, and stepped into the unknown. She put aside the ring and took Salman's hand. She placed it over her still flat belly and said, with a quiver in her voice, 'You deserve it all. We both do. And it's already started… A new life is growing in my belly—a tiny part of me and you…proof that there is a future for us.'

Salman looked awed, shocked. His hand tightened on her belly. 'But…how? I mean…when?'

Jamilah shrugged and smiled tremulously. 'Who knows? When we were careless that time in Paris?'

For a moment Jamilah saw joy and wonder mixed with fear and trepidation in Salman's eyes, and brought his hand to her mouth to kiss it. Her heart ached, and she said with husky remorse, 'I didn't mean what I said that day at the oasis, about you being a terrible father, and my not wanting the baby. Losing the baby devastated me, and I always feared I wouldn't have another chance. I think you would be the best father in the world… I was angry and I took it out on you.'

Salman groaned softly. 'I deserved it—and so much more. But perhaps this really is our second chance.'

Jamilah sat up straight and took Salman's face in her hands. 'You've paid enough dues to last a lifetime, my love. You have just as much a right to happiness as the next man—*more*. You've done your best to heal your own wounds and have helped countless others to heal theirs. Don't you think it's your turn now?'

Salman looked tortured for a moment. 'But I hurt you so badly—the one person I should never have hurt.'

Fervently Jamilah declared, 'It was worth it, Salman. Every heartbreaking second was worth it if it's brought us here now.'

'Where is here?'

Jamilah could have cried at the doubt still lingering in his eyes. 'It's brought me to you, my darling. I love you, Salman. I always have and I always will. You and our baby. All I want is to spend the rest of my life being happy and in *love*. And, yes, I'll marry you...'

He kissed her long and deeply until she moved against him, seeking more intimate contact. Then he pulled back for a moment and declared softly, 'I vow to spend the rest of my life loving you and trying to be a good father to our child and, God willing, to any more children we may have...'

Jamilah put a tender hand on his jaw and said with quiet conviction, 'You *will* be a good father, Salman. Don't doubt it for a second.'

Neither one of them noticed when Iseult knocked softly and entered a few seconds later. They were too engrossed in each other. They also didn't notice when Nadim appeared, and grinned, before pulling his open-mouthed wife back from the door and shutting it softly behind them.

* * *

Two months later, in a flowing strapless ivory gown that cleverly disguised her growing bump, Jamilah was married to Salman in a small, private civil ceremony on one of the rooftop terraces of the Merkazad castle.

Nadim and Iseult stood witness, with their newborn son asleep in a carrycot beside them, sharing their own private looks of love. Salman and Jamilah had wanted to wait to marry until after the birth and christening of baby Kamil Sean.

And when the ceremony was over, just as the stars were beginning to come alive in the skies, Jamilah and Salman went off for a quiet moment by themselves, before they went down to greet the guests who were waiting to congratulate them in the castle's lavishly decorated ballroom for the formal celebration.

Salman stood behind Jamilah, his arms crossed firmly around her belly, her hands tangled with his. She sighed happily and leant back into his embrace as they looked out over the view of the magical Arabian city. In the far distance it was possible to make out the construction crane which marked the spot where they were building a huge children's fairground.

Salman had taken the brave decision to come forward as the public face of his charity, and share something of his own painful experiences—which he'd never thought he'd be able to do.

He kissed her head at that moment, and Jamilah smiled. They didn't need words. They were together, and that was all they needed—for ever.

THE DESERT PRINCE

JENNIFER LEWIS

Jennifer Lewis has been dreaming up stories for as long as she can remember and is thrilled to be able to share them with readers. She has lived on both sides of the Atlantic and worked in media and the arts before she grew bold enough to put pen to paper. Happily settled in England with her family, she would love to hear from readers at jen@jenlewis.com. Visit her website at www.jenlewis.com.

For my sister Caroline,
whose adventurous spirit and creativity
are an inspiration.

Acknowledgement

Thanks once again to all the wonderful people who
read this book while I wrote it: Anne, Anne-Marie,
Carol, Cynthia, Jerri, Leeanne, Marie, Mel, my
agent Andrea and my editor Diana.

One

Did he know?

Celia Davidson took a deep breath and tried to stop her hands from shaking.

The Arabian Sea glittered outside the window of the elegant hotel offices, lapping against a ribbon of pure white sand.

The beach had probably been trucked in, along with the palm trees and the elegant hotel villas that lined its shores. With enough money you could remake anything.

Make it look as though the past had never happened.

The elaborately carved door in front of her opened and her stomach clenched in response.

"Mr. Al Mansur will see you now." His well-coiffed assistant smiled politely.

Celia brushed at her jacket, rumpled by the long journey from New York to Oman, and tucked a flyaway strand of mousy blond hair behind her ear.

Silly. He hadn't brought her here to rekindle their on-again, off-again romance.

Or had he?

That certainly wasn't going to happen. She wouldn't give him another chance to crush her heart beneath his heel.

And there was a lot more at stake now.

A rustling of papers from inside the office made her heart stutter, but she bravely took a step inside. Crisp white walls framed a high domed ceiling and two arched windows laid a spectacular view of the sea-lined horizon at her feet.

An antique desk filled the center of the room, its shiny surface devoid of clutter. Behind it, facing the windows, the broad back of a leather armchair concealed its occupant.

Her anxiety ratcheted up a notch as the chair swung to face her. Dark eyes locked onto hers. Black hair swept back from the aristocratic face and his wide, arrogant mouth sat in a hard line.

Unfortunately, he was every bit as handsome as when she'd last seen him, almost four years ago.

"Celia." He rose from the chair and strode toward her.

Blood rushed to Celia's head and she struggled to keep her feet steady on the thick carpet.

"Hello," she stammered. She extended her fingers and slid them into his large hand. A jolt of energy startled her, though it shouldn't since he'd always had that effect on her.

Her heart still ached from the last time he'd brushed her off and slammed the doors of his life against her—again.

Was that why she'd come? He'd finally invited her into the inner sanctum and she couldn't resist a chance to walk the glittering floors and fondle the treasures he'd never shown her before.

His eyes were expressionless as his palm pressed against hers, the formal gesture a stark contrast to the intimacy they once shared.

She pulled her hand back, skin humming.

Salim's stern good looks had always intimidated her as much as they'd attracted her. His tailored suit barely concealed the muscled body she remembered far too well.

"Thank you for coming." He smiled and gestured for her to take a seat. "As you've been told, I'm planning a land reclamation project. I understand that you specialize in sensitive treatment of ecologically challenging sites."

Celia blinked. Apparently he intended to gloss over the fact that they'd slept together the last time they met.

Focus. "I've worked on a number of desert projects, including an oil field in West Texas that I restored to native short grass prairie. I'm experienced with the issues involved and I—"

"Yes. I read your online portfolio." He turned and strode away from her. His broad shoulders tapered to his slim waist, accentuated by the well-cut suit.

He hadn't bothered to attend her presentation at the conference where they'd had their steamy tryst. No doubt he had more important things to do.

Silenced by his brusque comment, she scanned her surroundings. Pictureless walls and ornament-free shelves. The only decoration was a gold-sheathed dagger that hung on the wall.

Probably used to pierce his business rivals.

She knew he was capable of utter ruthlessness. He'd cut her adrift without a backward glance.

Twice.

Though, really, she had only herself to blame for letting it happen again. Their college relationship was long over, but she'd fallen back into his bed at the first opportunity like a lemming running for the cliff edge.

"The site is out in the desert." His deep voice jerked her back to the present.

He walked to the window and stood silhouetted against the bright view of the manicured bay. "My mother's people owned the land and it was explored and drilled in the 1970s. By the end of the decade it lay exhausted and abandoned and has remained in that condition ever since."

She steeled herself to ask the question landowners hated most. "Is the land polluted?"

"Probably." His eyes met hers, cool and dark, devoid of emotion.

Which was fine, because she felt enough for both of them. Sheer terror raced along her nerves at what still hung unspoken between them.

You don't have to tell him.

Her friends thought she was crazy to come here. They'd begged her to keep her distance and her secret.

Those sharp black eyes fixed on hers again. "I'll need to take you out to the site."

"Of course." She pulled her PDA out of her pocket,

trying not to think about being all alone with him, way out in the middle of nowhere. "That would be great. When would you like to go? I'm an early riser and I…"

"Right now." He rose from the chair as if ready to head for his car.

Not a question. A statement of fact. Apparently Salim Al Mansur was used to issuing orders and he expected her to jump.

"But it's afternoon. Won't the desert be awfully hot right now?" Couldn't she at least unpack and change? She was tired and disoriented. She'd come right here from the airport without even stopping to drop her bags off in her room at the hotel.

Though technically she was in the hotel right now. Salim owned it, part of his string of luxury resorts in the Gulf region. This office was his on-site throne room.

His eyes narrowed as he stared at her. For the first time the slightest flicker of humor seemed to glimmer in their lightless depths. "The desert is hot. It is in its nature."

She gulped. "You're right, of course." She forced a thin smile. "Might as well face things head-on."

She blanched.

The elephant in the room lumbered silently.

Had he summoned her here because he'd somehow learned the truth?

Salim strode toward his car. The desire to move— anywhere—surged through his limbs on a wave of thoughts and sensations.

He'd hoped that memories had deceived him, but unfortunately Celia Davidson was even more beautiful than he remembered. Although she'd come straight off a long flight, her skin glowed and her eyes shone blue as the Bahr al-Arab in the afternoon sun.

He dismissed the driver and pulled open the passenger door for Celia. His eyes strayed as she climbed in, and her boxy beige suit couldn't hide the lithe and shapely body he'd held in his arms.

Some memories were a curse that haunted you through all eternity.

"Buckle your seat belt." He started the ignition and pulled out of the hotel parking lot, leaving the sparkling oasis he'd created for the grittier and dustier world outside.

Celia belonged to that world, and he'd do well to remember it.

Funny how she still wore her golden hair pulled back in a tight ponytail, like the college student he remembered. She'd never been one to fuss over her appearance and he'd admired that at the time. Now it irked him that she glowed more than women who spent all day preening.

"Is it a long drive?" She stared straight ahead. Avoiding his glance, perhaps.

"That depends on what you're used to. Here in Oman almost everywhere is a long drive. Have you been to our country before?"

"No, never."

"You always said you wanted to come."

He watched as she turned, startled. She hadn't expected him to bring up the past.

"And I meant it." Her steady blue gaze stabbed him with accusation. Reminding him she'd expected so much more of him than he'd been able to give. She tore her eyes away with visible effort. "But that was a long time ago."

"I wasn't sure you'd be interested in this job." He shot a sideways glance. "I think I expected you to refuse."

He watched her neck lengthen. "Because of our history together?"

A moment of weakness had led him to her bed again after all those years apart. He'd been shocked at seeing her in the unfamiliar circumstances of a hoteliers' conference looking just as she had when they were in college together.

They'd been so young and innocent.

So foolish.

Celia had been deadly silent when he'd made it clear their renewed liaison had no future. She was a woman of reason. Surely she wouldn't expect a man in his position to continue an affair that could never end in marriage?

He glanced sideways at her, taking in the unchanged elegance of her profile. "I expected you to refuse because of the challenging nature of the project. I imagine most sensible landscape architects would laugh in my face."

Their encounter four years earlier was at a Manhattan conference on hotel design, so he knew she was in the landscape field. Still, he'd been surprised when his assistant had brought him her portfolio to consider as the landscape architect for this project.

The odd coincidence had presented an opportunity to face the past head-on—and push it from his mind forever.

"I enjoy taking on challenging projects." She sounded defensive, but he wasn't sure why. "And the location is a new one for me."

"You must travel a lot." He guided the car out of the hotel's palm-lined drive and onto the road.

"Yes. Manhattan is my home base work-wise. I live nearby in Connecticut, but I'm on the road two weeks out of most months."

Curiosity clawed at Salim. Or was it jealousy? "Your boyfriend doesn't mind you being away so much?"

She blinked. "I don't have a boyfriend." She tucked a strand of escaped blond hair nervously behind her ear.

"I'm sorry." Relief crept through his chest.

"Why should you be sorry? My life is very full." She stared straight ahead, jaw stiff as she uttered the words.

Why had he offered a condolence? She'd told him four years ago that she'd never married. Perhaps he felt guilty that he'd ruined her for all other men?

No doubt he gave himself too much credit.

But he'd never forgotten her. In fact, he blamed her for the demise of his first marriage, though she'd been at least three thousand miles away the entire time.

Their whirlwind romance at the conference had only deepened her infuriating hold over him. How could he take a suitable wife and hope for a successful marriage if he was enthralled by another woman?

Banishing Celia Davidson from his heart and mind would obviously be a challenge, but it must be done. The future of the Al Mansur dynasty depended on it.

Salalah's neat rows of boxy buildings gave way to plantations of palm trees. Celia couldn't help staring. How did they water this emerald forest of lushness out here in the desert?

"Salalah is naturally fertile. We get more rainfall than

the rest of the country." Salim's low voice penetrated her scattered thoughts.

"That must come in useful when you're landscaping your hotels. How many do you have?"

Phew. She'd managed to get the conversation back on a semiprofessional track.

"Twelve, at last count." He turned the steering wheel with a capable hand.

A big, leather-clad wheel, on what was obviously a very expensive car. Salim Al Mansur could probably buy and sell a few small nations with his pocket change.

"You must have bought quite a few palm trees."

The side of his mouth nearest her hitched slightly. A smile or a scowl, she couldn't be sure. "And I'll buy a few more if fate allows."

The palm trees receded behind them as the landscape opened up to the kind of bare, brown nothingness she'd expected. Some places were meant to be bare and brown, yet she could rarely persuade her clients of that. They'd rather install thousands of sprinkler heads in a quixotic attempt to create paradise in a place that was never meant to be one.

Celia squinted. Had the sun created a mirage, or was she staring straight ahead at a range of mountains?

"The Fog Mountains." His low voice interrupted her disbelief. Salim must have noticed her staring.

"Wow," was all she could manage.

A band of clouds hung low over the tree-cloaked crags, green as Vermont, like something out of a fairy tale.

She gulped.

She'd been so wrapped up in her personal angst about

coming here that she'd totally neglected to research the region. Better keep quiet about that, too.

Salim had always told her his country was full of surprises. Once upon a time she'd assumed they'd discover them together, but not like this.

How odd to be sitting inches away from him after everything that had happened. His solid, masculine presence next to her was only too familiar.

His unique scent, warm and spicy, drew her back into the past. He shared her bed for two whole years. They'd grown from childhood to adulthood together, sharing intimacies and joys and…incredible sex.

Her face heated at the memory. She'd fully expected to spend the rest of her life with him.

Then he'd ended it all in the most horrible way imaginable.

They climbed the lush green heights in silence and descended back to the rumpled beige floor of the desert. Relentless in its bleakness, it stretched to the heat-blurred horizon, broken only by the occasional isolated building.

As they drove, Celia found herself waiting for something marvelous to happen, like palm trees or mountains appearing out of the dusty haze.

Isn't that why she'd come here? Hoping for a miracle of some sort?

Salim turned off the main road and headed west on a dirt track to…nowhere.

After some minutes he pulled over, next to a dilapidated metal shed whose roof had fallen in, and climbed out in silence.

Confusion clouded Celia's mind as he opened her door and ushered her out onto the hot, sandy ground.

"This is the place?" Her incredulity showed in her voice.

Salim's face darkened. "It was beautiful, once."

Hard to believe. An abandoned jeep with no seats or wheels lay tilted on its side just to the left of them. Strange wheel-topped objects hunkered here and there amongst the rocky sand.

"Those are wellheads. All capped. There's an old pipeline running to the coast. It can all be removed. The oil is exhausted."

Salim strode amongst the detritus, his elegant dark suit an almost humorous contrast to the shabby surroundings.

"You're planning to build a hotel here?" Was this some kind of elaborate joke?

Beads of sweat broke out along her upper lip and she tried to dab them away gracefully.

"Come this way." The land gathered here and there into little rubble-strewn rises. She followed him behind one, and around the rise, signs of activity surprised her. Piles of dirt indicated a fresh excavation. She peered past a mound into a wide, shallow hole. The chiseled edges of dressed stone stood in sharp contrast to the rocky sand around them. "Stone blocks? Where did those come from?"

"There's a complex of buildings under the sand here. Maybe even a whole city."

Salim's gruff voice couldn't hide his enthusiasm.

"The famous lost city of the desert?" A rush of excitement danced over Celia's skin. She glanced up and realized that similar excavations surrounded them. Low walls emerged from the dusty terrain, tracing the ancient contours of buildings.

Ancient roads revealed themselves in the sand around them, cobbles worn smooth by time and the passage of many feet.

"We're on the frankincense trade route from the coast. There were caravan routes throughout the area, leading north into the Empty Quarter, to Saudi Arabia and beyond. Cities sprang up around oases where the merchants would stop to water their camels."

"But there's no water here." She glanced around, searching for the clichéd shimmering lake surrounded by palm trees.

"There was once." He kicked at a clod of rocky dirt with his black leather shoe. "It's still here, buried under the ground. The remains of an aquifer."

Celia stared at the arid soil. "There's enough water left to irrigate?"

"More than enough."

Something in his voice jerked her gaze to his. Was it her imagination or did triumph dance in his eyes? Anticipation, anyway.

It echoed like butterflies in her tummy.

"There's enough water to supply the hotel and staff housing. The excavations stretch over a five-hundred-foot area. I plan to reconstruct some of the buildings so visitors can see how people lived and worked back then."

"And perhaps you could leave some in a state of semi-excavation, so visitors could see how you found them. It's startling to see such perfectly made blocks emerging out of the sand."

He looked at her, thoughtful. "Yes. Let people see how the past lay hidden here for so many centuries."

His vision for this desolate wasteland animated his

features and made his eyes shine. He looked heart-achingly handsome, the sun burnishing his tanned features.

He peeled off his jacket and threw it down on a half-buried wall. Celia tore her gaze from the sight of his broad back straining against his thin white shirt.

Her faithless eyes tracked him as he strode, bold and athletic, across the rugged terrain. "Come here."

Celia scrambled over the rocky ground in her one pair of "smart" shoes. She certainly wouldn't be dressed like this if she'd known they were coming to the site.

"This is where the excavation started." He pointed to a wide, shallow pit, where layers of dirt had been brushed away to reveal the remains of several wide walls. "I hired a student to collect data about our family history. He became fascinated with this land and told me satellite imagery suggested signs of an ancient crossroads here. I hired an archeological team to excavate, and his suspicion was proven correct."

"What a find. Are you sure a hotel is the best use for the site? Perhaps archaeologists would like to study it in greater detail."

Salim's brow clouded. "I wish to bring this place back to life, not preserve it as a mummified corpse to be picked over by vultures."

"Of course," she stammered, chastened. She knew virtually nothing about his background. His home and family was a tacitly off-limits subject when they were in college.

She had found out why.

"I wish for people to travel here with a sense of purpose and anticipation. I want to share the history of our country and its people with anyone who cares to visit, not a few rarified academics." His dark eyes shone. "I hope people will come from other countries to visit."

He frowned and shoved a hand through his hair. She tore her eyes from the sudden clenching of his thick biceps when he looked back at her. "Perhaps you know that Oman's oil supply is limited. In a decade or two it'll be gone. It's my goal—personal and professional—to develop tourism as a well of riches for our future."

His zeal rose in the hot desert air like the frankincense that must have once perfumed it. Celia's chest swelled.

For a split second she saw a glimpse of the warm and excitable boy she'd once been so in love with.

She nodded. "The Salalah coastline is spectacular. The ocean is such an intense shade of blue. And those mountains...I'd never have imagined something like that here in the desert."

"Exactly. For every person who knows and appreciates the beauty of our country, there are untold millions who know nothing about it—yet." A wicked grin spread across his face. "I intend to change that."

Celia wiped another bead of sweat off her lip. Salim's mischievous smile was having a very unsettling effect on her.

He's dangerous, and don't you forget it. He'd already broken her heart twice.

And now there was another heart at stake, far more precious than her own.

"What kind of hotel design are you planning?" She managed to sound calm.

"Low rise. Buildings designed to blend with their surroundings, but to offer all the comforts a traveler would desire. Some will be luxurious—others will accommodate those with simpler tastes or a more modest budget. We shall welcome everyone."

He spread his arms in a generous gesture that tugged at somewhere deep inside her. She'd been so unwelcome in his life.

She cleared her throat. "And the landscape. What did you have in mind?"

That wicked smile played about his lips. "I don't. That's why you're here."

"Native plants or lavishly watered opulence?"

"They each have their own beauty. I imagine them coexisting here." He glanced around the strange half-dug excavations. "This was a meeting place of people, cultures and ideas. A place where anything was possible." His dark gaze fixed on hers. "And that's what I want you to create."

Her stomach fluttered.

Could she do it? Take this job and work with Salim Al Mansur after everything that happened between them? With a secret as hot and volatile as the desert air hovering between them?

The work sounded fascinating. To watch an ancient watering hole come back to life as a modern day resort, and to have free rein to plant it any way she saw fit…. The challenge was irresistible—almost.

"What's the budget?"

Salim's eyes narrowed.

Her question was crass—but she was in business.

"This project comes from my heart." He pressed a palm to his chest, broad fingers silhouetted against his fine white shirt. "I don't intend to put a number on the cost to restore it." He held her gaze just long enough to make her heart thud like a drum. "Whatever it takes."

Celia blew out a breath as his low voice reverberated around her brain.

What would it take?

If she worked with him she'd have to tell him.

Hell, she wanted to tell him. The secret ate her up inside. Every day she ached to tell him.

You have a daughter.

But the consequences might be unthinkable.

Two

As Salim piloted the car back to Salalah, he got the distinct impression Celia was trying to back out.

"How do you feel about honoring the land's history of oil production?" She glanced sideways at him, blue eyes alive with intelligence. "That's surely part of the area's heritage, too."

"You mean, incorporate the wellheads and pipelines?"

"Exactly." She crossed her arms over her chest. "I don't take a project unless I can implement my vision."

Ah. An uncompromising artist. He'd expect no less of Celia. Wasn't that part of her irresistible charm?

Salim turned and called her bluff. "Sure."

She blinked and her lips parted.

"Not all of them," she stammered. "I think an area's industrial history can be part of its magic. I designed a park two years ago around an old coal mine in England. We preserved the pithead as part of the project because that mine was the reason the town grew there in the first place."

Salim nodded as his hand slid over the wheel. "I appreciate original thinking. Too many tourist destinations are carbon copies of the same island fantasy."

"Aren't they? Sometimes it's hard to tell if you're in Florida or Madagascar. I have a heck of a time with some of my clients though. They don't want to use native plants because they don't see them as 'upscale.' I guess familiarity breeds contempt."

"We business types need educating."

Celia raised a blond brow. "Sometimes it's not worth the trouble. Many people aren't interested in being educated. They want business as usual."

Salim turned to stare out at the empty road ahead. She wanted him to be one of those unimaginative suits, so she could turn down his project without a qualm of conscience.

But he couldn't let that happen. "I'll pay triple your usual fee."

Celia froze. "What?"

"It's a big project and will take a long time."

She bit her lip, obviously contemplating the dilemma of turning down more money than she'd probably ever made.

He heard her inhale. "I'll need to travel back to the states regularly."

"Come and go as you please. I'll pay all your expenses."

She wanted to refuse him, but he'd make it impossible.

Seeing her again had already fanned that unfortunate flame of desire she kindled in him. It had never truly gone out. This time he wouldn't be done with her until it was extinguished—permanently.

A simple signature committed Celia to the uneasy partnership. A meeting with the architect and general contractor established they were all on the same page, and all systems were go by the time Celia headed back to Manhattan with her first check burning a large hole in her pocket.

She could fly back to visit Kira whenever she wanted. When this job was over she'd have enough money for a down payment on a house in Weston, near her parents. She could set down roots and have a real home base to share with her daughter.

She had thoroughly convinced herself that taking the job was a good idea—until Sunday lunch at her parents' house in Connecticut.

"But Mom, you're the one who said it was time for Kira to meet her father." Celia heard her voice rising to a whine the way it used to when she was a teen and they wouldn't lend her the car.

"I know, dear. But you met with her father. Did you tell him about Kira?"

Kira was napping in the upstairs bedroom she slept in when Celia was traveling.

"You know I didn't."

"Why not?" Her mother's clear blue gaze had never seemed more like an inquisitor's stare.

"I don't know." She sighed. "The time never felt right. It's a big thing. I should have told him when I was pregnant. I'm beginning to wish I had, but everyone talked me out of it."

Her mother nodded. "They had good reason to. He'd already told you there was no future between you. You know sharia law grants a father full legal custody of his children. He could have taken Kira from you and denied you the right to see her. He still could."

Celia frowned. "I don't think he'd do that."

"You've got solid gut instincts. If you didn't tell him, there was good reason for it."

"Your mother's right, dear," said her father, pushing a brussels sprout onto his fork. His soft voice rarely offered anything but support and encouragement, but she could see that he, too, was apprehensive about her taking this job. "He seemed like a nice boy when you two were back in college, but that was a long time ago. You don't know what he's capable of. He's rich and powerful."

Celia snorted. "All the money in the world doesn't turn him into a god. He was a little intimidating at first, but I was completely blunt about my ideas for the project and we came to an understanding."

"Except about the fact that you *bore his child*." Her mother stared intently at her white wineglass as she took a sip.

Celia bit her lip. "I do want to tell him."

"Just be careful. Once you tell him, there's no going back."

"I know, I know, believe me. Still, she's Salim's daughter. He has a right to know about her. It's cruel to both Salim and Kira to keep him in the dark about her existence. When the time is right, I'll tell him."

Fear curled in her stomach, along with the guilt that had been her constant companion since Kira's birth.

"*Salim,* huh? I see you're back on a first-name basis. Don't you fall in love with him again, either."

"I'd rather die."

Upstairs, she crouched beside Kira's "big girl bed." Her daughter's long, long lashes fluttered slightly, as dream images flashed across those huge brown eyes.

They looked so much like Salim's.

Celia bit her knuckle. So many things about Kira reminded her of Salim. Celia's own pale coloring had been shoved aside by genes demanding shiny dark hair and smooth olive skin. Kira had a throaty chuckle when something really amused her that sounded shockingly like Salim's laugh.

Already she was fascinated with numbers, and with money and business, and she certainly didn't get that from her mom. She'd even convinced her grandma to help her set up a lemonade—and lemon cupcake!—stand last summer, when she'd barely turned two. She'd fingered the shiny quarters with admiration and joy that made the family fall about, laughing.

Celia was sure Salim, who'd majored in business and run a consulting firm of sorts while still in college, would be amused and proud beyond words.

A soft, breathy sigh escaped from Kira's parted lips. Finely carved lips that were unmistakably an inheritance from one person.

It was wrong to deprive her daughter of her father. If it was awkward to tell him now, it would be much worse when Kira wanted to find him ten or fifteen years from now. It wasn't fair to keep them apart.

When Celia returned to Oman two weeks later, Salim was in Bahrain, opening a new hotel. Every day she expected his return with trembling anticipation, but the days stretched out into six weeks with no sign of him.

She could be offended by his neglect, but she decided to view it as a vote of confidence. Apparently, he trusted her completely and didn't even want detailed updates of her plans.

The archaeological team was hard at work reassembling structures and artifacts at the site. She'd put together a team of landscape professionals and made herself an expert in the unique local flora and fauna.

Suddenly word came from on high that his majesty was due back in three days. The coffee grew stronger and meetings stretched late into the night. Admins and accountants scurried faster from office to office. Celia found herself pacing the luxurious landscape nurseries, examining everything from specimen palm trees to prostrate ground covers with an increasing sense of alarm.

She planned to tell him about Kira at the first possible opportunity. She couldn't work for him and take his money while concealing something so vital. His loyal employees made it clear that he was a man of honor. He'd be angry, yes, but…

"He's here!" His admin burst into the conference room where Celia was organizing a set of drawings. "He's on his way up and he asked me to find you. I'll tell him you're in here."

Sunlight shone brighter through the elegant arched windows, and the sea outside seemed to glitter with a sense of menace. Celia straightened her new pinstriped suit and patted her hair.

You can do this.

It was going to be awkward any time she told him.

Disastrous, even, but she couldn't work for him under false pretenses. The longer she waited the worse it would be when the news finally came out.

He had to know. Now.

"Celia."

His deep voice resonated off the thick plaster walls and marble floors. Her breath stuck in her lungs as she turned to face him.

An unexpected smile lit his imperious features. He strode toward her and took hold of both her hands, then raised them to his mouth and kissed them. Shock rippled through her as his lips brushed her skin and sparked a shiver of sensation.

"Uh, hi," she stammered. "I was just organizing the plans."

"Ahmad tells me your designs are ingenious."

She smiled. "No more so than his." The architect was younger than her, but already accomplished and now apparently generous with praise. She made a mental note to thank him.

She made another mental note to rip her gaze from Salim's broad shoulders. Unlike last time he wore the typical attire of pretty much every man on the Arabian Peninsula: a long white dishdasha that emphasized the elegance of his powerful physique.

She cleared her throat. "I have some sets of plans to go over with you before I order the plantings."

And there's another little something I'd like to mention...

How on earth was she going to do this?

No time like the present. She screwed her hands up into fists. Drew a deep breath down into her lungs. Lifted her shoulders.

"Salim, there's something I…"

But the words dried on her tongue as another man entered the room. Almost a carbon copy of Salim, but with a stockier build. And this man wore Western clothing—jeans in fact.

"Celia, meet my brother, Elan."

Salim studied her face as she shook hands with Elan. She seemed nervous about something. According to Ahmad's daily reports her plans were brilliant: creative, stylish and ideally suited to the difficult environment.

So why did she look so…apprehensive?

Her eyes darted from Elan to himself. Her cheeks were pink and her lips appeared to quiver with unspoken words. The pulse hammering at her delicate throat suggested a heart beating fast beneath her high, proud breasts.

He cursed the thought as Elan's words tugged him out of his reverie. "I've heard so much about you."

"You have?" Celia's voice was almost a squeak.

"What do you mean?" asked Salim. Surely he'd never mentioned his long-ago American girlfriend to his brother. They hadn't even lived in the same country since Elan was sent away to boarding school at age eleven.

"Oh, yes. You were definitely the highlight of his college education," he teased. "I suspect you may have rose-tinted the entire college experience for him. He certainly enjoyed it a lot more than I did."

Salim's ears burned at hearing himself discussed so casually. "That's only because Elan is a man of action and not academics. I assure you my pleasure was entirely pedagogical." He shot a dark glance at his brother.

Elan's eyes twinkled with mischief. "Yeah, sure."

"Elan runs an oil services company in Nevada." Salim looked at Celia. "He's busy ripping up the landscape so that people like you can put it back together one day."

Elan shrugged. "The world still runs on oil, whether we like it or not. And as my brother knows, conserving the environment is a passion of mine."

Celia smiled. "That is refreshing."

Salim suppressed a snort of disgust. *A passion of mine?* He didn't remember his brother being such a flirtatious charmer. "Where are Sara and the children?"

"They're on the beach." Elan tucked his thumbs into his belt loops in another American gesture that made Salim realize how little he knew his own brother.

"Perhaps you should join them."

Salim glanced at Celia. Sun shone through the windows and illuminated her golden hair, picking out highlights of copper and bronze. He wanted to be alone with her.

To discuss the plans, naturally.

"I think we should all join them." Elan held out his arm, which Salim noticed with irritation was as thickly muscled as a dockworker's. "Celia, come meet my wife. She's never left the U.S. before so I think she'd be glad to hear a familiar accent."

Salim studied Celia's face as she absorbed the fact that his brother had married an American girl. A perfectly ordinary girl without an ounce of aristocratic blood. Elan bragged cheerfully about her impoverished background. A stark contrast to the type of woman tradition had expected him to marry.

But Elan was not the eldest son.

Celia pushed a hand through her silky hair. "Sure,

I'd love to come to the beach." She glanced nervously at Salim. "Unless you had other plans for me."

An alternate plan formed in his mind. It involved unbuttoning her officious pinstriped suit and liberating her lithe, elegant body.

He drew in a breath and banished the image before it could heat his blood. "None whatsoever."

She glanced down at her suit. "I'd better run to my room and change."

"Good idea." Elan smiled. "They're camped out near the snack bar. We'll meet you down there."

Salim bridled at the reference to his elegant beach café as a "snack bar," but he kept his mouth shut.

Elan was his guest and he'd resolved to end the long estrangement between the surviving members of their once-great family.

He may have failed in his mission to produce the son and heir his father demanded, but at least he could draw his scattered brothers back to their roots in Oman.

They were all he had left.

"Salim, I'm not leaving you here," said Elan. "You'll start working and that'll be the last we see of you until dinner."

Salim stiffened as his brother threaded his arm through his. Elan always had been affectionate. It was one of the reasons his father had sent him away to a spartan boarding school in England—to toughen him up.

It had worked, as he remembered from their guarded encounters afterward. And it had backfired badly. Salim recalled the forthright strength Elan had shown in refusing the bride their father had chosen and claiming he'd never set foot on their land again. A promise he'd kept until their father's death.

Apparently, Sara had un-toughened him again.

Salim snuck a sideways glance at his brother. Same strong nose, determined jaw, flinty black eyes. Even their close-cropped hair was similar.

But Elan's jeans and shirt were a striking contrast to Salim's traditional dress. A difference that spoke of the chasm opened between them.

Salim traveled regularly, but could not imagine living abroad.

Or marrying an American girl.

Even one as desirable as Celia.

Three

Celia couldn't stop laughing. A bright-eyed toddler was attempting to bury her feet in the sand, and the combination of sun and splashing seawater made her feel downright giddy.

Sailboats scudded on the sapphire horizon and, behind her, the elegant white buildings of the hotel reflected the magical afternoon sun.

Salim sat on the fine sand a few feet from her, his long white garment crisp and elegant in stark contrast to everyone else's swimsuits. He showered lavish praise on his young nephew Ben's elaborate sand castle, and smiled indulgently when nine-month-old Hannah tugged at the hem of his robe and sprinkled sand on his feet.

Unlike his brother Elan, he showed no inclination to run in the surf with them under his arm.

Elan's wife, Sara, was athletic, outspoken and almost as blond as Celia herself.

Hah. So much for the Al Mansur men being pledged from birth to marry a handpicked local bride. She couldn't help gloating a little, under the circumstances.

How different things might have been if Salim hadn't broken off their long-ago romance to marry the bride his father chose.

"I hear you're one of the top landscape architects in the world today." Sara's comment pulled Celia out of her reflection.

"Oh, I wouldn't say that. I've just had the good fortune to be offered some interesting projects."

"She's too modest," Salim cut in. "Her innovative approach has earned her an excellent reputation. I wouldn't have hired her otherwise."

"I'm impressed that you hired a woman," said Sara, looking straight at Salim. "Elan's told me the country is very traditional. I wasn't sure I'd see women in positions of influence."

"I wouldn't cheat my business of the skills and talents of half the population." Salim shifted position. "I've raised some eyebrows with my hiring practices over the years, but no one's laughing at the results."

"That's good to hear." Sara smiled. "Though I've noticed that even a man who believes in equality in the boardroom can be quite the knuckle-dragger when it comes to his private life." She shot a mischievous look at her husband. "Elan took a while to catch onto the idea of the emancipated woman."

"Really?" Celia couldn't disguise her fascination.

"It's true," said Elan ruefully. "I was all in favor

of women in the workplace, until it came to my own wife."

"And this after I'd already worked with him for several months. Somehow, once the ring was on my finger I was expected to lie around eating bonbons all day."

Elan shrugged. "I guess I still had all those old-fashioned traditions etched somewhere in my brain, even though I'd rejected them a long time ago. Almost losing Sara made me wake up."

"Lucky thing he came to his senses. I'd have missed him." Sara winked. "And we wouldn't have Hannah." She looked fondly at the baby, who sat on Elan's knee sucking on a sandy finger.

Elan stretched. "We Al Mansur men come with some baggage, but trust me, we're worth the trouble." He shot a glance at his brother.

Celia's eyes darted from one man to the next. Had his comment been intended for her?

Surely Salim hadn't told his brother about their long-ago relationship? With his hints about the past, he seemed to be trying to start something.

Salim sat, straight backed on the sand, brows lowered. Obviously the whole discussion made him uncomfortable.

As well it might.

Her breathing grew shallow. Elan had no idea of the bombshell she was about to lob at Salim.

"Salim," Elan flicked a bug from his baby daughter's arm. "Did I tell you Sara and I are eating out with one of my clients tonight? I hope you weren't counting on us for dinner."

Salim frowned. "I thought you wanted to eat that giant

fish you caught this morning in the harbor. You should enjoy it while it's still fresh."

"Oh, yeah. I forgot all about Old Yellow." He glanced up at Celia, a twinkle in his eye. "It's a yellowfin tuna. Maybe you two could share it?"

Celia gulped.

What was Salim's brother up to?

A cautious glance at Salim revealed his brow lowered in distaste.

"Goodness, I wouldn't dream of imposing," she blurted, anxious to dispel the tension. "I'm sure Salim is busy since he's been away so long. A lot has happened at the site."

"Yes, I need to visit it this afternoon." Salim's face was expressionless. "Perhaps you could accompany me and fill me in on the details."

"Absolutely. I'd be glad to." She met his poker face with one of her own.

Was that a grin of triumph spreading across Elan's rather arrogant features?

He'd be grinning out of the other side of his mouth if he knew the truth about her. He had no idea he was trying to set his brother up with a woman who kept his own child a secret from him.

She bit her lip as dread crept through her.

The excursion would present a perfect opportunity to tell Salim about Kira.

Now that they were working together, every day she didn't tell him made the secret weigh heavier. It was time to bite the proverbial bullet—or dagger, in this case—and face the consequences.

Salim chose a chauffeured car to drive Celia and himself to the site so there could be no suspicion of impropriety. His brother's bizarre hints made it sound as if he actually expected him to form a relationship with Celia.

Where would he get such an idea?

His unfortunate reunion liaison with Celia was entirely secret. He hadn't told a soul, and never would. He had no intentions toward her now, except to extinguish all thoughts of her from his heart and mind.

Celia stepped out of the car, her faded jeans giving away far too much information about her shapely legs. He glanced at his driver, but the man had tactfully averted his eyes.

"Guide me through the site as if it were built," he commanded. He cleared his throat as she walked past, determined not to be distracted by the tasteless and provocative way her pale pink T-shirt draped over her rather pert breasts.

Really, a mature woman should dress more modestly in a business situation.

It was entirely her fault that images of her snuck into his dreams and hung around his brain, ready to spear him with unexpected and unwelcome sensations.

It was annoying that his body responded so predictably to such simple and obvious stimuli.

She wore construction boots, too. Was there no limit to her desire to flaunt the expectations of feminine dress?

The boots were practical though, he couldn't argue with that. They picked their way across the rocky site until they reached an area where carved stone and mud-brick walls rose out of the soil.

"This will be the main entrance." Celia spread her arms, which had acquired a slight tan. "The road will be paved with stones to match those found at the site, and the drive lined with native plants like *simr* that need little water and provide nectar for honeybees. The original site appears to have been fortified, so the design incorporates a low wall and a wide, wooden gate, which will remain open."

"Unless invaders attack."

She glanced at him, surprised. A smile flickered across her shell-pink lips. "Always best to be prepared."

She strode ahead, long limbs covering the uneven ground with ease. "This open space will be the reception area of the hotel, and we've conceived it as the "marketplace." The various desks will be arranged like luxurious market stalls, and will in fact have handcrafted, traditional objects available for purchase."

The vision she conjured formed in Salim's mind. "A marketplace. I like it. We must have food available here, too. Coffee and dates."

"Date palms, bananas and coconut palms will be planted throughout the property. Of course they're not native, and will require irrigation, but it's likely they would have been grown here."

"Has the aquifer been tapped yet?"

"Come this way." Her mysterious smile intrigued him. He quickened his pace to keep up with her enthusiastic stride.

She paused at a circular section of wall, partially excavated from the surrounding ground. "The old well. And look inside."

Salim leaned over the edge of the wall. He inhaled deeply as the unmistakable, indescribable scent of pure, fresh water tickled his nostrils. It glittered below, just visible in the shadowed depths of the well. "Beautiful."

"Isn't it?" Excitement sparkled in her eyes. "I can imagine people sitting around this well a thousand years ago."

"People probably sat around this well three thousand years ago. Maybe even ten thousand years."

"Your ancestors." She peered into the depths.

Salim stiffened. The ancestors he'd let down by failing to sire an heir. But once he purged Celia from his mind he'd take a new wife and accomplish that, too.

"Perhaps they're all around us right now, invisible." Her soft voice drifted in the warm air.

"Ghosts?" His skin prickled.

"Or something like that. Can't you feel all the energy here?" She lifted her shoulders as if sensation trickled down her spine. The movement brought her pink T-shirt tight over her round breasts and drew his eye to where the nipple peaked beneath the soft fabric.

Heat flashed through him and a long-lost memory surfaced: Celia naked in his bed, sleepy-eyed and smiling.

Salim cursed the tricks of his brain. What would his ancestors think of that little vision? "The guest quarters?"

"This way." She walked on, aglow with confidence she'd enjoyed even back in college. "They're arranged along the patterns of the ancient streets. They were thoroughly excavated and all artifacts removed for study. As you can see, we've started rebuilding using the existing remains as the foundation where possible. It's moving to see the lost city rise from the sands again."

Salim nodded. Maybe that was why his flesh tingled

with unfamiliar sensation. Whole lives had unfolded here, only to disappear again into the dust.

"I've chosen plants that were indigenous at the time, or that could have been brought here by traders. Nothing from the Americas."

"Except yourself."

"Luckily I won't be a permanent feature." She kept her face turned from him.

"I'm sure you'd be a delightful addition, should you decide to install yourself." The words seemed to slip from his tongue. They both knew he didn't mean them.

Didn't they?

He saw her shoulders tighten. "I don't think I'd match the décor."

"I imagine that a desert oasis of this kind attracted travelers and merchants from all over the world. Perhaps even tall, blonde princesses from afar."

"I don't think anyone would accuse me of being a princess."

"If I recall correctly, you can be a little headstrong and demanding." He'd loved her effortless self-assurance and the way she always expected the world to come to its senses and see things her way.

"Oh, I still am." She flashed a smile. "That's how I get things done, especially with a crew of fifty to supervise. I'm impressed with the workers, by the way. They really are a diverse group. I have men from India, Africa, Saudi Arabia. They all have different skills and talents. You weren't kidding about this place attracting people from everywhere."

He shrugged. "People go where the work is."

Like her. He'd made it impossible for her to refuse this job. Not because he couldn't stand the thought of being rejected by her. Because she was the best person for the job.

And because he had unfinished business with her.

Celia marched forward, her construction boots striking the soil with determination. "Each guest will have their own house, arranged along the original streets and built in the traditional style. Each guest house will have a courtyard with a recirculating fountain."

"Perfect."

"I admit I'm nervous about how quickly we're forging ahead." She shoved a lock of hair off her face. "I know the archaeologists have been thorough, but there could well be more stuff down there."

"Then let it remain. This oasis probably has several layers of civilizations, each built on top of its predecessor. I wish for the tradition to continue, not for a lost way of life to be preserved in amber."

She smiled. "I think it's exciting that you're not afraid to embrace change and bring the oasis back to life. As you can see we're reusing a lot of the original building materials." She beckoned with her fingers. "The pool area is this way."

Salim let his gaze follow her for a moment before he started to walk. Her graceful stride revealed the power contained within her slim body. He knew all too well the energy and affectionate enthusiasm she was capable of.

Not that he'd fully appreciated it at the time. Perhaps he'd thought all women were such bewitching creatures in the intimacy of a bedroom.

Their regrettable meeting four years ago only reminded him too vividly of all he'd missed in the intervening years.

"An open body of water would have been pretty unlikely in the old settlement, so we racked our brains about whether to go for a natural free-form shape, or a more traditional rectangular form like a courtyard fountain. Right now we're thinking that a perfectly round pool would be an interesting combination of the two. Formal in its geometry, yet soft and natural in its outline so people can gather around it like a natural lake."

She marched briskly around its imagined shores. "It will be zero entry on one side so that small children can splash in the shallow water and the other side will have a gentle waterfall to circulate the water and provide filtration."

The setting sun made the rocky sand glow like candlelit amber. The workers had vanished for the day, leaving their excavator baking in the sun, and the oasis hung suspended in time. Celia stood on the shores of her imaginary lake, golden hair burnished by the rich light.

Salim cursed the ripple of thick sensation that surged through his body.

He was in control here.

It irked him that Celia could be so cool and businesslike.

He'd brought her here in the first place to remind him that she was just an ordinary woman, not the goddess of his fevered imagination.

Unfortunately, spending time with her had further unearthed the past he hoped to bury. Surely he wasn't the only one suddenly pricked by shards of memory?

"We must leave before it gets dark." His gruff tone seemed to startle her out of deep reverie. "You will have dinner with me."

* * *

Celia hovered in front of the mirror for a second.

Yes, it was her. She still had that little freckle next to her nose. Otherwise she might not have been so sure.

Her hair lay coiled about her neck in shimmering gold ringlets, arranged in her room by one of the hotel's hairdressers.

Her usual T-shirt had been replaced by a fitted tunic of peacock-blue silk, shot through with emerald-green.

She looked quite silly, but she hadn't wanted to be rude. She was now fit to be seen in the hotel's most exclusive dining room—at least according to the friendly staff member who'd bedecked her. Apparently, she and Salim were going to eat Elan's yellowfin tuna there, under the prying eyes of the hotel's wealthiest and snootiest guests.

Fun.

Especially since she *still* hadn't told Salim about Kira.

It seemed wrong to interrupt their work at the lost city with the news. The driver had invaded their privacy all the way back to the hotel. Now she had to smile and fake her way through a formal dinner, with the secret throbbing inside her like Edgar Allan Poe's telltale heart.

Her shoulders shook a little under the peacock silk covering. The dress was modest, Omani style, with embroidered gold trim at the neckline and cuffs, and matching pants underneath. The thick bangles on her wrists looked disturbingly like pure twenty-four-carat gold.

Naturally, she'd return them right after dinner.

She jumped when the phone on the bedside table

beeped. She shuffled across the floor in her gold-and-blue slippers and snatched up the receiver.

"I'm on my way to your room." Salim's bold tones sent a surge of adrenaline to her embroidered toes.

"Great. I'm all ready."

She plastered on her best fake smile.

Maybe tonight would present the perfect time to tell him.

Kira was the center of her universe. She spoke to her every day on the phone, sometimes several times. Twice now Kira had wondered aloud where her "Dada" was. She'd noticed that other kids in day care had one, and she didn't.

Celia was painfully reminded that two people who were father and daughter weren't even aware of each other's existence. The entire future of their relationship, possibly the whole direction of the rest of their lives, lay on her shoulders.

The door flung open and Salim stood framed in the soft glow from the hallway. His strong features had an expression of strange intensity, which deepened as he stared at her.

"Where did you get those clothes?"

"Aliyah brought them for me. From the gift shop. She said you'd…"

"I told her to find you whatever you needed. I didn't tell her to dress you up like an Omani." He himself had changed into Western clothes. A white shirt open at the collar and crisp dark pants.

Celia laughed, mostly out of nerves. "Kind of funny, isn't it? I look Omani and you look American."

Salim's gaze swept over her, heating her skin under the elaborate dress. A frown furrowed his forehead.

He hated it.

Her bangles jangled as she reached up to brush an imagined hair from her rapidly heating face. "If you think I should change I'm sure I can find something in my closet."

"No. You're fine. Let's eat."

He hesitated in the doorway then thrust his arm out for her to take.

Her stomach leaped as she slipped her arm in his. His thick muscle held rigid, unyielding, like he was steeling himself against something.

Celia drew a deep breath down into her lungs and tried not to trip over her embroidered slippers.

"Your work at the site," said Salim gruffly. "I'm very pleased with it."

"I'm amazed at how well it's coming together. Your team are magicians. I tell them what I want and they wave their magic wands overnight and make it happen."

"I've built and opened a lot of hotels."

She struggled to keep up as he strode along the hotel corridor, polished marble shimmering under their feet and lights glimmering in arched alcoves along the walls.

"Do you have a favorite, or is each new one the best and brightest?"

Salim frowned and his stride hesitated. "They're like children to me. I value each one for different reasons."

Celia faltered, tripping over her own feet as terror froze her blood at the word *children*.

"What's the matter?"

"I'm not used to wearing such a long dress," she stammered. "I spend too much time in jeans."

"You look different dressed up." His dark gaze

flickered over her face and body, leaving a trail of heat like a comet's tail.

Celia swallowed. "I guess almost anything is an improvement." She tried to walk gracefully, as the blue silk swished about her calves.

"I suppose that depends on the eye of the beholder."

Heat snapped between them, heating her arm where it lay inside his. Her skin tingled and she could feel her face, flushed like a schoolgirl on her first date.

It's not a date.

Why did it feel like one?

The hallway led into the hotel's main lobby, a well-lit atrium framed on all sides by the curved white arches characteristic of Omani architecture. Inlaid floor tiles glittered at their feet and hotel staff moved silently about, working their magic.

Celia's arm tingled inside Salim's as he guided her toward the restaurant. Her hand rested on his wrist, which she noticed was dusted with fine black hairs. His hand was broad and strong, more so than she remembered, but no surprise given all those hands had accomplished in the last decade.

She kept expecting him to withdraw his arm and push her politely away as they entered the restaurant, but he kept a firm hold as he nodded to his maitre d' and led her to the table.

Of course he probably behaved this way with business partners all the time. He was simply being polite. Nothing to get worked up about.

He pulled back her chair and she lowered herself into her seat as gracefully as possible. Glances darted to her from around the room, and she hoped it wasn't because she looked foolish in her getup. At least Aliyah hadn't suggested she wear a traditional gold headdress.

Salim frowned again. "You look beautiful."

His unexpected compliment left her speechless. It seemed at odds with his harsh demeanor. Almost like he was mad at her for looking nice.

"Thanks, I think." She grasped her water glass and took a sip. "You're not so hard on the eyes, yourself."

She wasn't sure whether Salim looked more breathtaking in Western clothes or in the traditional dishdasha. The truth was, it didn't matter what he wore. His strong features and proud bearing made any getup look downright majestic.

His stern expression only enhanced the handsome lines of his face. But he wasn't the boy she'd once loved. Something was different, changed forever.

What was it? A playfulness she remembered. The mischievous sparkle in his eyes.

Every now and then she thought she saw a shadow of it, but maybe she was just imagining things.

Something had died in her, too, the day he'd told her their relationship was over—because he'd married another woman. Just like that, over Christmas break, while she was sitting at home penning dreamy letters and looking forward to seeing him again.

"How come you never married again?" The question formed in her mind and emerged from her mouth at the same time.

She regretted it instantly, and waited for his brow to lower. But it didn't.

He picked up his glass and held it, clear liquid sparkling in the candlelight for a moment. "I never met anyone..."

"As wonderful as me?" She spoke it on a laugh, sure he'd respond with a jab.

But now he frowned. Stared at her with those impenetrable onyx eyes. "We did have something, you and I."

Her belly contracted. "I thought so, at the time." Her voice had gone strangely quiet, like the life force had been sucked out of her.

"The marriage wasn't my idea, you know." He put down his glass and wove his fingers together. "My father sprang the whole thing on me without warning."

"You could have said no."

He shook his head. "I couldn't." That odd look in his eyes again. A flash of...something. "Not then, anyway. I was still the eldest son, the dutiful one, my father's heir."

"So you had to do what he said, regardless of what you wanted." She frowned as a strange thought occurred to her. "Perhaps your marriage was doomed from the start because of the abrupt way you were forced into it."

"You mean, because I hadn't gotten over you?" Again, a gleam in those normally lightless depths.

What was she thinking? She'd never seen anyone so totally over her as the man who'd told her there would be no further contact between them—*ever.*

She waved her hand, dismissive. "Oh, I'm just rambling. As you said, you always knew your father would pick your bride, so it wasn't a surprise to you."

"You're right, though." His voice had an edge to it, almost as if his own thoughts took him by surprise. "I wasn't over you. I had to end our...relationship..." The word seemed to stick in his throat. "The way one snaps the shoot off a growing plant. Maybe it stunted the way

I grew after that. I couldn't be the husband my wife needed."

He leaned forward, frowning as he stared into her eyes with breath-stealing intensity. "Because I couldn't forget you."

Four

Celia almost fell off her chair. Except she couldn't move at all, because the blood drained from her body, leaving her brain empty, sputtering.

"I've shocked you." Salim sat back in his chair. "With the wisdom of hindsight I can now admit I couldn't love my wife. Maybe we could have grown into it slowly, as many people do, but she couldn't stand that I wasn't… romantic."

He inhaled deeply, chest rising beneath his shirt. "How could I be, when my heart still belonged to someone else?"

Two steaming plates of grilled yellowfin tuna materialized in front of them. Celia blinked at hers.

"Come on, eat. The past is the past and there's nothing we can do about it." Salim picked up a fork and speared his fish.

Celia managed to pick up her knife and fork and slice a piece of the tender flesh. She struggled for a way to turn his stunning revelation back into a normal conversation. "Does that happen a lot here, where arranged marriages are common? You know, people having romantic relationships with someone they can't marry, then having to go marry someone else?"

"Sure." Salim nodded and chewed. "All the time. But it's usually restricted to a quiet flirtation at a coffee shop, or in the poetry section of a bookstore, not the full-on, sleeping together kind of arrangement we had. That's simply not possible here."

"Do you think that's better?" She kept her eyes carefully on her plate.

"It certainly would have been in my case. I might have been a happily married father of four by now."

"You could still marry again." She spoke casually, as if to reassure him that she didn't care one way or the other.

"I intend to."

Celia's eyes widened. Salim simply took a bite of fish.

Why had he invited her to dinner and brought up the past? Her breathing was shallow. What did he want from her?

"The thing is—" he lifted his glass "—I'm honor-bound to continue the family name. I don't have a choice but to marry again."

"You'd marry just to have a child?" Celia worked hard to keep her voice even.

He nodded, his dark gaze unwavering.

You already have a child.

If there was a perfect moment to tell him, this was

it. She glanced around. Several tables were within easy earshot, and Salim's staff hovered all around.

No way could she drop a bomb like that here. She had no idea how he'd react.

"You think me old-fashioned." He rubbed a hand over his mouth. "But the failure of my marriage is my one big regret. I spend my days building a hotel empire, but if I died tomorrow, there'd be no one to hand it to."

"Hardly a big worry." She concentrated on her food, afraid to show him the panic in her eyes. "I'm sure you have a long life ahead of you. You'll have the heir you hope for."

She frowned. Would he consider a girl—illegitimate and American born—to be his heir? Probably not.

"Your confidence in me is inspiring. But then it always was." His soft gaze made her belly shiver. "Shame I didn't live up to it."

The confession—his admittance of guilt—touched her deeply. She had a sudden, typically feminine urge to smooth any ruffled feathers and reassure him. "What nonsense. You're one of the most successful men on the planet."

"You did say I'd succeed in business. I wasn't at all sure. I didn't speak English nearly as well as my brothers since I was educated at home while they went to school abroad. I wasn't comfortable around strangers." He rested his elbows on the table and studied her face. "But I grew very comfortable with you."

His voice lowered with what might be mistaken for a hint of suggestion.

She racked her brain for something to diffuse the tension thickening in the air. "I'll take some of the credit for improving your English. We used to stay up half the night talking."

"We had a lot to talk about." A hint of suggestion flickered across his striking features.

"True. I'd never met someone who read the entire *New York Times* from cover to cover every day. That's a lot of material."

"And you showed me that there's more to life than what you can read in the papers." A smile lit his eyes. "Do you remember the time you took me to the circus?"

She laughed. "How could I forget? You said the camels reminded you of home."

Salim's eyes narrowed. "They did. And when I was with you I forgot my home. I didn't think about where I came from. I was busy discovering new worlds and exploring them with you."

Celia blushed. "We were both virgins. Funny, isn't it?"

"Not really. I don't suppose that was as outrageous as we were led to believe. It did mean the first time was special for both of us."

His soft voice and tender words pulled at old chords of emotion. "Very special. And funny, too, considering that we'd approached it like explorers, armed with an illustrated Kama Sutra and a list of suitable positions."

Salim chuckled. "We did have a tendency to over intellectualize everything."

"We thought we were so darn smart, and that we could understand everything if we just thought about it and talked about it long enough."

"So true!" A smile tugged at his bold, sensual mouth. "No topic was off-limits."

"Well, except that you were going to take off and marry someone else."

The words fell from her lips, the accusation she'd never been bold enough to make. She was so shocked and hurt, at first. When they met again she was so surprised and delighted by their renewed connection that she didn't want to bring up the painful past.

Salim frowned. "You're right. I did avoid the subject of my future. I didn't like to think about it myself." His gaze drifted over her face, to her neck, which flushed under his attention. "And why would I, when it meant losing you?"

They hadn't talked much about his family at all. She'd assumed he didn't want to be reminded of the home that was so far away he only saw it once or twice a year.

He'd spent several weekends at her mom and dad's house and stayed with them once over spring break. Her parents had thought him sweet and funny. Being professors they were used to international students, many of whom stayed and settled in the States. They didn't think anything of her boyfriend being from another country.

It hadn't occurred to any of them that he had an entirely different life mapped out for him, thousands of miles away.

One that didn't, and never would, include Celia.

Salim's penetrating gaze locked onto hers. The flush rose over her face, and she let out a quick breath. "It might have been easier if I was prepared."

"How do you prepare to end a relationship?" He frowned. "I couldn't prepare for it myself."

"At least you knew it was coming."

Salim closed his eyes for a split second. When he

opened them they were dark as a starless night. "It wasn't easy for me."

He leaned forward, holding her attention with laser intensity. "That was, and remains, the worst day of my entire life."

"Mine, too." The words rushed from her mouth before she could stop them.

He'd seemed so cold and distant, like he didn't care. Like he'd changed into a different person overnight. One who'd never cared for her at all, let alone loved her.

She wasn't sure she'd ever recover from such a brutal rejection of all her affections. Such a firm and thorough crushing of all her hopes and dreams.

Maybe she hadn't recovered? She'd dated again, but never for long. She'd never married.

Now, suddenly everything was different.

He'd missed her.

He'd never forgotten her.

Memories of her, and their relationship, had ruined his marriage.

Shock—and something else—unfurled deep inside her.

Was this why he cut off their renewed affair four years ago? Because it had meant more to him than he was willing to admit?

Questions raced around Celia's mind. Questions about a Salim who'd been hidden from her.

A Salim who'd missed her and who still loved her and who might…

"Let's go." Salim swept up from the table without waiting for her reaction.

Celia rose, accidentally clattering her knife against her plate and almost knocking over her chair. Her heart pounded beneath her elegant silk dress and her pulse skittered beneath her bangles as she took his arm and swept out of the room on a tide of fierce and unexpected emotion.

Guests glanced up at them, curious, but she couldn't summon even a polite smile to greet them. She couldn't do anything except manage—just barely—to put one foot in front of the other.

They flew across the sparkling atrium and out through a dark arch toward the beach. Salim marched with such speed and concentration that no one even dared approach him, let alone speak. It was all Celia could do to keep up in her rustling dress and delicate slippers.

They stepped through the archway and walked down some steps to the sand. Warm evening air brushed her face like a breath. They hadn't even left the pool of light flooding from the atrium when Salim turned, wrapped his arms around her and kissed her with furious passion.

Celia melted into his kiss, rushed into it, her whole body cleaving to his, pressing against him from head to toe. Her hands fisted into his shirt and her nipples hardened against his powerful chest.

Salim's urgent fingers roamed into her elaborate hairstyle as he pulled her face to his and kissed her with breathless abandon.

"Oh, Celia," he murmured, when their lips finally parted for a second. "I tried to push you out of my mind." His words rang with pain, and tailed off as he crushed his mouth over hers again, a groan of relief shuddering through him.

Tears sprang to Celia's eyes. Fierce emotion threatened

to overwhelm her. "Me, too," she breathed into his ear, while he layered hot kisses along her neck.

She'd fallen so easily into his arms four years ago, despite how he'd hurt her. She couldn't help it. The connection between them was too strong to resist.

He grabbed her hand. "Come with me." He led her down to the beach, where she pulled off her hard-to-run-in slippers and let the cool sand welcome her toes. "My private apartment." He gestured to a small peninsula jutting out into the ocean's gentle waves. An elegant white building with typical Omani crenelations along the roofline—like a medieval castle in miniature—perched just over the rippling surf. Light illuminated a narrow arched window.

He ran so fast she could barely keep up.

Celia didn't protest. She couldn't even think, let alone talk.

He pushed open a carved door and ushered her inside. A lamp glowed in a corner, illuminating a simple, masculine space with bare white walls and a smooth stone floor. An ornate silver coffeepot glowed on a shelf, the only decoration besides the high arched windows shaded by carved wood screens.

Celia drank in the details, maybe because she'd been starved of information about Salim for so long. She'd wondered where he lived, and how, without her all this time.

He led her through a polished door in the far wall into what was obviously his bedroom.

A large white bed filled the center of the octagonal room. Tall windows punctuated each wall, providing slivers of ocean view where the moon danced over shimmering black water. Otherwise the space was ascetic as a monk's cell.

The space of a man who lived alone, with no woman in his life.

Salim closed the door behind her and slid his arms around her, muscles shuddering with urgency. His fingers roved over her back through the thin silk of her dress. He kissed her again and again, until her fingers plucked at his shirt buttons in thoughtless desperation.

"I missed you," his breath was hot on her neck. "Seeing you again four years ago only made it worse. I've craved you, wished for you."

Salim's blood hummed with tension so thick he felt he might explode.

He never forgot her. Not for want of trying. He'd done everything he could think of to expunge her from his body and soul.

He'd poured himself into his work, spent his time building an empire and filling it with people as passionate as himself.

But he never forgot Celia.

He'd had to try all over again after their fateful meeting in Manhattan. The very last person he'd thought to see there, she almost knocked him flat with her beauty and poise. He'd been helpless in the glow of her smile, and the warm greeting she'd offered, letting him know the past was gone and forgotten.

And he'd been forced to start over from scratch, trying to forget her again.

"It feels like heaven being here with you."

His words echoed off the walls, painfully true, as he touched her. She was so perfect, so precious, so totally unchanged, like time had captured her in amber and saved her for him, despite all his mistakes.

He lifted her diaphanous dress over her head in a swift movement and groaned at the sight of her breasts in their simple white bra.

Celia's hands gripped his upper arms with force as he lowered his mouth to her breasts, giving in to whatever primal forces drove him. He didn't fight the instincts he'd tried so hard to crush out of existence.

His lips brushed the cotton, tasting the shape of her thickened nipples through the soft fabric. Sensation kicked through him, firing his muscles and making his heart pound.

He unhooked her bra and slid her panties down her slender, muscled legs.

Celia laughed, a magical sound that filled his ears and echoed in his chest.

Laughter had been missing from his life for far too long. He'd tried so hard to do the right thing, to be the dutiful son and the upstanding businessman, when what he really wanted was...Celia.

Her hands tugged at his shirt and he realized that she'd undone all the buttons and was trying to remove it. Laughing again, he helped her, shrugging out of it and struggling with the fly of his pants.

Her face glowed in the soft moonlight, eyes closed and an expression of joy lighting her lovely features.

"You're perfect."

He said the words aloud right as he felt them, holding nothing back. Freed of his clothes, he pressed his skin to hers, enjoying the sweet, soft warmth of her in his arms.

His arousal was intense, agonizing, and if they

didn't make love right now, he wasn't sure what would happen. He did still have the presence of mind to don a condom. The last thing he wanted was for her to get pregnant.

He lowered her gently onto the bed, where a shaft of moonlight danced over the sheets and her soft skin.

Celia let out a little cry as he entered her. He opened his eyes, worried that he'd hurt her. Her face soothed his fears. A smile lit her features and her golden lashes fluttered as she writhed under him, clutching him closer.

Salim moved gingerly inside her—easing into a rhythm, then pulling back—wringing every second of sweet pleasure from the closeness he'd craved for so long. He ran his hands over her skin, pressed his fingers into her back and through the silk of her hair.

Years ago he might have rushed, eager to take his pleasure like a child with a bowl of candy. Back then, there was always more candy, maybe even sweeter, waiting for him tomorrow.

Now he was wiser and knew that life's sweetest moments must be savored, for that single perfect moment would never come again.

Her cheek, hot against his, felt so familiar. Her body, moving under him in quickening rhythm, was different and more delicious than ever. Her breasts seemed fuller and her belly softer. Her hips had more of a curve to them, as they lifted to meet his. Celia's slim, girlish body had ripened and filled out into delightful feminine perfection. He could swear her body had changed even since he'd last seen her.

"Your curves are fuller," he breathed.

Her breath caught for a second.

"It's a compliment," he reassured her. He'd forgotten Americans praised slimness above all else. "You become more lovely with each passing year."

"Or your sight gets dimmer with each year," she teased.

He released a ragged sigh as her long fingers dragged a trail of passion along his back.

"I'm not using my sight." He caressed her soft and seductive backside with his fingers. Pleasure rippled through him. "Even if I was blind, my other senses wouldn't lie to me."

He opened his eyes as if to reassure himself that the madness of his desire for Celia hadn't deprived him of his senses. In the dim light of the lamp he saw her delicate features, glowing gold, her lips parted in breathy moans.

He slowed the rhythm, layering kisses along her collarbone until her eyes opened. In the semidarkness they were blue as the night-dark sea outside.

A smile tilted her sensual mouth. "You've filled out, too. All muscle." She squeezed his bicep between her long fingers. "It seems cruel that you should get even more handsome as you get older."

"I could say the same for you, but I'd rather enjoy your beauty." He kissed her cheeks and her mouth, slow and gentle, relishing each brush of their skin. Her scent was intoxicating, like wild honey discovered just where you least expect it, filling the senses to the point of madness.

Madness. This must be madness. Wasn't he trying to cure himself of Celia?

Their tryst was having the very opposite effect.

A flare of anger—mixed inexorably with pure lust—flashed through him.

How did this woman have so much power over him?

Almost as if she heard his unspoken question, Celia angled one of her long legs over his, and deftly flipped their positions until she was on top.

Triumph flared in her eyes as she took him deep.

Salim moaned as pleasure cascaded through him. He'd always adored her sexual confidence—which they'd found and nurtured together—and the way she loved to take charge.

Her nipples hovered over him in the dim light, darker and fuller than he remembered, tempting his thumbs to strum their peaks. Celia sighed as he stroked her breasts, and she moved in a hypnotic rhythm, like a belly dancer, drawing him deeper and deeper.

She was taking him into a world where none of his senses functioned properly. A strange yet familiar place where his nerves were alive and tingling with pleasure so intense it felt like pain.

Celia bent and kissed him on the mouth, bold and beautiful, claiming him.

He kissed back, unable to stop himself. Lust and mischief soon had them clawing and nipping at each other. He was tempted to suck hard enough to brand her with the mark of his desire.

But he didn't. He was a gentleman, even in this moment of unbearable and delicious torture.

With a movement faster than her own, he grabbed hold of her thighs and maneuvered them both into a sitting position. Legs wrapped around each other, they sat face to face, with him still buried deep—and active—inside her.

She laughed. He'd picked one of the familiar positions from ancient India they'd studied and enjoyed all those years ago.

"It's a classic," he murmured, enjoying the face-to-face contact the position allowed. He kissed her on the mouth hard, then pulled back.

"It always slows things right down, doesn't it?" She looked at him through narrowed eyes. Her tongue flicked over her lips, tantalizing.

"Sometimes it's good to slow things down."

"When you're about to lose control?"

"I never lose control," he growled.

"Now that's an outright lie." Celia leaned forward, and brushed his chest with the aroused tips of her nipples.

"Okay," he rasped. "Only sometimes."

"Like when you're with me." She brushed her thumb over the curve of his mouth, daring him to argue.

"When I'm with you," he echoed. He seized her, flipping them again until he was on top, and sinking deeper into her hot and enticing depths.

Celia let out a long, shivering sigh and clutched him close.

Her muscles contracted around him when her climax seized her. In an instant he lost control.

He let out a tortured groan and clutched her to him while sensation rocked him like an earthquake. Colors and patterns burst in front of his eyes, and he clung to Celia as his whole world shook and shuddered and threatened to crumble.

He didn't want to let Celia go.

And that in itself was a big problem.

* * *

If Celia could stay right here, in Salim's warm, strong arms, she'd be fine. She was sure of it.

She could hear the sea outside the window, waves lapping against the soft white sand. The tide going in, or out, whichever it was, just as it did every day and night since the beginning of time.

If only she could stop the clock and hold them both here in this magical place where nothing else mattered but that they were together. But already, prying fingers of light crept around the blinds, ready to tug her back into real life.

She sat up with a start. Was it seven o'clock yet? She'd pledged to call Kira every day at 7:00 a.m. Salalah time, which was four in the afternoon in Connecticut, soon after Kira got home from daycare.

Salim stirred and his eyes opened a crack. His dark gaze sent a lightning bolt of guilt to her core.

She still hadn't told him.

And now she'd slept with him.

"I've got to go." She slid to the side of the bed, afraid he'd stretch out a muscled arm and pull her back into his embrace.

Salim lay sprawled on the pillows, broad chest bared, his seductive trail of black hair leading beneath the white sheet that barely covered his hips. "So soon? I think you should sleep in today. I'll talk to the boss." His mouth tilted into a sly smile.

A curl of fresh, hot desire unfolded in Celia's stomach. Which only deepened her sense of guilt. How could she do this to Kira, let alone Salim? Did she have no self-control at all?

Apparently not, at least as far as Salim was concerned.

She tugged her gaze from his dark, sleepy eyes and tousled hair and cleared her throat. "I wish I could, but I have a meeting at the job site. I don't want to mess up other people's plans."

"You're very devoted to your work." His low, seductive voice seemed to suggest that was a bad thing. He shifted onto his side, giving her an eyeful of his sculpted chest and hard biceps.

"Isn't that why you hired me?"

Something glittered in his dark eyes. "Not really."

Celia's belly tightened. Had he truly brought her here because he wanted…her?

He wouldn't have done that if he knew she'd concealed his own daughter from him.

Adrenaline propelled her from the bed. "I've got to get moving." She bit her lip at the sight of her crumpled blue finery. "I'm going to look pretty silly sprinting across the hotel complex in this."

"I'll call and have some of your clothes brought here." Salim stretched again, bronzed muscle pressing against the soft mattress.

"Are you crazy? Then everyone will know."

He shrugged. Maybe he did this sort of thing all the time.

Celia drew in a long, fortifying breath. "No thanks, I'll take my chances. It's still early. I'll sneak around past the tennis courts."

Salim laughed. "You have no need to 'sneak.' You're not married, and neither am I. We have nothing to be ashamed of."

She gulped. "I'm sure that's true in an ideal world, but

in this one I still need to be able to give instructions to the landscapers without them all falling around laughing because they're picturing me in bed with the boss."

He tilted his head back and surveyed her through narrowed eyes. "It's a pretty picture."

Her nipples stung with unwelcome arousal. In fact, her whole body still hummed with the memory of his touch. She needed to get out of here…now.

She shrugged into the blue dress and stepped into the sequined slippers.

"Come, kiss me before you go." He lay stretched on the bed like a sultan, sheets wound around his sturdy thighs. Celia's stomach flip-flopped.

She climbed onto the bed and leaned down to brush her lips to his. Salim captured her in his arms and claimed her mouth with a forceful kiss.

Desire surged through Celia, powerful and invincible. Her skin heated and her limbs trembled with arousal as she kissed him back. A low groan rose from Salim's chest, calling to a dark, sensual part of her that only he'd ever awakened.

Then the thought of Kira—possibly waiting by the phone—cracked in her mind like a whip.

She pulled her mouth from his with considerable effort. "I have to go."

"Shame." He lolled back into the fine sheets, propping muscled arms behind his head. "Since the project's going so smoothly I'm afraid I may lose you before we have time to become properly reacquainted. I find myself wanting to hinder your progress."

His words were a splash of icy water on Celia's lust heated skin. He spoke so easily of "losing her." No doubt if she didn't get lost by herself, he'd give her a neat shove out of his life again.

She stumbled for the door and pushed out into the sunlight, raking a hand through her long, tangled hair.

Why did she let this happen?

She came here to participate in an interesting project, earn good money…and tell him about Kira.

She certainly hadn't come here to sleep with him at the first opportunity.

Common sense deserted her entirely when Salim was around. She knew that. So why had she let herself be tempted into his bed?

Salim clearly saw this as an opportunity to enjoy her body and revel in the warm light of old memories, before he left her behind—yet again—and got on with his own life. Which, as she knew from long, painful experience, did not include her.

Or Kira.

How could she do anything so stupid? Had she thought that suddenly everything was different and he loved her?

A hard blast of air escaped her lungs. What an idiot she was!

She hurried along a neat brick walkway under a row of lush palms, keeping her eyes down so as not to make contact with any of the gardeners pulling dead fronds from the trees and sweeping the paths.

And what was her excuse now for not telling him about his daughter? They'd been alone all night in bed and she could have blurted the truth at any moment.

But the moment never seemed right.

Dammit, the moment would *never* be right.

She lowered her eyes as two hotel managers passed

her on the path, with a hushed glance at her rumpled finery. Shadows slashed like knives across the path, as sun crept through the palms.

Oh, how he'd hate her if he knew the magnitude of the secret she still kept hidden while she lay naked in his arms.

How in the world would she ever tell him now?

Five

Salim's chest filled with pride as they approached the gates of the lost city. He was driving the new seven-seater SUV he'd bought to accommodate his newly expanded family, and the children played cheerfully in the rear-facing backseat, while Elan and Sara exclaimed over their first sight of the new complex.

"It's amazing the way it just rises up out of the sand," Sara said as she leaned forward. "I love the crisp whiteness of the buildings here. Maybe we should paint our house white?" She turned to Elan. "I think you painted it the exact same color as the land around it so that no one could find you."

Elan chuckled. "You're probably right. I didn't want anyone to find me, until you came along."

Salim smiled. His brother was obviously very happy,

despite his unconventional marriage. He hoped he'd soon feel as settled and content himself.

"How come Celia isn't with us?" Sara's question deflated his momentary joy.

Guilt pricked him.

Sleeping with Celia last night was wrong on so many levels.

"She's here already. At least that's what my assistant told me. She came to supervise a delivery of plants. I'm sure we'll run into her." Would he even be able to look her in the eye in front of his family?

He'd taken advantage of her, knowing full well that their relationship—as always—had no future.

Sometimes he cursed the fact that he was the eldest son. That the burden of tradition and the future of the Al Mansur family rested with him.

But it did. Simple as that.

He pulled up inside the open gates and helped everyone out.

"It's loud." Little Ben covered his ears with his hands. Salim didn't usually notice such things, but there were quite a few pieces of machinery in motion.

"That's the sound of progress," Salim said as he bent down to pick him up. "You can't make things beautiful without some noise. Haven't you been to your dad's work sites?"

"No!" Sara laughed. "He's too young. And so far he's looking more like an artist than an oilman."

"You like to draw?" Salim peered into Ben's bright eyes.

The child nodded. "And paint. And I like to make up stories, but I don't know how to write them down yet."

"He's a genius," proclaimed Elan proudly.

Salim nodded. "He'll be the next Leonardo da Vinci." He stroked the boy's soft cheek. "You'll put the Al Mansur name on the map, won't you?"

"I think you're doing a pretty good job of that yourself," said Elan.

Salim snorted. "A few hotels, nothing more. I hope to make this area a popular tourist destination. It's good for our economy and provides work for the people."

"It's a lot more than that," Sara gushed as she walked forward, wide-eyed. "This is incredible. It's a whole city out in the middle of the desert."

Warmth surged inside him. "I can't take all the credit. The city was always here—we just found it and dusted it off again."

"It's breathtaking. Look at the artistry." A ribbon of painted frieze ran along the wall of a building next to them, and turned the corner onto another crisp, cobbled street.

"My architect hired talented craftsmen. It's been a joy to bring so much talent together in one place."

"Speaking of which, there's Celia. Goodness, look at those beautiful trees. What kind of bush is that?"

"I have no idea. Celia knows far more about Omani plants than I do at this point." Her knowledge and expertise floored him. And the pleasure she took in her work made it a joy to behold.

Salim's heart ached with trepidation as they approached. What a night they'd spent together. A taste of heaven in the one pair of arms he could never resist.

He cursed his own weakness.

His torment was worsened by the sight of those faded jeans she wore. They hugged her long, strong legs and cupped her firm backside. She was reaching up to prune a branch as they approached, and her pale yellow T-shirt lifted to reveal a sliver of slim waist.

Arousal flashed through him, heating his blood and bruising his ego.

Had he no self-control around this woman?

"Hello, Celia." He managed the gruff greeting with a poker face. "Hard at work, as usual."

He didn't want the others to know about their tryst last night. Elan might tease him mercilessly, or worse, try to make more of it than it was.

She turned. Her face glowed with exertion, and he could swear her cheeks grew pinker at the sight of him. "What are you doing here?"

Her blue eyes glowed with excitement that only fanned his desire.

"What kind of question is that?" He tried to act casual. "It's my newest resort, not to mention the home of my ancestors." He attempted a smile. "This is where I *should* be."

He tried to keep his eyes on her face, to ignore the way her thin cotton T-shirt draped over her chest.

She pushed a strand of damp hair off her face, and dusted off her jeans as the others approached, apparently self-conscious. "What do you think of the lost city?"

"I'm thinking it's very happy to have been found again," Sara said with a grin. She held little Hannah in her arms, and the baby reached out for a dangling branch. "It's so beautiful. And rather mystical, too. If I rub on that pot over there, will a genie pop out?" She gestured to a tall reproduction oil jar beside a nearby doorway.

"No, but I'm hoping the vine I planted in it yesterday will pop out soon if it gets watered often enough."

"It's hot, Mommy," whined Ben. "Can we go inside?"

"Won't help, I'm afraid," said Celia. "They're not turning on the air-conditioning until next week."

"Ben, you must learn to enjoy the heat." Salim set him down and ruffled his hair. "We Omanis don't need artificially cooled air to live our lives." He'd make sure his own son didn't grow up too dependent on modern conveniences. There was a lot to be said for living according to tradition. He'd worn a long, white dishdasha today, perhaps to remind himself of his place in the world.

He averted his eyes as Celia leaned forward to offer Ben a cool Thermos, revealing a flash of cleavage. If she had on traditional Omani attire, such mutually embarrassing moments would be avoided.

Then again, she was wearing traditional Omani attire last night, and look what happened.

Apparently there was no helping him.

"I love the heat," Sara exclaimed. "It took me a while to get used to it when I moved to Nevada to work for Elan, but now I can't imagine living somewhere that never gets hot."

"Maybe I'll convince the two of you to move back to Oman." Salim let slip the words that had danced in his mind ever since they arrived.

"That would take a lot of convincing. I'm not sure my employees would be too thrilled." Elan chuckled. "But I can see Celia's taken to the place already. I heard her speaking flawless Arabic yesterday."

Salim frowned. Was Elan trying to paint Celia as his perfect mate again? Couldn't he see that only did more harm than good?

"My Arabic is hardly flawless." Celia flushed a shade darker. She snuck a glance at Salim, who pretended not to notice. "I know just enough to make myself understood."

"Yours is probably better than mine," Elan said with a smile. "I've lived in the U.S. so long I've forgotten a lot."

"It's coming back, though," said Sara. "You did a fantastic job haggling over that rug for the dining room yesterday."

"Raw instinct. I'm sure you'd have gotten it for even less if you tried." Elan looked at Celia. "Sara's a demon negotiator. I think that's how she really won my heart. We Al Mansur men like our women made of pretty stern stuff."

Elan looked approvingly at Celia's work attire. Salim felt a twinge of annoyance—surely not jealousy?

Salim realized his brow had furrowed into a frown. He cleared his throat. Celia fidgeted, no doubt uncomfortable with this discussion of what kind of woman Al Mansur men needed.

"Would you like me to show you the plantings?" Celia's voice was a little squeaky. "The shrubs are *sarh*. They're native to the region and can go long periods between watering." She darted forward to stop Ben from plucking one of the berries. "They're not poisonous, but they might have been sprayed with something at the nursery." She looked at Sara. "I always check that plantings are nontoxic if they're in an area where children may find them."

"That's very thoughtful." Sara made a silly face at Ben, who grinned in response, then glanced up at Celia. "I'd almost suspect you of being a mother yourself."

Celia stood openmouthed. Salim could swear her skin turned pale. When she finally spoke, her voice was low and breathless. "Just being practical. My clients hate lawsuits."

She didn't glance up at him, the client. "She's right. I hate lawsuits. Such a time waster and so…unfriendly." He smiled. "I'm about to give Elan and Sara and the kids a tour of our found-again lost city. Will you join us?"

"Uh, sure." Celia glanced around, as if looking for an excuse not to.

He couldn't blame her. It was awkward trying to act normal after the night of heady passion they'd shared.

If he could turn back the clock and undo their sweaty, embarrassingly emotional tryst, he would.

What kind of idiot thought that sleeping with a woman he craved would help him get over her?

He'd plunged the arrow of longing even deeper into his flesh. He doubted even a knife could cut it free now.

He couldn't begin to imagine how Celia felt. Didn't dare even let his mind wander in that direction.

"This way, everyone," he called, aiming for cheerful confidence. "Celia could tell you how the city rose up out of the desert, stone by stone. She's seen a lot more of the process than I have."

"It's been truly amazing." Celia marched boldly ahead. "I was nervous that a lot of construction would destroy the site, but Salim's crew really know what they're doing. They were so careful to preserve the past."

"Salim's very big on the past." Elan shot a narrow-eyed glance at his brother.

"Speaking of which…" Salim said as he paused in front of a two-story building of white stucco, shaded with native date palms.

Elan turned and frowned. He blinked up at the pale walls, ornamented with a strip of painted diamonds. "It looks like...our house. Where we grew up."

"It is." Salim paused, watching his brother's face. "Come inside."

He led them through the shady arched doorway, into the cool interior. "I know you don't have the happiest of memories from here, but that house is gone now, and for some reason I wanted to recreate it here."

Elan's mouth hung open as he surveyed the stone floor, the smooth stuccoed walls, all exactly like the home they'd shared long ago. "Wow," Elan said softly as he blew out a breath and ran a hand through his hair. "This takes me back."

"We were happy in that house once."

Elan frowned. "When we were all together. Before father sent me and Quasar as far away as possible and screwed up all our lives."

Salim swallowed. Their father's action had abruptly ended their happy childhoods. With his fun-loving and energetic brothers banished to distant boarding schools, Salim lived a lonely and cloistered existence. His mother had died soon after, leaving him alone with the harsh father who never had a kind word for him.

So what? He'd survived. And prospered.

Elan cocked his head. "You've recreated our home, and now you've brought me back to it." His eyes twinkled. "If Quasar was here, we'd be a family again. Of sorts."

"We are a family." Salim spoke gruffly. He was determined the Al Mansurs would face the future together. "Quasar will come one day." Their wild younger brother was hard to keep up with. One day he'd settle down.

Or at least Salim hoped so.

Sara gazed up at the high ceilings, ringed with a simple painted frieze. "It's beautiful. Simple and elegant. I'm sure you'll recreate a happier version of the past here."

"I'm not nearly that ambitious." Salim crossed his arms, trying to ignore the rush of emotion in his chest. "It was a typical Omani building that seemed suitable for the site."

"Sometimes you have to confront the past in order to move forward," Elan said slowly, glancing around the familiar—yet unfamiliar—space. Salim's stomach clenched at his words. "I avoided the past like a dog that hunted me. I just ran faster to get away from it. Put as much distance between me and…home…as I could. I locked all that hurt and disappointment away, and vowed to never feel anything like it again."

Sara leaned forward. "Until one night in the desert, I pried open the lockbox of his emotions."

"And I've been a changed—and far happier—man ever since." Elan slid his arm around Sara's waist.

Salim swallowed. "I'm very happy for you. Naturally, since I've been here in Oman all the time, I've been surrounded by the past and have had no need or desire to run away from it."

He looked sideways at Celia. She stood rigid as a statue. No doubt she felt herself an unfortunate intruder in this family tableau. He quickly glanced out the window.

"Sometimes you can run from something without even knowing it." Elan's low voice penetrated the fog of his thoughts. "It's even harder to find your way back, in that case."

Salim frowned. "You speak in riddles, brother. I'm simply glad you're here and I intend to keep you here as long as possible."

"I'll tell you, it feels really good to be back. We'll have to make a habit of it." Elan smiled at Sara.

She nodded. "I'd love Hannah and Ben to grow up knowing their Omani family, and being aware of their heritage." Her eyes shone. "We should visit as often as possible."

Salim watched his little niece, now crawling across the stone floor with impressive speed. His heart filled with joy, and a sense of purpose fulfilled. "You're welcome here every single day, literally. Nothing could mean more to me than to bring our family together again."

A sudden fit of coughing took Celia by surprise, and she struggled to get it under control. "Sorry! I don't know what happened," she stammered, when she finally managed to stop and take a sip from the shared Thermos.

"The dry air," said Elan, reassuring, as usual. "Can you believe that a family of five and at least five servants lived in this house?"

Celia's eyes widened. "Are there more rooms?"

"There'd better be." Elan chuckled. "Can't have men and women in the same room. Anything might happen." He winked.

Salim narrowed his eyes. Some traditions had rather fallen by the wayside, at least in the bustling coastal cities. Still, better for Celia to see how different life was here than in the States.

Salim held a curtain aside so they could walk through the doorway into the next room. "Our room," Elan said as he stared, then glanced up at Sara. "Though Salim forgot the bed. We brothers shared one. We used to make up crazy stories in here, while the grown-ups were still sitting out in the courtyard. Wow, that was a long time ago. Probably the happiest time of my life, until I met Sara."

Sara glanced at Celia, who still stood there as if she'd seen a ghost. "He was far too busy working to be happy, until I sorted him out."

"Look who's talking, Miss Workaholic." Elan prodded her with his fingertips.

"That's Mrs. Workaholic, to you." Sara gave him a playful shove. "It's true, though. We both helped each other mellow out. I think when you enjoy your work it's good to marry someone else who's career-oriented. Then no one's left moping at home. What do you think, Celia?"

Celia's elegant throat contracted as she swallowed. "I suppose so." Her voice was scratchy. "I've never been married."

"It's not easy to meet the right person," mused Sara. "And sometimes they take some time to realize it themselves."

Salim frowned. Were they trying to cook up mischief again? Couldn't they see that Celia would rather be anywhere but here? No doubt all this talk of family and Omani traditions made her want to run for cover.

He frowned. "Let's go."

Salim and his family had left Celia at the site to finish her work. She'd almost died during all the talk of family and togetherness.

How would they feel about her if they knew she was hiding a member of their own family from them?

It hurt that she was depriving Kira of her own family

and heritage. Not to mention depriving Salim of the family he so openly craved.

She'd decided to tell him about Kira tonight. Whatever happened between them had happened, and she couldn't do anything about that now. All she could do was try to make the future brighter for all of them.

She was sure he'd come see her.

But he didn't.

Probably busy with work. She knew he had business dinners several nights a week. And he did have family visiting. Maybe they needed some time to themselves.

At least that's how she tried to reassure herself.

After a fitful night of broken sleep, she decided to go for a quick run on the beach to shake off stress. Exercise made almost anything easier to cope with.

Sensitive to Oman's conservative sensibilities, she dressed in light cotton pants and a shirt rather than her usual jogging bra and shorts. It was actually cooler to keep herself covered, she'd discovered. Which no doubt explained why most people in this region didn't expose their bare skin to the punishing sun.

No one paid attention to thermometers here. There were only two temperatures: hot, and very, very hot. Compared to the misery of the Connecticut winter she was missing, she wasn't complaining.

Once dressed, she picked up the phone for her daily call to Kira. Her daughter's garbled hello greeted her. This was Celia's usual time to call, so her grandparents allowed Kira to answer the phone. "Hi, sweetie."

"Mama come home."

"Mama will be home soon, sweetie. Two weeks. That's not long, is it?"

It felt like an eternity.

"Mama come home *today*." Tears thickened the words.

"I wish I could, lovie, but Mama has to work."

"Kira come, too, and help you work." Her little voice brightened and Celia could picture those dark eyes filled with excitement at her new idea.

Celia's chest constricted. "I wish you could, my baby. I wish you could." Tears threatened and she sucked in a deep breath.

"Why can't I?" Her brave voice sounded suddenly so grown-up.

Why couldn't she? She was too young to *need* to attend school. There was truly no reason why she couldn't "help" while Celia arranged potted portacula plants and studied the fall of shade over garden walls.

Except that this was her father's home.

And he didn't know she existed.

"I...I..." Celia's voice shook. She needed to get control of herself quickly and reassure Kira there was nothing wrong. "One day you'll be big enough to help me."

"When?" Again, the forceful clarity of a child far older than three.

"Soon," she lied. What was one more lie? Except that each one seemed to eat another hole in her soul. "Do you want me to sing you a song?"

"Okay Mama." Her reply didn't conceal her disappointment. "You sing 'Rock-a-bye Baby.'"

Celia gulped and inhaled. The song was so familiar she usually didn't pay attention to the words, but today they rang with threatening prescience, echoing from one side of the world to another. "...When the bough breaks, the cradle will fall, down will come baby, cradle and all." Her voice wavered and she tried to turn it into a laugh.

She was so afraid of breaking that bough. Of rocking the safe world she'd tried to create for Kira thousands of miles away in Connecticut. But she was learning that sooner or later it had to break, and she'd just have to do her best to catch her.

Brushing away tears, she hung up the phone with promises that she'd send more pictures from her cell phone and tell Kira exactly what she ate for breakfast.

Running shoes laced, she pushed out into the invigorating morning warmth. Her shoes sank into the sand as she ran, and her calves enjoyed the extra work as she filled her lungs with fragrant sea air.

A high rock outcropping marked the end of the hotel property. She ran to it, then stretched in the shade on the far side for a few minutes. She was about to turn and run back, when she heard familiar voices.

"Celia's more beautiful than I thought she'd be." It was Elan's jovial voice.

The object of their conversation blanched and ducked behind the craggy rock. A fissure near eye level allowed her to see the beach beyond, stretching to the hotel complex. She shifted until a sliver of visibility revealed Salim and Elan.

"You thought I'd spend years pining over an ugly woman?" Salim sounded in good humor. Again he wore a long, white dishdasha, this time with the traditional ornamental *khanjar* dagger at the waist. Morning sun reflected off the hard planes of his handsome face.

He'd spent years pining? Well, he'd admitted as much to her at their dinner together.

Celia bit her lip and listened.

"I'm glad you're finally coming to your senses where she's concerned." Elan wore jeans and a white towel wrapped around his neck. Sweat shimmered on the thick muscle of his back.

"What do you mean?" She couldn't see Salim's face, but she could picture his thoughtful frown.

"You know, getting back together with her. I know the two of you spent the evening together the night before last. How come Celia wasn't with us at dinner last night?"

"She had something to do."

Celia bit her lip.

"Make sure you don't let her get away a second time."

"A third time, actually." Salim sounded somewhat embarrassed.

"What?"

"I didn't tell you we had a little...reunion...four years ago at the Ritz Carlton in Manhattan."

"And what happened after that?"

"I flew back here. She has her own career, her own life. It was obvious there was no future between us."

"She told you that?"

"No, but it was understood."

"You told her that." It wasn't a question. Apparently Elan understood his brother, despite their years apart.

"I don't like confusion."

"Brother of mine, you have a talent for screwing up your love life. I'm going to personally see to it that you don't mess things up this time."

Salim laughed. "Don't worry, I've got it all under control."

Celia's ears burned. What on earth did he mean?

She gulped. He'd be horrified if he knew she was listening in on their private conversation.

"How, exactly, do you have it under control?" Elan's voice grew closer.

Celia shrank against the rock, its rough surface digging into her palms and knees.

"Isn't it obvious? She'll go back to the States, and I'll stay here."

"How does that solve anything?"

"It's a clean break."

"Yeah, except that's not what you need. She's the one, Salim. You know it, don't try to tell me different."

Salim laughed, but it wasn't a genuine laugh, more of a forced guffaw. "No, Elan. Your romantic American notions are touching, but Celia is not the one. I intend to marry Nabilah Al Sabah."

Celia's jaw dropped as her ribcage tightened around her painfully swollen heart.

"Who's Nabilah Al Sabah?" Elan's skepticism showed in his tone.

"She's the daughter of Sheikh Mohammad Al Sabah."

"The guy who owns that big shopping mall in Dubai."

"Among other things. He has a large retail empire."

"So this proposed marriage is something of a business arrangement?" Elan didn't try to hide his distaste.

"Not at all." Salim had the decency to sound offended. "I've chosen her because I think she will be an ideal wife and will make a good mother for our children."

"How many children do you two have together?"

Celia gulped.

"Don't be ridiculous. I've never even kissed her."

Elan laughed. "Then how do you know she'll be a suitable wife?"

"She comes from excellent stock."

Elan let out a long dismissive snort. "Brother of mine, you know I have a strong appreciation for excellent stock. I pay close attention to it—when selecting my stallions and mares. With women and marriage it's entirely different, let me assure you."

"I've been married before."

"Not successfully."

Celia's breathing was in danger of becoming audible, as she crouched painfully against the rock, a few feet from the brothers. Sweat trickled down her face.

She heard some movement in the sand, and when they spoke again they were farther away.

"I was young then, and unprepared for the responsibilities of marriage and family. I tried to fulfill them as best I could, but only disappointed a wife who wanted an affectionate husband, as well as a reliable head of household."

"Because you were still crazy about Celia and didn't want to make love to another woman."

The long silence made Celia aware of the pounding of her own heart, louder than the surf hitting the sand a few yards away.

"At the time, yes."

"And what makes you think that will be different now?"

"Because I'm older and wiser. I've accepted that I cannot marry Celia and I must choose a suitable wife and do everything in my power to make the relationship work."

"Do you have any idea how insane that sounds?" Elan's incredulity rang across the sand.

Probably his own brother was the only person to

express an honest opinion to a man as powerful and revered as Salim Al Mansur.

"Why can't you marry her?" Elan demanded.

"She's American, free-spirited, she doesn't care about tradition."

"I can tell you from personal experience that such women make very fine wives and mothers." She could almost hear Elan's grin.

"It's different with you and Sara. You live in America. Celia would never live here in Oman."

"How do you know? Have you asked her?"

"Of course not. Besides, she wouldn't fit in. You've seen how she dresses. She'd never go along with all the arcane social rules and regulations we have here."

"You certainly don't. At least from what I've observed so far. I've seen you drinking wine, for a start."

"I may not always agree with traditions, but as head of the family I have a duty to uphold the best of them. I'm proud of the customs and mores of our country, and I want my children to be raised accordingly."

"Brother." She heard a rustling sound, like Elan taking hold of Salim. "If you plan to marry another woman, then why are you playing around with Celia? Why did you bring her here?"

"To purge her from my system." He had the decency to sound sheepish.

Tears sprang to Celia's eyes.

He hadn't hired her because he wanted to revive their relationship, nor even because he wanted her landscape design expertise.

He'd hired her because he wanted to develop immunity to her.

"And how's that working for you?" Elan's snide tone gave Celia a moment of satisfaction.

"Fine."

Elan blew out a snort. "Yeah. Right."

They moved along the beach, and she had to struggle to catch their words above the sound of the waves.

Still, she heard Salim's final words: "In two weeks she'll be gone. I promise, on my honor, that I'll never see her again."

Celia peeled herself back from the hard surface of the rock and for the first time let an audible whimper escape her mouth. Her skin stung where she'd pressed it against the uneven surface. Her whole body ached, sickened by a destructive cocktail of rage and pain.

How could she have let herself imagine—even for a moment—that there could be anything between them but steamy sex and temporary intimacy followed by heartbreak?

She'd fooled herself into thinking that she'd come here to tell Salim about Kira, and she hadn't accomplished even that.

I'm proud of the customs and mores of our country, and I want my children to be raised accordingly.

Wasn't that the reason she'd kept Kira secret? She knew Salim was a man of tradition—it was why he'd dumped her in the first place. She'd always suspected he'd insist his child be raised in Oman by him.

Without her.

Her heart forcefully rejected the notion.

Kira deserved to be raised by someone who cared about her, not a bunch of centuries-old customs.

Maybe she wouldn't tell him. She'd finish the job—

she had a contract and she wouldn't break it—and then she'd leave.

Her chest filled with anger and hurt.

And then I promise, on my honor, I'll never see him again.

Six

Celia managed to avoid Salim and his family for the rest of the day. She spent time driving to nurseries, looking for the last few elusive plants she needed, and going over paperwork in her room. When the phone rang, she didn't answer it.

She ordered dinner in her room, and by 9:00 p.m. she was fairly confident of being left in peace for the rest of the night.

A knock on the door made her start.

She frowned. If it were Salim she'd say she had a headache and send him packing. She certainly wasn't going to give him another chance to *purge her from his system.*

"Who is it?" she said in a forced whisper.

"It's Sara. Can I come in?"

Celia bit her lip. What did Sara want?

She couldn't think of a good reason to turn her away. "Sure." She unlocked the door with fumbling hands. "Come in. It's kind of messy. I've been catching up on some spreadsheets."

She had a printer hooked up to her laptop, and the results were spread unartistically over the large bed and part of the tiled floor.

Sara wore a simple silver-gray dress that accentuated her pretty roses-and-gold coloring. Her dark blond hair was pulled back into a ponytail. She smiled warmly at Celia. "We missed you at dinner. I was hoping to pick your brain about landscaping our house in Nevada. We have a heck of a time getting anything to grow because it's flaming hot in the summer and under several feet of snow in the winter."

Celia laughed, glad for the familiar subject matter. "I always advise my clients to start with native plants. At least you know they'll grow."

"Yeah, but you can get tired of sagebrush. It's pretty much all there is and we have plenty of it already."

"How about a nice sculpture?" She lifted a brow.

"Elan's horses are the most beautiful sculptures. We've got plenty of those. I guess you're right and I should focus on what works. Who's this?"

Celia's heart almost stopped as Sara leaned forward and picked up a photo from the cluttered bedcover.

A picture of Kira that she'd been mooning over earlier that afternoon, reminding herself to count her blessings.

"Uh…Kira." Her brain had frozen, and it was all she could come out with.

Sara peered at the picture. "She's adorable." She glanced up at Celia, expectant.

"Yes," managed Celia. She turned to stack some scattered papers, as fear stung her fingertips.

"She looks a lot like Ben." Sara tilted her head, holding the picture at arm's length. "He's a boy, of course, and I can tell from the dress that this is a girl, despite the short hair, but there's a striking similarity about their eyes and the shape of their mouth."

"Oh." Celia pretended to busy herself shoving papers into a manila folder, while her pulse drummed at her temples.

The long silence finally made her turn to look at Sara.

Who stared right at her.

"She's your daughter, isn't she?"

"Yes." The simple word exploded from her mouth.

What mother could deny her own child?

Sara blurred as tears sprang to Celia's eyes.

"I knew it immediately." Sara pressed a hand to her mouth for a moment, staring at the picture. "She looks so like Salim. She is Salim's, isn't she?"

Celia nodded mutely.

"She looks like you, too. You can tell she'll have your lovely bone structure. And what a sweet smile. I think that's yours, too."

She handed the picture back to Celia, who accepted it with shaking fingers.

"Salim doesn't know about her, does he?" Sara's voice dropped, serious.

"He doesn't. I wanted to tell him. I was going to… but…."

"How old is she? She looks about two in that picture."

"She just turned three. She's started nursery school.

She's living with my parents in Connecticut while I'm here."

The useless facts did nothing to cover over the bald reality that she'd kept her daughter's existence from the girl's own father.

"You have to tell him." Sara's intense stare—her eyes were an unusual pale green color—did not brook contradiction.

"I'm not so sure." Celia tucked the photo into her shirt pocket, and wiped her perspiring hands on the back of her jeans. "Sometimes it seems like a good idea, then something happens and…" She trailed off.

Heat rose to her cheeks as she recalled the humiliating confidences overheard on the beach that morning.

"What are you afraid of?" Sara rose and put a cool hand on Celia's arm. "I haven't known him long, but Salim's obviously a good man."

"He could take her. It's the law here—in any Islamic country, I think. A child belongs to its father."

"He wouldn't do that. Besides, from what I know, even in cases of divorce the child lives with its mother until it's eight or so. One of our business partners from Saudi told me that."

"Would you be willing to give up Hannah when she turns eight?" Tears threatened and were audible in Celia's voice.

"God, no." The very thought seemed to make Sara shiver. "Still, to not tell him…" She looked up at Celia, still holding her arm. "It took me a while to pluck up the courage to tell Elan about Ben. I was his assistant at the time and our liaison had been a total accident—just one night, with no prospect of any relationship. He was so horrified by his lapse of judgment that he left the

country afterward for several days without even telling
me. I was sure I'd lose my job and be left pregnant with
no health insurance. It wasn't easy, that's for sure, but
I told Elan the truth, and look how wonderfully things
have turned out." She shone a warm gaze on Celia. "That
could happen for you and Salim."

Celia swallowed. "I don't think so."

"Why not? I know Salim wants to get married. He's
absolutely charmed by Ben and Hannah and has said
several times that he can't wait to have children. And—"
she squeezed Celia's arm "—anyone would have to be
blind not to notice that he's madly in love with you."

Celia blew out. "He isn't, really. We can't keep our
hands off each other, and then it ends in tears. Trust me,
it's a been-there-done-that situation."

"I don't know what's happened between you in the
past, but I truly believe things will be different if you
tell him about his daughter."

"So we can get married and be a happy family?"
Celia's voice rose to something between a whine and
laugh. "Never happen. He likes me between his sheets,
but I'm not what he considers suitable wife material."

"Perhaps he needs to have some sense drummed into
him. As Elan said on the beach that day, sometimes the
Al Mansur men can be a tad slow on the uptake. But
they need our help. They had a deprived childhood."

"All that money can buy and very little else."

"At least after their mother died. They had no family
life, just a cruel father bossing them around. No one
helped them grow up into decent family men. Salim's
proud and stubborn, I can see that, but he's got a good
heart beating under that long white robe he wears. I
think you can dig past all the baggage and find your way

into it. Especially once he knows you share a beautiful daughter."

"Oh, boy." Celia shoved a hank of hair off her face. "I do want to tell him, but…" The overheard conversation made doubts stretch out like shadows. "Maybe Salim would prefer not to know. He has a whole life planned out. One without me in it."

"You know what? It doesn't matter what he has planned. Seriously, it's not fair to keep something like that a secret. It's not fair to your daughter, either. Kira will want to know her father one day. Why not now, when there's still a bright future possible for all of you?"

Celia inhaled a shaky breath. Sarah's words struck a painful chord of truth inside her. Not that they could live happily ever after, but that she had to tell him, no matter what.

"I'm not optimistic about the bright future, but I swear I'll tell him tomorrow, come hell or high water."

Sara smiled. "I guess either is a possibility, given that we're in a burning desert and on a beach at the same time." She gave Celia's arm a supportive squeeze. "Elan and I will be here for you. Everything will turn out okay."

Doubt sent a cold shiver down Celia's spine. "I hope so."

Celia called Salim on his cell first thing in the morning. She didn't even say hello. She didn't want to lose her nerve. "Can we drive to the site together at nine?"

"Um, I have a meeting at ten and a… Perhaps Hanif can drive you."

"Can you meet me at the site?" Maybe that was better. Less chance of causing a major road accident.

"Sure, I can be there by four. I'll drive you home."

"Fine." She hung up, fingers trembling. No turning back now.

As four o'clock rolled around she began to regret not telling him back at the hotel. At least there it was cool and she didn't have grit under her fingernails and no place to wash it out. She shoved a lock of damp hair off her forehead.

Luckily there weren't many people around as she'd sent her staff home early. The construction crews had knocked off for the day. A few painters and electricians worked here and there in the complex of elegant white buildings.

The muffled purr of an expensive engine made her skin prickle.

I have something to tell you.

How did you come out and say it? Each time she tried to find the words, it sounded more dramatic and shocking, and she felt more ashamed that she'd kept the truth to herself for so long.

The engine stopped.

He's here. No turning back now.

She strode toward the parking area in front of the future "marketplace" with her head held high and her courage screwed down tight. "Hi!" She hoped her breezy wave hid the sheer terror throbbing in her veins.

Salim climbed from the car with a warm smile. "Hello, Celia. Things have been busy the last couple of days. I've missed you."

He wore khakis and a white shirt with the sleeves rolled up, looking deceptively Westernized and infuriatingly handsome. His dark eyes flashed with pleasure, as if he was genuinely pleased to see her.

Which she knew he wasn't. He just wanted to flush her out of his system like a nasty virus.

Shame he was about to find it had lingering effects—like fatherhood.

"Salim, there's something I have to tell you." Her heart hammered against her ribs.

"Oh?" He cocked his head, his expression quizzical. He strode closer, the outline of his sturdy thighs visible inside the thin khakis. A smile tugged at his powerful mouth. "I'm all ears."

If only he was. Ears would be a lot easier to deal with than bronzed muscle and chiseled cheekbones. "Three years ago…" Her voice trailed off.

Come on, you can do it.

"Yes?"

"A little over three years ago, I had a baby."

His eyes narrowed. "What?"

"A baby. I gave birth." Why on earth was she explaining like an idiot? He knew what a baby was.

"I don't understand." His proud bearing had stiffened, as if he knew something was up, but he couldn't figure out what.

Celia swallowed hard. "After our…reunion at the Ritz Carlton, I learned I was pregnant."

His lips parted, but no words came out.

"We have a daughter. Her name is Kira."

"Impossible." The word shot from his mouth.

Celia felt like she'd been slapped. "It's not only possible, it happened."

"You never mentioned a child." He spoke slowly, as if trying to unravel a mystery.

"I didn't mention her at the time because you were too busy brushing me off like a piece of lint. I tried to tell you. I called your office twice, and all I got in return was a brusque message reminding me that our weekend fling was over, and we'd better get back to our normal lives. So I did, except by then my normal life had a growing baby in it."

Salim blew out a long breath. "A baby?"

"Yes, the human kind, with two legs and two arms. And dark hair and eyes exactly like yours."

"It can't be mine."

Her spine stiffened. "She's not an it. She's a sweet and funny little girl."

His proud forehead creased. "We always used... protection."

"Apparently it wasn't effective." Her blood heated. How could he argue with her about this?

There was incontrovertible proof. She reached into the back pocket of her jeans and pulled out the photo Sara had seen in her room. She held it out, hand shaking.

Salim looked at the picture like a snake that might bite. Or perhaps a scorpion.

His chest rose as he took in the image. She watched him frown as he raised it to his eyes and stared for a full minute. "*Alhamdulillah.* She is mine."

He didn't take his eyes off the picture. Adrenaline and emotion made Celia so punchy she had to fight the urge to scold him for doubting her.

When he finally looked up, his eyes were wide, stunned. "You should have told me."

"I wanted to, but you didn't let me."

He raised a broad hand and wiped it over his face. "Three years old, and I never knew she existed. You should have found a way." He growled with indignation.

Which only fuelled her own.

"Why? So you could try to take her away from me? You'd made it abundantly clear that you had no interest in pursuing a relationship with me."

And she knew from the previous morning's conversation with Elan that nothing had changed on that score.

She drew in a shaky breath. "I wanted to protect her. To protect myself."

Salim's brain felt numb, stunned by this new and shocking revelation.

A daughter.

The picture was all the proof he needed. Unmistakably a member of the Al Mansur family, the toddler already bore the distinctive mouth they'd all inherited from their mother.

How could Celia keep his own daughter a secret?

She trembled, despite the heat. Anxiety tightened the lines of her lovely face and wound her hands together.

He fought the urge to reach out and reassure her. "You didn't trust me."

"How could I? You'd betrayed me once already, when you married another woman without even telling me. Then I got my hopes up again and…" She closed her mouth as if anxious to stop the flow of words that revealed too much.

"I had no idea. How could I?"

"You could have asked." Her bright gaze blazed with accusation. "You didn't care how I was doing, if I was even alive, as long as I was out of your life."

The ugly truth made his skin prickle. Celia got under his skin and made him itch and burn late at night. She made him ache in a way no salves or cold compresses could cure.

And he'd been looking for that cure for years.

"I was just trying to be practical, sensible." He frowned. What was the sensible course of action now?

He could handle executive problem solving—trouble-shooting and issuing orders—but this situation called for tact and delicacy beyond his command.

A daughter. His own child.

Something clawed at his heart, a sense of desperation. His own child was out there, somewhere, without even knowledge of her father.

His anger—mingled with the strong emotions Celia always roused in him—made him want to shout and accuse her, but he knew that was foolish and counter-productive.

Celia brushed a stray wisp of hair from her high forehead. "I was also trying to be practical. It seemed best for both of us. I raise Kira and support her, and you get back to the life you were so keen to keep me out of."

Salim blew out hard. "It's not that I *wanted* to keep you out of my life, it's that…"

That what?

A vision of his lovely Celia, holding his child—their child—in her arms, assaulted his brain. Unnameable feelings, powerful and hypnotic, stole all words from his mouth.

The sound of an engine made them both turn. A black Mercedes pulled up the curved brick road near them and stopped.

A rear door opened and a woman, dressed in yellow-and-black with a scarf revealing only a few inches of her glossy black hair, stepped out.

He stifled a curse. "A friend of mine. I told her to come here to look around sometime. I had no idea she'd come now. I suppose someone at the office told her I was here."

Surely the universe was playing some kind of joke on him. He'd been formally courting Nabilah Al Sabah for months and she'd shown no interest in visiting the site. Now that his careful plans for the future had been tossed to the desert wind, she appeared like an ill omen.

This situation was certainly beyond even his considerable competence. As Nabilah walked toward them, elegant silk billowing in the wind, he decided to leave it to the fates to sort things out.

He tucked the precious photo in his pocket and crossed his arms over his chest.

"Nabilah. I'm glad you were finally able to come see the results of all our hard work."

"I've been dying to come for ages. I should have asked for better directions. My driver got lost twice on the way!"

Nabilah had a smile fixed to her beautiful face like it was painted on. Salim had thought this a charming feature in a young lady—until Celia appeared with her ready and mischievous grin.

"Celia, this is my...friend, Nabilah Al Sabah."

Celia's whole body stiffened. Which was odd. He'd never so much as mentioned Nabilah or his future plans, to Celia.

"Nabilah, this is Celia Davidson. She's the landscape architect for the project and...an old and dear friend of mine." The unexpected need to affirm his relationship with Celia took him by surprise.

Both ladies looked appropriately alarmed as they shared a cautious handshake.

Salim experienced a sudden, intense urge to vanish into the hot desert air.

He decided to act on it.

"I must go. Celia, please give Nabilah a tour of the site." He shot her a meaningful glance.

He had no idea at all what it meant. Probably something like *I can't believe you just told me I have a daughter. Help.*

Not, perhaps, the most heroic approach, but better than several alternatives that threatened the gathered trio.

Celia swallowed. "Sure." Her voice was hollow.

"Salim, I'd hoped you would give me a tour yourself." Nabilah's treacly voice sent a crawl of aversion down his spine. Why had he never noticed that arrogant tilt to her eyebrows before?

"Another time, perhaps. I'm afraid I must run. Celia, I'll send Hanif to pick you up."

"Don't worry, I brought my own car. I suspected I might need it." Her cool gaze told him to get lost.

And he was more than ready to do so.

Fighting the urge to literally run, he nodded to the two beautiful, frowning women and strode for his car.

A daughter.

Kira.

A fist of emotion clutched his heart. A little girl, with big brown eyes and a dimpled chin, who needed a father's love.

He'd always suspected there was something real—

magical and painful at the same time—but undeniable, between him and Celia.

And there was. Now he'd seen her with his own eyes.

He couldn't feel more disoriented if his world had literally turned upside down and he'd banged his head on the hot desert floor. The unrelenting sun beat down on him from the bright sky, just the way it always did, but suddenly everything had changed.

Everything.

His life would never be the same again. He was sure of it.

"Men." Celia shrugged. "Just when you really need them, they turn and run."

She glanced at Nabilah to gauge her reaction. The other woman was as tall as she was. Her traditional attire fluttered against a slender yet flawlessly female body.

Nabilah Al Sabah was breathtakingly beautiful. She laughed, a melodious tinkle of sound.

No doubt that was the appropriate reaction for a woman of taste.

Celia fought to control the adrenaline charging through her veins. This was the woman Salim had chosen instead of her. "Well, where shall we start?"

"Wherever you prefer." Nabilah's smooth, unlined face revealed nothing but pleasure.

"How about right here?" She swept her arm around, to encompass the space of the marketplace. "As you can see the buildings are up, but still need a few finishing touches. Nearly all of the plantings are in the ground at this point. We're working on getting them established so we can remove any stakes and other unsightly props before the hotel opens."

"Fascinating." Nabilah beamed with more distilled delight. "I've always been intrigued by desert horticulture."

Celia didn't believe a word of it. "Your English is very good."

"It should be. I had a private tutor in the language for six years. I also speak French, Spanish and Japanese. It's important to be well-versed in world languages, don't you think?"

"Oh, yes." Celia mustered a chilly smile. "I often wish I spoke Chinese. One of these days I must learn. What aspect of our project are you interested in?"

She'd been unable to resist the possessive "our." A catty female urge to lay claim to Salim crept through her and sharpened her claws.

Which was idiotic, since this was the woman he intended to marry.

"Oh, I'm interested in all of it." She shone Celia a syrupy smile. "A lost city in the sands. Rather a fairy tale, don't you think?"

"Not a fairy tale at all, I assure you. It's quite genuine. It looks brand-new with all the fresh stucco, but underneath the bright veneer the bones of the old city are still there."

"Along with the history of Salim's family. His mother's family, anyway. I believe his father moved here from Egypt."

Celia hid her surprise. She'd never heard any mention of Egypt in his past. But why would she? Salim told her nothing about his family history. He'd never intended for her to be part of it.

Her heart sank even lower in her chest.

"His mother's family is very ancient. They controlled most of this area at one time. Their lineage dates back thousands of years." Nabilah lifted her proud head to survey the landscape.

"I think everyone's lineage dates back thousands of years, to the beginning of mankind. We wouldn't be here if it didn't."

"You know what I mean." Nabilah adjusted her headscarf to display more of her luxuriant dark hair. "They were influential."

Like your darling daddy, no doubt. Celia struggled to keep her claws sheathed. "Are you from Salalah?"

"Oh, no." Nabilah's laugh dismissed this idea as ridiculous. "I grew up in Muscat, the capital. For the last few years we've been living in Dubai. Salalah's so sleepy by comparison."

"It's spectacularly beautiful, though, don't you think?"

Celia was beginning to wonder whether Salim had chosen his bride carefully. He openly adored Salalah.

"People do go on about the mountains, and they are unusual for the Arabian Peninsula, but nothing like Switzerland, let's face it. Have you been to Switzerland?"

She clearly expected Celia to say no, and busied herself with rearranging her black-and-yellow finery.

"Yes, I designed the grounds for a bank headquartered in Zurich. Would you like to see the pool area?" She shot a bright smile at Nabilah.

Her rival's eyes narrowed for a split second. "A pool out here in the middle of nowhere? How quaint. I suppose it is just a hotel, after all." She strode alongside Celia, elegant nose high. "Salim said you were old friends. How did you meet?"

Her breezy tone didn't fool Celia.

Who couldn't resist turning the knife.

"Oh, we've been friends for donkey's years. We met back in college."

"That is a long time ago." Her voice dripped with the first hint of deliberate malice.

Celia stifled a chuckle. "Yes, Salim and I are both ancient."

That tinkling laugh. "Oh, that's not what I meant at all! Though, I am rather younger." She cleared her throat. "And you've kept in touch all this time?"

Ah. Now she's getting down to business. "On and off. I guess that thread of connection has always been there."

Though most of the time I'd have liked to strangle him with it.

"I don't imagine you'll see each other again once the project is over." Nabilah stared straight ahead, at the dry concrete shell of the empty pool.

Celia's stomach clenched. "What makes you say that?" she blurted, before she could stop herself.

"As a married man he won't be gallivanting all over the world consorting with all kinds of people." She said the last words with marked distaste.

But it was the words "a married man" that jolted Celia. Nabilah was laying claim to Salim, and warning her off.

"He didn't tell me he was getting married," she said, as calmly as possible. She walked around the curved pool, lined by lush palms, which would soon shade guests basking in lounge chairs.

Nabilah's laugh echoed off the bare concrete. "Oh, yes, everyone knows that Salim and I are getting married. It's a perfect match. A profitable union of two important families and two successful businesses."

She turned her elegant profile to survey the guest cottages around the pool. Her perfect nose wrinkled. "I don't imagine we'll be spending much time here, though. No matter how much you paint and plant it, it's still a howling wilderness."

Celia frowned. "Thousands of people have lived and laughed and eaten and slept in this place. Soon, thousands more will come. Can't you feel the energy?"

Her skin prickled with it. It wrapped itself around her as soon as she came to the site. The buzz and hum of humanity lingered in the air even when the workers had left for the day. Even the hot desert sand whispered with the bustle of life.

Nabilah laughed again, a tinny sound that hurt Celia's ears. "I think the unaccustomed heat is affecting your brain."

"Salim loves this place." She said it slowly, watching Nabilah's striking features for a reaction.

Nabilah simply waved her hand in the air. "Men fall in love with whatever wanders in front of them. Sometimes they make quite ludicrous choices." She adjusted her headscarf. "Besides, we'll be living in Dubai. Daddy is building me a house on one of the palm frond islands. I doubt we'll spend much time in Oman."

Celia stared, unable to formulate a response. She was pretty sure Salim had no idea of his future wife's plans.

Then again, there was the possibility that if he married Nabilah, he fully deserved to be miserable.

Something he might deserve anyway, just for leaving her alone here with this woman.

An uncomfortable knot formed in her stomach. He'd been so shocked by her news he hadn't been able to stay and act normal.

He'd just learned he had a daughter.

How would Nabilah Al Sabah react to that news?

Nabilah marched around the empty pool. "I think it will be good for Salim to get away from past associations and influences. The world of business can bring one into contact with all kinds of inappropriate people." She cast a dismissive glance at Celia's work attire.

"Like me, you mean?" She couldn't help herself.

Nabilah raised a sculpted brow. "I hardly think that Salim's association with you is significant."

Celia's lips parted in astonishment as the rude comment stung her.

Except that we have a child together.

She had to marshal all her self-control to keep the words in her mouth. She wanted desperately to whip out the picture of Kira and watch Nabilah's reaction as the monkey wrench of reality clanked down into the perfectly oiled machinery of her future plans.

Then she recoiled at the very idea. Kira wasn't a pawn to be played in a jealous game of one-upmanship. She was a little girl who depended on Celia to protect her and keep her safe.

And Salim had taken the picture with him.

"You must excuse me, but I believe my insignificant presence is expected back in Salalah," Celia murmured. "I do hope you don't mind me cutting our tour short."

"Not in the least." Nabilah lifted her neat chin. "I've seen enough already." She brushed imaginary dust from her silk-clad arm with an expression of distaste. "I doubt you and I will see each other again."

"I certainly hope not." Celia flashed a bright smile.

As Nabilah turned, she regretted her rash rudeness. What if Salim did marry Nabilah? She'd be forced to endure that woman's smirk as she shared her own child with her.

She shivered with revulsion.

The truth was out and the wheels of fate were turning. She bit her knuckle hard, hoping and praying with every fiber of her body that she and Kira wouldn't be crushed under them.

Seven

Celia had barely pulled into the forecourt of the hotel when Salim appeared. Brows lowered, he approached the still-moving car.

She stopped in front of the valet and climbed out, trying to look normal while blood thundered through her veins.

"We must talk." Salim's low voice revealed nothing of his emotions.

"Of course," she replied, attempting to sound business-like.

"Come with me." He turned and strode along a walk toward the beach. Bright blue sea glittered beyond the white sand.

Paradise.

Except that it felt more like hell. "Are you still angry?"

She kept her voice low, not wanting to cause a scene in front of the employees.

Or maybe she should cause a scene? She deserved one.

He'd used her again, with every intention of casting her aside.

He'd left her to entertain his future bride.

She certainly had every right to the anger that simmered in her belly.

"No, I'm not angry." He turned and shot a glance in her direction. His stern gaze did nothing to comfort her. "It was my fault that you didn't tell me. I can see that now."

He waited for her to catch up with him. For an instant his arm twitched, as if he planned to thread it through hers, but he didn't. "What happened and didn't happen is in the past. We must talk about the future."

Celia nodded. Her stomach tightened. The future shimmered with frightening possibilities.

"I apologize for abandoning you with Nabilah." A wry glance softened his grim expression. "I suspect you two had a lot to talk about."

"Not really." Celia swallowed. "I didn't say anything about Kira, if that's what you mean. She did tell me you two are getting married." She lifted her chin and braced for his reaction.

He frowned. "Nothing is formally arranged."

His cool reply, so formal and unemotional, flipped the cap off her hurt feelings.

"It wasn't *formal* yet? You slept with me while you were promised to someone else!" Her rasped whisper shot through the air. "How could you do that?"

"I'm not promised to her or anyone else."

"She seemed to think you were." She wanted to mention the conversation she'd overheard on the beach, but that would reveal too much. "Did you know she expects you to move to Dubai and live on one of those dredged islands in the shape of a palm tree?"

The look of horror that flashed across Salim's face should have made her laugh. But she was in no mood for laughing.

He inhaled sharply. "What I did was wrong."

"You were wrong to sleep with me? Or wrong to leave me to entertain your intended bride?" The words shot from her tongue. She glanced around to see if anyone heard. They were almost out on the sand now, and few people were nearby.

"Both." Salim narrowed his eyes. "I apologize sincerely. Leaving you with Nabilah was terrible, but I didn't have the mental reserves to pretend everything was normal right then."

"Why pretend? What is normal, anyway?"

Salim stared at her. "Nothing is normal. Everything has changed." He shoved a hand through his dark hair. "I don't know where to start, or should I say, how to proceed, since everything between us started so long ago."

He looked out at the ocean. Its blue, endless depths shimmered in the blazing sun. Then he turned back to her. "I must meet our daughter."

The pronouncement, swift and certain, deprived her of speech. His dark eyes shone with excitement. "I've missed so much time with her already, and I ache to meet her."

A throb of emotion echoed deep inside Celia. Excitement mingled with fear. "She's so lively and curious and affectionate. And she'll be so thrilled to meet you."

His brow furrowed. "What does she know about me?"

"Nothing, really." Celia's voice sounded thin. "She's been too young to understand until lately. Now she's noticed that her friends have daddies and that she doesn't, but I don't think she's figured out the right questions to ask."

"She'll be able to ask me any question she likes." His expression brightened. "I've had plenty of practice with little Ben. He has a very inquisitive mind." A smile tugged at the edges of his mouth. "Can I keep the picture of her?"

"Sure. You can have it. I'll print out another."

Salim pulled the now-crumpled image out of his pocket and held it gingerly, like something precious.

"She has your smile. And I think she has your infectious optimism."

"Me? I don't think I'd call myself that optimistic. If I had been, I'd have told you about her." She glanced up at him, wary.

He rubbed his other hand over his mouth, staring at the picture. "You wanted to protect her. I don't blame you. I hurt you and you didn't want her to experience that pain." He glanced up at her, eyes black with emotion. "I promise you I won't do anything to hurt her."

Or you.

She read the words in his gaze.

"Would you join me for dinner tonight? Somewhere private. We can talk and...figure things out."

"Or try to figure things out." Celia crossed her arms over her chest, which swelled with some relief that he was at least being honest and admitting the situation was tricky and the way forward unclear. The future was all any of them had, and it was her responsibility to make Kira's future as bright as possible, regardless of her own reservations. "Okay."

"I'll pick you up at your room."

Celia was scrubbing the last of the day's grit from under her fingernails with a nailbrush when she heard a knock on the door of her suite. Was he early? She hadn't finished getting ready. She strode toward the door. "Come in."

She heard someone struggling with the handle. The kids? She hurried to open the door and was greeted by a wall of flowers.

"Delivery for Miss Davidson," came a muffled voice behind the barrage of lilies and orchids. Celia's eyes fixed on a particularly rare speckled orchid just center left of the design. The delivery man staggered into the room and carefully lowered the enormous bouquet onto a polished table. "There's a card."

He handed it to her, bowed and vanished, before she thought to tip him.

They've got to be from Salim. She should be mad at him for having rare orchids yanked from their habitat just to mollify her, but oh, boy…. Lush leaves wound through stunning specimen blooms, creating a magical garden that rose like smoke from a hand-painted vase.

"Celia, I can't apologize enough for my behavior this afternoon. Please accept these flowers as an offering of contrition." Handwritten in a familiar black script.

She couldn't resist a smile. What an offering. And a detailed note from the florist explained that these were hand-raised blooms, not wild specimens. It also gave a detailed history of each unique flower—further investigation revealed that their roots were in water so they could be repotted and kept alive—that kept Celia riveted for a full fifteen minutes, almost causing her to forget about getting ready. How well he knew her!

Another knock on the door made her drop the note card. "It's me, Sara," she heard through the heavy wood.

Celia tugged open the door to see Sara grinning. "You told him."

"I finally did. Thank you for pushing me."

"He admitted to Elan that he refused to believe you, then he abandoned you in the desert with Nabilah Al Sabah."

"All true." She tried not to smile as she gestured to the flowers. "This forest is his idea of an apology."

Sara raised a brow. "I'm glad it's big. It should be. Still, he's very excited."

"I know. It took a while for the idea to sink in, but I think he's really warming to the idea of being a father."

"He'll be an awesome dad," Sara said with a smile.

Celia's shoulders tightened. How would that work? Could one be an "awesome dad" on occasional visiting weekends, or even extended summer vacations?

"I'm having dinner with him tonight," Celia said. "Hopefully we'll figure out some of the details. I know he wants to meet her as soon as possible." Her stomach contracted again. There was so much to worry about.

"Of course he does. And she'll have him wrapped around her plump pinky in seconds," Sara added.

"Speaking of seconds, he'll be arriving in a few and

I'm still not ready. I'd better at least put some aloe on my sunburn."

"You look radiant."

"I suspect being on the verge of hysterics has that effect."

Sara chuckled. "You can't fool me. You're a tough customer who can handle whatever life lobs her way."

"Yeah, like a dozen rare orchids in a froth of lilies."

"Or an Al Mansur man."

Celia shot a doubtful glance at her. Just then, a knock sounded on the door.

"You look ravishing," whispered Sara. "Enjoy your evening."

"Hopefully I'll survive," murmured Celia with raised brows. She turned to face the door. "Come in!"

Sara smiled and waved as Salim entered. "Yes, there's a conspiracy in progress," she confessed.

"What nonsense!" protested Celia.

Salim looked unfortunately devastating in crisp, dark pants and a collarless linen shirt.

Celia drew in a silent breath. "I'm almost ready. I just keep getting interrupted." She shot a wry glance at Sara. "Will you excuse me a moment?"

Without waiting for a reply, she darted to the bathroom and slammed the door. The enormous mirror revealed a face that was indeed glowing, with either good health or total panic.

She slapped some mascara on her sun-bleached eyelashes and brightened her lips with gloss. There was no need for blush on her hot, pink cheeks, so she quickly twisted her hair up into a knot and stuck a couple of pins in it.

Ack. I look like I'm getting ready for a date.

This was not a date. This was dinner with a man who'd trampled on her heart and smashed it flat.

Again.

At least she was one hundred percent sure she wasn't going to sleep with him tonight.

She burst out of the bathroom, a cheery smile fixed to her face. Sara had gone. Salim stood alone, apparently relaxed and pleased to see her, in front of the elaborate arrangement of flowers.

"The flowers are lovely," she said.

"You know they're alive? I suspected you'd hate cut flowers."

"You're absolutely right. Plants are only beautiful when they're alive and growing."

That bouquet had probably cost as much as the GDP of several developing nations, but she managed not to comment on that. It was the gesture that counted. "Do you want to see more pictures of Kira?"

"I'd love to." His voice was gruff with enthusiasm.

She reached for the mini-album she took on trips. It was freshly updated with pictures from her last return home: Kira rolling in the snow; building a tower of blocks; playing a toddler game on the computer and— her favorite thing—talking on her pink cell phone. In each picture her eyes glowed with joy and interest.

"She's a busy girl. She makes the most of every moment. And have you noticed she has far more fashion sense than me?" She gestured to a picture of Kira in an outfit composed of four different kinds of stripes. "She likes to set a trend."

"She's perfect." Salim sounded almost breathless. "Anyone can see how happy she is. You've obviously given her a warm and nurturing family environment."

"You've met my parents. They're sweethearts. And they have a lot of energy for people in their sixties. Which is good since they need it to keep up with Kira. She loves the outdoors. She told me this morning that she's building a garden in the snow for me."

"She's thoughtful, too." A smile tugged at his mouth. He stared at each picture for a long time. He was enchanted. "She'll be great friends with Ben."

Celia frowned. How would Kira meet Ben? Would she have to bring Kira here? She wasn't sure such a long flight was a good idea—or even survivable—with a toddler. Though Sara and Elan had obviously managed. It was probably easier when there were two grown-ups.

Salim apparently noticed her hesitation. "Let's go to dinner."

Celia had never seen the roof garden. Available for rental by the day or hour, it was a popular spot for lavish weddings. As she left the elevator—which opened directly onto the roof—she could see why.

White marble glittered in the last rays of sun. Porticos of pointed arches ringed the wide terraces, framing a stunning view out toward the watery horizon, where colorful fishing dhows returned to port with the day's catch, or set out to cast nets under the moon.

An elegant white gazebo shaded a single table, set for two. A bottle of champagne sat open in a bucket of ice, and a brass pot brimmed with white lilies in the center of the gleaming linen tablecloth.

"I figured we'd have some privacy up here. I asked the chefs to leave us a buffet to pick from." Elegant dishes piled with tasty hors d'oeuvres sat on two small tables that flanked the main dining table. Marinated shrimp kebabs rested on a steaming bed of saffron rice.

"Kira loves shrimp." Celia picked up a plate and helped herself to the delicacies.

"Does she? That sounds very sophisticated."

"Of course she's sophisticated. She's your daughter." The words sounded strange—but wonderful—coming from her mouth, like they'd been bursting to be free this whole time.

"So she is. Tell me more. Does she sleep well, or does she wake up all the time, like Hannah?" He glanced up, almost shyly, from spooning braised vegetables on his plate.

"Oh, she was a terror as a baby. She woke so many times during the night that finally I just let her sleep with me in my bed."

Salim laughed. "That's the norm in most countries."

"So my friends kept reassuring me. Anyway, around nine months I finally convinced her that her crib wasn't a prison cell by putting her there for naps. She loved a music box I hung on it that played 'Rock-a-bye Baby.' Pretty soon I got her sleeping in there at night, too, and soon she slept like a log, right until morning."

"That must have been a relief." He pulled her chair back and seated her at the table. His elbow brushed hers as she slid past him, and unwelcome heat shimmered over her skin.

"I didn't know what to do with myself. It was a couple of months before I actually grew bold enough to sleep through the night."

Salim filled her tall flute with champagne. His eyes sparkled more than the golden liquid. "And I was enjoying uninterrupted nights of peace the whole time. I suppose I should thank you for that." He raised his glass. "To you, Celia, for bringing Kira into the world and taking good care of her."

Celia clinked her glass against his, a little nervous. She didn't hear any accusation in his voice, but surely it had to be there. By her deception, she'd deprived him of the first years of his daughter's life.

But Salim glowed with enthusiasm. "Does she go to school?"

"She's only three. School in the U.S. doesn't start until age five. She goes to a kind of nursery-school-day care now. She loves it there. She likes to be around people, in the center of the action."

"She'd love a hotel, then, wouldn't she?"

"Um, sure. I suspect she would." This was the next step. Where they'd meet. Somehow she hadn't dared to think that far ahead.

"Will you bring her here? Next week perhaps?" The hopeful look in his dark eyes tugged at something inside her.

"It's a long flight. It might be better if you came to Connecticut."

"But she must see her country. And she can meet Elan's family. They're staying until the end of the month. Think how much fun it would be for her to play with Hannah and Ben."

Celia bit her lip. "It would be nice for her to visit. Let me think about the logistics and come up with a plan."

They chatted about the hotel and the final changes to be made at the lost city site, as well as about Kira, and the air between them crackled with excitement. Candles glowed around them as the sun set behind the liquid horizon, and bright stars and a slim crescent moon decorated the dark canopy overhead.

They rose from the table to fetch coffee from an elaborate urn on one side of the roof garden, but Celia was arrested by the shimmering lights of Salalah down below. "It's strangely quiet up here. It almost feels like we're in a magic kingdom up in the clouds."

"We are." Salim shot her a sly glance. "Except this one's man-made. You worked the magic to bring the lost city to life. It was nothing but empty buildings and unnamed streets. Now leaves rustle in the wind and cast lively shadows on the paths. The scent of nectar fills the air and brings bees and birds out into the desert again. And with even more powerful magic, you've brought me a daughter."

Celia's eyes widened. "It's not really magic."

"Nature is magical, don't you think?" A look of enchantment replaced his usually stern demeanor. "You think you know what to expect, what the usual rhythms and seasons are, when it will rain and when it will be dry, then suddenly…" He fixed her with a dark gaze that stole her breath. "Everything changes."

Celia's skin tingled under his intense stare. Was it magic that crackled in the air between them? Or something altogether more predictable? Her fingertips vibrated with the urge to wind into his soft linen shirt.

"You've always brought magic into my life, Celia. I've just been too blind to see it. Or too busy looking for something else."

"Oh, I don't know, I…" Her brain couldn't pull together a sensible thought. Her body was too overwhelmingly aware of his nearness.

He took a step closer and she could smell his scent

in the dark: a rich, masculine fragrance that tormented her senses.

"We weave a spell together, you and I." His expression was serious, confused even, like he was trying to figure out some mystery. "It's dangerous, because I have no power to resist."

Before her scattered thoughts could gather into words, their lips met in a swift, fierce kiss. The simple sensation of his skin on hers brought a low murmur of relief that met and mingled in their mouths. In an instant her hands were fisted into his shirt, and his long, strong fingers slid around her back, pulling her closer.

Don't do this, screamed every last grain of sense left in her.

But her body didn't listen. Salim's solid arms felt like the only safe place in this confusing world where everything shifted and altered from minute to minute, and where dreams and nightmares seemed interchangeable.

I can't help it.

Her lips trembled with passion under his kiss. His hard body crushed deliciously to her breasts and belly. Her fingers wove into his thick hair as she inhaled the intoxicating scent of his skin. He was her first love and she'd never felt the same about anyone else.

Not even close.

His face lit up while she talked about Kira, and she saw once again the bright-eyed boy she'd fallen so hard in love with. The young man who'd held her tight in the privacy of her off-campus apartment, and told her he loved her.

She'd told him she loved him, too, and meant it. Everything that had happened between then and now didn't change that one simple fact.

Their kiss deepened and she shuddered with longing as he wrapped his arms tight around her. Her fingers roamed into the collar of his shirt, feeling the strong shoulders that carried so much weight each day. Her skin ached to touch his, to claim the passion he always roused in her.

Salim's thick arousal pressed against her tummy, quickening her desire into a tight coil of need. She writhed against him, fighting the urge to unbutton his shirt and reveal the hot skin beneath.

Could this be a new start between them?

Salim was clearly thrilled to be a father, once he got over the initial shock. Maybe Sara was right and they really could be...a family.

The word caused a fierce pull of emotion deep in her chest. How much she'd love that for Kira. She'd enjoyed the support of two loving parents, and she still relied on both of them more than she could say. Would Kira grow up with that gift, now that the truth was out?

Salim caressed her, their lips still locked in silent, sensual communication. So much less complicated than the kind with words. She could feel the beat of his heart and the pulse of the emotion that ran between them like a spark jumping between two electrodes.

For a second the buzz of arousal seemed so intense that Celia wondered if they'd started a chemical reaction. Then she realized Salim's phone was vibrating.

"I told them to make sure I wasn't disturbed." Confusion and irritation warred on his handsome face.

"It might be important." Celia smoothed the front of her rumpled blouse as they moved apart.

Salim pressed a button and put the phone to his ear with a barked, "What?" Celia looked around, head still spinning with desire and emotion. "Don't be ridiculous. Don't you have your own life to worry about? Yeah. Fine. Good night, Elan."

He pushed the phone back into his pocket. A wry expression crept across his sensual mouth. "He wanted to make sure we weren't getting carried away."

"Uh-oh. Guilty as charged."

"He thinks it will mess things up between us."

"It usually does." She blew on a strand of hair that had escaped from her bun. "I think we should call it a night."

Salim pushed a hand through his disheveled hair. The moonlight revealed his frown of frustration. "All my baser instincts tell me otherwise, but I suppose you're right. We do have a tendency to get out of control."

"All that magic." She couldn't help smiling. "As you said, it's dangerous."

"In the best possible way." A smile crept across his mouth, revealing a sliver of his perfect white teeth. "But we are both rather on edge right now. I suppose my brother is right."

"He seems a sensible man." She blew out a breath. The collar of her dress was all twisted and her belt had slipped sideways. She tugged at them and tried to straighten the seams. "More than I can say for some." She glanced up.

Salim's eyes sparkled with mischief. "I'm perfectly sensible most of the time. In fact, I'd go so far as to say I'm the very model of prudence—except when a certain Celia Davidson is in evidence."

She shrugged. "Sorry. You might want to fix your shirt." She pointed to where two buttons had somehow come undone.

"See? My clothes even fall off when you're around."

"Nothing I can do. It's the magic." She blew on her fingers as if to disperse any dangerous rays that might be lingering there.

"Let me escort you to your room."

"I suspect it would be safer if I escorted myself there. But I promise, tomorrow I'll make arrangements to bring Kira here."

Salim's expression grew serious. He nodded, and excitement brightened his eyes and warmed her heart. "I can't wait."

Eight

Celia woke up in a cold sweat. The fan above her bed slashed in slow circles, swiping her with a breeze that made goose bumps rise on her skin.

She'd promised to bring Kira to Oman. She'd dreamed of this moment and dreaded it. She knew that, one way or another, it would change their lives forever.

A knock on the door made her clutch the damp sheets to her chest. "Who is it?"

"Sara. Can I come in, just for a sec?"

Celia grabbed the yellow silk kimono she used as a dressing gown and slipped it on. She opened the door and ushered Sara in. Her new friend's green eyes sparkled. "I heard it went well last night. I can't wait to meet Kira. Salim's so excited, it's adorable."

"Yes, I promised to bring her as soon as possible. In the blistering light of day, though, I'm nervous. He *is* really excited and I know he'll adore Kira. What if he won't let me take her home?"

Sara chewed her lower lip for a second. "What makes you so sure you'll want to go home?"

"You're getting carried away with romantic visions again, aren't you?" Celia put her hands on her hips.

"Well, did Elan's call interrupt anything, or not?"

Celia let out a long sigh. "It did, which I should be totally ashamed of, since it seems crazy under the circumstances."

"It's not crazy. The two of you have an undeniable connection. You're nervous, and trust me, I know how scary it is when there's another life on the line, as well as yours. It made me defensive and anxious when Elan and I were trying to figure things out, but having a child together really does mean a lot. I realized that in the end. That's what made me decide to put my doubts aside and take a chance on the love we shared. You're a family now, whether you admit it or not."

Celia raised a brow. "He hasn't made any promises to me. He has all kinds of grand ideas about a suitable marriage and the respectable heir he's so set on. Kira's a girl, so she's not going to carry on the Al Mansur dynasty. Maybe he'll decide to keep her and marry that horrible Nabilah anyway." Her voice grew thin.

"Oh, come on, you don't really think he's capable of that, do you?"

Celia swallowed. "He left me to marry another woman once already. I'd be crazy to think it couldn't happen again. I'm a survivor, so I'm not worried about me...."

A sudden image of her heart, patched and nailed with bits of soldered metal, filled her mind. "But I'm truly nervous about Kira. I can't just ignore the sharia laws. If he wants to take her from me, he can."

Sara walked farther into the room and crossed her arms over her chest, staring out the window. "Well. We're both businesswomen, so perhaps that's the way to approach the situation. He has screwed you over before, so you have a perfectly legitimate reason for caution." She spun and looked right at Celia. "How about a contract?"

"What do you mean?"

"A document in which you spell out exactly what you require. You must have the right to take Kira home as you see fit. Salim must relinquish the right to keep her here against your will."

Celia's eyes widened. "That'll make him furious."

"Only if he intends to hurt you. If he plans to tread carefully—as he certainly should—it won't be a problem."

"You're very optimistic."

"Let's just say I became optimistic the hard way." She winked. "You know what? I'll arrange it all. You go about your business and book the flights, and I'll draw up the contract. I do that all day long at work so it'll be easy as pie. I'll show it to you when it's done, and if you're on board with the terms, I'll take it to Salim myself."

Celia stared at her. "You'd do all that for me?"

"Not just you." She smiled. "For Salim, for Elan, for Hannah and Ben and for me. For all of us."

Thick warmth rose in Celia's chest. Could she and Kira really find a place in this growing family? "Okay."

* * *

Salim stared at the black-and-white printed words until they blurred. His blood heated at the idea of signing a contract relinquishing rights to his own flesh and blood. Rights that had been kept from him for far too long already.

Sara stood very still on the other side of the large desk in his office.

"Why are you asking me to sign this?" He glanced up at Sara. "Where's Celia?"

"She's working. I convinced her to tell you about Kira with the assurance that nothing bad would happen. Now I'm just making sure nothing bad does happen." Her innocent smile did nothing to conceal the sharp mind he'd heard so much about.

"Does Celia know about this? Did she tell you to make me sign away my rights?"

"She knows about it." Sara was calm, her gray-green eyes rarely blinking. She tilted her head. "You must admit it's only prudent. You've let Celia down before."

Salim recoiled from the accusation. "That was different. There were no commitments between us."

"And are there commitments between you now?" Sara lifted a slim brow.

"No formal arrangements, no." He bristled. How could she pry into his personal life at a time when even he didn't know what would happen from minute to minute?

"Maybe you should make some." Sara's eyes narrowed. "Celia has feelings, you know."

"She told you this?" He leaned forward in his chair, fighting the urge to get up and pace around the room.

"No. That's my personal view. Celia expects nothing

from you at all. And why would she, given what's happened between you in the past?"

Salim shifted in his chair. "I had no choice. I had
family obligations to fulfill."

"And have you fulfilled them?"

Her rhetorical question poked him like the tip of a
sharp knife. He had failed in his one duty to take a
proper wife and provide the Al Mansur house with an
heir.

"No." Now he did rise, swiftly, and planted his hands
on his desk. "I've made mistakes, done things I regret."
He narrowed his eyes. This small woman wasn't the
slightest bit intimidated by him. She formed her own
opinions and spoke her mind readily.

And she made his brother very happy.

Elan had taken charge of his own destiny. He'd chosen
the mate who captured his heart and they were building
a happy life together.

Both Elan and Sara obviously thought he and Celia
were meant to be together.

And was that so crazy? According to tradition and
convention, yes. But according to his own desires, the
needs and hopes that still ached in his time-hardened
heart...

Signing this contract went against everything he'd
ever been told about how to conduct himself as a man.
He was taught to seize control and hold it tight. To set
the agenda and ignore or banish those who objected.

But now the stakes were far too high.

His own daughter, Kira, was out there, looking at
something with those big brown eyes—or were they
closed tight in dream-filled sleep? Her plump cheeks
might be creased in a smile.

A smile he'd never seen—and might never see if he chose to stand his ground.

Everything was different now. He was different. And he couldn't wait to meet his little daughter.

"I'll sign."

The week spent fetching Kira was the longest of Celia's life. Salim hadn't wanted to speak to Kira on the phone—he said he wouldn't know what to say in such an awkward situation. He did want to meet her the moment she arrived at the airport.

The journey had taken almost twenty-four hours, on three planes, with lengthy stopovers in Dubai and Muscat. Kira had slept little. Instead, she'd played and listened to stories and eaten Goldfish crackers and stared at her fellow travelers and listened to songs on the iPod, and, finally, when Celia was too exhausted to stop her, she ran up and down the aisle, laughing.

Kira was now completely wiped out and—naturally—fell into a deep sleep just as the wheels touched down on the tarmac.

"Wake up, sweetheart. Wake up!"

Eventually she abandoned efforts at stirring Kira and managed to hoist the toddler onto her shoulder while wrestling with her purse, her large carry-on bag and Kira's backpack filled with toys. As she stepped out of the arrival gate into the bright, gleaming airport, she had a momentary wish that she'd remembered to put on lipstick, but she shoved it to the back of her tired brain.

Kira woke up as they went through Passport Control, and was begging for milk by the time they got her bag and walked out to where the waiting drivers and relatives stood behind a rope.

Celia scanned the crowd, heart pounding. Salim had told her he'd meet them at the airport. Did he get cold feet? Kira's tiny hand clutched hers tightly.

Please don't let her down.

She'd told Kira they were coming to meet her father. Kira had been astonished at first, then delighted. Now the little girl toddled bravely beside her, looking distinctly worried.

"Celia!" A low voice called from the rear of the crowd.

She saw Salim push through, tall and regal, dressed in a crisp white shirt and dark pants. His eyes immediately swiveled to Kira, and he stared at her unabashedly. Then he ducked under the rope and walked up to them.

They all stood there for a second, as Salim and Kira gazed at each other. He held out his hand. "You must be Kira. I'm pleased to meet you." He spoke slowly, like someone talking in an unfamiliar language.

Kira stared at his hand, alarm in her wide, dark eyes.

"I don't think she knows about shaking hands," Celia blurted. "They don't do that much at nursery school."

Salim withdrew his hand, and crouched down to Kira's level. "How silly of me. Still, I am pleased to meet you."

Kira peered at him, frowning slightly. "Are you my daddy?"

"Yes, I am."

"You're very tall."

His face creased into a smile. "And so will you be, one day."

Salim looked as if he wanted to pick Kira up, but Celia hoped he wouldn't try, because Kira's hot little hand gripped hers like a clamp.

"Maybe we should go get in the car," she stammered. "It's been a long flight."

"Good idea." Salim stood and took Celia's bag. "I drove here myself so we could be alone." He glanced down at Kira, an odd sparkle in his eyes. "Just the three of us."

Celia did her best not to hyperventilate on the way out to the car. The Omani heat enveloped her in a warm hug as they left the chill of the airport.

"It's hot, Mama!"

"Yes, sweetie. It's always hot here."

"I like it." A big smile spread across Kira's face. "Look, palm trees. Like in *Babar*."

"*Babar* is a kids' book series," explained Celia to Salim.

"I know." Salim smiled as he held the rear door open for them. "I read them in French. My tutor brought them from Paris. I was always a big fan of Zephyr the monkey."

Celia laughed.

"I like Zephyr, too," said Kira, quite serious. "Are we in Paris?"

"No, we're in Salalah, Oman."

"Salalalalah." Kira tried to wrap her tongue around the word.

"Climb in, sweetie." Celia prodded her gently. People swirled around them, and cars honked and weaved through the airport. Kira and Salim, however, felt no sense of urgency.

"That's right. Salalah. I know you're going to love it here."

Kira finally climbed in. No car seat. Of course Salim wouldn't have thought of it. Celia managed to buckled the lap belt over her and move the shoulder strap out of the way.

Salim climbed into the driver's seat and started the engine. Kira watched intently out the window as they pulled away from the curb and out onto the streets of Salalah, with their crisp, whitewashed buildings. "Mama, are we going to live here now?"

"Oh, no. We're just visiting." The words flew out of her mouth as the breath rushed from her lungs. She glanced at Salim and saw his brows lower.

"But don't people usually live with their daddies?" Kira glanced up, a frown puckering her tiny forehead.

Her heart pounded like the jackhammer on a nearby street. "Some people do, and some people don't. Everyone's different." Celia prayed for a change of subject.

When they arrived at the hotel, Salim asked a porter to take their bags upstairs. Unbeknownst to Celia, who'd left her room a mess, he'd moved them into a vast penthouse suite with several bedrooms and a wraparound terrace with a panoramic view of the ocean.

Kira ran around, exclaiming. "It's a castle! I'm a princess!"

"Don't run so fast, sweetie!" called Celia. "The marble floor is slippery."

"She'll be fine." Salim beamed. "She's full of energy after her long flight."

"She might fall and bang her head."

"Nonsense. She's graceful as a gazelle."

Celia frowned. "Are we having our first parental argument?"

Salim let out a snort of laughter. "I think we are. And in that case, you win." He winked. "Kira, come here. I want to show you off to everyone. You can run around and frighten your mother later."

Kira took his offered hand. "Are you a king?"

He grinned. "No. But you're definitely a princess."

"I know. Mama calls me princess sometimes." She smiled and twirled in the new pink dress she'd chosen. "I like living here."

Celia's heart seized.

Salim looked up, an expression of quiet triumph on his face.

"This is Kira, my daughter." Salim said it over and over again, as they walked around the hotel and grounds. Everyone, from the maids to the head chef, exclaimed over her and complimented her dress or her smile and sometimes even her stuffed bear. Kira handled it like a true princess, with charming thanks and giggles.

Celia stumbled along, wondering what people were really thinking. They must be shocked that Salim had a daughter, yet no one gasped or started babbling nonsense. Had some informative memo been circulated?

Kira's hand, tight in her own, probably informed them of Celia's role in the drama. What did they imagine was the story of her relationship with Salim? What did they think would happen next?

She certainly had no idea.

She should be happy that Kira seemed to settle in so well here. Instead, she felt a sense of foreboding. What if Kira didn't want to leave and go back to their life in America? What if she wanted to stay here with Salim?

Icy fear gnawed at her gut, but she hid it behind a bright smile.

Salim strode around with the easy grace of a king. If he felt the slightest bit flustered by the odd circumstances, it was entirely invisible. Pride and obvious joy lit his handsome features and made him laugh readily.

Whenever Kira saw something new, like a fountain, he'd stop and crouch down next to her, patiently explaining all the details of what it was and how it worked. He listened to her often outlandish questions and answered them with thoughtful consideration.

Celia's chest filled with happiness and anxiety as she watched Kira blossom in the strange new environment. Always talkative and friendly, her daughter was delighted by her bustling new surroundings and legions of admirers.

She'd worried that Salim might want to keep their relationship secret, that he'd be circumspect about Kira's origins.

Quite the opposite was true. He claimed her at every available opportunity, and took pride in pointing out countless similarities between them, real or imaginary.

"Kira's naturally suited to running a hotel, look!" Salim beamed as Kira ran across a wide plaza near the beach, toward another toddler carrying a shovel and pail. "She's welcoming the guests."

"She's not shy, that's for sure." Celia sipped the cool drink they'd picked up at the bar. "It's really sweet of you to introduce her to everyone."

"It's my very great joy." He stared at Kira as he spoke. Emotion thickened his voice.

Guilt soaked through Celia. "I feel terrible that I waited so long."

Salim turned to her. "I feel terrible that you were forced to wait so long. The guilt doesn't lie with you." He waved a hand in the air. "But it's the past. Let's enjoy the glorious present." And he strode across the plaza after Kira, who was now attempting to rip the shovel and pail from her new acquaintance's hands.

The present was one thing, but soon enough they'd have to talk about the future. They both seemed to be avoiding it, treading carefully around it. And with good reason.

That's when things would get messy.

Kira got on famously with Ben. Equally active, they ran up and down the beach and in and out of the shallow surf, with their mothers running after them, beseeching them to slow down and be careful.

Celia shot an exasperated glance at Sara. "I think we need a drink with an umbrella in it."

Sara laughed. "I'm terrified of Hannah learning to walk. I haven't figured out how to run in two different directions at the same time." She glanced back to where Hannah played on the beach under Elan's watchful gaze.

"At least I don't have that problem." Celia gasped and leaped forward to stop Kira diving under a wave.

"Not yet."

"Seriously. Not going to happen."

"So you say now." Sara's mouth twisted into a sly smile. "Time will tell."

"Thanks for the clichés."

"Don't look now, but he can't take his eyes off you."

Hairs prickled on the back of Celia's neck. "I'm sure he's just looking at Kira."

Kira squealed and splashed Ben again, totally ignoring the conversation.

"Maybe he's watching both of you."

Celia angled herself to the beach and peered behind the lenses of her sunglasses. Sure enough, there was Salim, standing a few feet from Elan. A tall, elegant figure, fully dressed among the reclining sunbathers.

He was too far away for her to see where he was looking, but she could feel his gaze on her. Suddenly self-conscious in her swimsuit, she crouched and lifted Kira up. Kira waved her legs in the air, splashing water everywhere, her excited squeal pealing across the water. "Mama! Lift me higher!"

"I can't, my arms aren't long enough." She lowered Kira down into the water.

"I bet my daddy could lift me higher." Kira stared at the beach. "Daddy!" She tugged on Celia's arm, dragging her through the shallow water toward the shore. "Daddy!"

Salim loped across the sand and into her outstretched arms. "Yes, my princess." He picked her up and twirled her around, while seawater soaked into his expensive shirt. "Are you sure you're not a mermaid?"

"I don't have a fishy tail." She pressed her chubby fingers to his cheeks. "But I like to swim."

Celia laughed. "She's not kidding. I'm turning into a prune from spending so much time in the water."

"You're the loveliest prune I've ever seen." Salim glowed with good humor. It heated Celia's wet skin like the warm sun. "And I'm hoping you'll join me for dinner tonight, after Kira goes to bed."

"I could come, too," chimed in Kira.

"You need some sleep." Salim pushed strands of wet hair off her flushed face. "You've been on the go nonstop all day."

"Will you read me a bedtime story?"

"Any story you like." Salim looked at her, his expression serious. "I'd be delighted." He turned to Celia. "What time?"

Somehow the idea of Salim reading Kira a story—a favorite part of their daily routine—struck fear into her heart. Kira was growing attached to Salim.

Too attached. Leaving him would be very hard for her, even now.

Every moment they spent together made their inevitable parting more ominous.

But he was her father.

Celia swallowed. "She usually goes down around seven o'clock. Of course with jet lag, anything could happen."

"I was actually inquiring what time I should pick you up for dinner." His eyebrow lifted, a hint of flirtation.

Celia's stomach clenched. Why did she have to feel excited and apprehensive at the prospect of dinner with him? "Why don't you come at six-thirty for story time and we'll see what happens."

Nine

Kira was already asleep when Salim arrived. She'd passed out on the bed while watching cartoons, and Celia watched, smiling and biting her lip at the same time, while Salim gently lifted her and carried her into her room.

The nanny he'd arranged settled herself in an armchair and promised to phone them if she woke up.

"Where are we going?" whispered Celia, once they stepped out into the hall. "I had no idea what to wear." Aware of conservative Omani sensibilities, she'd put on a tiered skirt and a thin, long-sleeved blouse. She probably looked like a cartoon peasant.

"You look breathtaking, as always." Salim's admiring gaze made her skin shimmer.

He was infuriatingly gorgeous himself, dressed in

black from head to toe, his hair swept back from his bold features.

"We're going out on my boat." He pressed the elevator button and the doors opened instantly. Probably someone downstairs at the controls made sure an elevator was always at his majesty's disposal. "I've arranged for dinner to be delivered."

"I didn't know you had a boat," Celia said and then frowned, looking down at her skirt and wondering if she should have worn pants.

"There's a lot you don't know about me." A mysterious smile lifted one corner of his mouth. "But little by little, I'm letting you in on my secrets."

Heat flickered in her belly. "Why do I have a feeling there are thousands of them?"

"You're a woman of mystery yourself. If you can keep a daughter secret, who knows what else you might be hiding." The gleam in his eye revealed no hint of hostility.

"I can't tell you how relieved I am not to be keeping that secret anymore. Secrets don't sit at all comfortably with me. And she's so enjoying her time here."

"I don't have words to express how I feel getting to know her." He glanced up at the mirrored elevator ceiling for a moment, as if searching his mind for the missing words. His chest heaved. "She's more wonderful than I could have imagined."

The doors opened, and Celia managed to govern her face into a blank expression as they strode through the glittering lobby. She didn't want to reveal any of the confusing mix of emotions that roiled in her chest: pride at how well her daughter had handled the strange new surroundings, admiration for Salim's complete and enthusiastic acceptance of his new role as a father…and anxiety about the future.

Smartly dressed patrons milled about, greeting their guests and friends and heading for the restaurant. Salim ushered her out onto one of the brick walks, heading toward the hotel dock.

"This day has been…astonishing. I could never have imagined what it would feel like to be a father. Kira has left me speechless."

His expression of fatherly delight brought a smile to her mouth. "You don't need much speech around Kira." She raised a brow. "You may have noticed she talks a lot."

"And runs a lot, and laughs a lot and smiles a lot."

"She's very bright." They walked along, side by side. "She knows the whole alphabet already."

"We'll have to teach her the Arabic alphabet."

Celia swallowed. How far would this go? Would he really want her to come visit regularly? Familiar fear clutched at her heart. Now he'd met Kira, could he stand to let her go?

At least she had the contract.

He'd signed it, and she had the copy locked in her file cabinet back home.

They'd never spoken about it.

Guilt tightened her muscles. "They do say it's good to learn a new language while you're still young. It wouldn't surprise me if Kira figures out Arabic pretty fast."

"Naturally she will. She's an Omani." Salim marched forward, proud chin lifted, a smile tilting his mouth.

Celia didn't contradict him. She didn't want to. He looked so…happy.

It couldn't last, of course. Sooner or later they'd have

to confront the ugly, sticky details of child visitation rights and haggle over where Kira would spend spring break. But for now she wanted him to revel in the simple joy of being a father.

She'd deprived him of that for long enough.

Salim leaped onto the dock in a single, powerful move, then turned to offer Celia a hand. Heat flared in her palm as she took his fingers. Why did she still have to be so attracted to him? It wasn't fair.

She stepped up onto the dock, avoiding his fierce gaze. Her own eyes were soon fixed on the gleaming white yacht floating before them. "That's quite a boat."

"She's capable of a long ocean voyage."

"Why do people call boats *she?*" Celia felt a twinge of jealousy. Which was way too silly. It's not like the boat was her rival for Salim's affections.

"Perhaps because they're beautiful, and they can take us to places we'd never discover by ourselves."

"That sounds rather exciting."

"Tonight we'll only go out a mile or so, but some other time I'll take you and Kira to Muscat or to Yemen. We Omanis have always been a seafaring people. It's obvious that Kira loves the ocean."

Celia nodded. "The ocean in Connecticut is freezing cold and gray. She always used to scream if it so much as touched her toes. Here I can barely get her out of the water to eat."

"Not many places in the world compare favorably with Salalah."

Salim's smile warmed her to her toes as he helped her aboard.

The deck was huge, at least thirty feet across, and lined with padded seats. Every inch of the ship was polished to a high shine. Brass railings gleamed in the sunset and colorful flags fluttered high above.

A smell of delicious cooking came from somewhere inside the mahogany paneled bowels of the boat. "Yusef is cooking our dinner. He'll steer the vessel, too. We can be frank in our conversation around him."

"He's discreet?" Celia wondered what Salim was telling his staff about her and Kira.

"Yes. And he speaks about eight words of English, most of them filthy." His infectious grin made her stomach quiver. "Let's go see what he's prepared for us."

Dinner was arranged on a lower deck, inches above the rippling surface of the water. Moonlight danced across tiny waves on an evening breeze that blew away the day's heat and made Celia draw her silk shawl around her shoulders.

"Are you cold?" Salim shrugged off his suit jacket, "Here, put this on."

"Oh, no. I'm fine. Perfect." The last thing she needed was to be surrounded by his seductive masculine smell. It was bad enough sitting directly opposite him while he glowed with joy and enthusiasm about the daughter they shared. "I like the breeze."

Yusef, an older man in a dark dishdasha and a brown turban, served the meal with a smile.

Tender spiced fish on a bed of saffron rice made Celia's mouth water just to look at it. "Omani food is sensational. I don't know how I'll survive without it."

Salim frowned slightly, as if he wanted to say something.

But he didn't. He tore off a hunk of freshly baked flatbread and chewed it silently.

No doubt neither of them knew quite what to say.

They were walking along a delicate bridge between the past and the future.

Salim had made no mention of Nabilah or his plans for the future. Celia didn't dare look beyond the end of the week.

Her landscaping project was nearly done. She'd return to the States soon, and take Kira with her.

Neither of them wanted to talk or think about that.

It was easier to exist here in this magical realm, suspended between realities, where anything seemed possible.

They sat at the table like…a couple.

But she didn't dare to imagine a possible future between her and Salim.

She glanced out over the silvery water, to where lights shone on the distant shore. "I can understand why you wanted to come back here. Life in Massachusetts must have been pretty grim compared to your existence here. You never told me you had people waiting on you hand and foot in your regular life."

Salim shrugged. "The experience did me good. I learned how to do things for myself, how to make my own decisions." Something flickered in his dark eyes. "Though I'm not sure I would have survived without your help."

"We had some really good times together." For years she'd suppressed the happy memories of their halcyon days in college. It hurt too much to remember how it all ended. "I guess everything good has to come to an end some time. That's just how life works."

"And sometimes an ending isn't really an ending, as proved by our tryst four years ago and its very delightful results."

Celia smiled. *Don't go getting your hopes up.* "We do have a colorful history, you and I."

Salim placed one broad, tanned hand on the white tablecloth. If she'd wanted to—or dared—she could have placed her own on top of it, to seal the connection between them.

But she didn't.

An ancient wood fishing dhow moved slowly through the water close to them. She could make out its curved outline in the moonlight. Fishermen on the lamp-lit deck called out and waved and Salim replied something in Arabic with a grin. "They're jealous."

Celia laughed. "Who wouldn't be? This boat is like a floating palace."

"It's not the boat they're jealous of." Mischief glimmered in his eyes. "They said I've caught a very beautiful fish."

Celia struggled not to squirm with pleasure under the idle flattery. "How silly. I'm sunburned like a fisherman myself. If it wasn't for the flattering candlelight I'm sure they'd be saying something quite else."

"You don't enjoy being beautiful, do you?" Salim cocked his head.

Celia stiffened. "If I actually was beautiful, maybe I'd have an opinion on that subject."

"Or perhaps you feel you won't be taken seriously if you look too feminine?"

"I prefer to let my work speak for itself. I'd expect to be taken just as seriously in chandelier earrings. In fact, maybe I'll wear some tomorrow." She raised a brow.

"I'll be sure to take you seriously." His smile revealed his perfect white teeth.

She couldn't get a rise out of him tonight. Apparently

he, too, was determined to enjoy their evening. "I wish Kira was here." She sighed. "It's so lovely."

"We'll bring her. We'll come out for a long sail along the coast. I do know how to sail her, you know."

"I believe you. I suspect that you could do just about anything you put your hand to." She glanced down at Salim's sturdy, capable hand, where it rested on the white linen.

Oh, how she'd like to put her hand in his and leave it there for a lifetime.

But that was another lifetime than this one.

And maybe now, while things were calm and cordial between them, and Kira was tucked up quietly in bed, was the best time to plan the future. "Kira and I can come visit regularly. Whenever there's a school holiday, really. My schedule is usually pretty flexible, since I set it myself."

She wanted to make it clear that if Kira came, she would, too.

Salim's brows lowered. "I don't want to see Kira only two or three times a year."

"You could come to the States whenever you want. I'm sure you have business to do there. You'd be welcome to come visit anytime." Her cheerful invitation rang hollow in the sea-scented night air.

"I don't want to be 'welcome to visit' my daughter. I want to be a *father* to her. Those things are very different."

"I know, but the situation is complicated. We live on different continents. You're rooted here, and Kira and I have friends and family there."

"You have friends and family here." His voice was almost a growl.

Only you. And I've learned better than to depend on you for my happiness.

She kept her thoughts silent, not wanting to stir up more trouble.

"You can see how happy Kira is here. How well she fits in. We have excellent schools here in Salalah. She will grow up surrounded by people who care about her and want the best for her."

Panic flashed through Celia. And a flare of indignation. "She's already growing up surrounded by people who care about her. That's why she's so happy and outgoing." She straightened her shoulders and braced herself. Her hands were shaking and she hid them under the table. Things were about to get ugly. "And I told you, I'm taking her back home."

"Home. Isn't there an American saying, 'home is where the heart is?'"

"Maybe one's heart can be in more than one place, but I'm Kira's mother and she belongs with me." She couldn't hide the tremor in her voice.

"And that's why you had me sign that *contract*." Salim's eyes narrowed to dark slits.

"Yes." She lifted her chin. "I knew that sooner or later we'd have this discussion. I needed to protect my rights, as you can see."

"Why didn't you bring it to me yourself?"

Because I'm afraid of what a pushover I am where you're concerned. "I didn't want to get overemotional, or have us get into an argument."

"You mean, like we're doing now?" He raised a brow. "Surely you didn't think I could meet Kira, get to know her and then simply kiss her goodbye?"

Guilt and fear knotted in Celia's stomach. "I knew you wouldn't. That's why I was afraid. Why I am afraid."

Salim stood, scraping his chair on the deck. Water lapped against the side of the ship, punctuating the thick silence. "You must think about what's best for Kira."

He loomed over her. Moonlight picked out the hard lines of his jaw and cheekbones in silver.

"I am. There's no neat solution. There never has been."

Salim blew out a hard breath and stared out over the water. It shimmered in the bright streak of moonlight that lit its heaving surface.

He frowned, then extended a hand to her. "Come, let's walk on the deck."

Celia stared at his hand, broad palm and long, sturdy fingers, reaching out to her.

If she took it, was she somehow agreeing to his terms? Or would she get sucked into the vortex of madness that gave him such infuriating control over her mind and body?

She didn't want to make trouble. Really, she wanted this to go as smoothly as possible, so rejecting a friendly gesture didn't make sense.

She stood slowly and extended her hand to meet his.

Energy snapped between them and shot up her arm as her fingertips met his. He wrapped his fingers around hers, taking hold of her gently but firmly. "From the far side of the deck we can see the lights of Salalah."

She let him lead her across the polished wood deck with its brass railing. The flags fluttering overhead in the starry darkness echoed the rapid beat of her heart. They passed the stairs leading down to the galley and cabins, and the shore came into view. The city lay spread before them, flickering dots of golden light in the distance.

"It's beautiful," she admitted. "It looks like a floating city." The ocean shimmered and rippled like a flying carpet in the space between the yacht and the glowing shore.

"You can see why I had to come back here. Why staying in the States was never an option for me."

"Yes, of course. I understand everything now. You were always going to come back here. I was young and naive and it didn't occur to me that we weren't entirely in charge of our own destiny."

"Salalah could be your home, too." He spoke low, looking out into the far distance, rather than right at her.

A mix of terror and longing rose inside her. *Oh, stop it! He doesn't mean for you to all be a family. He'll probably set you up in a nice out-of-the-way house somewhere and treat you like a maiden aunt, while he gets on with his "suitable marriage" to someone else.*

Did she imagine it, or did his fingers just tighten around hers? Her palm heated and a tingling sensation crept up her arm and rippled to her breasts and belly.

Maybe he did mean for them to be romantic?

She drew in a shaky breath.

"I never truly thought about the joys of being a father." Salim spoke, gazing out over the silver water. "I knew it was my duty, and that I would have children one day." He turned to look at her. His dark eyes held hers fixed on his. "I didn't realize she'd capture my heart and carry it with her every moment."

His words shot a bolt of fierce emotion to Celia's core. She knew exactly how he felt. And that was why everything they said, everything they did, was so important.

And so very difficult.

He turned to her and captured her other hand, holding them both tight in his. "Thank you for bringing Kira into the world." He spoke with force. "Thank you for raising her to be the bright and happy child she is. You're a wonderful mother."

Celia gulped as a rush of feeling threatened to choke her. She'd felt his censure that she continued to work and travel and spend time away from Kira. His praise now warmed her more than she wanted to admit.

"Thanks," she managed.

"So you must realize that Kira needs both of us."

His statement hung in the night air for a moment as his gaze held hers.

"Yes." She knew he was right. But how could they make it happen?

His eyes drifted to her mouth, which twitched under his stare. Heat sizzled in the air between them, heating their clasped hands and stinging her taut nipples.

Uh-oh.

Their mouths moved inexorably closer. Her lips tingled with awareness of his mouth, hovering close to hers in the darkness. His eyes darkened as passion flared between them.

Then Salim dropped her hands and turned abruptly away.

He strode across the deck, leaving Celia standing there by herself, lips parted in unkissed astonishment.

Ten

The next morning, Celia guided Kira out of the sunlit breakfast room where they'd both had freshly made crepes with fruit. She planned to let Kira play on the beach for a while, then take her to the site so she could look over a few final details.

Her evening with Salim had ended abruptly after their almost-kiss. He'd gruffly suggested they should return to shore, and she'd agreed, glad the darkness hid her flush of humiliation.

Where had she thought that kiss would lead? Nowhere sensible, to be sure.

She should be glad Salim had put a stop to it.

Still, the rejection—on top of all the other rejections she still smarted from—hurt.

Kira stopped and cried out in distress. "We forgot my water wings!"

"You can't swim right after breakfast, sweetie. You could get a cramp."

Kira's lower lip stuck out, and she looked up with big, imploring eyes. "I won't go in deep."

"You're darn right you won't." Celia grinned. "We'll build a sand castle."

Kira was at stake. Kira's future happiness depended on both her parents coming to some kind of sensible arrangement. And breathless kisses were anything but sensible—at least between the two of them.

"Miss Davidson!" A female voice behind her made Celia turn around. She squinted in the morning sun as a woman with red hair rushed across the open courtyard toward her. "Mr. Al Mansur would like to see you in his office."

"Oh." She frowned.

Why didn't he just call her? She always had her phone with her.

"He asked me to take Kira to the Kids' Club. We're making clay sculptures this morning."

Celia frowned. What was he up to? She didn't know this particular hotel employee and she wasn't too delighted about handing Kira over to a total stranger.

"I'm Lucinda Bacon, director of the children's activities." She thrust out a hand. Celia shook it. "How silly of me not to introduce myself. I was a nanny for tots in England for eight years before I came here. I'll make sure Kira has a lovely time." Her bright smile and warm gaze gave Celia some reassurance.

Still…

"She might need a nap soon. She's had an exciting couple of days."

"Not a problem at all!" Lucinda squatted to Kira's

height. "We've got a lovely nap room with the prettiest beds you could imagine." She looked right at Kira. "And we sing lullabies. Do you have a favorite bedtime song?"

"'Rock-a-bye Baby,'" said Kira.

"Oh, that's one of my favorites. And did you know, one of our beds rocks, just like a cradle?"

"Can I try it?" Kira looked up at her mom, eyes wide with excitement.

Celia's stomach tightened. "Um, sure, I guess so. Salim is in his office, you said?"

"Yes, he's waiting for you. He asked us to look after Kira until you're done. No rush at all, we're open until ten in the evening." She beamed, and took Kira's hand.

Celia wiped her empty palms on the back of her pants. "Okay." She wrote down her number for Lucinda and watched as she led Kira away.

A nasty feeling of foreboding crept over her.

Was this how it would start? Kira being pried from her and seduced into a new world of unimagined luxuries— things that she could never provide for her daughter, but Salim could produce with a snap of his powerful fingers.

She swallowed and lifted her chin. *He's waiting for you.*

Celia felt as if she'd been summoned to the principal's office.

The feeling only increased when she was ushered into his spacious office, and found him sitting behind the desk, attired in a crisp, dark suit.

Salim rose and nodded, a formal greeting. His grim expression deepened the churning in her stomach. "Please, take a seat."

He gestured to the richly upholstered chair beside her, and she managed to lower herself into it. Her knees were wobbly and she had a sudden urge to diffuse the tension in the air. "Kira was so excited to go to the Kids' Club. I didn't even know there was one here. Every time I turn around, I find something new at this hotel. It's really amazing."

The nonsensical babbling hung in the air as Salim simply stared at her, eyes narrowed. Something in his gaze was more focused, more intense than usual.

Her stomach tightened.

Salim leaned forward in his chair, which magnified the sensation of being in a laser sight. "As you know, I consider family to be of great importance."

Uh-oh. Celia squirmed under his hard stare.

He frowned before continuing. "I originally broke off our relationship because I considered my responsibility to my family to be paramount. I was the eldest son, and therefore it is my duty to sustain the family into the next generation."

Celia straightened her back. *Here we go again.* All the reasons why she could never be a suitable wife and must thus be banished from his life, yada, yada.

She should be used to it by now. But apparently she wasn't.

Pain lanced through her and she swallowed hard. Had he summoned her here to reject her—yet again? She hadn't even suggested or hinted that she expected anything of him.

Rapid blinking shoved back any tears lurking behind her eyelids.

"I have always intended to fulfill my father's wishes and take an Omani bride of good family."

Didn't you try that once already?

His words stung, but she managed to keep her retort to herself. What good could come of bickering with him? He was still Kira's father, even if he was a heartless clod where she was concerned.

"But now I've decided that, once again, I must put my family first."

Celia's heart clenched. Did he mean to break the contract? It might not even be legally enforceable here. What did she or even confident and chipper Sara know about such things? She struggled to keep her breathing under control.

He hadn't arrived at his point yet.

"I have a daughter now. I believe it is important—in fact, I feel it is essential—that she is provided with a proper family. To that end I have decided that we must marry."

His words hung in the air above his polished desk.

All thoughts deserted Celia's brain. Had he just said what she thought he said?

And who exactly did he mean by *we?*

Salim's frown deepened. "As my wife you will no longer have the burden of supporting yourself and Kira. You will not need to travel, or to be away from her for long periods of time, as you are now. You can stay at home and take care of our daughter, which, I'm sure you will agree, is the most sensible course of action."

Celia stared at him, unable to form a coherent idea, let alone speak a sentence.

"Naturally we must be married as soon as possible. The wedding can take place here at the hotel. I have a full staff of wedding planners and caterers who can take care of all the arrangements. Is there any particular day you prefer?"

"No."

Salim frowned. Celia had been silent while he made his proposal. Not the reaction he'd expected. He was sure she'd be thrilled. "Do you mean, no, you don't have a particular day in mind?"

"No." She sat up straight in her chair, blue eyes flashing. "I mean no to all of it. No, I won't marry you."

Her response hit him like a punch to the gut and he found himself braced against his chair. "What?"

"How can you reduce our whole lives to a business arrangement?" Her hands shook as she gripped the arms of her chair. "You want to marry me entirely out of a sense of duty or some old-fashioned, wrongheaded idea of responsibility. You don't want to marry me. You're just offering because you feel you *have* to." Her voice rose to a high pitch and color flushed her neck. "I don't need to marry you. I can support myself and my daughter and I don't *want* to marry you."

Her words crashed over him, smashing his plans and his vision of their happy family life.

Adrenaline surged through him. "But why not? Surely you can see it's for the best?"

"Best for who? Best for Kira? Best for you? It surely isn't best for me."

"It could be. I know you'll have to leave friends behind to come live here, but you'll make new ones. You can see we have a busy, friendly environment with people from all over the world here at the hotel, and the new property will bring even more visitors."

"I don't want to be a hotel guest in your life." She tossed her head, and gold hair flew around her face. "Can't you see that? It's not enough for me."

Salim frowned. Why wouldn't she see sense? Panic crept over him. "We don't have to live at the hotel. We can build a house, together. You can design the grounds exactly how you like."

"Design the grounds?" Her voice rang with incredulity. "You don't understand me at all." Tears glistened in her eyes. "I don't want my life to be a project, organized according to deadlines and budgets, with all the limits carefully set out from the start. I don't want my marriage to be a carefully orchestrated contractual agreement." Her voice started to crack. "I can't live like that, and I won't have Kira live like that."

She rose from the chair, which screeched on the marble floor.

Salim stood, horror exploding in his chest.

How could she reject him? That would ruin everything. Didn't she see that all of their futures depended on this?

She was totally irrational. Was she reacting emotionally because he'd rejected her in the past? "I know I've hurt you. I wish I could turn back the clock and handle things differently—"

"How?" Celia cocked her head to one side, steel glinting in her blue eyes. "By never getting involved with me in the first place? That would have been the sensible thing to do. No mess, no fuss, no broken promises. No disappointed brides or illegitimate children." She crossed her arms over her chest. "Yes, that would have been much easier. You could have married your suitable bride and lived with her happily ever after."

I didn't want to marry a suitable bride. I wanted to marry you.

The truth of it crashed across his brain. But he didn't say the words.

He'd asked her to marry him—and she'd said no.

His pride smarted and stung. Maybe she took pleasure in causing him the pain he'd once given her.

Except this was far worse, because she had the power to keep his own daughter from him.

His heart ached, too full to express the hopes and fears now lying crushed inside it.

Celia turned and strode across the room. "And you think I should stop working and stay home. Where would I be if I'd done that when Kira was born?" She wheeled around and stared at him. "After I'd called you to tell you about her, and you brushed me off?"

"I didn't know about her or naturally I would have paid all your expenses."

"Oh, how gracious of you." Fury flashed in her eyes. "I do hope I would have been suitably grateful. Perhaps you could have paid to have us hidden away somewhere. Your secret second family. The one no one knows about, except you."

"That's ridiculous, and you know it. I'm not asking you to be a second wife." He paused and frowned. "Well, I suppose technically you would be my second wife, but I'm long divorced from the first. You would be my only wife."

"I don't think I could ever be *appropriate* enough for your needs." She lifted her chin. "I want my daughter to be raised seeing women support themselves and fulfill their ambitions. I want her to know that she can shape her own life however she pleases."

She shoved a stray lock of hair off her forehead. "My parents take excellent care of her when I travel. She's surrounded by friends and family at all times. As you've seen with your own eyes, she's happy and well-adjusted." Her eyes, still blazing like the sea in the noonday sun, defied him to argue.

"She should grow up knowing her father." His voice emerged as a low growl he hardly recognized. Words were so inadequate to express his feelings.

"I agree." She paused and frowned.

Hope unfurled in his chest.

Celia put her hands on her slim hips. "She should grow up knowing her father. And I'm sure we can come up with some mutually acceptable *contract*..." She spat the word. "To provide for that."

She inhaled and he watched her chest rise, cursing the lust that licked at him, even now. "But there is no need for either of us to commit to a loveless marriage that will diminish us both." Her voice rang, clear and resolute, across the wide space of his office.

She turned and walked to the door.

Salim sprang from his chair.

"Don't worry, I'll be discreet," she said, her expression stony. "I won't tell anyone that I turned down your *generous* proposal. I've all but fulfilled the terms of our original contract, the one that brought me here. There are just a few small details to take care of. Then Kira and I will return to the States, as planned."

Her golden hair flew out behind her as she swung the door open and stepped out. It closed behind her with a decisive slam.

Salim rushed for the door. Then stopped.

He couldn't *make* her stay. Which was an unfamiliar

sensation, since there was so little in his life that he didn't have total control over.

He didn't have any control—or any influence at all—over Celia.

A mix of indignation and frustration pricked his muscles. Could she simply leave and take his daughter with her?

Of course she could. He'd signed that stupid contract agreeing to let her.

He wasn't sure what hurt more. The prospect of losing Kira, his bright-eyed and affectionate daughter who'd already crept into his heart.

Or the prospect of losing Celia—again.

No matter how hard he'd tried to shove her out of his mind, there she was, lingering somewhere in the dark nether regions of his consciousness, an eternal temptation.

He could never resist his attraction to her. It was gut level, visceral and raw in a way that pushed reason and sense aside.

All his carefully cultivated plans fell into disarray as soon as she walked into the room. He could never marry Nabilah now. Celia had ruined him for any other woman.

She was all wrong—foreign, outspoken, bold and driven. She didn't even seem to notice convention, let alone conform to it. She never had.

And the way she dressed…

She was all wrong for him.

But tradition be damned, he loved her. And she was the only wife he wanted.

Eleven

Celia jogged across the hotel complex, heart pounding and breath coming in unsteady gasps.

Salim had just asked her to marry him.

And she'd turned him down.

A proposal from Salim was something she'd once dreamed of and hoped for. But not one like this, a crude business arrangement to suit his idea of propriety.

A sob caught in her throat.

He didn't love her.

He didn't even care about her. Not if he thought she'd be happy to give up her career to sit quietly at his feet in some blond-haired, blue-eyed imitation of a "suitable wife."

The cruelty of the situation choked her with anger and sadness. The man she loved had asked her to be his wife—in a way that made it impossible for her to accept.

She had to get Kira. Who knew what orders Salim might issue to his staff. Here in the hotel compound he was surrounded by his friends and allies, his loyal family members. All of them might gang up against her and try to convince her to leave Kira here.

Even to force her, contract be damned.

Fear pricked her nerves as she hurried past the plate-glass windows of the beauty salon and the store selling local arts and crafts. She scanned the signs for the Kids' Club and was relieved to see it just past the massage parlor.

Breathless and sweating, she pushed open the door, her whole body pulsing with terror. She scanned the interior, decorated with elaborate fairy-tale murals and painted furniture.

Where was Kira?

She needed to leave now, today.

And she intended to keep Kira at her side until she did.

Kira burst through a door in the middle of a Little Bo Peep mural and ran to her. "Mama!"

Relief washed over her in a tidal wave. Kira's bright eyes sparkled. "It's so fun here!" Celia hugged her, and clutched her to her chest, careful to conceal her own trepidation.

"They read stories and I learned a new song."

"That's great, sweetie, but we have to go now." She wiped her palms on the back of her pants. "We'll grab some lunch and I'll take you out to the site. Remember how I told you about the old city?"

"With the castles and everything?"

"Exactly. We're going to see it right now." She needed to wrap up a few final details, and leave some last instructions for planting and maintenance with the crew. Then she'd fulfilled her obligations and could leave with a clear conscience.

At least as clear as it ever would be.

"Come on, sweetie."

Kira pouted. "Can't I stay for nap time? I didn't get to try the cradle."

"Another time, okay?"

Would there be another time? She couldn't keep Kira from Salim. She didn't want to, but maybe he wouldn't want a relationship on any terms other than his own. Sooner or later he'd take his "suitable" bride, who probably wouldn't want anything to do with the illegitimate child of a former liaison.

"Okay." Kira's glum face sent a stab of guilt to her chest. Was she doing the right thing for Kira?

On the other hand, she couldn't be a good mother to Kira if she was living a lie, married to a man who saw her as nothing but an obligation.

Celia helped Kira into her pink ballet flats and picked her up. Her baby was obviously ready for a nap. "You can sleep in the car, so you'll be awake to see the ancient city."

"Okay, Mama."

Kira trusted her completely. In her innocence she still saw her mom as her protector and savior and someone who always did the right thing. Celia inhaled deeply, and wondered how long she'd inhabit that role in her daughter's imagination.

"I love you, sweetie," she whispered into Kira's dark hair.

She thanked the nursery staff and left the well-appointed facilities with mingled feelings of relief and sadness. What a lovely place for Kira to play and interact with other children.

If only her father hadn't issued his impossible demand.

She rushed to their hotel room and threw their few belongings into her duffel bag. She hurried down the outside staircase, anxious to avoid the staff. At first Kira protested, wanting to go to the beach, but perhaps something in her mom's tone let her know that this was no time for play. She held Celia's hand as they hurried along the palm-shaded path to the car park, where Celia bundled her into the back of her rented Mercedes and strapped her into the car seat she'd borrowed from the rental agency.

"If you stay awake a little while, you'll see the Fog Mountains."

"Okay, Mama." Kira must be really sleepy. What had happened to the feisty terror who resisted her car seat with energy and persuasive arguments? Maybe all the action and events of the last few days had sucked the chutzpah out of her, too.

Too many ups and downs. Too many high hopes and foolish fantasies.

She started the engine and pulled out of the hotel complex. She'd miss the bright, white walls of Salalah, and the backdrop of blue sea shining in the background. She'd miss the tall, graceful palms and the friendly people.

She'd miss Salim.

But she'd missed him—and survived—most of her adult life. She should be used to that by now.

Her heart ached with longing for everything that could never be.

She and Salim just weren't destined to be together. The gulf between them was wide and windswept as the Rub' Al Khali. That desert wilderness was once criss-crossed by caravans of brave and hopeful traders who visited the lost city on their journey. Now it was virtually impassible, and even the Bedouin no longer walked its sand-choked passes.

Things changed, and there was no going back.

The mystical environment of the Fog Mountains engulfed her like a hug as she drove through their now-familiar passes. Then the desert floor welcomed her again, with its austere mysteries and quiet beauty.

The lost city rose, majestic, through the haze of midday heat that shimmered over the sands. Bright walls enclosed the lush oasis that would soon welcome visitors back to its ancient streets.

Already she'd seen it come alive again as a crossroads of cultures and peoples. She rolled down the window as she pulled up alongside one of her crews, mulching freshly planted date palms. "Faisal, do you have a few minutes? I need to go over some final details. Turns out I have to leave…very soon." She gulped. The crew chief frowned and nodded.

She parked and spent a few minutes in her makeshift site office—soon to become a luxurious bedroom—going over maintenance details. Plants didn't survive long in rainless desert conditions without carefully planned care.

Celia kept her voice steady while she gave instructions for watering and fertilizing. Kira slept quietly on a soft pillow nearby. Would either of them see the majestic date palms in maturity, heavy with rich fruit?

Or would the rebuilt lost city live on only in her imagination? Suspended in time just the way it was when she last saw it.

Which might well be today. She intended to drive her rental car directly to the airport in Muscat and get on the next available flight to the States.

Her stomach clenched at the thought of leaving all this behind. Of tearing Kira from the new surroundings she'd grown to enjoy. But it was better to make the break now, so they could start rebuilding their lives.

She left Kira sleeping and took Faisal outside to go over instructions for fertilizing a new ground cover. As he typed the name of it into his PDA, a car engine roared into earshot.

"I can't get used to the way people drive around here," she exclaimed. "In the U.S. pedestrians have the right of way. Here they have the right to get out of the way—and fast."

She stepped back off the road as the car squealed around the corner.

Salim's sedan.

It screeched to a dramatic and noisy halt, sending a cloud of dust into the air around it.

"I've got to go." Instinct fired her veins with adrenaline, and she turned to run toward the building where Kira slept.

She wouldn't let him talk her around. She wouldn't let herself fall for his fatal charms.

He'd caused her too much pain already.

"Celia." His voice rang out behind her as he leaped

from the car. "Stop." His command boomed through the air.

She ignored it and kept marching. She was done being told what to do by Salim Al Mansur.

Footsteps on the path behind her made her heart pound harder.

"Celia, wait." His words stuck her like a knife and every muscle in her body yearned to respond.

How did he have such power over her?

Still, she kept walking, steeling herself against whatever appeal he might be ready to launch.

A hand grabbed her upper arm, jerking her to a halt.

"Let go!" She spun around.

"No." He grabbed her other arm and held her, facing him. Her first instinct was to fight—

Then their eyes met.

His were blacker than she'd ever seen them, piercing and intense. His gaze locked onto hers, fierce and pleading. "I won't let you go."

Breath fled her lungs.

"I love you." His eyes narrowed, their fierce stare penetrating to her core. "I *love* you and I need you." His voice cracked as raw emotion spilled out.

His words crashed over her, draining the strength from her muscles. She struggled to resist them. "You don't," she whispered.

Her skin burned under the heat of his palms. Already the forceful—and purely physical—attraction between them threatened to overwhelm her. "You don't love me," she managed. "You just want me."

She frowned, fighting the emotion—the sobs—that hovered just beneath the surface of her voice. "You want to make things right, and you think you can do that by capturing me and keeping me here. Me and Kira…" Fear flared in her heart as she thought of Kira sleeping, innocent and unsuspecting, just a few yards away. "You can't. You can't make yourself love me no matter how much you might want to, and you can't make me stay."

"Make myself love you?" The words exploded from his tongue, "I've been trying for over a decade to make myself *stop* loving you. I've always loved you and I always will love you."

A groan issued from somewhere deep inside him, and echoed off the white buildings around them. "I'll love you until my last breath."

Desperation—and passion—flashed in his dark eyes. "Can't you see that? Can't you see that I can't live without you?" He inhaled a shaky breath. "I don't want to live without you."

Celia stood, unable to move, held up only by the strong hands that kept her captive.

The force of his words had turned her blood to vapor. She felt weightless, breathless, helpless.

"But you… But you…"

"I've been a fool." He lifted his head to the sky and let out a curse. "I've been a stubborn idiot who wouldn't know paradise if he fell into it."

His eyes fixed on hers, this time wide with wonder and brimming with raw emotion. "I've lived an empty, soulless life since I lost you—since I threw you away out of my own cowardice and stupidity." He made a strange sound, somewhere between a howl and a growl, primal and piercing.

Then he drew in a sharp breath, frowning as if in agony. "I should have fought for you, claimed you, and told my father that *you* were the only bride I could take." His voice rose to a crescendo, echoing off the buildings.

Celia swallowed. His words wrapped around her like the warm desert air.

Like the siren call of madness.

Then he let go of her arms and fell to his knees at her feet. He took her hands in his. "Don't leave, Celia. Please don't leave." His words were muffled in her shirtfront. Breathless and rasped, they scratched at her skin and clawed inside her. "I crave you with my heart and I love you with all my body and soul. Stay with me."

His strong hands held her tight.

And she had no desire to push them away.

He looked up, his handsome face taut with emotion. "Will you be my wife? Will you share my life and help me be the man I should have been all along? I can't do it without you."

Dark and shining, his eyes implored her.

"Oh, Salim." She fought the almost overwhelming urge to shout yes.

But she knew she couldn't. "I'm still the Celia you couldn't marry. The one who didn't fit and wouldn't work in your life." Her voice shook. "I'll always be that person."

She gestured to her work shirt and her dusty jeans. "I couldn't ever be the polished and proper bride you need. It's just not me. You may think you can change me, but you won't."

She narrowed her eyes and girded herself against his emotional appeal. "I don't want to change. I don't want to live a lie. That's not fair to me or the people around me."

"I know." Salim dropped her hands. Losing their warmth left her cold, even in the desert heat.

He sat back on his heels and looked up at her. "I know you won't change. That you can't change. That you don't want to be anyone but just you." She saw his Adam's apple move as he swallowed. "And it just makes me love you more."

His words, spoken so low as he stared up at her from the dusty pathway, gripped her guts like a clenched fist.

"I love you, Celia Davidson. I love your work and your passion…" Wearing a serious expression, he picked up one of her hands and pressed his lips to it. "And the grit under your fingernails."

Warmth swept through her.

"Everything about you is precious to me." A flicker of pain crossed his face, and he closed his eyes for a second. "When you turned me down and walked out of my office, I felt like my heart had been torn from my chest."

He clasped her hand in both of his. "I tried to tell myself—*you can live without a heart. You've gone this far without it. You don't need it.*" He frowned. "But I knew I couldn't."

He climbed to his feet, still holding her hands fast in his, eyes riveted to hers. "You've shown me that I do have a heart, and that I can't keep acting a role I've learned the lines for, but that I don't believe in."

He let out a long, shuddering breath. "I've tried to live my life for my family, for its honor and pride and for the future of our line.…" He shook his head, confusion sparkling in his eyes, then bursting into a laugh. "When all along, *you* were my real family. You, and now Kira.

You're the people I should care about and love and cherish."

Celia's breath came in unsteady gasps. "We're family." She tested the words aloud as the truth of his passionate words echoed in her core.

"You were always meant to be my wife. That's why we fell in love and were so happy together. In my youthful stupidity, I had no idea what a mistake I was making to toss that away and go along with someone else's plan." He squeezed her hands. "You are my wife. You always have been and always will be, whether you like it or not."

Mischief—or was it sheer conviction—glinted in his eyes.

Celia bit her lip. "I ruined you for everyone else."

"You did. And I wouldn't have it any other way. We're husband and wife and we don't need any contracts or ceremonies or rings to prove it."

Eyes wide, she stared at him. "So you don't even want to marry me?"

He shook his head. "I'm already married to you. I don't need a piece of paper to make it real."

She stared at him. The hard lines of his regal face seemed softer than usual. He glowed with...hope.

But maybe they were getting carried away. "But what about the practicalities? We can't live together."

"Of course we can." He raised her hands to his mouth and pressed his lips to her fingers. Her skin shivered in response. "We can live together here, and in New York, and in Muscat, and Bahrain and...wherever your work takes you. We'll be nomads, like my Bedouin ancestors." His eyes sparkled. "I think that will suit us very well."

"But what about Kira? Where will she go to school?"

"Life is school for the Bedouin." A smile tugged at his arrogant mouth. "And we'll hire a tutor. I had one, and I still got into the same college as you, with your genius-professor parents."

Celia smiled. "You do have a point there."

She racked her brain for more objections. All sensible thoughts seemed to have departed on the hot, blossom-scented wind. "So, this would be our home base, but we could travel to, say, New Zealand, if I had a job there?"

She peered at him, unable to believe this was really possible. It was just too perfect. With Salim and a tutor she really could bring Kira with her when she worked.

"Of course. Wherever we travel to, we'll always be home because we'll have each other."

She stared at him, openmouthed. Why not? The genius—and beauty—of it swelled in her heart.

"Mama!" Her daughter's high-pitched voice rang through the air. Celia turned to see her standing at the door of the building where she'd left her. Tears streaked her face and her mouth was turned down in an expression of dismay.

Celia tugged her hands from Salim's and ran to her. "Sweetheart, what's the matter?"

"We're leaving, aren't we? That's why you packed my toys." A fat tear rolled over her plump cheek.

"Um, actually…" She couldn't seem to find words. Her mouth hadn't caught up with her brain.

"I don't want to leave." Kira blinked, eyes wide and brimming. "I'd miss my daddy too much."

Kira glanced behind her, and a rumble of emotion

emerged from Salim's chest. "I'd miss you far too much, as well, my princess."

"So we're not leaving?" Kira's eyes brightened.

"No," Celia said firmly. "At least not unless we're all together."

"And Daddy could come with us to America?"

"Of course. He knows America well."

"My two favorite people in the world are from there." Salim smiled and brushed away a glittering tear with his thumb. "And we'll go to other countries, too. Now, when your mommy gets a new job, we'll go with her. And we'll all manage my hotels together, as well. I think you'd be a big help with that."

"Me, too." Kira's tears had vanished, replaced by her sparkling smile. "I'll help you get rich. I'm good at that."

Salim guffawed.

Celia smiled and hugged Kira close. "She's right. I told you about her lemonade stand. Watch out or she'll set one up by the pool."

"That sounds like an excellent idea."

"And you have to have a wedding so I can wear a flower girl dress. My friend Rachel wore one with little blue flowers." Kira frowned. "But I want pink flowers."

Celia's eyes met Salim's. His twinkled. "What do you say? Does she get to wear the flowers?"

Celia bit her lip, willing tears not to pour from her own eyes. "Yes. I'd like that very much."

Epilogue

"The guys are here!" Sara poked her head from behind the beaded curtain separating Celia from the prewedding festivities outside.

"What? I thought today was a no-guys-allowed thing." Celia glanced down at the fresh henna, drawn in swirling organic patterns on her arms and hands. She couldn't move until it dried. It was rather fun being propped up on cushions while everyone came behind the curtain to see her.

Everyone female, that is. Today's wedding celebration was the party for women, and hundreds of them milled about in colorful finery, laughing and chatting and picking their way over the cobbled stones of the lost city in high heels.

"We're only sticking with the good traditions, remember? What fun would your wedding party be if your husband-to-be couldn't share it?"

"You're right." Celia giggled. "He does know he can't touch me, I hope."

"I'll fight him off with a stick." Sara cast her eyes around for a weapon. "Maybe one of those sticks they all carried in the men's ceremony yesterday. Look out, here they come."

Salim and Elan burst through the curtain. Salim swept forward, careless of her elaborate paint job, and pressed his lips to hers. Heat rushed through her, mingled with excitement and elation that the wedding was finally underway after all the weeks of planning.

With effort, she pulled her lips from his and drew in a shaky breath. "Farah spent nearly three hours on my arms. Don't smudge the henna!"

"It's nearly dry." He leaned forward, and his hot breath caressed her ear as he whispered, "And when it is I'm going to trace each precious line with my tongue."

"Salim." She glanced over his shoulder. "We're not alone."

"We'll be alone soon enough," he murmured. His eyes flashed with desire that echoed inside her.

She glanced behind him, as Sara walked in with the children. "I'm not so sure. There must be a thousand people staying here and in Salalah."

"As well there should be. It's the celebration of the century." Salim beamed proudly. He did have the decency to step back. He stood next to Elan, both of them tall and regal in long white dishdashas, with the traditional curved *khanjar* dagger tucked into a sash at the waist.

"Elan's not wearing jeans!" Celia exclaimed.

"I'm getting in touch with my heritage." He grinned. Ben tugged at the long robe and Elan turned to pick him up. "Next thing you know, I'll be riding a camel."

"Can we, Dad? Oh, please!" Kira ran into the

curtained tent like a blast of air, her sequined dress sparkling.

"Of course you can." Salim picked her up and whirled her around. "Anything for my princess."

"Those camels are more dressed up than I am." Celia glanced ruefully at the embroidered silk dress she was trying not to get henna on. "I think I need a few more tassels to compete."

"I think the camels look adorable." Sara smiled. "Where on earth did you get them, Salim?"

"Faisal brought them from his village. His uncle owns them. They walked for five days to get here."

"The lost city welcomes camel trains once again." Celia grinned. "They look right at home here, too, nibbling on those native trees I picked out so carefully."

"Speaking of the lost city." Salim cocked his head. His intense gaze made heat flash over Celia's skin. "It's been found again and it needs a real name."

"But the archaeologists couldn't seem to figure it out." Celia sighed. She'd put quite a bit of effort into tracking it down herself. "They kept calling it 'the city of the Ubarites' which is more a description than a name."

"I'd imagine the name changed over time," cut in Elan. "Depending on who was living here and running the place. They'd name it after whatever was important to them."

"And I intend to do the same." A sheepish smile tilted Salim's arrogant mouth. "We shall call it Sal-iyy-ah." He pronounced the syllables slowly.

Sara burst out with a laugh. "Ce-l-ia! I love it."

Celia gasped as surprise and embarrassment reddened her face. "You can't! I'm not even from here."

"No one is from here." Salim crossed his hands over his broad chest, eyes glittering. "It was abandoned. Empty, lying in ruins. You helped bring it back to life, and now we shall all enjoy it together." He lifted his chin, defying her to disagree.

"That's crazy…" Celia fanned herself, henna be damned.

"It's perfect." Elan hoisted Ben higher on his waist. "It's both Arab and Western at the same time. Just like our family."

"The city is our vision come to life, just as the rest of our lives will be." Salim kissed Kira's cheek, and she giggled. "And Kira likes the name."

"Well, if Kira likes it, who am I to argue?" She felt a goofy smile spread across her face.

This was all a bit too much, and the actual wedding wasn't even until tomorrow!

"Someone bring this woman a cocktail!" exclaimed Sara.

"No, please, I'm far too light-headed already. The frankincense is making me giddy." She gestured to the aromatic lump smoldering in an open brazier. "I know it's fabulously valuable and the entire city was built around its trade, but I'm starting to think it's possible to suffer overexposure."

"Maybe you're just delirious with happiness," Sara said as she winked.

"Yeah. That could be it." She grinned and leaned back in her cushions.

Salim could honestly say the wedding was the most spectacular event he'd ever attended, let alone hosted. Over a thousand people joined in the festivities, many of them from the States, including Celia's friends and relatives, Salim and Elan's younger brother, Quasar, and Sara's large troupe of brothers and sisters and their children. They danced and sang and feasted and shared a four-foot-high cake decorated with candied lilies and orchids, until the stars twinkled over Saliyah.

The noise of revelry still filled the air as Celia and Salim hurried, hand-in-hand, along a lamp-lit stone path toward their lavishly decorated honeymoon suite.

Once inside, Celia closed the door behind them and clicked the lock. "Alone at last." Her eyes shone. "It's past 3:00 a.m. They're never going to leave, are they?"

"Why would they? They're having the time of their lives." Salim's chest swelled with pride and happiness. "As am I. Especially now that I have you all to myself."

Kira was happily settled in a suite with Sara's children for the night.

Celia threw off the emerald silk shawl that covered her shoulders. "Why did we both have to wear green?" She stretched and her delicate gold dress clung to her curves.

Heat stirred inside him. "It's traditional." His words were a throaty growl. "For fertility."

Celia raised a slim brow as she strolled toward him, limbs lithe. "I'm not sure that's a problem for us."

"Not in the least." He slid his hands around her waist.

Mischief lit her eyes as she wrapped long, slender fingers around the hilt of his *khanjar*. "Is an Omani wife allowed to grasp her husband's...dagger?"

"Only in the privacy of the bedchamber." Heat roared through him. "And only if she's looking for trouble."

Celia licked her lips. "Trouble is exactly what I have in mind. We haven't had nearly enough time for that lately." She tugged at his elaborate embroidered sash, pulling until it came loose and tumbled to the floor.

Salim's fingers plucked at the delicate shell buttons on her dress to reveal glowing, silky skin. He sighed at the rich, floral scent that filled his senses as he stripped off her elegant layers. "Gold underwear," he breathed, as the wickedly scant lace bra and panties revealed themselves.

"Got to match." Celia's cheeks glowed, and her breath came in unsteady gasps through parted lips. Together they removed his formal dishdasha with unsteady hands, until he stood naked, and very aroused, before her.

Celia wore nothing but her sensual gold satin lingerie—and a single green silk garter just above her left knee.

Salim slid a finger inside the unfamiliar but strangely erotic accessory. "Why do women wear these?"

"To drive men crazy."

"It works." He frowned. His arousal thickened as he slid his hand up her thigh and cupped her soft backside in its delicate satin and lace shell.

"Good." Her eyes flashed. "About this fertility thing.…" She cocked her head slightly. One henna-decorated hand strayed to her belly. "What if it works?"

"All the better." Emotion filled his chest. "Kira should have siblings, don't you think?"

"Absolutely. And this time you'll get to enjoy each glorious second of…" She slid a finger over the muscles of his chest, and down over his stomach. The muscles contracted as shivers of sensation shot to his groin. "My labor and delivery."

Her eyes flashed as she tossed her head, flicking her golden hair behind her shoulders.

"I'll put up with every word of abuse you hurl at me." He rubbed his palms over her nipples. She wriggled, enjoying the sensation. "I'll enjoy it."

"And when the baby cries at night…" She laid a line of kisses along his collarbone.

"I'll call for the nurse." He peered at her, hiding a smile.

She laughed. "You'll go get our baby for me."

"Unless she's lying between us."

"Which she probably will be." Celia's smile lit her lovely face. "Unless she's a he."

"Either one would bring me great joy." Warmth filled his body and the rich scroll of possibilities unfolded in his mind. "As long as we're all together."

Heat seared him as their lips met. His erection throbbed against Celia's soft belly, shoving all thoughts from his mind. In an instant they were on the bed, and her delicate undergarments fell to the floor. She shuddered when he entered her, and he let out a soft groan of sweet relief.

Could he really be lucky enough to have won the bride of his dreams?

The evidence lay in his arms.

Well, not exactly *lay*.

Before he knew what was happening she'd somehow reversed their positions and taken charge. Salim moaned aloud as she rode him hard, driving him to new heights of pleasure. Outside the window, traditional music mingled with a thumping dance beat, and revelers laughed and called to each other in many languages. He gripped Celia and moved with her, challenging her and flipping them into a third position, where each could guide their sensual dance in turn. Celia cried out as the first shocks of her orgasm crashed through her and drew them both into a realm of shuddering bliss.

"I wonder how long it's been since someone made love here?" she rasped as they lay panting on the sheets.

He couldn't take his eyes off her. Her golden hair sprawled on the embroidered pillow and her skin glowed in the lamplight.

"A thousand years. Maybe more."

Her eyes sparkled. "Then we'd better get cracking. We've got a lot of lost time to make up for."

He wrapped his arm around her waist and leaned in until his lips brushed her ear. "There's no time like the present."

* * * * *

SAVED BY THE SHEIKH!

TESSA RADLEY

Tessa Radley loves travelling, reading and watching the world around her. As a teen Tessa wanted to be an intrepid foreign correspondent. But after completing a bachelor of arts degree and marrying her sweetheart, she became fascinated by law and ended up studying further and practising as an attorney in a city firm.

A six-month break travelling through Australia with her family reawoke the yen to write. And life as a writer suits her perfectly—travelling and reading count as research and, as for analysing the world…well, she can think 'what if?' all day long. When she's not reading, travelling or thinking about writing, she's spending time with her husband, her two sons or her zany and wonderful friends. You can contact Tessa through her website, www.tessaradley.com.

This is for the readers who wrote asking about the fate of Shafir's brothers, Rafiq and Khalid. Rafiq's story is for you. Enjoy!

One

A male hand beckoned through the swirling silvery wisps generated by a smoke machine.

Tiffany Smith squinted and located Renate leaning against the white marble bar flanked by two men. Relief kicked in. The Hong Kong club was crowded—and a lot busier than Tiffany had expected. The harsh, beating music and flashing strobe lights had disoriented her. And the spike of vulnerability she had experienced in the aftermath of having her bag snatched yesterday with her passport, credit card, traveler's checks and cash returned full blast.

Picking up two cocktail menus, Tiffany headed through the mist for the trio. The older man was vaguely familiar. But it was the younger of the two men who watched her approach, his dark eyes cool, assessing—even critical. Tiffany switched her attention to him. He wore a dark formal suit and had a distant manner. Taking in the high cheekbones and bladed nose that gave his face an arrogant cast, she lifted her chin to stare boldly back at him.

"I'm not sure what Rafiq wants but Sir Julian would like a gin and tonic," Renate said, smiling at the older man who must have been at least three inches shorter than she. "And I'll have a champagne cocktail—the Hot Sex version."

Sir Julian. Of course! That would make him Sir Julian Carling, owner of Carling Hotels. If this was the kind of clientele Le Club attracted, tips would be good.

"Sure I can't get you something a little more adventurous?" *Expensive,* Tiffany appended silently as she passed the men the cocktail menus with her sweetest smile.

Not for the first time she thanked her lucky stars for the chance meeting with Renate when she'd checked into the hostel yesterday after her return from the police station and the embassy. Last night's accommodation had used up her last twenty Hong Kong dollars.

This morning Renate had generously shared her breakfast cereal with Tiffany and offered to bring her along to Le Club tonight to make some quick cash as a hostess serving drinks.

It had been Renate who had showed her where the trays of "champagne cocktails" were kept. Lemonade. *Cheap* lemonade. For the hostesses. Geared at getting the well-heeled patrons to order and imbibe more of the elaborate, expensive cocktails with outrageously sexy names for which Le Club was apparently famed—as well as billing them for the hostesses' over-priced lemonade cocktails. Tiffany had silenced her scruples. Renate had done her a favor. Anyway, Sir Julian seemed untroubled at the prospect of footing the bill for Renate's bogus champagne cocktails.

It was none of her business, Tiffany told herself. She

would keep her mouth shut and do as ordered. She was only here for the tips. For that she would smile until her face hurt. She glanced at the younger man, about to give him a glittering grin but his expression deterred her. His eyes were hooded, revealing none of his thoughts. Even in the crush of the club he seemed to create a ring of space around him. A no-go area.

She dismissed the thought as fanciful and forced a smile. "What can I get you to drink?"

"I'll stick with the gin and tonic." Sir Julian gave her a smile and passed back the cocktail menu.

"A Coca-Cola. Cold, please. With ice—if there's any that hasn't melted yet." The man Renate had called Rafiq curved his lips upward, lighting up the harsh features and giving him a devastating charm that had Tiffany catching her breath in surprise.

He was gorgeous.

"Sh-sure, I'll be right back," she stuttered.

"We'll be in one of the back booths," said Renate.

Tiffany found them easily enough a few minutes later. She handed Renate and Sir Julian their drinks before turning to the man seated on the other side of the booth.

Rafiq, Renate had called him. It suited him. Foreign. Exotic. Quintessentially male. Wordlessly Tiffany passed him the soda, and the ice he'd requested rattled against the glass.

"Thank you." He inclined his head.

For one wild moment Tiffany got the impression that she was expected to genuflect.

Renate leaned forward, breaking her train of thought. "Here."

Tiffany took the cell phone Renate offered, and gazed at the other woman in puzzlement. With two hands Renate mimicked taking a photo, and realization dawned. Tiffany studied the phone's settings. Easy enough. By the time Tiffany glanced up, Renate had draped herself over Sir Julian, so Tiffany raised the phone and clicked off a couple of shots.

At the flash, Sir Julian came to life, waving his hands in front of his face. "No photos."

"Sorry." Tiffany colored and fumbled with the phone.

"Are they deleted?" Rafiq's voice was sharp.

"Yes, yes." Tiffany shoved the phone behind the wide leather belt that cinched in her waist, vowing to check that the dratted images were gone the next time she went to get a round of drinks.

"Good girl." Sir Julian gave her an approving smile, and Tiffany breathed a little easier. She wasn't about to get fired before she'd even been paid.

"Sit down, Tiff, next to Rafiq."

The younger man sat opposite—alone—that ring of space clearly demarcated. Pity about the grim reserve, otherwise he would certainly have fitted the tall, dark and handsome label.

"Um…I think I'll go see if anyone else wants a cocktail."

"Sit down, Tiffany." This time Renate's tone brooked no argument.

Tiffany threw a desperate look at the surrounding booths. Several of the hostesses Renate had introduced her to earlier sat talking to patrons, sipping sham champagne cocktails. No one looked like they needed assistance.

Giving in, Tiffany perched herself on the edge of the padded velvet beside Rafiq, and tried to convince herself that it was only the gloom back here in the booths that made him look so…disapproving. He had no reason to be looking down his nose at her.

"They should put brighter lights back here," Tiffany blurted out.

Rafiq raised a dark eyebrow. "Brighter lights? That would defeat the purpose."

Puzzled, Tiffany frowned at him. "What purpose?"

"To talk, of course." Renate's laugh was light and frothy. "No one talks when the lights are bright. It's too much like an interrogation room."

"I would've thought the music was too loud to talk." Tiffany fell silent. Now that she thought about it, it wasn't quite so loud back here.

Rafiq was studying her, and Tiffany moved restlessly under that intense scrutiny. "I'm going to get myself something to drink."

"Have a champagne cocktail—they're great." Renate raised her glass and downed it. "You can bring me another—and Sir Julian needs his gin and tonic topped up."

Rafiq's mouth kicked up at the side, giving him a sardonic, world-weary look.

He knew. Tiffany wasn't sure precisely *what* he knew. That the hostesses' drinks were fake? Or that the patrons would be billed full price for them? But something in his dark visage warned her to tread warily around him.

She edged out of the booth, away from those all-seeing eyes.

It was ten minutes before Tiffany could steel herself to return with a tray of drinks.

"What took so long?" Renate glanced up from where she was snuggled up against Sir Julian. "Jules is parched."

Jules?

Tiffany did a double take. In the time that she'd been gone Sir Julian Carling had become Jules? And Renate had become positively kittenish, curled up against the hotelier, all but purring. Tiffany slid back into the booth beside Rafiq and thanked the heavens for that wall of ice that surrounded him. No one would get close enough to cuddle this man.

"That surely can't be a champagne cocktail?" Rafiq commented.

She slid him a startled glance. Was he calling her on Le Club's shady ploy to overcharge patrons?

"It's water."

That expressive eyebrow lifted again. "So where's the Perrier bottle?"

"Water out of the tap." Although on second thought, perhaps it might've been more sensible to drink bottled water. "I'm thirsty."

"So you chose tap water?"

Was that disbelief in his voice? Tiffany swallowed, suddenly certain that this man was acutely aware of everything that happened around him.

"Why not champagne?"

She could hardly confess that she was reluctant to engage in the establishment's scam, so she replied evasively, "I don't drink champagne."

"You don't?" Rafiq sounded incredulous.

"I've never acquired the taste."

More accurately she'd lost the taste for the drink that her mother and father offered by the gallon in their society home. The headache it left her with came from the tension that invariably followed her parents' parties rather than the beverage itself.

An inexplicable wave of loneliness swamped her.

Those parties were a thing of the past....

Yesterday she'd tamped down the fury that had engulfed her after speaking to her mother, and called her father. To have him wire her some money—even though the thought of asking him for anything stuck in her throat—and to give him a roasting for what she'd learned from her mother.

This time he'd broken her mother's heart. He'd been tearing strips off that mutilated organ for years, but taking off with Imogen was different from the brief affairs. Imogen was no starlet with her eye on a bit part in a Taylor Smith film; Imogen had been her father's business manager for years.

Tiffany *liked* Imogen. She *trusted* Imogen. By running off with Imogen, her father had sunk to a new low in her estimation.

But Taylor Smith could not be found. No one knew where he—and Imogen—had gone. Holed up in a resort someplace, enjoying a faux honeymoon, no doubt. Tiffany had given up trying to reach her father.

"What else don't you like?" Rafiq's voice broke into her unpleasant thoughts. For the first time he was starting to look approachable—even amused.

What would he say if she responded that she didn't like arrogant men who thought they were God's gift to womankind?

The diamond-cutter gaze warned her against the reckless urge to put him down. Instead she gave him a fake smile and said in dulcet tones, "There's not much I don't like."

"I should have guessed." His mouth flattened, and without moving away, he managed to give the impression that he'd retreated onto another planet.

Had there been a subtle jibe in there somewhere that she'd missed? Tiffany took a sip of water and thought about what he might've construed from her careless words. *Not much that I don't like.* Perhaps she'd imagined the edge in his voice.

Across the booth Renate whispered something to Sir Julian, who laughed and pulled her onto his lap.

Conscious of the flush of embarrassment creeping over her cheeks, Tiffany slid a glance at Rafiq. He, too, was watching the antics of the other couple, his face tight.

What in heaven's name was Renate up to?

The rising heat resulting from the crush of bodies in Le Club and the sight of Renate wriggling all over Sir Julian compounded to make Tiffany feel…uncomfortable… unclean.

She downed the rest of the water. "I need the bathroom," she said in desperation.

In the relative safety of the bathroom, Tiffany opened the cold water tap. Cupping her hands, she allowed the cool water to pool between her palms. She bent her head and splashed her face. The door hissed open behind her.

"Don't." Renate's hand caught at hers. "You'll ruin your makeup."

"I'm hot." And starting to fear that she was way out of her depth.

"Now we'll have to do your face again." Renate sounded exasperated.

Tiffany held her hands up to ward Renate off. She didn't want another thick layer of foundation caked onto her skin. "It was too hot. My face doesn't matter. I'm not here to find a date," she said pointedly.

"But you need cash," Renate responded, her makeup bag already open on the vanity counter. "Jules says that Rafiq is a business acquaintance—he must have a fat wallet if he's associated with Jules."

"Fat wallet? You mean I should steal from him?"

Disbelief spiked in Tiffany. She turned to look at her newfound friend. Was Renate crazy? Tiffany was certain that Rafiq's retribution would be swift and relentless. She was feeling less and less comfortable about Renate's idea of easy money. "I could never do that."

Renate rolled her eyes. "Don't be dumb. I don't rip them off. You don't want to get arrested for theft. Especially not here."

"Certainly not here—or anywhere," Tiffany said with heartfelt fervor. As desperate as she was, the idea of a Hong Kong jail terrified her witless. "Yesterday's visit to the police station was more than enough."

She'd had her fill of bureaucracy after spending the entire day yesterday and most of today reporting the loss of her purse to the police, followed by hours queuing at the embassy, trying to secure a temporary passport... and a living allowance for the weekend. All hope of cash assistance from the embassy had been quashed once the official had realized who her father was. A father who was nowhere to be found.

On Monday a shiny new credit card would be couriered to her by her bank back home. And her temporary travel documents would be ready, too. For the first time since leaving home, Tiffany almost wished she had access to the allowance her father had cut off when she had chosen to do this trip with a friend against his wishes. What had started out as an exciting adventure was turning into a nightmare, costing much more than she'd ever dreamed.

But buying an air ticket home was Monday's worry. For now she only had to make it through the next two days.

Thank goodness for Renate.

Despite her sexual acrobatics in the booth, the other woman had saved Tiffany's skin by offering her this chance to earn some cash tonight. She owed her. "Renate, are you sure flirting with Sir Julian is a good idea? He's old enough to be your father."

"But he's rich."

Renate was fiddling in her purse, and Tiffany couldn't read her expression.

"That's what you want? A rich man? You think he'll marry you?" Concern made her say, "Oh, Renate, he's probably already married."

Renate drew out a lipstick tube and applied the glossy dark plum color then stood back to admire the dramatic effect against her pale skin and bleached-blond hair. "Of course he is."

"He is?" Shocked by Renate's nonchalance, Tiffany stared. "So why are you wasting your time on him?"

"He's a multimillionaire. Maybe even a billionaire. I recognized him the instant he arrived—he's been here before, but I've never gotten to—" Renate broke off and shot Tiffany a sidelong glance "—I never got to meet him. He's already promised to take me with him to the races later in the week."

Tiffany thought of the aching hurt she'd detected in her mother's voice yesterday when her mom had blurted out that Dad had taken off with Imogen.

"But what about his wife, Renate? How do you think she'll feel?"

Renate shrugged a careless shoulder. "She's probably too busy socializing with her country-club friends to notice. Tennis. Champagne breakfasts. Fancy fundraisers. Why should she care?"

Tiffany was prepared to stake her life on it that Sir Julian's wife did care. Speechlessly, she stared at Renate.

"The last girl he met here got a trip to Phuket and a wardrobe of designer dresses. I'd love that." She met Tiffany's appalled gaze in the mirror. "Don't knock it—maybe Rafiq is a millionaire, too. He might be worth cultivating."

Cultivating? An image of Rafiq's disdainful expression flashed before Tiffany's vision. He was so not her type. Too remote. Too arrogant. And way too full of his own importance. She didn't need a gazillionaire, much less one who had a wife tucked back in a desert somewhere.

All she wanted was someone normal. Ordinary. A man with whom she could be herself—no facades, no pretence. Just Tiffany. Someone who would learn to love her without drama and histrionics. Someone with a family that was real...not dysfunctional.

"Tiff, you need money." Renate flashed a sly look over her shoulder as she turned away to a soap dispenser set against the tiled wall. "What could be wrong with getting to know Rafiq a little better?"

Getting to know Rafiq a little better? Could Renate possibly mean that in the sense it had come across? Surely not.

"Here." Renate pressed something into her palm.

Tiffany glanced down—and despite the cloying heat, she turned cold. "What in heaven's name do I need a condom for?"

But she knew, even as Renate flipped back her short blond hair and laughed. "Tiffany, Tiffany. You can't be that innocent. Look at you. Big velvety eyes, peachy skin, long legs. You're gorgeous. And I'll bet Rafiq is very, very aware of it."

"I couldn't—"

Renate took both her hands, and brought her face up against Tiffany's. "Honey, listen to me. The quickest way to make some cash is to be as nice to Rafiq as he wants. You'll be well rewarded. He's a man—a rich one judging by that handmade thousand-dollar suit. He came here, to Le Club, tonight. He knows the score."

Horror surged through Tiffany. "What are you saying?"

"The men who come to Le Club are looking for a companion for the night. The whole night."

"Oh, God, no." She wrenched her hands free from Renate's hold and covered her face. The clues had been there lurking under what she'd seen as Renate's friendliness. *You can borrow my minidress, Tiff, it does great things for your legs. Your mouth is so sexy, a red lipstick will bring out the pout. Be nice, Tiff—you'll get more tips.* How had she missed them?

Stupid!

She'd been so grateful for what she'd seen as Renate's friendship…her help.…

Tiffany dropped her hands away from her face.

Renate's features softened a trifle. "Tiff, the first time is the worst. It'll be easier next time."

"Next time?" She felt absolutely and utterly chilled. And infinitely wiser than she had been even an hour ago. Renate was no well-meaning friend; she'd misled Tiffany. Purposefully. A sense of betrayal spread through her.

"There won't be a next time." Tiffany had no intention of ever setting a foot back in this place.

Renate picked Tiffany's tiny beaded purse off the vanity slab and slid the condom inside. "Don't be so sure."

Tiffany snatched her purse up and looped the strap around her wrist. "I'm leaving."

"First shift ends at ten," Renate pointed out. "If you leave before that, you won't get paid for the hours you've worked. Work another shift and you'll earn even more."

Tiffany glanced at her watch. Nine-thirty. She had to last another thirty minutes. She needed that cash to pay for her bed at the hostel. But another shift was more than she could manage. She met Renate's gaze. "I'll wait it out."

"Think about what I said. It's no big deal after the first time—I promise." For a moment something suspiciously akin to vulnerability glimmered in Renate's eyes. "Everyone does it—there's a lot of demand for young foreign female tourists." Renate shrugged one shoulder. "Rafiq is good-looking. It won't be too bad. Would you rather be broke and desperate?"

"Yes!" Tiffany shivered. Rafiq's disdain suddenly made sense. He thought—

Her hand froze on the door handle.

God. Surely he didn't intend… No, he hadn't even exhibited any interest in her. She'd only served him a drink—there'd been no hint of anything more. "At least Rafiq isn't expecting to sleep with me."

"Of course he is." The look Renate gave her was full of superiority. "Although sleeping will have little to do with it—and he will undoubtedly pay well."

The chill that had been spreading through Tiffany froze into a solid block of ice. It took effort to release the door handle she was clutching. "I'd rather starve!"

"You won't starve—not if you do what he wants."

"No!" Tiffany clenched her fists, a steely determination filling her. "And I won't starve, either." She'd foolishly trusted Renate. But she intended to make the best of the situation. "I'm only a waitress tonight—and he still owes me a tip."

Right now that tip meant tomorrow's food, and when she walked out of there at ten o'clock with her shift money, it would be with a generous tip, too.

Rafiq found himself blocking out Julian Carling's overloud voice as he focused on the archway to the right side of the bar where Tiffany and Renate had reappeared.

Tiffany wasn't the kind of woman Rafiq would ever

have expected to meet at a place like Le Club. Her face had a deceptive freshness…an innocence…at odds with the scarlet lipstick and the frilly, short black dress. He snorted in derision. It only went to show the ingenue act was exactly that—an act.

Yet as she neared the booth, Rafiq could've have sworn he saw her gulp.

She handed him a tall iced soda and stared at him with wary eyes.

"Thank you." Rafiq's body grew tight. He wasn't accustomed to evoking that kind of look on a woman's face. Usually there was admiration, a yearning for the worldly goods he could bestow. And a healthy dose of desire, too.

But Tiffany wore none of the too-familiar expressions.

Instead her pupils had dilated and transformed her eyes to dark holes in a face where her skin had lost its lotus-petal luminescence.

Apprehension. That's what it was. A touch of fear. As though someone had told her he trafficked in human beings—or worse.

He switched his narrowed gaze to Renate. Had *she* told Tiffany something to result in that pinched expression?

While the statuesque blonde had instantly identified Sir Julian, who was something of a celebrity in Hong Kong, much to Rafiq's relief she had not recognized him. Rafiq had wryly concluded that royal sheikhs didn't have the same cachet as hoteliers. In fact, he'd been ready to call it a night as soon as he'd realized what kind of a place Le Club was. One celebratory drink with Julian out of politeness to seal the first stages of the proposal they'd put together for a hotel in his home country of Dhahara, and he'd intended to leave.

Then Tiffany had chosen water over fake champagne cocktails and he'd been intrigued enough to want to find out what kind of game she was playing.

Flicking his gaze back to her, he took in the stiff way she held herself. Only the tilt of her chin showed something of the woman he'd glimpsed before, the woman who had demanded more light in this tacky made-for-seduction booth.

Rafiq intended to find out what had disturbed her. Shifting a little farther into the booth to give her space to sit, he patted the seat beside him. She ignored the velvet upholstered expanse, and fixed him with the same dazed stare of a rabbit confronted by a hunting hawk.

His frown deepened.

She swallowed, visibly uneasy.

"Sit down," he growled. "Contrary to popular opinion, I don't bite."

Her gaze skated away from his—and she blanched. He turned his head to see what had caused such an extreme reaction.

Renate was stroking a finger over Julian's fleshy lips and the hotelier was nibbling lasciviously at the pad of her thumb. Even as they watched, Sir Julian took it into his mouth and sucked it suggestively.

Rafiq compressed his lips into a tight line. Only yesterday he'd been invited to Sir Julian's home for dinner. The hotel magnate had proudly introduced his wife of almost three decades as the love of his life…and produced a daughter with whom he'd tried to match Rafiq.

"Nor do I devour thumbs," he murmured to Tiffany. To his surprise, relief lightened her eyes. Surely a sucked thumb was tame for a place like Le Club?

For the first time he saw that her eyes were brown with gold streaks. Until now it had been her hair and peachy skin that had snagged his attention. Not that he'd been looking—he wasn't interested in a woman who earned her living the way Tiffany did.

Abruptly, he asked, "Why do you choose to work here?"

"Tonight is my first time. Renate brought me—she said it was a good place to make cash."

He withdrew imperceptibly at her confession. She'd come prepared to barter her body for cash? "You want money so desperately?" When she failed to respond, disappointment filtered through him like hot desert sand winnowing through his fingers, until nothing remained save emptiness. "You should leave," he said.

A flush crept along her cheekbones. She looked down at the table and started to draw patterns on the white linen tablecloth with her index finger.

Rafiq looked away.

Across from them Julian's hand had weaseled its way under the neckline of Renate's dress, and Rafiq could see the ridges under the stretchy electric blue fabric where the other man's fingers groped at her rounded breasts. Renate giggled.

This was what Tiffany was contemplating?

"Will it be worth it?" he asked her.

She didn't answer.

He glanced down at her. Her attention was riveted on the couple on the other side of the table. She looked distinctly queasy.

"You'd let a man paw you for money?" He sounded harsher than he'd intended. "In front of a roomful of strangers?"

"I think I need the bathroom again."

She looked as if she were about to throw up as she bolted from the booth. Good. His deliberate crudity had shaken her. She'd said tonight was her first night. Maybe he could still talk sense into her. Perhaps there was still a chance to lure her away from such a recklessly destructive course of action.

His mouth tight with distaste, Rafiq threw a hundred-dollar note down on the table and rose to his feet to follow her.

Two

Rafiq was leaning against the wall when Tiffany emerged from the bathroom, his body lean and supple in the dark, well-fitting suit. He straightened and came toward her like a panther, sleek and sinuous.

Tiffany fervently hoped she wasn't the prey he intended hunting. There were dark qualities to this man that she had no wish to explore further.

"I'm going to call you a cab."

"Now?" Panic jostled her. "I can't leave. My shift isn't over yet."

"I'll tell whoever is in charge around here that you're leaving with me. No one will argue."

She assessed him. The hard eyes, the hawk-like features, the lean, whipcord strength. The way he had of appearing to own all the space around him. Yes, he was right. No one would argue with him.

Except her. "I'm not going anywhere with you."

Something flared in those unfathomable eyes. "I wasn't intending to take you anywhere…only to call for a cab."

"I can't afford one," she said bluntly.

"I'll pay for your damned cab."

Tiffany started to protest, and then hesitated. Why shouldn't he pay for her fare? He'd never coughed up the service tip she needed. Though the disquieting discussion with Renate had made it clear that tips in this place required more service than just a little company over drinks. Renate was clearly going to end up in Sir Julian's bed tonight. For what? A visit to the races tomorrow…and a wad of cash?

Tiffany had no intention of following suit. She'd rather have her self-respect.

Yet she couldn't afford to be too proud. She needed every cent she could lay her hands on. For food and accommodation until Monday. If Rafiq gave her the fare for a cab, she could sneak out the back while he was organizing it and hurry to her lodgings on foot. It wouldn't be dishonest, she assured herself. She'd earned the tip he'd never paid.

"Thanks." The word almost choked her.

He was suddenly—unexpectedly—close. Too close. Tiffany edged away and suppressed the impulse to tell him to stick his money. Reality set in. The cab fare, together with the miserly rate for tonight's work, which she'd be able to collect in less than ten minutes, meant she'd be able to pay for her accommodation and buy food for the weekend.

Relief swept through her.

All her problems would be solved.

Until Monday…

Over the weekend, she'd keep trying her father. Surely he'd check his e-mail, his phone messages, sooner or later? Of course, it would mean listening to him tell her he'd been right from the outset, that she wasn't taking care of herself in the big, bad world. But at least he'd advance her the money to rebook her flights and she'd be able to get back to help her mom.

"I'd appreciate it," she said, suddenly subdued. Tiffany halted, waiting for him produce his wallet.

"Let's go."

His hand came down on the small of her back and the contact electrified her. It was the humidity in the club, not his touch that had caused the flash of heat, she told herself as she tried to marshal her suddenly chaotic thoughts.

Her money.

"Wait—"

Before she could finish objecting he'd propelled her past the bar, through the spectacular mirrored lobby and out into the oppressive heat of the night. Of course there was a cab waiting. For a men like Rafiq there always were.

"Hang on—"

Ignoring her, Rafiq opened the door and ushered her in and all of the sudden he was overwhelming in the confined space.

"Where to?" he asked.

He'd never intended to hand her cash. And she hadn't had the opportunity to collect her earnings, either.

"I didn't get my money," she wailed. Then it struck her that he shouldn't be sitting next to her with his thigh pressed against hers. "You said you weren't coming with me."

"I changed my mind."

His smile didn't reach his midnight-dark eyes. Then he closed the door, dousing the interior light. Tiffany didn't know whether to be relieved or disturbed by the sudden cloak of darkness. So she scooted across the seat, out of his reach, trying to ignore his sheer, overwhelming physical presence by focusing on everything she'd been cheated of. Food. Lodgings. Survival.

She could *survive* without food until Monday. It wouldn't kill her. When she went back to the embassy she wouldn't let pride stop her begging for a handout for a meal. But she needed a roof over her head.

"I'm not going to be able to get that money back." She hadn't worked out her shift. "I doubt they'll take me back tomorrow now." There were strict rules about telling the management when you were leaving—and with whom. Tiffany had thought it was for the hostess's protection.

"You don't want to work there—find somewhere else." Rafiq murmured something to the cabdriver and the vehicle started to move.

Tiffany didn't bother to explain that she didn't have a visa to work in Hong Kong, that she'd only turned up at Le Club for the night as a casual waitress. Worry tugged at her stomach. "I *need* the money for those hours I spent there tonight."

"A pittance," he said dismissively.

Anger splintered through her. "It might be a pittance to you but it's *my* pittance. I worked for that money."

"And for what do you so desperately need cash? An overloaded credit card after frequenting the boutique stores at Harbor City's Ocean Terminal?"

His drawling cynicism made her want to smack him. Instead she tried to ignore him and huddled down into the corner as far away from him as she could get in the backseat. He was *so* overbearing. So certain that he was right about everything. Assuming she was a shopaholic airhead. Making decisions for her about where she should work, about when she should go home.

God help any woman silly enough to marry him—he'd

be a dictator. Maybe he was already married. The thought caused a bolt of shock.

What did she care whether he was married?

That fierce, dark gaze clashed with hers. "I'm waiting."

Trying frantically to regroup, she said, "For what?"

"For you to tell me why you're so desperate for money."

Tiffany cringed at the idea of telling him. "It makes me sound stupid."

He arched an eyebrow. "More stupid than working at Le Club?"

She supposed he was right. So she hauled in a deep breath and said reluctantly, "I was mugged yesterday morning. My passport was stolen *and* my credit cards *and* my cash."

It was mortifying. How many times had she been told to keep one card and a copy of her itinerary and travel insurance separate from the rest? How she wished she had. It would have saved a lot of grief. And a host of I-told-you-you-wouldn't-survive-alones from her father, when she finally managed to locate him.

"All that I had left was twenty Hong Kong dollars that I had in my pocket and I used that for last night's accommodation."

"How convenient."

The mocking note in his voice made it clear Mr. Arrogant Know-all thought she was lying.

"You don't believe me."

The seat gave as he shrugged. "It's hardly an original story. Although I prefer it to a fabricated tale about an ailing grandfather or a brother with leukemia."

He thought she was angling for sympathy. She stared

across the backseat in disbelief. "Good grief, but you're cynical. I hope I never become like you."

In the flash of passing lights she glimpsed a flare of emotion in his eyes. Then it vanished as darkness closed around them again. "And I hope, for your sake, that you are not as naive as you pretend to be."

"I'm not naive," Tiffany said, annoyed by the nerve he'd unwittingly struck. He sounded exactly like her father.

"Then come up with a better story."

"It's true. Do you think I'd voluntarily make myself look like such an airhead?"

"The helpless, stranded tourist might work on some."

She glared at him under the cover of night.

His voice dropped to a rasp. "Perhaps I'm the fool. I find myself actually considering this silly tale—against my better judgment."

"Well, thanks." Her tone dripped affront.

Unexpectedly he laughed aloud. "My pleasure."

The sound was warm and full of joy. The cab pulled up at a well-lit intersection and the handsome features were flooded with light. Tiffany caught her breath at the sudden, startling charm that warmed his face, and somewhere deep in the pit of her stomach liquid heat melted. For a heady fragment of time she almost allowed herself smile, too, and laugh at the ridiculousness of her plight.

Then she came to her senses.

"It's not funny," she said with more than a hint of rebellion.

Rafiq moved his weight on the seat beside her. "No, I don't suppose it would be—if your story were true."

Rafiq's brooding gaze settled on the woman bundled up against the door. If she moved any farther away from him, she'd be in serious danger of falling out. Was she telling the truth? Or was it all an elaborate charade?

The lights changed and the vehicle pulled away from the intersection. "Don't you have anyone you can borrow money from?"

She turned her head and looked out into the night. "No."

Frowning now, Rafiq stared at the dark shape of her head and pale curve of her cheek that was all he could see from this perspective, highlighted every few seconds by flashes from passing neon signs.

"What about your friend Renate? Can't she help you out?"

She gave a strangled laugh. "Hardly a friend. I only met her today. She lodges at the hostel I'm staying at."

Aah. He started to see the light. "There's no one else?"

She shook her head. "Not someone I can ask for money."

Rafiq waited for a heartbeat. For two. Then three. But the expected plea never came.

"You're traveling by yourself." It was a statement. And it explained so much, Rafiq decided, the reluctant urge to believe her growing stronger by the minute.

Tiffany shifted, and he sensed her uneasy glance before she turned back to the window.

She'd be a fool to tell him if she was. Or perhaps this was part of an act designed to make him feel more sympathy for a young woman all alone and out of her depth.

Had he been hustled by an expert? To Rafiq's disquiet he wasn't certain. And he was not accustomed to being rendered uncertain, off-balance. Particularly not by a woman. A young, attractive woman.

He was far from being an impressionable youth.

Three times he'd been in love. Three times he'd been on the brink of proposing marriage. And each time, much to his father's fury, he'd pulled away. At the last moment Rafiq had discovered that the desire, the sparkle, had burnt out under the weight of family expectation.

Rafiq himself didn't understand how something that started with so much hope and promise could fizzle out so disappointingly as soon as his father started to talk marriage settlements.

"So how much money do you need?" He directed the question to the sliver of sculpted cheek that was all he could see of her face.

This should establish whether he was being hustled.

A modest request for only a few dollars to cover necessities and shelter until she could arrange for her bank to put her back in funds would make it easier to swallow her tale.

"Enough to cover my bed and food until Monday."

Rafiq released the breath that he hadn't even been aware of holding.

As head of the Royal Bank of Dhahara he was familiar with all kinds of fraud, from the simplest ploys that emptied the pockets of soft-hearted elders to complex Internet frauds. Tiffany would not be seeing him again, so this was her only opportunity to try stripping him of a substantial amount of money and she had not taken it. She was in genuine need. All she wanted—and she hadn't even directly asked him for it yet—was a small amount of cash to tide her over.

This was not a scam.

The first whisper of real concern for the situation in which she found herself sounded inside his head. He had a cousin who was as close to him as a sister. He'd hate for Zara to be in the position that Tiffany was in, with no one to turn to for help. Rafiq knew he would make sure Tiffany would be looked after. "Tell me more."

"Except…" Her voice trailed away.

Every muscle in his body contracted as he tensed, praying that his instincts had not played him false.

"Except…*what?*" he prompted.

She averted her face. Even in the dark, he caught the movement as her pale fingers fiddled with the hem of the short, flirty dress. "I'm not sure that I'm going to have enough available on my credit card to pay for the changes to my flight."

"How much?"

Here it was. Rafiq forced his gaze up from the distraction of those fingers. She'd just hit him with the big sum—a drop in the ocean to him if she'd but known it—and he couldn't even see her face to read her eyes as his hopes that she was the real deal faded into oblivion. The tidal wave of anger that shook him was unexpected.

It shouldn't have mattered that she was a beautiful little schemer.

But it did.

Rafiq told himself it was because he wasn't often wrong about people, that he'd considered himself too wily to be taken in by a pretty face. *That* was why he was angry.…

Because of his own foolishness.

Not because he'd hoped against all odds—

She turned her head toward him, and her gaze connected with his in the murky darkness of the backseat. He almost convinced himself that he sensed real desperation in her glistening eyes.

Anger overpowered him. Damn her. She was good. So good, she belonged in Hollywood.

How nearly had she hooked him with her air of innocence and lonely despair?

And so much smarter than Renate. He would never have fallen for the platinum blonde's sexual promise of a one-night stand…but this woman… By Allah, he'd nearly bought everything she'd sold him. With her wide waif's eyes, her hesitant smile…she'd suckered him. Like Scheherazade, she was a consummate teller of tales.

Rage licked at his gut like hot flames. He was wise to her now.

He would not be deceived again.

No one made a fool of him. *No one.* And he hadn't fallen into her trap—he'd been fortunate enough to realize the truth before it was too late. No, not fortunate, he admitted, shamed. He'd almost been duped. A slip of a female had drawn him so close to the claws of her honeyed trap, and proven that he was not as wise as he liked to believe. He could still be taken in by a pair of heavily lashed eyes.

Tiffany had been a little too confident. The mistake she'd made had lain in her eagerness to reel him in too quickly.

"Where are we?"

The cab had slowed. Rafiq glanced away from her profile to the imposing marble facade lit up by pale gold light. "At my hotel."

"I never agreed to come here." Her voice was breathy, suddenly hesitant. Earlier he might have considered it uncertainty—even apprehension; now he knew it was nothing more than pretence.

"You never gave me any address when I asked." He opened his door and hid his anger behind a slow smile as he consciously summoned every reserve of charm he possessed. "Come, you will tell me your problems and I will buy you a drink, and perhaps I can find a way to help you."

This was the final test.

If she'd been telling him the truth, she would refuse. But if she was only after the money, she would interpret that smile as weakness, and she would accept.

Rafiq couldn't figure why it was so important to give her a last chance when she'd already revealed her true colors.

She hesitated for a fleeting moment and gave him a tremulous smile designed to melt the hardest heart. Just as he was about to surrender his cynicism, she followed him out of the cab.

The taste inside his mouth was decidedly bitter as she joined him on the sidewalk. Rafiq hadn't realized that he'd still had any illusions left to lose.

Inside the hotel, he headed for the bank of elevators. "There's an open pool deck upstairs that offers views over the city," he said over his shoulder as she hesitated.

Once in the elevator, Rafiq activated it with the key card to his presidential suite.

He brooded while he watched the floors light up as the car shot upward. A sweetly seductive fragrance surrounded him—a mix of fresh green notes and heady gardenia—and to his disgust his body stirred.

Rafiq told himself he wasn't going to take her up on what she was so clearly here for—he only wanted to see how far she was prepared to go.

Yet the urge to teach Tiffany a lesson she would never forget pressed down on him even as the sweet, intoxicating scent of her filled his nostrils. When the elevator finally came to rest, he placed his hand on the small of her back and gently ushered her out.

Balmy night air embraced Tiffany as she stepped through frosted-glass sliding doors into the intimate darkness of the hotel's deserted pool deck.

Overhead the moon hung in the sky, a perfectly shaped crescent, while far below the harbor gleamed like black satin beyond lights that sparkled like sprinklings of fairy dust.

Tiffany made for a group of chairs beside a surprisingly small pool, a row of lamps reflecting off the smooth surface like half a dozen full moons. She sank into a luxuriously padded armchair, nerve-rackingly conscious of the man who stood with his back to her, hands on hips, staring over the city...thinking God knew what. Because he was back in that remote space that he allowed no one else to inhabit.

When he wheeled about and shrugged off his suit jacket, her pulse leaped uncontrollably. He dropped into the chair beside her, and suddenly the air became thick and cloying.

"What would you like to drink?" he asked as a waiter appeared, as if that slice of time when he'd become so inaccessible had never been.

Tiffany rather fancied she needed a clear head. But she also had no intention of showing him how much he intimidated her. Her chin inched higher. "Vodka with lots of ice and orange." She'd sip it. Make it last.

Casting a somewhat mocking smile at her, Rafiq ordered Perrier for himself. And Tiffany wished she'd thought of that herself.

By some magic, the waiter was back in seconds with the drinks, and then Rafiq dismissed him.

She shivered as the sudden silence, the silken heat of the night and the sheer imposing presence of the man beside her all closed in on her senses. They were alone. How had this happened? He'd offered to buy her a drink...to lend a sympathetic ear. She'd imagined a busy bar and a little kindness.

Not this.

He turned his head. The trickle of awareness grew to a torrent as she fell into the enigmatic depths of his dark eyes.

Tiffany let out a deep breath that she'd been unaware of holding, and told herself that Rafiq was only a man. *A man.* Her father was a well-known film director. She'd met some of the most sought-after men in the world; men who graced covers of glitzy magazines and were featured on lists of women's most secret fantasy lovers. So why on earth was this one intimidating her?

The only explanation that made any sense was that losing her passport, her money, had stripped away the comfort of her identity and put her at a disadvantage. No longer her parents' pampered princess, she was struggling to survive…and the unexpected reversal had disoriented her.

Of course, it wasn't *him*. It had nothing to do with him. Or with the tantalizing air of reserve that invited her to crash through it.

This was about *her*.

About her confusion. It was easy to see how he had become appealing, an unexpected pillar of strength in a world gone crazy.

The rationality of the conclusion comforted her and allowed her to smile up at him with hastily mustered composure, to say in a carefully modulated tone, "I'm sorry, I've been so tied up in talking about me. What brings you to Hong Kong?"

His reply was terse. "Business."

"With Sir Julian?"

A slight nod was the only response she got. And a renewed blast of that do-not-intrude-any-further reserve that he was so good at displaying. He might as well have worn a great, big sign with ten-foot-high red letters that read Danger: Keep Out.

"Hotel business?"

"Why do you think that?"

Tiffany took a sip of her drink. It was deliciously sweet and cool. "Because he's famous for his hotels—are you trying to develop a resort?"

"Do I look like a developer?"

She took in the angled cheekbones starkly highlighted by the lamplight; his white shirt with dark stripes that stood out in the darkness; his fingers clenching the glass that he held. Even though he should've appeared relaxed sitting there, he hummed with tension.

"I'm not sure what a developer is supposed to look like. People are individuals. Not one size fits all."

He inspected her silently until she shifted. "What do you do, Tiffany? What are you doing in Hong Kong?"

"Uh…" She had no intention of confessing that she didn't do very much at all. She'd completed a degree in English literature and French…and found she still wasn't sure what she wanted to do with her life. Nor did she have any intention of telling him about her abortive trip with her school friend, Sally. About how Sally had hooked up with a guy and how Tiffany had felt like a third wheel in their developing romance. She'd already revealed far too much; she certainly didn't want Rafiq to know how naive she'd been. So she smiled brightly at him, took a sip of her drink and said casually, "Just traveling here and there."

"Your family approve of this carefree existence?"

She prickled. "My family knows that I can look after myself."

That was debatable. Tiffany doubted her father would ever believe she was capable of taking care of herself. Yet she also knew she had to tread carefully. She didn't want Rafiq to know quite how isolated she was right now.

"I've been keeping in close touch with them."

"By cell phone."

It was a statement. She didn't deny it, didn't tell him that her cell phone had been in the stolen purse. Or that she didn't even know where her father was right now. Or about her mother's emotional devastation. Far safer to let him believe that she was only a text away from communicating with her family.

"Why don't they send you money for the fare that you need?"

"They can't afford to."

It was true. Sort of. Tiffany thought about her mother's tears when she'd called her yesterday to arrange exactly that. Linda Smith née Canning had been a B-grade actress before her marriage to Taylor Smith; she hadn't worked for nearly two decades. The terms of her prenuptial agreement settled a house in Auckland on her, a far from liquid asset. It would take time to sell, and Mom needed her father's consent to borrow against it. In the meantime there were groceries to buy, staff to pay, bills for the hired house in L.A....and, according to her mother, not much money in the joint account. Add a husband who'd made sure he couldn't be found, and Linda's panic and distress had been palpable.

So, no, her mom was not in a position to help right now. She needed a lawyer—and Tiffany intended to arrange the best lawyer she could find as soon as she got back home. The more expensive, the better, she vowed darkly. Her father would pay those bills in due course.

But Rafiq wouldn't be interested in any of that.

"How did we get back to talking about me?" she asked. "I'm not terribly interesting."

"That's a matter of opinion." His voice was smoother than velvet.

Tiffany leaned a little closer and caught the glimmer of starlight in his dark eyes. A frisson of half fear, half anticipation feathered down her spine. She drew sharply back.

She must be mad....

Sucking in a breath, she blurted out, "Sir Julian was born in New Zealand. He owns a historic home in Auckland that often appears in lifestyle magazines." The change of subject seemed sudden, but at least it got them back onto neutral territory. "His father was English."

Unexpectedly, Rafiq didn't take the bait to find out more about his business acquaintance. "So you're from New Zealand? I couldn't place your accent."

"Because of my father's job, some of my schooling took place in the States, so that would make it even harder to identify." Her parents had relocated her from an Auckland all-girl school while they'd tried to juggle family life with her father's filming schedule. It had been awkward. Eventually, Tiffany and her mother had returned to live in Auckland. But her mother had frequently flown to Los Angeles to act as hostess for the lavish parties he threw at the opulent Malibu mansion he'd rented—and to keep an eye on her father. Tiffany had been seventeen the first time she'd read about her father's affairs in a gossip magazine. Like the final piece in a puzzle, it had completed a picture she hadn't even known was missing an essential part.

"Your father was in the military?"

She didn't want to talk about Taylor Smith. "No—but he traveled a lot."

"Ah, like a salesman or something?"

"Something like that." She took another sip of her drink

and set it down on a round glass-topped table. "What about you? Where do you live?"

He considered her. "I'm from Dhahara—it's a desert kingdom, near Oman."

"How fascinating!"

"Ah, you find me fascinating...."

Tiffany stared at him.

Then she detected the wry mockery glinting in his eyes. "Not you!" She gave a gurgle of laughter and relaxed a little. "Where you live fascinates me."

"Now you break my heart."

"Are you flirting with me?" she asked suspiciously.

"If you must ask, then I must be losing my touch." He stretched out his long legs and loosened his tie.

The gesture brought her attention to his hands. In the reflected glow of the lamplight his fingers were lean and square-tipped, and dark against the white of his shirt. The gold of a signet ring winked in the light. His hand had stilled. Under his fingertips his heart would be beating like—

"You might not think I'm fascinating but most women think I'm charming," he murmured, his eyes half-closed, his mood indecipherable.

She reared back. Did he know what was happening to her? Why her pulse had gone crazy? "You? Charming?"

"Absolutely."

Tiffany swallowed. "Most women must be mad."

A glint entered his eyes. "You think so?"

Danger! Danger! She recklessly ignored the warning, too caught up in the surge of adrenalin that provoking him brought. "I know so."

"You don't believe I could be charming?" He smiled, his teeth startlingly white in the darkening night, and a bolt of metallic heat shot through Tiffany's belly.

"Never!" she said fiercely.

"Well then, I'll have to convince you otherwise."

He bent his head. Slowly, oh, far too slowly. Her heart started to pound. There was plenty of time for her to duck away, to smack his face as she'd earlier in the cab told herself he richly deserved. But she didn't. Instead she waited, holding her breath, watching his mouth—why hadn't she noticed how beautiful it was?—come closer and closer, until it finally settled on hers.

And then she sighed.

A soft whisper of sound.

He kissed with mastery. His lips pressed against hers, moving along the seam, playing…tantalizing, never demanding more than she was prepared to give. No other part of him touched her. After an age Tiffany let her lips part. He didn't take advantage. Instead he continued to taste her with playful kisses until she groaned in frustration.

He needed no further invitation. He plundered her mouth, hungrily seeking out secrets she hadn't known existed. Passion seized her. Quickly followed by a rush of hunger. His hand came up and cupped the back of her neck. The heat of his touch sent quivers along undiscovered nerve endings.

Tiffany swayed, eyes closed beneath the sensory onslaught.

At last, an eternity later, he lifted his head and gazed down at her with hooded eyes.

"So," he said with some satisfaction, his fingertips rubbing in soft circles against the sensitized nape of her neck, "you will agree that most women are right. You are charmed."

Tiffany reeled under the deluge of what could only be cool calculation.

"*I* think that you are the most arrogant and conceited *playboy*—" she spat that out "—I have ever met."

For an instant he stared at her, and she steeled herself for retaliation…of a sexual kind.

He threw his head back and laughed.

"Thank you," Rafiq said when he was finally through laughing, bowing his head with mock grace, his eyes still gleaming with hilarity. "I am honored."

And Tiffany wished with wild regret that she'd smacked his face until her hand stung while she'd had the chance. Through lips that still burned from his kiss, she said, "You don't charm me."

Three

His amusement instantly evaporated.

Rafiq suppressed the flare of annoyance and studied her dispassionately. Her hostility surprised him. He'd thought she'd leap at the opportunity to seduce him. Had she gauged he was not easily swayed? Intrigued by the idea, he assessed her. Was the taunt a ploy to capture his attention? Was it possible that she'd known exactly who he was? Researched him?

He shook off the sudden concern.

No, she might be street-smart. But she was a nobody—an insignificant foreign girl illegally working in a dubious club in the backstreets of Hong Kong. He dismissed his apprehension.

"Don't look at me like that, you arrogant jerk."

No one talked to him like that. Certainly not a woman like her. With a growl he grabbed her hand and yanked her toward him. She made a little squeaking sound as she landed in his lap. Rafiq softened his hold, stroking his fingers in long sweeps along her spine. Bending his head, he nuzzled the soft skin of her neck, murmuring sweet words. Her gasp quickly turned to a moan of delight. He marshaled every seductive trick he knew. She responded like a moonflower opening, overwhelming him with her sweet response.

Rafiq fought against the intoxicating pleasure her soft body unlocked. Told himself he was still in control. After all, he'd only teased her...flirted with her...*kissed* her to determine how far Tiffany was prepared to take this scam.

It was a test.

He told himself she'd failed. Dismally. Even as she'd kissed him like angel. He should've been thrilled he'd been proved right.

Instead he drowned in her unresisting softness.

When she shoved at his chest, he blinked rapidly in surprise and shook his head to clear it. "What?"

She scrambled to her feet, her breathing unsteady, her eyes blazing. "You misled me. I didn't come here for this. I'm not so desperate for a place to sleep."

Before she could spin away, he caught her arm.

"Tiffany, wait. You insult both of us. You might think I'm a jerk but I never assumed you came with me to find a bed for the night." Although perhaps the possibility should've occurred to him.

There was something about her that made him want to believe she wasn't like that. Maybe it was her wide brown eyes that gave her such an air of sincerity. Or the baby-soft skin beneath his fingertips...

He brushed the observation aside. She was a woman—of course her skin was soft. It made her no different from a million other women.

Time to get rid of her, before she had him believing the tales she'd spun. He dropped her arm and drew his wallet from the back of his pants, flipping it open to extract a five-hundred-dollar bill. To his surprise his fingers still shook from the aftershocks of the kiss. "Here, this is your tip for serving me drinks—that should help cover your accommodation for a couple of nights." If indeed, that story was true.

Bowing her head, Tiffany mumbled, "I can't take that."

"Why not?" By Allah, she drove him mad. What did she want from him? "I always intended to give you something to tide you over."

Rafiq tried to figure out her agenda. He still wasn't sure what she was after. She was such a curious mix of sophistication and spontaneity. On the one hand she'd almost convinced him her purse and passport had been stolen and all she wanted was a few dollars for a couple of nights' budget accommodation. Hah, he was even ready to give it to her. In the next breath she'd told him she couldn't afford the airfare home, leaving him certain that he was being manipulated by an expert.

He couldn't work out whether she was simply a victim or extremely smart.

But his conscience wouldn't allow him to leave her homeless in case she really had been the victim of petty crime. He thought of his cousin Zara, of his brother's wife, Megan. What if it had been one of the women of his family in such a predicament? He would hope that someone would come to their aid.

"Take it, please."

She stared down at the note in his hand. "It's too much. After that kiss it would feel…wrong," she mumbled, her hair blocking him from seeing her face.

He couldn't help noticing the catch in her voice.

"Okay." Growing impatient with himself, for being so aware of the woman, he opened the billfold again and extracted a twenty and a ten before shoving the other note back. "Take this then—it's not as good a tip as you deserve, but at least you won't suspect my motives."

She tilted her head back and stared at him for a long moment. "Thank you for understanding."

Tears glimmered in her eyes.

"Oh, don't cry," he said roughly.

"I can't help it." She sniffed and wiped her fingers across her eyes. "I'm sorry for calling you a jerk."

Rafiq found himself smiling. She enchanted him, this woman whom he couldn't get a fix on. One minute he had her down as the cleverest schemer he'd ever met, the next she appeared as sweetly innocent as his cousin Zara.

She leaned forward. The scent of gardenias surrounded him. She rested her palm against his chest, her hand warm through the fine cotton of his shirt. Rafiq's breath caught in his throat.

But the hunger he felt for Tiffany bore no resemblance to the sisterly love he showered on Zara.

By the time Tiffany rose on tiptoes and pressed soft lips against his cheek, he was rigid with reaction.

"Thank you, you've saved my life."

She smelled so sweet, the body brushing against him so feminine, that Rafiq couldn't stop his arms from encircling her. He drew her up against him. "Oh, Tiffany, what am I supposed to make of you?"

"I'm not very complicated at all—what you see is what you get," she muttered against his shirt front.

He felt her smile against his thundering heart, heard her breath quicken as his arms tightened convulsively around her…and was lost.

* * *

A long time seemed to pass before Rafiq lifted his lips from hers.

As Tiffany's fingers crept up his shirt and hooked into his loosened tie, Rafiq forgot that he'd started this driven by perverse curiosity and affronted male pride, to see if Tiffany would kiss him when she'd vowed that she wasn't affected by his brand of charm.

It had all changed.

His tightly leashed control was in shreds.

All he could think about was tasting her again...and again.

Her fingers froze. "What are we doing?" She sounded as befuddled as he felt. "Anyone could walk in on us through those sliding doors."

"No." He shook his head. "That's not true. This private pool and deck are part of my suite—my key card activated the entry doors onto the deck."

Her breath caught—an audible sound. "Your suite? You said we'd have a drink.... I would never have entered your suite."

She'd withdrawn. Her eyes had grown dark and distrustful. Rafiq gathered she was making unfavorable assumptions about his motives. He couldn't blame her. "The bar downstairs is noisy—and full of inebriated men at this time of night. We wouldn't have been able to hear ourselves think." Much less talk.

"Oh..."

Unable to help himself he stroked a finger along the curve of her jaw. Soft curls trailed over the back of his hand. "You are very beautiful, do you know that?"

"Not beautiful." She sounded distracted.

He stilled his fingers, and cupped the side of her face.

Tilting it up, he looked down into her wide eyes. "Beautiful."

She shook her head. "Not me. Pretty, maybe, at a stretch. But in this light you wouldn't even be able to tell."

No one could call her vain. "My eyes are not the only senses attuned to you. I don't need bright intrusive light to remember that your eyes are the haunting tawny-brown shade of the desert sands streaked with the burnished gold of the setting sun. I don't need light to feel." Gently he rubbed her bottom lip with the pad of his thumb. "Your mouth is the crushed red of the satiny petals in the rose gardens of Qasr Al-Ward." His fingers explored her cheeks. "Your skin is softer than an almond blossom. Your cheekbones are carefully sculpted by a masterful hand to ensure that as you grow older you will only grow more beautiful."

Tiffany felt herself color.

A beat of time elapsed. Tiffany tried to summon the anger that had scorched her only a moment before when she'd discovered he'd brought her to his suite, but it had vanished. His touch, the heat of his lean body, the force of his soft words had overwhelmed her. She couldn't think of a single thing to say. She'd never met anyone remotely like him. He was way out her league.

Finally she gave up trying to understand the emotion that flooded her. Linking her fingers behind his neck, she pulled his mouth back to hers, his hair thick and silken under her fingers. His thigh moved against her hip, making her aware of the hard, muscled strength of him. When the kiss ended, Tiffany discovered that her heart was pounding.

Tilting her head back, she looked up into his face. His eyes glowed, he'd warmed, he was a long way from being the remote, distant stranger. A heady sense of being on a precipice of discovery overtook her.

Before she could speak, Rafiq grasped her hand. "Come."

He led her through a pair of French doors into a darkened room. A flick of a switch and dim lighting washed the room, revealing a king-size bed in a sumptuously decorated room.

Tiffany hesitated for a microsecond as Rafiq shrugged off his shirt. Then he turned her in his arms and the moment of cool analysis was gone.

Her wide, elasticized belt gave.... She heard something fall, and dismissed it. The zip on the back of her borrowed dress rasped down. His hands closed over the shoulder straps and eased them down her arms along with the tiny, dainty bag looped around her wrist. She didn't have any time to feel exposed...or naked. Only relief that the tight dress was gone. Rafiq drew her against his bare torso, his skin smooth and warm against hers.

His fingers tangled in her hair, before moving in small circles down her back, setting flame to each inch of flesh he massaged.

Tiffany flung her head back. A moan escaped. Desire flared uncontrollably within her and her nipples peaked beneath the modest black bra she wore. She didn't even feel Rafiq loosen the back before the plain bra gave and he removed it, tossing it over the bed end. Then he was on his knees in front of her, easing her heels off, sliding the cotton briefs down her legs, his touch trailing fire down the insides of her thighs.

She started to shake.

The explosive hunger that consumed her was unfamiliar. Powerful. Incredible. A new experience. He buried his face in her belly. Goose bumps broke out over her skin as sensation shook her to her soul. Her hands clutched at his hair, the texture rough as she closed her fingers over the short strands.

"I'm going to pleasure you—but we're not going to make love," he murmured.

Relief, instantly followed by a crazy kind of disappointment spread through her. "Why won't we make love?"

Did he think he was too good for her?

"I'm not…equipped."

"Equipped?" Then it struck her what he meant. "Oh."

The next thought was that if he didn't carry condoms around with him, then he didn't do casual sex, either. It made her almost start to like the man who had her in such a sweat.

Perversely, it made her want him to make love to her.

Tiffany reached for the puddle of her dress on the floor and found her bag. Opening it she extracted the condom that Renate had stuck in. "I only have one."

"Better than nothing," he growled.

Then he had her on the bed and everything started to move very fast. She closed her eyes as his mouth teased her nipple, arousing sensations she'd never experienced. A wild, keening sound broke from her throat as his teeth teased her burgeoning flesh. His hands were everywhere.… He knew exactly what to do to reduce her to a state of quivering arousal. Her body turned fluid. It seemed to know exactly what he wanted…how to respond to his every move.

When he finally moved over her, her legs parted. Opening her eyes, she glimpsed the tense line of his jaw, the fullness of a bottom lip softened by passion. He shifted into the space between her legs, his body so male, so unfamiliar against her own. He moved his hips, and Tiffany tensed, fighting the instinct to resist.

The pressure. Her breath caught in the back of her throat. He wasn't going to fit. Staring at the mouth that had wreaked so much pleasure, she waited uncertainly. Suddenly her body gave, and the pressure eased. The shudders subsided. Her heart expanded as he sank forward. A glow of warmth swept her. Her hands fluttered along the indent of his spine as a powerful, primal emotion swept her.

Tiffany thought she was going to cry with joy, at the beauty of it all.

The warmth spiraled into a fierce, desperate heat as he moved within her. As the friction built, she could feel herself straining to reach a place she'd never been. Her body tightened, no longer hers, taken over by the passion that ripped through her.

"Relax," he whispered in her ear. "Let it happen."

She didn't know what he was talking about. Yet the warmth of his breath against her ear caused a fresh wave of shivers to race up and down her spine, spreading out along every inch of her skin.

This time she didn't fight the sensation. She allowed it to sweep her away. Pleasure soared.

He grew still. Then he moved, his body driving in quick thrusts into hers, his breath fast.

A cry of shock caught in her throat as her body convulsed. Waves of heat broke, rippling through her, a tide of inexorable sensation that left her limp.

Tiffany opened her eyes and blinked against bright sunlight.

Disorientation was quickly followed by a suffocating sense of dread. *What had she done?* Slowly, she turned her head against the plump oversized pillow.

The space beside her in the giant king-size bed was

empty. Rafiq was already awake…and out of the bed. With any luck he'd stay closeted in the bathroom until she could escape. Except she could hear no sound. Perhaps he'd gone to have breakfast…a swim…to work out. Anything.

Tiffany didn't care so long as she didn't have to confront him.

A movement drew her gaze to the floor-to-ceiling windows where the drapes had already been thrown back. Squinting against the gauze-filtered sunlight, Tiffany made out the dark shadow of a backlit figure.

Rafiq.

She shifted and he must've heard the movement, because he wheeled around and spoke. "You're awake."

Too late to squeeze her eyelids shut and fake sleep.

"Yes." She offered him a tremulous smile, and tried to read his expression, but bright light behind him frustrated her attempt.

"Good."

Was it? She wasn't so sure. He moved closer and came into focus. The passionate lover from last night's dark, delicious world had vanished. Replaced by the aloof man she'd met—was it only the evening before?

Tiffany shuddered.

"You're already dressed." Did she have to sound so plaintive?

He shrugged. "I have a busy day planned."

And it was time for her to make herself scarce.

He didn't need to speak the words out loud. It was painfully obvious.

But she had no intention of getting out of bed with him standing less than three feet away. She was naked under the sheet. And he was impeccably, immaculately dressed. She'd exposed more of herself than she'd ever intended, and she had no one but herself to blame. He would not see another inch of her body. A fresh flush of humiliation scorched her at the memory of what had passed between them last night.

Tiffany raised her chin and bravely met his granite gaze. "So why are you still here?"

"I've been waiting for you to awaken."

The harsh features that had been aflame with desire last night had reverted to keep-out coldness. Any hope that he'd wanted to tell her something momentous withered. Her stomach balled into a tight knot.

"Why?"

He reached into his jacket pocket.

His fist uncurled. A cell phone lay there—slim and silent.

Tiffany frowned, trying to make sense of the tension that vibrated from him. And what it had to do with her. "That's Renate's phone. I slipped it into my belt—"

"You took pictures last night."

Oh. Darn. She'd forgotten all about that. "I meant to delete—"

"Yes." His mouth curled. It was not a nice smile. "I'm sure you meant to. But you didn't. And you assured Sir Julian that you already had deleted the images."

She'd been scared of losing her job—now she'd been caught in a lie. She wriggled under the sheet, trying to think of how to explain. In the end she decided she'd probably be better off remaining silent, before she dug herself into a deeper hole. What a mess.

"Nothing to say?"

"Why do you care?"

"Oh, I care." He brandished the phone at her. "One of the photos is of me with Sir Julian—and enough of Renate to make sure the viewer knows exactly what kind of relationship she's contemplating with him."

"I didn't mean—"

"Of course, you didn't." He sneered. "You were very interested in talking about Sir Julian Carling last night, too."

"I was making conversation." Tiffany was utterly bewildered by the turn the conversation had taken. "So what?"

His eyes darkened. "So what? That's all you have to say for yourself?"

Tiffany drew the top sheet more securely around herself. What had possessed her to let this daunting stranger get so close last night?

"You are wise to be nervous."

"I'm not nervous," she lied. "I'm confused."

The silence swelled. Tiffany *was* growing decidedly nervous. Her gaze flitted toward the door. Even if she made it out the room, she wouldn't get very far without any clothes. And she doubted she'd have time to scoop up her dress and bag off the floor.

She turned her attention back to him and decided to brazen it out. "Why are you angry?"

His eyebrow shot up. "You expect me to believe you don't know? Come, come, it's enough now."

Tiffany decided it would probably be better to say nothing. It would only enrage him further. So she waited.

"There's a text message from your friend on her phone asking how your night went."

The expression of distaste on his face told her that he'd jumped to the conclusion that she'd discussed sleeping with him with Renate.

Damn Renate. "You're misunderstanding—"

He held up a hand. "I don't want to hear it. How much do you want?"

"*What?*"

"To forget that you ever saw me with Sir Julian."

Her mouth dropped open. He was delusional. Or paranoid. Or maybe just plain crazy. That was enough to make her say hastily, "Just delete the images—it's what I meant to do last night. I forgot…and then I forgot to give the phone back to Renate."

"How convenient."

Tiffany didn't like the way he said that.

"When you didn't respond, your friend's texts make it clear she's decided you must've stolen her phone." He smiled, but his eyes still smoldered like hot coals. "That you're planning to sell the images yourself."

"I wouldn't do that!"

He made a sound that sounded suspiciously like a snort. "Sell the images or steal her phone? Since when is there honor among thieves?"

What on earth was he getting at? She gave him a wary glance, and then said, "Just say what you mean."

"You and your friend intended to blackmail me and Sir Julian. Your friend has decided you've decided to proceed alone. I think she's right."

"Blackmail?"

He was definitely, certifiably crazy. Her eyes flickered toward the door again. Maybe, just maybe she could get out of here…and if she yanked the sheet along, she'd have cover.

"You're not going anywhere," he growled and sat down on the bed, pinning her under the sheet that she'd been planning to escape in, wrapped around her like a toga.

"I know." She gazed at him limpidly.

His eyes narrowed to slits. "That look won't work. I know you're no innocent."

If he only knew.

"Uh…" Tiffany's voice trailed away. No point telling him, he wouldn't believe her.

"So what were the two of you intending to do with the photos?"

"Nothing."

He shook his head. "You take me for a fool. Your friend was desperate to know whether you still had the phone and the photos. Someone was ready to buy them. You were in on the deal."

She wasn't going to argue with him. Not while he was looming over her, and she wasn't wearing a stitch under the scanty cover that the hotel's silk sheet provided. No way was she risking sparking the tension between them into something else…something infinitely more dangerous.

Panic filled her. "Get off me!"

He didn't budge. "Here's what's going to happen. I'm going to delete the images from the phone. Then I'm going to buy you the ticket that you were so desperate for last night. Then I never want to see or hear from you again. Do you understand?"

Tiffany nodded.

He sat back and she breathed again.

"I'm not going to give you the money you so badly want. I'm going to take you to the airport and pay whatever it takes to get that ticket changed—so I hope you really need a flight to Auckland."

"I do," she croaked.

He pushed himself away from her. "It will be waiting for you downstairs when you are ready to leave."

As he rose from the bed, her bravado returned. Her chin lifted. "I don't need you to take me to the airport—it won't help. My temporary travel documents will only be ready on Monday. I'll take a cab back to the hostel."

"I want you out of Hong Kong."

"I have no intention of staying a minute more than I have to. Nor will I cause you any grief. I promise."

He gave her one of those narrow-eyed glances that chilled her to the bone. "If I learn that you have—"

"I'm not going to do anything. I swear. And, believe me, I intend to pay you back," she said fervently. Tiffany had no intention of being beholden to this man.

He waved a dismissive hand. "Please. Don't lie."

"I *will* repay you. But I'll need your bank details."

"To further scam me?" The bark of laughter he gave sounded ugly. His eyes bored into hers. She didn't look away. The mood changed, becoming hot and oppressive. Something arced between them, an emotion so intense, so powerful that she lost the ability to think.

Without looking away, Rafiq reached into his pocket for his wallet. This time he extracted a small white card. "Here are my details. You can post me a check...but I don't want to see you again. Ever."

It stung.

Determined to hurt him, she flung the words back at him. "I have no intention of seeing you again." Then, for good measure, she added defiantly, "Ever."

She bit her lip hard to stop it trembling as he swung away, and she watched him head for the door with long, raking strides. When the door thudded shut behind him, she glanced down at the card she held.

Rafiq Al Dhahara. President, Royal Bank of Dhahara.

She should've known. He wasn't any old banker. He was the boss. The man who had showed her a glimpse of heaven would never be an ordinary man.

Four

Rafiq could not settle.

He'd been restless for weeks now. He told himself it was the fierce desert heat of Dhahara that kept him awake deep into the heart of the night. Not even the arctic air-conditioning circulating through the main boardroom of the Royal Bank of Dhahara soothed him.

"Stop pacing," Shafir said from behind him. "You called us in to talk about the new hotel you've financed, but now you wear holes in that kelim. Sit down and talk." He tapped his gold pen against the legal pad in front of him. "I'm in a hurry."

Swiveling on his heel, Rafiq put his hands on narrow hips, and scowled down at where his brother lounged in the black leather chair, his white robes cascading about him. "You can wait, Shafir."

"I might, but Megan won't. My wife is determined to spend every free minute we have at Qasr Al-Ward." Shafir flashed him the wicked grin of a man well satisfied by that state of affairs. "Come for the weekend. Celebrate that the contracts for the new Carling Hotel are in place. It'll give you a chance to shed that suit for a couple of days."

Shaking his head, Rafiq said, "Too much else to do. I'll resist the call of the desert." He envied his brother the bond he had to Qasr Al-Ward, the desert palace that had been in the family for centuries. Since his marriage to Megan, Shafir had made Qasr Al-Ward their home.

"Don't resist it too long—or you may not find your way back."

"Why don't you take our father?" Rafiq wasn't eager to engage in the kind of analysis that Shafir's sharp gaze suggested was about to begin. In an effort to distract his brother, he tipped his head to where King Selim was intent on getting his point across to his firstborn son. The words "duty" and "marriage" drifted across the expanse of the boardroom table. "That way Khalid might get some peace, too."

Shafir chuckled. "Looks like our father is determined not to give him a break."

"You realize your marriage has only increased the pressure on Khalid?"

Stabbing a finger at his brother's chest, Shafir chuckled. "And on you. Everyone expected you to marry first, Rafiq. Unlike Khalid, your bride isn't Father's choice. And unlike me, women don't view you as already wed to the desert. You spent years abroad—you've had plenty of opportunity to fall in love."

"It wasn't so straightforward." Rafiq realized that was true. "There were no expectations on you, Shafir. No pressure. You've always done exactly what you want."

His brother had spent much of his life growing up in the desert; he'd been allowed rough edges, whereas

Rafiq had been groomed for a corporate role. Educated at Eton, followed by degrees at Cambridge and Harvard. There had been pressure to put thought and care into his choice of partner—someone who could bear scrutiny on an international stage. A trophy wife. A *powerful* trophy wife.

How could he explain how a relationship that started off as something special could deteriorate into nothing more than duty?

"Take it." His father's rising voice broke into his thoughts.

Rafiq refocused across the table. His father was trying to press a piece of paper into Khalid's hand. "All three of these women are suitable. Yasmin is a wealthy young woman who knows what you need in a wife."

"No!" Khalid's jaw was like rock.

"She's pretty, too." Shafir smirked.

"I don't want pretty," his eldest brother argued.

Pretty. Rafiq shied away from the word. Tiffany had thought she was pretty. Not beautiful. Pretty. Rafiq had considered her beautiful.

"I want a woman who will match me," Khalid was saying. "I don't care what she looks like. I need a partner... not a pinup."

"Hey, my wife is a partner," Shafir objected. "In my eyes she's a pinup, too."

Newly—and happily—married, he'd become the king's ally in the quest to seek a suitable wife for his brothers. Although Rafiq suspected that Shafir was only trying to drive home how fortunate he'd been to find his Megan. If he could find a woman as unique, as in tune with him as Megan was with Shafir, he'd get married in a shot....

Khalid bestowed a killing look on Shafir, who laughed and helped himself to a cup of the rich, fragrant coffee that the bank's newest secretary was busy pouring into small brass cups.

"Thank you, Miss Turner." To his father Khalid added, "I don't need a list. I will find my own wife."

Rafiq craned his neck, peering at the list. "Who else is on there?"

"Farrah? She's far too young—I don't want a child bride."

"Leila Mummhar."

Rafiq's suggestion had captured his father's attention.

"Pah." The King flung out his arms. "Don't *you* give him advice. I was certain you'd be married long before Shafir. Now look at you—no woman at your side since your beloved departed."

"Shenilla and I had...differences." It was the best way to describe the pushy interest that Shenilla's father had started to exert as soon as they'd considered him hooked. Shenilla was a qualified accountant, she was beautiful, her family was well respected in Dhahara. On paper it was the perfect match.

Yet he'd run....

"Differences?" His father growled. "What is a little difference? Your beloved mother and I had many differences while we were courting. We overcame them and—"

"But your marriage was expected," Rafiq interrupted. "It was arranged between your families from the time you were very young. You could not end such a relationship."

The king shook his head. "It made marriage no easier. But we worked at it. Happiness is something to strive for, my son, every day of your life. And you were so in love. Ay me, I was so certain that this time it would be right."

How could Rafiq confess that he'd been sure that Shenilla had been perfect for him, yet once their families had become involved as quickly as he'd fallen in love with her, he'd fallen out again? And it hadn't been the first time. Before that there had been Rosa and before her, Neela. He wasn't indiscriminate. His cautious courtships lasted for lengthy periods—that was expected after the care he put into the choice. But just when they got to the point where formalities like engagements became expected, when the pressure to set a wedding date was applied, the love dwindled, leaving only a restless need to escape the cloying trap the relationship had become.

"Khalid, you may object now but you know your duty." The king patted his firstborn son on the shoulder. "Choose any one of those women and you will be richly rewarded."

Rafiq eyed the list and thought of the requirements he'd set for women he considered in the past—after all he was a practical man, his wife would have to fit into his world. Wealthy. Beautiful. Well connected. "Yasmin comes from a powerful family."

Khalid shook his head fiercely. "No, it's not her family I'd be marrying. And I want more than power, wealth and looks in a bride. She must be able to keep me interested for many years, long after worldly goods are forgotten."

Interested? Rafiq's thoughts veered to the last woman who had occupied his bed.

Tiffany had kept him interested from the moment he'd met her. Yes, he'd told her she was beautiful. And he'd meant it. But she was nothing like the other beauties he'd dated. Her features reflected her every emotion, and the graceful way she moved had held him entranced. She certainly fulfilled none of the other criteria he looked for in a wife…she'd never be suitable.

It shamed him that in one short night with little effort she'd stripped him of the restraint and control he prided himself on. It had disturbed him deeply that a woman whom he didn't love, held no fondness for, a woman he suspected of being a con artist, a blackmailer, could hold such power over him.

She'd insisted she'd had no intention of bedding him; she'd been as deliciously tight as a virgin, yet she'd produced a condom at the critical moment. And she'd lied about deleting the photos she'd taken of him and Sir Julian. The more he thought about it, the more he decided he'd been played for a fool by an expert.

He'd given her his business card.

Fool!

He stared blindly at the list he held until Shafir stretched across the boardroom table and snagged it. His brother studied it…and hooted with laughter, pulling Rafiq out the trance that held him immobile. "I can't believe Leila is on here—she's more work than all the bandits that hide on the border of Marulla."

"It would make political sense—we would be able to watch her relations," the king growled.

"Father, we don't want the trouble that her uncles would bring." Rafiq shook his head as he referred to the spats that the two sheikhs were infamous for waging. "Pick someone with less baggage."

Khalid fixed his attention on Shafir. "Maybe I should do what you did…choose a woman with family on the other side of the world. That way I will have no problem with my inlaws."

Suppressing the urge to grin, Rafiq waited for his father to launch into a tirade about the sanctity of family. But his father wore an arrested expression. "Rafiq, did you not say that Sir Julian Carling has a daughter?"

"Yes." Rafiq thought of the woman he'd once met. "Elizabeth Carling."

Despite the dislike he'd taken to Sir Julian, there'd been nothing wrong with the daughter. Elizabeth had everything he usually looked for. Wealth, beauty, connections. Yet there'd been no spark. Not like what he'd experienced with Tiffany—if such a wild madness could be termed a spark. It had been more like a conflagration.

At last he nodded. "Yes, she would be a good choice for Khalid."

"Add her to the list," his father commanded Shafir. "Rafiq says her father is coming to Dhahara to inspect the site for the new Carling Hotel. Her father is a very wealthy man." King Selim gave his eldest son an arch look, and leaned back in his chair. "I will invite Lady Carling and his daughter, too."

Even as Khalid glared at him, the young secretary reappeared in the doorway, concern in her eyes. "The CEO of Pyramid Oil is here for his appointment. What shall I tell him?"

"That's right, run, before I kill you for adding to the pressure," his brother muttered, but Rafiq only laughed.

"Discussing your future took the heat off me, so thanks."

Khalid snorted in disgust.

Still grinning, Rafiq turned to the young secretary. "Miss Turner, give us five more minutes—by then I will be done."

Tiffany stepped out of the cab into the dry, arid midday heat of Dhahara. Hot wind redolent of spices and a tang of the desert swept around her. In front of her towered the Royal Bank of Dhahara. The butterflies that had been floating around in her stomach started to whip their wings in earnest.

Sure, she'd known from his gold-embossed card that

Rafiq would be an important man. President, Royal Bank of Dhahara. But not *this* important.

Yet coming here had been the right thing to do. She'd never doubted her path from the moment the doctor had confirmed her deepest fear. But being confronted with the material reality of where Rafiq worked, knowing that it would be only minutes before she saw him again, made her palms grow moist and her heart thump loudly in her chest.

She paid the driver and couldn't help being relieved that she'd had the foresight to check into a city hotel and stow her luggage in her room before coming here. Pulling a filmy scarf over her hair, she passed the bank's uniformed guard and headed for the glass sliding doors.

Inside, behind the sleek, circular black marble reception counter, stood a young, clean-shaven man in a dark suit and white headgear. Tiffany approached him, determined to brazen this out. "I have an appointment."

His brow creased as he scanned the computer screen in front of him, searching for an appointment she knew would not be listed for today…or any day. Finally he shook his head.

But Tiffany had not come this far to be deterred. She held her ground, refusing to turn away.

"Call Rafiq Al Dhahara." Her conjuring up the name she'd memorized from the business card caused him to do a double take. "Tell him Tiffany Smith is here to see him." She mustered up every bit of authority that she had. "He won't be pleased if he learns you sent me away without bothering to check."

That was stretching the truth, because Rafiq might well refuse to see her. Even if he did agree to speak to her, he would certainly not be pleased to find her here in Dhahara.

But the bank official wasn't to know that.

Tiffany waited, arms folded across a stomach that was still behaving in the most peculiar fashion, as it fluttered and tumbled over.

He picked up a telephone and spoke in Arabic. When he'd finished, his expression had changed. "The sheikh will see you."

The sheikh?

Oh, my. This time her stomach turned a full somersault. "Sheikh?" she spluttered. "I thought he was—" she searched a mind gone suddenly blank for the impressive title on his business card "—the president of the Royal Bank of Dhahara."

The bank official gave her a peculiar look. "The royal family owns the bank."

"What does that have to do with Rafiq?"

He blinked at her casual use of his name, and then replied, "The sheikh is part of the royal family."

Before she could faintly repeat "royal family," the elevator doors to the left of the marble reception counter slid open, and Rafiq himself stepped out.

His face was haughtier than she remembered, his eyes darker, his cheekbones more aristocratic. Sheikh? Royal family? He certainly looked every inch the part in a dark suit with a conservative white shirt that even in this sweltering heat appeared crisp and fresh. Yet his head was uncovered, and his hair gleamed like a black hawk's wing. After all the soul-searching it had taken to bring her here, now that she faced him she couldn't think of a word to say.

So she settled for the most inane.

"Hi."

"Tiffany."

The sphinxlike gaze revealed no surprise. He'd told

her he never wanted to see her again. *Ever.* Now she stood before him, shifting from one foot to the other. The displeasure she'd expected was absent. Typically, he showed no emotion at all. The wall of stony reserve was as high as ever.

He bowed his head. "Please, come with me."

If it hadn't been for one never-to-be-forgotten night in Hong Kong, she'd never have known that his reserve could be breached.

That night…

The memory of the catastrophic extremes, heaven and hell, pleasure and shame, still had the power to make her shudder.

Tiffany had been sure nothing would make her contact him again. Nothing. But she'd been so wrong. She pressed her hand to her belly.

Her baby…

He ushered her into the elevator. Unexpectedly, the elevator dropped instead of rising. Her stomach rolled wildly. Tiffany gritted her teeth. Seconds later the doors opened to reveal a well-lit parking level where a black Mercedes-Benz idled, waiting. Rafiq strode forward and opened the rear door.

She hesitated. "Where—?"

His dark gaze was hooded. "There is no privacy here."

He was ashamed of her.

Despite a tinge of apprehension Tiffany swallowed her protests and, straightening her spine, stepped past him and slid into the leather backseat.

She'd come to Dhahara because of her baby. Not for herself. Not for Rafiq. For their unborn child.

She couldn't afford to let fear dominate her.

For her daughter she had put aside her desire never

to encounter Rafiq again. For the baby's sake, she would keep her relationship with Rafiq cordial. Unemotional. Her daughter deserved the right to know her father. Nor could she allow herself to indulge in wild notions that he might kidnap her child, hide her away.

He was a businessman. He'd told her he'd been educated in England and the United States. He headed a large bank. Even it if was a position he'd gotten through nepotism, neither he—nor his royal family—could afford the kind of international outcry that would come from taking her baby from her. He was a single man—or at least she hoped he was—what would he do with a baby?

The silence was oppressive. Fifteen minutes later the Mercedes came to a smooth stop, and the rear doors opened. Rafiq's hand closed around her elbow—to escort her or ensure she didn't escape? Tiffany wasn't sure. As he hurried her up a flight of stairs, she caught a glimpse of two guards in red berets standing in front of stone pillars that flanked a vast wooden front door. Then the door swung inward and they were inside a vaulted entrance hall.

She gazed around, wide-eyed. Despite the mansions she'd seen, this dwelling took luxury to new heights. "Where are we?"

"This is my home."

A hasty glance revealed magnificent dark wooden floors covered in Persian rugs, original art hanging on deep blue walls. Refusing to be impressed, Tiffany focused her attention on Rafiq. "Is there somewhere we can talk?"

His lips quirked, and something devilish gleamed in his eyes. "Talk? Our best communication is done in other ways. I thought that must be why you are here."

Damn him for the reminder.

Tiffany compressed her lips. "I need to talk to you."

"Whenever we talk, it seems to cost me money." The humor had vanished, and he gave her a brooding look.

His words only underscored what she already knew: he thought her the worst kind of woman. What would he say when he discovered she was pregnant with his child? A frisson of alarm chilled her.

"I haven't come all this way for money, Rafiq."

"I'm very relieved to hear that."

He strode down a hall hung with richly woven tapestries that held the patina of age. Tiffany resisted the urge to slow and inspect them.

"But for the moment I will reserve judgment," he was saying. "I will be more convinced of that once I have heard what you have to say to me."

He didn't believe her. He thought this was about money.

"Hey, I sent you a check for what you gave me," she protested. She hadn't wanted to be in his debt.

"Sure you did."

"I sent it last week. Maybe it's still in the mail." She'd meant to send it earlier. Discovering she was pregnant had wiped all other thoughts out of her head. But now she was seriously starting to wish that she had called…not come all this way to give him the news about his impending fatherhood.

Yet it had seemed the right thing to do. She'd wanted to break the news in person, not over the phone separated by thousands of miles, unable to register the nuances of his expression. And certainly not by an e-mail that might go astray.

This was too important. Her child's whole life, her baby's relationship with her father, would be determined by the course of this conversation.

And she wasn't about to let Rafiq Al Dhahara cause

her to regret the decision she'd made to come here to tell him.

Pushing open a door, he gestured for her to precede him. Tiffany entered a book-lined room that was clearly a man's domain. *His* domain. Before her nerve could give out, she drew a deep breath and spun to face him.

"I'm pregnant," she announced.

Rafiq went very still, and his eyes narrowed to dark cracks that revealed nothing.

All at once the dangerous man she'd seen glimpses of in Hong Kong, the man she'd known lurked under the polite, charming veneer, surfaced.

"We used a condom," he said, softly.

She spread her hands helplessly. "It must've been faulty."

"Did you know it was faulty?"

"What's that supposed to mean?"

"Did you tamper with it?"

"How?" Outrage filled the question. "It was sealed!"

"Nothing a pinprick couldn't have taken care of."

"You're sick."

His mouth tightened. "Be careful how you talk to me."

Tiffany's front teeth worried at her bottom lip. His gaze flickered to her mouth, before returning to clash with hers. "How much do you want?"

"What?"

She stared at him, not sure she'd heard right. His eyes were fixed on her, his mouth tight. No sign of softness in the features that were so difficult to read. He'd pay money so that he'd never have to see his child again?

What kind of man did that?

Tiffany turned away, defeated. At least she would always carry the knowledge in her heart that she'd tried. And if her daughter one day wanted to know who her father was, she'd tell her. Rafiq might be a sheikh. He might be desert royalty. But he would be the loser…he'd have forfeited the chance to know his child.

But he'd been given the choice.

"I've been a fool."

Tiffany spun back and focused on him. He'd positioned himself behind an antique desk. One hand was raking through his hair. Straight and dark, it shone like silk under the overhead lights.

Unable to bear to look at him, she closed her eyes.

He'd been a fool? What did that make her?

"And I have absolutely no excuse. I even know how the scam works. Start with small amounts, get the idiot hooked and then, when he can't back out, increase the amount."

Her mouth fell open as she absorbed what he was saying. "You honestly think I'd travel *here* to blackmail you?" Her hand closed protectively over her belly. "That I'd blackmail the father of my child?"

From beyond the barrier of the desk, his glance fell to her still-flat stomach, and then lifted to meet her eyes. Black. Implacable. Furious. Tiffany felt the searing heat of his contempt. "Enough. Don't expect me to believe there is a child."

Rafiq thought—

She shook her head to clear it. "You really do think I came all this way to blackmail you."

He arched a brow. "Didn't you?"

"No!"

"Previous experience makes that impossible for me to believe."

What was the point of arguing that she hadn't wanted to blackmail him in the past, either? Tiffany placed her fingertips to her pounding temples. God, why had she allowed her conviction that she was doing the right thing to persuade her to come? He didn't care about the child. All he cared about was protecting himself.

There was nothing here for her daughter…nothing worth fighting for.

She started to back away.

"Where are you going?"

"To my hotel. I'm pregnant. It was a long flight. I'm tired. My feet ache. I need a shower and a sleep." She listed the reasons in a flat, dead tone.

He was around the desk before she could move and caught up to her with two long strides. Planting himself in front of her, he folded his arms across his chest. "You will stay here."

Tiffany shook her head. "I can't stay here." He was a man—an unmarried man. It would not be sanctioned. "Besides, my luggage is already at the hotel."

His jaw had set. "I am not letting you stay in the city alone. I want you where I can watch you. Give me the name of the hotel and I will have your luggage sent here."

"I'd be your prisoner."

"Not a prisoner," he corrected, "my guest."

"It's hardly appropriate for me to stay here, even I know—"

Holding up a hand, he stopped her mid-sentence. "My aunt Lily will come stay. The widow of my father's brother, and the perfect chaperone. Zara, her daughter, is away studying at present, and Aunt Lily is missing her. She's Australian, so you should get along well. But don't think you can wind her around your little finger. I will be there all the time you are together. Rest tonight, and I will escort you back to the airport myself tomorrow."

Taking in his hard face, Tiffany made herself straighten. She'd come all this way, and he didn't even believe she was pregnant. Right now she was too weary to argue further but she'd be damned if she'd let him see that. He'd only interpret it as weakness. Tomorrow she'd be ready to fight again.

At least she'd have a chance to meet a part of his family, his aunt. For her daughter's future relationship with her father, Tiffany knew she would do her best to get along with the woman.

Before he took her by the scruff of her neck and threw her out of his country.

Five

Tiffany hadn't been lying about being weary, Rafiq saw that evening. Seated across from him at the dinner table, alongside his aunt Lily, who was clearly bursting with curiosity about her presence in his home, Tiffany barely picked at her food.

There were shadows beneath her eyes. Pale purple hollows that gave her a heart-wrenching fragility that tugged at him—even though he refused to put a name to the emotion.

The array of dishes at her elbow remained untouched. The succulent pieces of skewered lamb. The breads baked with great care in his kitchens. The char-roasted vegetables on earthenware platters. Even her wineglass remained full. Something of the fine spread should have tempted her. But nothing had.

Finally, his aunt could clearly contain herself no longer. "My daughter is at university in Los Angeles. Did you meet Rafiq when he studied abroad?"

Rafiq answered before she could reply. "Tiffany and I are...business acquaintances. She's been traveling—and decided to visit." It didn't satisfy his aunt's curiosity but she wouldn't ask again.

"You look tired, dear."

"I am." Tiffany gave Lily a smile. "I can't wait to go to bed."

"After dinner I'll show you where the women's quarters are."

"Thank you."

The subdued note in her voice made Rafiq want to confront the turmoil that had been whirling around inside his head. He'd been rough on her earlier. Even his aunt could see that her travels had worn her out.

A trickle of shame seeped through Rafiq, then he forced it ruthlessly aside. What else was he supposed to have done? Accepted the lie that she was pregnant? Paid through the nose for the privilege of silencing her new blackmail attempt?

Never.

He'd taken the only course of action open to him: he'd brought her here, away from the bank, away from any possible contact with his father, brothers and staff to learn what she wanted.

Pregnant? Hah! He would not let her get away with such a ruse. Now she was confined to his home. And he would make sure she wasn't left alone with his aunt. He made a mental note to assign one of the maids to keep the women company. His aunt would never gossip in front of the servants.

Tomorrow she would leave. He'd escort her to the airport himself. He certainly wouldn't allow himself any regrets. Tiffany was not the stranded innocent she'd once almost managed to con him into believing she was. He'd already allowed her to squeeze him for money once.

By foolishly possessing her, taking her under a starlit sky, he'd made a fatal mistake. One that she would milk for the rest of her life—if he let her.

Rafiq had no intention of becoming trapped in the prison she'd created with her soft touches and sweet, drugging kisses.

He became aware that Tiffany was talking to his aunt. He tensed, and started to pay attention.

"You must miss your daughter," Tiffany was saying.

Lily nodded. "But I'll be joining her when the holidays come. She wanted a little time to find her feet."

"How lucky for her that you respect her need for independence."

"I still worry about her. She had a bad romantic experience a while back."

That was enough! He wasn't having this woman interrogating his family, discovering pains better left hidden.

"Wine?" Rafiq brusquely offered Tiffany.

She shook her head, "No, thanks." And focused on his aunt. "Do you have any other children?"

"No, only Zara."

"I'm an only child, too."

"Oh, what a pity Zara wasn't here for you to meet. You would've gotten along like a house on fire."

Rafiq narrowed his gaze. If Tiffany even thought she might threaten his family's well-being she would learn how very ruthless he could be.

"I would've liked that."

She sounded so sincere. His aunt was glowing with delight. Lily put a hand on his arm, "I'm sure your father and brothers would like to meet Tiffany."

"I'd like that but—"

His killing glare interrupted the woman who had caused all this trouble. "Tiffany will not be staying for very long," he said with a snap of his teeth.

Aunt Lily looked crestfallen. "What a pity."

Rafiq wished savagely that he'd been less respectful of Tiffany's modesty. He should've known better than to introduce her to any member of his family.

"She'll be leaving us tomorrow."

The bedchamber Lily and the little plump maid called Mina showed Tiffany into was rich and luxurious. Filmy gold drapes surrounded a high bed covered by white linen while beautiful handwoven rugs covered the intricately patterned wooden floors. On the opposite walls, shutters were flung back to reveal a view of a courtyard containing a pool surrounded by padded loungers. Water trickled over a tiered fountain on the far side of the pool, the soothing sound adding to the welcome.

It felt as if she'd been transported into another, far more exotic, world.

Alone, Tiffany stripped off her crumpled clothes and pulled on a nightie. She felt dazed and disoriented and just a little bit queasy. Jet lag was setting in with vengeance.

Through an open door, she caught a glimpse of an immense tub with leaping dolphins—dolphins!—for faucets before weariness sank like a cloud around her. She padded through to the large bathroom to brush her teeth before heading for the bedchamber and clambering between the soft sheets where sleep claimed her.

The next thing she knew she was being wakened by the loud sound of knocking. Seconds later the door crashed open.

Tiffany sat up, dragging the covers up to her chin, thoroughly startled at being yanked from deep sleep.

"What do you want?" she demanded of the man looming in the doorway.

"Neither of the maids could awaken you." Whatever had glittered in Rafiq's eyes when the door first opened had already subsided.

"I was tired," she said defensively. "I told you that last night."

"It's late." He glanced at his watch. "Eleven o'clock. I thought you might've run out—" He broke off.

Eleven o'clock was all she heard. "It can't be that late."

He strode closer, brandishing the square face of his Cartier timepiece in her direction. "Look."

The wrist beneath the leather strap was tanned, a mix of sinew and muscle. Oh, God, surely she wasn't being drawn back under his thrall?

"I believe you," she said hastily, her grip tightening on the bedcovers as she pulled them up to her chin so that no bare flesh was visible. Her stomach had started its now-familiar morning lurching routine.

"Will you please *go?*"

And then it was too late. Tiffany bolted from the bed and into the adjoining bathroom, where she was miserably and ignominiously sick.

When she finally raised her head, it was—horror of horrors—to find Rafiq beside her, holding out a white facecloth. She took it and wiped it over her face, appreciating the cool wetness.

"Thanks," she mumbled.

"You look terrible."

This time her "Thanks" held no gratitude.

"I don't like this. I'm going to call a doctor." He was already moving away with that sleek, predatory stride.

"Don't," Tiffany said.

He halted just short of the bathroom door.

"There's nothing wrong with me." She gave him a grim smile.

"Maybe it was something you ate." Two long paces had him at her side. "You may need an antibiotic."

"No antibiotic!" Nothing was going to harm her baby. "I promise you this is a perfectly normal part of being pregnant."

His hands closed around her shoulders. "Oh, don't try that tall tale again."

"It's the truth. I can't help that you're too dumb to see what's right in front of your nose." She poked a finger at his chest, but to her dismay he did not back away. Instead she became conscious of his muscled body beneath the crisply ironed business shirt. A body she'd touched all over the night they had been together...

She withdrew her finger as though it had been burned.

"I'm not dumb," he growled.

Right. "And I'm not pregnant," she countered.

"I *knew* you were faking it."

The triumph in his voice made her see red. "Oh, for heaven's sake!"

Tiffany broke out of his grasp and, slipping past him, headed for the bedroom. Grabbing her purse off the dressing table she upended it onto the bed and scrabbled through the displaced contents. Snatching up a black-and-white image in a small frame she spun around to wave it in front of his nose.

"Look at this."

"What is it?"

Couldn't he see? He had to be blind...as well as obtuse.

"A photo of your daughter."

"A photo of my daughter?" For once that air of composure had deserted him. "I don't have a daughter."

She pushed the picture into his hands. "It's an image from a scan. A scan of my baby—" *their baby* "—taken last week. See? There's her head, her hipbone, her arms. That's your daughter you're holding."

His expression changed. When he finally raised his head, his eyes were glazed with shock.

"You really *are* pregnant."

Six

"No, I'm only faking it. Remember?"

Rafiq glared at Tiffany, unamused by the flippant retort—and the sharp edge he detected beneath it. He tightened his grip on the photo, conscious of a sense that his world was shifting.

"So how do you know it's a girl? Can they tell?"

She stared down her nose at him in a way that made him want to kiss her, or throttle her. Then she said, "My intuition tells me she is."

Her intuition? The ridiculous reply brought him back to reality, and he shut down the string of questions that he'd been about to ask. Rafiq almost snorted in disgust at how readily he'd crumbled. She was softening him up—and worse, it was working.

"You don't think I'm going to fall for this?" He shoved the picture back at her. "This could be any man's baby."

Her fingers closed around the small framed image with

great care. She slid it into the bag and walked back to the dressing table where she set the bag down. Her back to him, she said, "Doctors will be able to estimate the time of conception close enough to that night—"

"They won't be able to pinpoint exactly. The baby could've been conceived anytime around then." He paused as she wheeled around to face him. "It doesn't mean it is *my* child." He sneered. "I hardly met you under the most pristine conditions."

The gold flecks in those velvet eyes grew dull. "I told you that it was my first night at Le Club."

"I don't know you at all." He shrugged. "Even if it was the truth, who knows what's behind it?"

Tiffany flushed, and the gold in her tawny eyes had brightened to an accusatory flame. She looked spirited, alive, and Rafiq fisted his hands at his sides to stop himself from reaching for her. Instead he said, "I want to have DNA tests done before I pay a dollar."

"Have I demanded even one dollar from you since I got here?" she asked, her eyes blazing with what he realized in surprise was rage. Glorious, incandescent rage that had him blinking in admiration.

"I'm sure you intend to demand far more than that."

"There's no trust in you, is there?"

"Not a great deal," he said honestly. "When you grow up as wealthy as I have there's always someone with a new angle. A new scam."

"Everyone wants something from you?"

He shrugged. "I'm used to it."

There was a perturbing perception in her gaze. As if she understood exactly how he felt. And sympathized. But she couldn't. He'd found her in the backstreets of Hong Kong—hardly the place for someone who could have any insight into his world.

Crossing to the bedroom door that he'd left wide open, he paused. "I'll arrange for the DNA tests to be done as soon as possible." That would give him the answer he wanted and put an end to this farce.

"But you were going to take me to the airport."

Rafiq's gaze narrowed. Tiffany looked surprisingly agitated. "You're not staying in Dhahara long. You'll be on the first plane out once I have confirmation that your child is not mine. You're not going to hold that threat over my head for the rest of my life."

Once a week Rafiq met his brother Khalid for breakfast in one of Dhahara's seven-star hotels. As the two men were heavily invested in the political and economic well-being of the desert kingdom, talk was usually lively. But Rafiq was too abstracted by the rapidly approaching appointment for his and Tiffany's DNA tests that he'd arranged after their argument yesterday.

Before he could temper it, he found himself asking, "Khalid, have you ever thought what might happen if you get a woman who is not on father's list pregnant?"

His brother's mouth fell open in surprise. He looked around and lowered his voice. "I take great care not to get a woman pregnant."

So did Rafiq. It hadn't helped. He'd been a fool. "But what if you did," he pressed, pushing his empty plate away. "What would you do?"

Khalid looked disconcerted. "I don't know. One thing is for sure, an abortion would be out of the question. I suppose it would depend on the situation. The woman in question would have to be suitable for me to consider marrying her."

Suitable. Just thinking of the night he'd met Tiffany

made Rafiq squirm. She couldn't have been more totally *un*suitable if he'd scoured the entire earth. "That is true."

And there lay his problem.

"Of course," continued his brother, then pausing as a white-garbed waiter filled their cups with black, fragrant coffee and waiting until he'd left, "there has never been an illegitimate heir in our family. That's something else to consider. I suppose even an unsuitable marriage would be better than that," mused Khalid. "Later I could always find a second, more suitable wife who would perform the state duties."

Rafiq had never considered marriage to Tiffany an option. As he sipped his coffee, another thought occurred to him. "If there's a marriage, then there's divorce, too."

Khalid frowned. "As a last resort. It's never popular for a ruler to divorce a consort."

But, even though his brother didn't know it, they weren't talking about Khalid. They were talking about *his* situation. And Rafiq was not heir to the throne. It wouldn't attract the same degree of censure.

Marriage to legitimize the child followed by divorce might work…*if* the child turned out to be his.

Rafiq set his cup down and flicked back a starched cuff to glance at his Cartier watch. Time to go. Tiffany would be waiting for him to collect her from his residence. "It's later than I thought. I have an appointment—I must go."

"If I divorced her, I'd make sure the child—if it was a boy—was well out of her control," said Khalid thoughtfully.

Arrested, Rafiq turned to gaze at his brother. *Of course.* "Thank you."

While Khalid shook his head in bemusement, Rafiq strode across the dining hall with a light heart. Sometimes the solution to a seemingly insurmountable problem was far simpler than a man dreamed.

The doctor's rooms were surprisingly modern. A glass desk paired with crisp-white walls hung with framed sketches of flowers gave the room a contemporary feel. Nothing like the heavy dark furniture Tiffany had expected. Even more astonishing was the fact that the doctor was female. Although on second thought, that shouldn't have surprised her. No doubt many Dhaharan men preferred their wives to be examined by a woman doctor.

Yet it was the doctor's words that had caused the tension that presently gripped Tiffany. Shaking her head until her hair whipped about her face, she turned to Rafiq and said defiantly, "I'm not agreeing to that."

Rafiq gave Dr. Farouk a charming smile. "Excuse us for a moment, please."

The doctor rose to her feet. "Of course, Your Highness. I'll be next door when you need me."

A few words and a smile from him, and the doctor simply obeyed? Vacating her own office? Tiffany was taken aback at the display of his power.

No wonder Rafiq believed he could get whatever he wanted.

"I'm not signing the consent for surgery." Tiffany gestured to the paper that lay on the desk.

Rafiq raked a hand through his hair, rumpling the sleek perfection. "I was prepared to undergo the indignity of a test—why can't you be more cooperative?"

"A swab taken from your inner cheek?" She snorted. "That's nothing. If it was just a simple DNA test, I wouldn't have a problem. But you heard the doctor. Getting the baby's DNA is not going to be that easy."

The doctor had laid the options out for them. Getting the baby's DNA would require a surgical procedure. Because Tiffany was only ten weeks pregnant, amniocentesis could not be performed. Instead, a thin needle, guided by ultrasound, would pass through her cervix to retrieve little fingers of tissue from the wall of the uterus beyond. Like her baby, the tissue, which the doctor had called chorionic villi, originated from the egg that Rafiq's sperm had fertilized.

"You're not going to change my mind," she warned him.

"Be reasonable—"

"Reasonable? You heard the doctor. The procedure holds risks to my baby."

He waved a hand. "Very slim percentages."

"Miscarriage is not a percentage I'm prepared to risk."

Rafiq's eyebrows lowered to form a thick line over his eyes, making him look fierce and formidable. "How else am I supposed to find out whether the baby is mine?"

She glared at him, determined not to let him know that her heart was knocking against her ribs. "You're prepared to risk this life growing within me, so that you can evade the responsibility of fatherhood?"

"That's not true—"

"Of course it's true." She averted her gaze. "You could easily wait until the baby is born, *then* have the necessary tests done. But no, that doesn't suit the great sheikh. So you want to risk my baby's life to get the answer you're expecting. Well, I'm not going to let that happen!"

"You're hardly in a position to dictate terms," he breathed from barely an inch away.

"I'm in the best position," she fired back. "I'm not signing that consent form."

"Then you'll lose any chance of a quick cash settlement."

"I don't need your monetary support. I just wanted you to know…" Her voice trailed away.

How to explain? Her childhood had been less than perfect, disrupted by her father's affairs. Rafiq might've been distant, but he'd struck her as honorable. She'd wanted her daughter to have a father. Resting her fingertips on her stomach, Tiffany said softly, "One day this baby will want to know who her father is—and I would never keep that from her."

"Nor would I. This is not an attempt to evade responsibility."

It appeared her accusation had irked him.

He leaned toward her. "Tiffany, understand this, as long as a child is mine, I will take care of it."

"It?" His use of the derogatory term revealed the disparity between them. "No baby of mine could ever be an 'it.' She's a person. Infinitely precious."

"That's why you have no choice but to take this test. So that I can give the child the best if it is mine." But he was looking less certain than he had only minutes ago.

"You could take my word," she snapped, but already Rafiq was shaking his head, his eyes beginning to glitter with what she recognized as annoyance. She held her ground. This was not an issue she was prepared to negotiate. "Then you have no choice but to wait until the baby is born."

Rafiq got to his feet and started to pace. "Neither of those are options I'm prepared to accept. I want hard evidence that your child is not mine—so I can escort you out of the country."

"I'm not risking a miscarriage. You can't force me to

undergo this procedure," she stated, and hoped like hell she was right. Nor could he make her stay.

Or could he? This was his domain, after all. When she'd come to Dhahara she hadn't known the extent of his power...that he was the king's son, a royal sheikh. And when she'd discovered that, she'd convinced herself that he wouldn't be interested in bringing up the child.

But now she was starting to get cold feet. His family made the laws in this country. Rafiq could do what he wanted to her—with her—and get away with it. Could he force her to have surgery against her will? Would he keep her in Dhahara if she wanted to leave?

Before her first flutterings of fear could develop into full-fledged panic, Rafiq had turned to face her. He stood still and erect.

Tiffany took in the magnificence of the man. The harsh hawk-like features. His dark suit that had to be handmade. The shine of his shoes. He could've stepped out of a magazine spread. Yet she didn't like what he was trying to persuade her to do.

"Look," she said, tempering her voice, "I told you my passport was stolen—you didn't believe me. Yet it was true."

"You blackmailed me."

"That's the interpretation you put on it." She pushed the fringe of her bangs out her eyes. "I bet you never thought you'd see the cash again. But I've paid you back in full. Now I'm pregnant—and you think that's a scam, too. Yet here we are in the doctor's office and it's true."

"How convenient."

She ignored his sarcasm and continued, "As much as you tell yourself I slept with the whole of Hong Kong, you must know that it's possible that you're the father of my child—"

Nothing she said appeared to be denting that shell. His eyes were still hard with suspicion. "We used a condom."

"And, of course, you'd like to put your faith in the percentages that say overwhelmingly that they're fail-safe?" She shook her head. "Because it suits you. Well, not this time. Something went wrong. Just like something could go wrong when the doctor takes the chorionic villi sample."

A frisson of unease slithered through her. She moved from one foot to the other under his stare. The fact that he was selfish enough to be prepared to jeopardize their daughter, a living being, had made her realize that maybe he wasn't the kind of father she wanted for her baby. How could she even contemplate occasionally leaving her daughter in his solo care?

The sooner she—and her unborn baby—left this country, the better for them both.

He didn't believe the baby was his, so he had no reason to stop her. The decision made, the tension that had been building within her started to ease.

"I'll leave Dhahara now. Today, on the first flight I can get. Once the baby is born, taking a sample from inside her cheek will be a breeze, compared to this invasive procedure. The solution is simple. Let's defer this discussion until then."

But instead of looking happy at the thought, he frowned. "Where would you go?"

His concern must stem for the prospect of the scandal he would face once it became known he'd fathered her unborn child. She knew all about gossip and scandal—it had been part of her world for too long. The best way to deal with it was to lie low.

"I can go to my parents' home in New Zealand." She

hesitated, contemplating telling him more about her parents, then decided it wasn't relevant, not now. She didn't even know where her father was. Thinking about her parents made her realize that soon there would be no home in Auckland. Her mother needed the money that the sale of the house would bring. "Although my mother will probably need to sell up the house in Auckland."

"Tiffany—"

She didn't need his pity. She rushed on. "There's a quiet seaside village I used to visit as a child." Her vision blurred at the memory of those carefree days. Everything had been so simple then. So happy. That was what she wanted for her child. "I'll go there."

He didn't look any happier. "I thought you wanted to meet my family. At least, that's what you had my aunt believing."

"I did. I mean, I do," Tiffany hastily amended her reply. "They're my daughter's family, too. But you've made it clear you can't wait to get rid of me. Why the sudden about-face?"

Tension quivered through him. "So why leave now? After coming all this way? What if it *is* my baby?"

Her daughter didn't deserve a father who would risk her very existence to evade paternity. No father would be better than that. She'd make up for her baby's lack of a father. She'd do everything in her power to be the best parent her daughter could have.

Rafiq was waiting for her response. She shrugged. "Do you care?"

Anger ignited in the back of his dark eyes, giving them a feral depth. "Yes. I care."

Sensing she'd miscalculated, she said quickly, "Well, after the baby is born, and once the tests have been done and your paternity confirmed, then you can decide whether you want a part in her life."

"You can bet your life on it I will."

Her instinct to flee wavered. Just as she'd decided he didn't want this baby, he ruined it by getting all passionate and showing her a glimpse of caring.

"My child will not be born illegitimate," he whispered. "There's never been an illegitimate heir born in my family." His carved features revealed no emotion. "That's why I need to know if the child is mine."

The unease deepened to panic. He didn't care about the baby at all. Only about legalities.

"It doesn't matter that the baby will be illegitimate. *She* will be loved." Tiffany gave *she* a not-so-subtle emphasis. "I'd never subject her to a marriage between parents who care nothing for each other." Her own parents had been wildly in love when they'd gotten married. Yet their marriage had become a battleground. Her father had been unable to resist other women, had helped himself to them like a child to candy.

When she married she would choose carefully. A nice, ordinary family man.

"It matters." His fist closed around her wrist.

Tiffany shuddered under the pressure of his fingers. "Well, this appointment is over. I'm not having this test done now, so this whole discussion is irrelevant until the baby is born."

In the meantime she was going to get her baby out of this country, out from under his control. She pulled her hand free of his and rose to her feet.

"Then I'm going to have to take your word that it's my baby." His features were stern as gazed up at her from where he sat, master of all he surveyed, in the doctor's office. "If you are lying to me, you will regret it."

"I'm not lying—"

He cut across her heated denial. "There's no option but for us to get married in the meantime."

"Get married?"

Tiffany was staring at him as if he'd taken leave of his senses.

Perhaps he had. Rafiq suppressed the urge to smile grimly at her wide-eyed shock. Did she not grasp the honor he'd offered her? But what choice did he have? He would use every advantage offered by his country's laws if the baby proved to be his own—he would marry her, divorce her and keep the baby as his own.

"I'm not marrying *you*."

She made it sound as if he were a particularly offensive variety of the male sex. As she pushed past him, he snagged her fingers between his, and growled, "Think of it as your lucky day. Lots of women want to marry me."

Tiffany opened her mouth, shut it and made a peculiar sound.

Rafiq leaned closer until her tantalizing fragrance enveloped him. "You wouldn't be thinking of claiming that you're so different from all those women, would you, Tiffany?"

The brief flash of awareness in her eyes turned quickly to something darker. He could see she remembered quite clearly what had happened the last time she'd vowed she was so different from the women who considered him charming. In fact, his determination to prove conclusively that she *did* find him charming was what had led to this present blackmail attempt of hers.

That realization alone should've leashed the reckless impulse to provoke her. But it didn't. Instead he remembered what she'd tasted like…the softness of her skin beneath his fingers…and every detail of what had followed on that hot, balmy night.

She was irresistible.

With a silent curse he realized he wanted to kiss her again. "Tiffany…"

He got to his feet and placed his hands on her shoulders, felt the shudder that quaked through her.

She didn't pull away. So he drew her closer. Breathed in the soft seductive scent of her. Filled his senses with her sweetness until he could wait no more.

Kissing Tiffany was like rediscovering a secret, shaded oasis filled with fragrant gardenias and leafy green trees. He hadn't even known that he'd missed her as intensely. Yet now he found himself drowning in her.

His eyes closed, he took his time to rediscover the softness of her mouth. When the kiss ended, the strength of the yearning to claim her mouth once again blindsided him. As he acted on the impulse, she shoved him away.

"Hey." He steadied her as the force of her shove caused her to stumble. "Steady."

She touched a mouth that, to his immense satisfaction, looked ripe and very well kissed.

"I don't want this!"

Rafiq quelled the impulse to prove her passionately wrong. Instead, he arranged his features into an expression of concern. "There's nothing wrong with enjoying kissing one's future spouse."

"No." She shook her head. "That's just it. We're not getting married."

He smiled to mask the impatience that surged. He wanted her. He would have her—once they were married. He'd sate himself then cut her loose. But she need not know that yet.

"Let's not play games, Tiffany. Marriage was the

ultimate prize you hoped to secure by coming here. You say it wasn't about blackmail or money. So that leaves only marriage." His lip curled. "Well, *you've* gotten all you could ever have wanted."

"I don't want to marry you!"

"You came here because you wanted to marry someone else?" Rafiq's mocking retort was met with silence. His gaze narrowed. A lightning-fast glance took in the slender fingers clenched into fists, her wary, defiant eyes.

There was someone else.

A blaze of possessiveness roared through him, the need to stake his claim, to mark her as his, now and forever. He yanked her up against him, tangled his hands in the tumbled waves of hair and captured her mouth roughly with his.

He was aware of the fine tremors that shimmered through her, of the way his thigh fitted between hers and how the cradle of her hips rocked against him. The intoxicating scent and taste of her filled his senses, and her tongue danced with his.

He was aware of everything about her. Only her. The rest of the world receded.

He was so far gone, that he didn't care about control, about leashing it, about the fact that Dr. Farouk might walk back into her office and discover him alone with her, kissing her. There was just Tiffany...and him.

And she was going to marry him.

Only him.

He broke the kiss and set her away from him with shaking hands. "There," he said, making his point. "You can't possibly share what we have with any other man."

"I don't."

Confused, he shook his head. Had he imagined the

expression on her face? No, it had been there. A look of yearning—and it hadn't been for him. He narrowed his gaze in a way that anyone who knew him well recognized. "Where is this fool who allows you to roam the bars of Hong Kong alone, untended? Who leaves you vulnerable to other men?"

"I haven't met him yet."

"What?" Rafiq felt like the world had tipped upside down. "We're arguing over a man who does not even exist?"

"Oh, he does exist." She wore a dreamy expression. "I know he does. Otherwise why was I put on earth? He's out there somewhere. I couldn't believe in love as much as I do, and have it not happen." A shadow passed over her face. "But I can promise you one thing—he's nothing like you. Suspicious. Distrustful. Emotionless."

"So what's he like then?" he scoffed.

Her eyes had gone soft and dewy. "He's ordinary. He's not famous. Or wealthy. He doesn't live in an obscenely ornate home, nor does he have movie-star looks—"

He bowed his head, and said with irony, "Thank you."

"I'm not referring to you," she said crushingly. "I'm trying to explain how ordinary he is. A white picket fence and two-point-four children kind of guy."

"Then what makes him so special?"

"He'll love me," she said simply. "And I'm the most important person in his whole world. In fact, I am his world. There's none of the pomp and circumstance that fills your existence."

The red tide that crashed over him couldn't possibly be jealousy. By Allah, the man did not even exist. Incredulous, he glared at her. Rafiq gazed into her clear, desert-and-sunshine eyes. His chest tightened.

Tiffany was speaking the absolute truth. She didn't want him. She wanted someone else…someone he could never be.

Seven

Tiffany might have won the skirmish about having a DNA test done, but the tension that filled the back of the chauffeur-driven limousine as they left the doctor's office warned her that there were still plenty of battles to come.

Rafiq broke the silence that stretched between them by leaning forward to issue instructions in Arabic through the intercom to the chauffeur.

"Let's walk," Rafiq said abruptly, as the Mercedes-Benz came to a stop and the back doors opened.

Tiffany followed him out and caught her breath at the sight of the park that sprawled in front of them, tall trees shading open green lawns and a forest of roses beyond. "Where is this?"

"These are the botanical gardens that lie between the hospital and the university. They were laid out by one of my ancestors. She loved gardens and roses."

"It's beautiful. So green. So unlike anything I ever expected to find in a desert."

"The unexpected surprise surpasses the expected."

"Is that a proverb?" she asked, and for a moment there was absolute accord, a sense of intimacy between them, as their eyes met and he gave her a slight smile.

"No, it's original. You can claim it if you wish."

The awful tension that had started in the doctor's rooms began to ease. She smiled back at him. "What a wonderfully romantic place."

"Don't hope to find your dream man here." Rafiq's face grew taut. "You may as well accept you're going to marry me."

Biting her lip, Tiffany walked swiftly away from him and considered her options. Marriage to Rafiq would make her parents' marriage look like a picnic at Disneyland by comparison. But the set of his jaw warned Tiffany to tread carefully. He might not believe the child was his, but he feared the slur of illegitimacy. Rafiq had decided to keep the scandal—and her—within his control.

She'd reached the rose gardens. She halted beside a bed of pale pink flowers. Rafiq stopped beside her. "Rafiq, be reasonable—"

"I'm being perfectly reasonable." He tipped his head back, and gave her a particularly arrogant look.

She gave a little laugh of disbelief. "You don't even believe I'm carrying your child." She touched her stomach. "Yet you're prepared to marry me. That's reasonable?"

"You didn't want to do the tests necessary to establish the baby's paternity, and I didn't force you. I'm prepared to take your word that it's my child and marry you, so that the real truth can be determined once the baby is born—as you suggested. How can you possibly accuse me of being unreasonable?"

He wore such a fake-patient expression that Tiffany ground her teeth. How had he managed to twist it all to make her the unreasonable party here?

To temper her rising agitation, Tiffany sucked in a steadying breath and tried to let the soft, warm wind that blew over the rose beds, releasing their sweet scent, soothe her frayed nerves. "All I wanted was to make sure that my daughter had a right to know who her father was. And to find out whether you would be prepared to acknowledge her—if she feels the need to seek you out one day. I had hoped we could visit. When she's older," she added hastily as his brows shot up, "she'll want to know who her father is."

He inclined his head. "Of course. I should've expected this. You came here to have me sign some sort of acknowledgment of paternity. A document that would enable you to claim maintenance, too."

"Coming here was never about money!" Tiffany almost stamped her foot. This was not about his ego. Or hers. It was about their daughter.

He spread his hands. "It no longer matters, Tiffany. Marry me, then as soon as the child is born we can test for paternity. If she is mine, I will support her. It is my duty."

Money. Duty. Those were the reasons a man like Rafiq married. It wasn't the kind of marriage she wanted for herself. Nor had she ever intended to marry a man of his wealth and position. She'd seen the strain a high-profile lifestyle had placed on her parents' marriage—a show-biz union—not a royal wedding, and her father didn't even have the kind of power this man did.

"Marriage between us would be a mistake," she argued desperately.

Rafiq was arrogant—even more arrogant than her

father. Tiffany shivered. Her father had trampled all over her mother's feelings with little respect. Given that the man before her had been treated like a proper prince since the moment he'd been born, she could expect even less from Rafiq.

If she were foolish enough to marry him...

"Why should it be a mistake?" His frown cleared. "We will work on it. All marriages take work."

Tiffany goggled at him, unable to believe what she was hearing. "You're prepared to put *work* into our marriage?" That was more than her father had ever done.

For a moment he hesitated, then he smiled, a charming smile that, despite all her reservations, caused tiny electric quivers to shoot through her. "Of course, I will work at it," he assured her.

So what if she reacted to his smile? She wanted the man. No problems there. Her body adored him. Just as well she wasn't ruled by her senses. "You'll really work at it?"

Rafiq's gaze bored into her. "You don't believe me, do you?"

She shrugged. "I'm sure you have great intentions."

"Why?"

"Why what?"

"Why can't you believe me?"

Okay, so maybe she'd been wrong. Her gaze slid away from his. Maybe marriage to him would work for their child. But it was a big decision to make—probably the biggest decision of her life. A group of students dressed in denim and some in traditional dress sauntered past them, chatting and laughing.

Tiffany drew a deep breath, weighing up whether to confide in Rafiq what a dreadful mess her parents' marriage had been, then dismissed the impulse. Why would Rafiq care?

When she turned her attention back to him, it was to find that he'd moved. He stood before her now, blocking her way, formidable and intimidating.

"I'm prepared to marry you, Tiffany. What have you got to lose?"

He said it as though she should be grateful for his largesse. It irked her that he thought she'd be such a pushover. "I'm not quite the nobody you think. My father is Taylor Smith."

He didn't react to the name. Finally he shook his head. "Should I know him?"

"In some circles he's very well-known. He's a film director."

"A film director." He raised an eyebrow. "What kind of film director?"

"He doesn't make skin flicks, in case that's what you're thinking." His films might be respectable, but her father's private life was a different story. The scandals that followed him would not meet the approval of someone as upstanding as Rafiq. "He's quite successful. He directed *Legacy*." Tiffany named a film that had taken the world by storm a couple of years ago. Recognition lit Rafiq's eyes.

"I watched that movie on the jet—it was about two years ago."

"That must've been when it first came out." His casual reference to flying by jet made Tiffany realize that while her father might travel by jet as part of his work, this man owned one. Help, his family probably owned a fleet of Lear jets!

"If your father is wealthy and successful, why were you working in Le Club?" he was asking.

Tiffany braced herself to hold his gaze. "After my purse was stolen, I called home. I discovered my father had left my mother for another woman the day before I met you in Hong Kong."

A host of unidentifiable emotions flickered over his face. "That would've been a shock."

"It was," she agreed, reaching blindly past him to touch a full, pink bloom, to give herself something to do. The velvet smoothness of the petals under her fingertips steadied her as she stroked them. "But there was nothing I could do. I could hardly add to my mother's stress at the time by telling her about the fix I was in—or asking her for money she didn't have. And my father was nowhere to be found. Nor could I have his business manager arrange it—because that was who he chose to run off with."

"So that's why—" He broke off.

"That's why what?" she prompted, glancing up at him.

The bitter chocolate of his eyes had turned black. "You had no one you could ask for money."

"I would've gotten out of there."

"By continuing to work at Le Club…by selling your body?" He looked suddenly, murderously angry.

"No, I would never do that!"

"Okay, I shouldn't have implied that you would. But now I understand why you are so reluctant to marry me."

"What do you mean?"

"You don't trust any man not to let you down."

Tiffany forced herself not to flinch. "That's ridiculous! You expected me to leap on your proposal? To marry you without thinking it through?" At his glowering expression, she said, "Oh, you did! I can see it on your face. Rafiq, how arrogant!"

Dark brows lowered over his eyes. "But when you think it through, you'll realize that it's the best option you have open to you." Rafiq reached forward and plucked one perfect, pale pink bloom then handed it to her. "Think of the child. This way the baby starts its life with both its parents."

Clutching the stem, Tiffany bent her head and inhaled the fragrance of the flower.

Yes. Rafiq was right. She had to think about her baby. Not about herself, what she wanted, but what would be best for her baby. She'd wanted to give her daughter the chance to have a meaningful relationship with her father, unbroken by the estrangement of living in separate countries she'd had with her father growing up.

Rafiq was offering that.

Raising her head, Tiffany said, "I need time to marshal my thoughts. Let me think about your proposal."

"I have a function tonight. I can afford to give you one night." He gave her a slow, incredibly sexy smile that caused her heart to roll over. "But be warned, I will demolish every one of your objections."

The Mercedes swept out of the forecourt of his home, returning Rafiq to the bank for the meetings that lay ahead for the rest of the day. Uncharacteristically, instead of pulling out his laptop and busying himself with the necessary preparation, he leaned back against the butter-soft leather headrest and stared out the window.

Tiffany came from a family that had wealth—and, possibly connections. It should've delighted him. It certainly made it easier to present her to his father as his prospective bride. The king would relish the red-carpet connection. Instead Rafiq felt as though someone had claimed a private treasure, one that he'd prided himself on discovering and appreciating when no one else did, and exposed it to the world.

Of course, the revelation meant that Tiffany didn't need

his resources, his wealth—as he'd mistakenly believed. She had no need to marry him, except for the baby's sake. She didn't even particularly want to marry him....

It was a startling realization. And it changed everything. Because he wanted her, had no intention of letting her go—at least not yet, and certainly not because of some fairy-tale notion of love that she desired.

They had so much more. She'd woken a fire, a depth of passion, that he'd never suspected existed within himself. He intended to stoke that fire, feed the flames and experience the full blast of the heat.

Tiffany *would* marry him.

The extent of his determination astonished him. What had happened to the part of him that withdrew when his paramours wanted a commitment and his father demanded a wedding date be set? Where had the voice of reason gone that anxiously warned him to take a step back before he got boxed in and caged for life?

Perhaps it was silent because this time he had an escape hatch. He stared unseeingly at the streetscape, not noticing the busy market as the Mercedes cruised past. Tiffany had even sensed it when she'd expressed her doubts about his promise to work on their marriage. The solution that had seemed so crystal clear after his discussion with Khalid was starting to become murky.

Because of this desire she roused in him.

Rafiq tried to tell himself this want wouldn't last. By the time the baby was born, the desire would be spent. Then he would do as he'd intended. *If* the DNA tests proved the baby was a member of their family, he would keep the baby—and divorce Tiffany. He'd have done his duty. The baby would be legitimate. In terms of the marriage contracts, he'd settle a fair sum of money on Tiffany.

He'd support his child. Make sure it—he, Rafiq

amended—went to the right schools, was given a fitting education and upbringing. The fact that Tiffany's father had wealth was an inconvenience, but Rafiq had no doubt he had the resources, the power, to win any legal battle her family chose to mount to seize the child. He would start by having Taylor Smith investigated to find out exactly what kind of financial resources the man had, and whether he possessed an Achilles' heel.

If the baby wasn't his…?

The Mercedes slowed to turn into the bank's underground car park. Still he hadn't started up his laptop, opened his calendar to view his coming appointments. The conundrum of Tiffany held his full attention. Rafiq didn't even want to think about how he would feel if it had all been an elaborate lie, if the baby wasn't his.

If she'd lied to him—he'd make Tiffany rue the day they'd ever met.

The night was long. Tiffany barely slept. Restlessness had taken hold of her.

Yes?

Or no?

What answer to give Rafiq?

Tiffany rolled into a ball, huddling her belly, and stared blindly into the darkness. If she refused to marry him and left Dhahara, while her daughter would have a mother, she'd grow up never knowing her father. Then what if Rafiq wanted nothing to do with her baby later…when she was older? At least if she married Rafiq now, he'd see the baby every day. A bond would form. How could it not?

Did she really have a choice?

With a sigh Tiffany flopped over onto her back. The man she'd met again in Dhahara was every bit as arrow-straight as the first time she'd met him. Suppressing her anxieties that she might lose her child, she'd come to Dhahara to establish contact with a banker...and discovered a sheikh. A royal prince.

Rafiq was a busy man. An important man. Tiffany already knew he traveled extensively. Would he take time out to spend with a family he'd never wanted? A baby daughter who was not the male heir he expected? Or would it be a reenactment of her own childhood with a father who was never home?

Through the window she could see only the brightest stars sprinkling the darkness. The moon was fuller than the sliver that had hung in the sky the night her baby had been conceived. If she married Rafiq, she would be the moon to his sun...barely meeting and separated by vast chasms of yawning space.

That realization made the decision so much easier. She did not want that kind of marriage. She would refuse his offer of marriage, and take her chances alone. One day she would tell her daughter who her father was. They didn't need Rafiq to be a family.

The decision that had been tormenting her made, Tiffany finally drifted off to sleep.

Tiffany's decision to turn down Rafiq's proposal was reinforced the next morning when she went down to breakfast and Lily hastily closed the newspaper she'd been leafing through—but not before Tiffany had caught a glimpse of Rafiq's handsome features spread over the page.

"May I?" She gave Lily a grim smile and reached for the paper.

Lily must've seen something in her face because she spread her hands helplessly. "You must realize, it's not my nephew's fault—women have been throwing themselves at him since he was a teenager."

So much for Rafiq's explanation to his aunt that they were business acquaintances. Lily had clearly read much more into their relationship.

Yet Lily's words brought no comfort. Tiffany stared at a series of photos of Rafiq at what was obviously a society event, a beautiful dark-haired woman clinging to his arm. This was why he hadn't been home for dinner last night. He'd generously given her time to make her decision, while he'd escorted another woman to a function.

Most women think I'm charming.

It appeared Rafiq had been right.

"She's beautiful," said Tiffany expressionlessly, her stomach tightening into a hard knot. *So this is how it begins.* It was her father all over again. There would always be women. The knowledge hurt more than she'd ever thought it could.

"It's the opening of the new wing of the hospital. Her family is well-known in Dhahara—and I'm sure Rafiq allowed himself to be photographed with her because of the large donation her family made to the new wing."

That possessive hand on his sleeve was a world away from polite. The tilt of the woman's head, her kohl-outlined eyes and society-goddess smile all announced her confidence in securing the man beside her to the world. Tiffany had never wanted a high-profile man who attracted women like bees to a honeypot. She had no intention of enduring what her mother had put up with.

Marriage to Rafiq was her idea of hell on earth.

She was going to say no—not only because her daughter deserved more than an absentee father, but also because she wasn't prepared to tolerate a string of photos with women that caused her to feel sick with doubt. Now she just had to communicate her decision to Rafiq. No doubt, he'd be glad to be rid of her. By tonight she'd be gone.

Turning her head away from Lily's concerned glance, Tiffany helped herself to apricots and dates and spooned over creamy yogurt and honey, sure that if she tried to eat anything more substantial she would gag—despite the beautiful display.

By the time Rafiq strode in minutes later, the offending newspaper had been folded and tucked away. Yet not even the flash of his white smile and his warm greeting could bring any softening to Tiffany's resolve. Her stomach started to churn, and nausea rose in the back of her throat.

Her spoon clattered into her bowl, and Tiffany pushed her chair back.

"Not so fast," Rafiq's tone made her pause. "Stay. We must talk."

Lily glanced at him. "I've got a few calls to make. I'll make them in your study if you don't mind, Rafiq."

Tiffany wanted to scuttle after Lily, anything to avoid the coming unpleasantness. Then she stiffened her spine. She'd sit across the table from Rafiq and give him her answer.

The sooner she got it over with, the better.

"I have one thing to ask of you," Rafiq said after his aunt had left them alone, his voice pure liquid. He'd pulled a chair up beside her, turning it so that he was so close that she could inhale the scent of lemon and soap.

Jolted out of her thoughts, Tiffany stared at him.

"We will create a tale of how we met. No one need ever know of our ignominious start. We will keep to the story that we are business acquaintances…who met during your time at university."

"You mean lie?"

He ignored her angry comment. "You did go to university, didn't you?"

He hadn't asked her that in Hong Kong. "I studied English literature and French. Our paths were unlikely to have crossed."

"You speak French?"

She nodded.

"Good," he said. "We will say that you assisted me with some translation."

He was sweeping her objections aside. Tiffany knew she had to make a stand, before he walked all over her. "I haven't said I'll marry you."

"Oh, we both know what your final answer will be. I only want to whitewash our meeting so that our families are not hurt by the scandalous nature of our first encounter."

Her father was far from an angel. And once Rafiq discovered Taylor Smith's affairs, he'd be trying to protect his family from the taint of her father's reputation. "Now that you know my family is wealthy, you're obviously no longer worried that I might blackmail you and Sir Julian," she said with a bite in her voice, the memory of the image of him and the beautiful woman still burning like salt in a raw wound.

He shook his head. And her heart leaped. Then he killed the hope. "The deal with Sir Julian has already been announced. It can no longer be jeopardized."

Already hurting with an emotion she didn't want to label for fear of admitting what she dared not confront, it stung that he hadn't admitted that he'd been wrong to doubt her.

"I'm not going to marry you," she said baldly.

There was a silence.

"I beg your pardon?" His voice turned ominously soft. To her relief he made no move to shift closer.

"I can't marry you."

As Taylor Smith's daughter, Tiffany was every bit as unsuitable as a blackmailing club hostess he'd met one night in Hong Kong. Her father might be a film director, but Tiffany had no doubt that his list of affairs had made him too scandalous for Rafiq's conservative family to tolerate.

He raised a brow. "You must marry me."

"The only reason for our marriage is to legitimize the daughter you're not even convinced is yours." It irked her to remind him of that, but right now she needed every argument she could muster.

"The DNA tests will tell the truth when the time comes." He reached out and took her hand. "But you're mistaken, Tiffany. The baby is far from the only reason I have for desiring to marry you," he argued, his eyes glowing with a light she was starting to recognize.

Oh, no!

Tiffany tried to free her hand, waving the other to ward him off. But when he trailed a finger down the side of her face, little quivers of delight followed in its wake. "Rafiq, that's not going to work," she said rather breathlessly.

"This always works for us."

Not today. Jealousy mushroomed into rage. "You haven't seen the photos in today's paper."

"What, a photo of me with the daughter of a man who donated to a cause I am a founding patron for?"

"It didn't look that innocent."

"Her hand was on my arm. I did not touch her. Pah, that's the paparazzi—always on the lookout for a scandal."

There was a ring of truth in his impatience.

But Tiffany had learned young that there was no whiff of smoke without a raging inferno someplace. A picture of her father with an adoring starlet in the gossip rags usually escalated into a passionate affair with the young actress in question not long after.

And Rafiq had admitted the first night they met that women found him charming. She had been warned.

Turning in her chair, Tiffany pulled the newspaper out from where she'd tucked it away on the seat beside her and unfolded it, spreading it out on the table, to glance at the image again.

She stared hard. Rafiq was facing into a camera, his expression carefully blank. No smile for the woman at his side. No glow of romance. Was Rafiq really different from her father? She wanted desperately to believe he was, but she had no intention of fooling herself that she could change such a man.

Perhaps the woman in the newspaper was indeed no more than a woman whose family he knew, a family who had donated a large sum to a good cause he sponsored.

She set the paper aside.

Rafiq was watching her. He hadn't even spared the paper a glance—he obviously didn't care what she believed. The ache in her chest that had begun when she'd first seen that picture intensified. It was an ache that was starting to concern her greatly.

"Have you ever been in love?" she asked suddenly.

"The kind of love that the poets wail about?" Rafiq grimaced. "Probably not. But the kind of love that makes me desire a woman? Then yes, several times—with a number of highly suitable women."

His candor caused a fresh stab of sharper pain.

Well, she'd asked, hadn't she? She could hardly complain when she didn't like the reply.

Shoring up optimism, she said, "But you never married any of them."

"I considered marrying one or two."

Tiffany blinked. "You did? So what stopped you?"

He shrugged, then glanced away, his lashes falling to mask his unfathomable eyes. His hair shone in the light of the morning sun that streamed through the high windows above and into the dining room. "The pressure of expectation. I only had to show a small amount of interest in a woman for my family, her family and the newspapers to start setting wedding dates."

His honesty startled her. She wished she'd never asked. "You felt trapped."

He met her gaze squarely. "Yes."

"Yet you have asked me to marry you—demanded that I marry you, in fact. After what you just told me, how do I know you're not going to back out at the last moment if you start to feel pressured?"

"I *have* to marry you," he pointed out. "You are with child—my child, you assure me." Then he smiled, his eyes crinkling, and her breath snagged in her throat. "And, at this stage, you have the advantage that your father hasn't produced marriage agreements for me to sign."

"And I'm supposed to be relieved by that?"

He laughed.

Tiffany didn't.

It was starting to occur to her that she had a much bigger problem on her hands than she'd ever dreamed. The man who'd asked her to marry him had been caught by the oldest trick in the book: pregnancy. And, worse, he was every bit as terrified of being trapped as she was of being cheated on.

"Do you expect a marriage of convenience?" he asked.

She did a double take. "You mean no sex?"

Rafiq was a passionate man. Their night together had proved that beyond a shadow of doubt. She wouldn't have picked him for a man who could survive the sexless wasteland that a marriage in name only would be. Unless he planned to go to other women…despite his marriage vows. The ache inside her intensified.

With a firm shake of her head, she said, "I don't know why I said that. It's irrelevant. I don't want the kind of marriage we'd have."

"Then we can have a different kind of marriage." His eyes grew lazy and he tugged the hand that he was holding, propelling her closer. Her chair scraped across the highly polished wooden floor. "With lots of sex."

"That's not what I meant—"

Before she could finish setting him right, his mouth closed over hers, full of ardor. Tiffany tasted coffee and desire. Deliciously tempting. She edged nearer. Closing her eyes, she sagged against him.

His body was hard against hers. He was aroused, she realized. She pulled away. "No!" Her voice was sharp. "I don't want that kind of marriage, either."

"You might think a marriage of convenience would work for the child's sake. You might think you want a romantic fairy tale." His eyes had darkened, coal-black, piercing. "But what I'm offering is the exactly the kind of marriage you want."

She wrenched herself out of his arms. "You don't know me. You have no idea what I want!"

His lips curved up, and his eyes smoldered. "Then why don't you tell me exactly what you want, and I will do everything in my power to give it to you."

Little frissons of excitement ran up and down her spine. It annoyed her that he could control her body's response so easily. "I've told you before—I don't want *you*. I want to marry a different kind of man altogether, someone—"

"Ordinary." The sexy smile vanished. "You're chasing

a chimera, Tiffany. Maybe you even believe it, but one day you will discover what I know already—that you have deceived yourself. You do not want anyone ordinary."

Tiffany pushed her chair back and rose to her feet. Forcing herself to laugh, the kind of light, careless laugh her mother gave when she pretended to dismiss her father's flirtations as inconsequential, she said, "So I suppose you're going to tell me exactly what kind of man I do want?"

"You want *me*."

Eight

As his stark words disappeared into a void of resounding silence, Rafiq knew at once he'd been far too forthright. Honeyed sentiments about love were what women wanted, not the honest, unvarnished truth.

Tiffany looked shaken. She opened her mouth, then closed it again. At last she found her voice. "Your arrogance knows no bounds."

Heat expanded inside his chest. "Have you forgotten where the conversation ended up last time you called me an arrogant jerk?" he asked softly, getting to his feet.

By the golden fire in her eyes he saw that she remembered. Perfectly.

"It won't end up in the same place this time."

He cocked an eyebrow, and gave her a slow smile as he advanced. "You are certain of that?"

"Absolutely!"

"I relish a challenge." And he watched the dismay dawn on her face with masculine satisfaction.

"Wait…" Tiffany backed up until the table was behind her. She held up her hands. "I didn't mean for you to interpret my statement that you were arrogant as a challenge to get me back into your bed—"

"You agree it will be too easy?" He kept coming, until her hands were flat against his chest. Could she feel the thud of his heart against her palms? He was intensely aware of the touch of her fingers through the silk of his shirt.

"Definitely not."

Despite his growing arousal, Rafiq was starting to enjoy himself. He suppressed a grin. "And that is a challenge for me to prove how easy it will be?"

She did a double take.

"No! I mean—" She paused, clearly fearful that he'd taken her denial as a fresh challenge.

"Hush." He placed a finger against her lips. "It's why I'm such a good negotiator."

This time he allowed himself a smug grin.

Her retort was cut off by the appearance of an aide at the door. "Your Highness, your office called. The first appointment for the day has arrived."

Rafiq glanced down at his watch. He had no intention of telling Tiffany that Sir Julian had arrived in Dhahara, not while he was trying to convince her to marry him. "He is early. My secretary is away. Please let Miss Turner, her assistant, know I will be in shortly."

After the aide had left, all teasing humor faded. Leaning forward he said, "Tiffany, what happened between you and me that night in Hong Kong—" Rafiq caught her hand in his "—should never have happened. It was dishonorable."

She stared levelly back at him. "I've got as much to lose

as you—I have no intention of telling the paparazzi about our night together…or the life we created."

Rafiq threaded his fingers through hers, aware of the quiver of her fingers. "I'm relieved to hear that." She opened her mouth to object. He continued quickly, "That night should never have happened. I don't know why—" He broke off and shook his head.

He still didn't understand what had happened to him that night. How he'd lost control so fast. Why it lingered in his mind…tempting him to repeat the experience, to the point where he couldn't wait to marry Tiffany and get her back into his bed.

Finally he said, "It doesn't change the fact that I will take responsibility for my actions."

She glanced up sharply. "Are you saying that you're prepared to believe that the baby is yours?"

Rafiq shook his head slowly. "I do not say that." *Yet.* "But I am prepared to concede that it is possible, and for that reason I am prepared to marry you."

"Even though it makes you feel trapped?"

He hesitated, then decided to let her believe it. He'd already told her he wanted her. She didn't need to know the full extent of the sexual power she held over him. He thought of her every waking moment. He'd never experienced anything like it. What harm would it do to let her think he was marrying her only out of duty? "We will discover the truth when the baby is born. Until then we will not talk of this again. It is about time you met my family, don't you think?" He smiled at her. "I will arrange for them to gather at Qasr Al-Ward, my brother's home—I think you will like it there."

Her eyes widened. "Wait—you can't drop a bombshell like that and leave."

"I'll answer your questions later."

Rafiq raised her hand and kissed the back. She gasped. It seemed as if he wasn't the only one affected by the sensual tie that bound them.

"If I don't leave now, I will be late for my appointment. I will send a car for you at five o'clock. Be ready. Tonight we will plan our wedding."

Rafiq had spoken the truth.

Tiffany lay in the marble bath with its dolphin faucets, soaking to relax her aching neck muscles, and admitted the truth to herself. She'd been fooling herself, she wanted him, only him. Only he had ever aroused an emotion that she could label possessiveness. Only Rafiq had ignited the heat within her that made her melt when he was near her.

She'd come to Dhahara to build a bridge to the future for her unborn daughter. She'd discovered a man she was no longer sure she would be able to walk away from.

So why didn't she throw caution to the wind and marry him? Because she still clung to part of her dream. She wanted more than a father for her child, and a lover for herself.

She wanted a man to marry her not because she was pregnant, not because she carried a royal heir, but because he loved her. But that dream was the biggest fairy tale of all.

The reality was that once Rafiq discovered how much the tabloids stalked her fickle father, it would outweigh the scandal of an illegitimate heir being born into the royal family. It was unlikely that he would need any second urging to drop her like a hot potato.

Sir Julian Carling had an agenda.

Rafiq sensed it as soon as the other man greeted him

as he stepped into the bank's wood-paneled boardroom. As soon as the discussions about the new hotel were out the way, Sir Julian pounced.

"My daughter, Elizabeth, was very taken with you, Rafiq."

Rafiq could barely recall the debutante he'd met at Sir Julian's home months ago. Across the wooden boardroom table, he gave the older man a noncommittal smile and put his slimline laptop back in its case. "I'm sure any man would be flattered by her attention."

Sprawled in the leather-backed chair, Julian said, "She's coming to Dhahara—the only reason she didn't come with me now is a work commitment. She's very involved in the Carling Hotel group, but she'd like to get to know you better. Perhaps, once Elizabeth arrives, we can talk about building a second hotel in one of the desert cities."

It was a bribe.

Rafiq had not managed to remain unwed for more than three decades without developing an uncanny sixth sense about matchmaking parents. But this time he got the feeling that he was being craftily boxed in by a master operator. Getting to his feet, he made it clear that the meeting was at an end. "Julian, I must inform you that I'm getting married. My bride and I will probably be away when your daughter arrives."

"Married?" Sir Julian sat up and planted his elbows on the boardroom table, displeasure written all over his florid features. "When I spoke to your father only a few days ago, he suggested I bring Elizabeth to spend time with you. He said nothing about your marriage."

Because, at the time, his crafty father hadn't known. Rafiq could have throttled the king. So much for taking up his joking suggestion that Elizabeth Carling might suit Khalid; his father had had another plan altogether.

"My bride and I will be married before the week is out." Speaking with utmost confidence, Rafiq bent to pick up his laptop case. He would give Tiffany—and the king—no choice in the matter. She'd become a temptation he could not withstand.

"I'll have to make sure I'm here to celebrate the event."

"My fiancée wants a quiet, family wedding." As he spoke, Rafiq wondered whether Tiffany would agree to a marriage without her parents present to give their blessing.

Tiffany didn't know what she'd expected, but it certainly wasn't the fortress of sun-bleached sandstone that rose out the surrounding desert. She peered through the window of the Mercedes-Benz to get a better look.

"Good heavens."

"Qasr Al-Ward," Rafiq announced as the black car came to a stop in the graveled forecourt.

"Your brother and his wife live here?"

"Yes, my brother has made his home here—he spends as much time as he can away from the city with his wife."

Only one wife?

But Tiffany bit back the sarcastic retort as the chauffeur opened the door for her. The stifling heat of the late afternoon closed around her. Alighting from the backseat, she started to worry about the simple white dress she wore. "I'm not dressed up enough."

"Don't worry. More often than not Shafir is covered in desert sand. My brother won't even notice what you are wearing." There was a gleam of humor in Rafiq's eyes. "But if what you are wearing concerns you, I am sure clothes can be found that will be more to your liking."

Shafir Al Dhahara wore flowing white robes with not

a speck of dust. But his wife was a surprise. Tiffany found herself enchanted by Megan—and it was clear that Shafir adored his wife.

"I have heard all about you," said a tall, dark man with liquid-gold eyes coming up to stand behind the couple at the top of the stone stairs that led to the vast front door. "Rafiq, aren't you going to introduce us?"

Well, Tiffany had heard nothing about him—she didn't even know who he was.

Rafiq waved a careless hand. "Tiffany, this is my brother, Khalid."

She smiled, and wondered how many more brothers Rafiq had.

As if Khalid had read her thoughts, he said, "There are three of us. I am the eldest and Shafir here is the middle son. Rafiq is the baby of the family."

Ha. Some baby!

Tiffany waited for Rafiq to object; instead he gave his brother a rough hug. "Father will be here later. He had a meeting with the council of elders. Now let us go inside."

The thought of meeting Rafiq's father, the king, was enough to give Tiffany the shakes. But before she could worry about it any further, Shafir's wife came up beside her.

"Would you like something to drink?" Megan asked. "It's going to be a hectic few hours."

A hectic few hours?

Despite her bemusement Tiffany requested a glass of soda.

"What did Megan mean by 'a hectic few hours'?" she asked, dropping back to speak to Rafiq.

He avoided her gaze.

She put a hand on his arm to stop him moving away. "Answer me."

"Ah, look at the lovebirds," chortled Shafir.

"Let Tiffany and Rafiq alone," Megan scolded her husband. "Rafiq, you can use your usual suite of rooms. Tiffany, for now, I've given you a chamber in the old harem—but don't let that freak you out."

Megan's statement did indeed freak her out. But not the bit about the harem. "A chamber?"

Did Megan mean a bedchamber? They weren't staying the night, were they? Rafiq had said nothing about that.

Megan nodded. "I'll send one of the maids to help you dress for the party."

Help her dress? Tiffany suddenly knew exactly how Alice must've felt when she blundered down the rabbit hole. "What party? I didn't think to bring a change of clothes with me."

"Your clothes—"

"Megan," her husband grasped her arm, "you talk too much."

Megan glanced around, a resigned expression on her face. "Have I put my foot in it again?"

Turning away from his family to confront a silent Rafiq, Tiffany demanded, "What is going on?"

Behind her she could hear Megan saying, "Dammit, I *have* put my foot in it. Why did none of you bother to tell me that she didn't know?"

Tiffany's sense of ire grew. "Don't know what?"

"Er—" Rafiq started to move past her. "Come through to the salon."

"Rafiq?" She grabbed at his sleeve. "Tell me."

"My family—every one—is here to celebrate our engagement this evening."

Tiffany's mouth fell open. *"Our engagement?"*

"You should've tried seduction, Rafiq." The male voice was followed by hoots of laughter.

Oh, dear God! "Do they know I'm pregnant?" she whispered, humiliation creeping over her in a sickly wave at the thought of their night together being the subject of ridicule.

A flare of color seared his cheekbones, but he didn't drop his gaze. "Ignore Shafir, he knows nothing. It's a joke—I once told him he should seduce Megan—he's simply trying to score points."

"Did he?" she asked in a low tone.

"By your expression, it looks like he did."

She shook her head impatiently. "Not now. Did he seduce Megan?"

"No, he decided to kidnap her instead."

"Kidnap her?" Tiffany's eyes stretched wide as they followed the rest of the party into a large room that overlooked lush gardens with tall palms and pools of water. *"Really?"*

He nodded. "He brought her here—and kept her under lock and key."

"You've got to be joking! Right?"

Rafiq shook his head. "No, I'm not. Ask Megan."

Megan's voice piped up, "What must Tiffany ask me?"

"Hush, wife," said Shafir, and everyone laughed.

"Did your husband kidnap you?" Tiffany stared at the other woman, sure that she was being mercilessly teased.

"Oh, yes. Except he wasn't my husband back then."

"And he kept you here until you agreed to marry him?"

Megan shook her head, and reached for Shafir's hand before casting him a loving glance. "He didn't force me to marry him—he was trying to stop me from marrying Zara's fiancé."

"Zara's fiancé?" Tiffany did a double take. "But Zara's Lily's daughter. Isn't she in L.A.?"

Shafir only laughed. "It's a long story."

"Sounds like one I should hear," Tiffany said darkly.

"Not before you marry me," objected Rafiq. "Although maybe I'll have to take a leaf out of Shafir's book and lock you up here."

She spun around. *"What?"*

Rafiq glanced at her annoyed face and then around at their attentive audience. "Excuse us, please."

He wrapped one arm around her shoulders, hooked the other behind her knees and swept her off her feet. He hoisted her high against his chest. Tiffany buried her face against his throat to drown out the whoops of laughter as he exited the room.

When they reached a sitting room where scimitars adorned a wall, he lowered her to her feet.

Tiffany couldn't restrain herself. "How could you do that? *In front of your family?* And how could you announce our engagement to them? I haven't even said I'll marry you."

His eyes were guarded. "Of course you will."

Tiffany threw her hands up. "But I haven't said 'yes.'"

He arched a brow in a gesture that had become endearingly familiar. "So say it."

After seeing how Shafir doted on Megan, Tiffany was wildly tempted to give in and let herself be dragged down the aisle. When she'd come to Dhahara to tell Rafiq about his baby, marriage was not what she'd expected. Yet she was unbearably tempted.

A pang pierced her.

"Don't look so desperate."

She lifted her head. "I'm not desperate."

"Only love makes you desperate." His mouth twisted. "And this match isn't about love."

He paused, and Tiffany wondered how he expected her to respond. When he remained silent, she said, "You will regret our marriage."

"What do you mean?"

This time there was no hesitation. It wasn't right to let him walk into a marriage without at least warning him. "The tabloids adore my father. He can always be relied on to deliver a story."

"Do you mean that he feeds them Hollywood leaks?"

"No, no. Nothing like that. He has affairs with actresses—much to my mother's grief." She clenched her hands at her sides. "Your family will not be happy."

"Tiffany." His hands closed over her shoulders. He pulled her up against his chest. He felt so unabashedly solid and male. "You need to understand that I am marrying you—not your father."

"He will cause you a lot of embarrassment."

Rafiq shrugged against her. "That is not your doing."

The last bastion of her line of defense crumbled. A warmth spread through her, and tears pricked at her eyes. Her hands crept up his shirt front and a fierce emotion shook her.

"Thank you," she whispered.

What did she have to lose? Pulling back a little, Tiffany met his melting gaze, and said, "Okay, I'll marry you."

Nine

The wedding contracts had been signed.

Once Tiffany had accepted his proposal, Rafiq had wasted no time in the week that followed to arrange their wedding.

He thought about their unborn child. His daughter perhaps...

How would he have felt if some stranger had gotten his daughter pregnant after a one-night stand? Rafiq realized he would've been furious!

With a little trepidation he'd approached inviting her parents, but Tiffany had decided against it. Her mother had a lot of adjusting to do, she'd explained, and right now she didn't feel like seeing her father.

Rafiq hadn't agreed, but he'd gone along with it. For Tiffany's peace of mind.

Now, oblivious of the knot of people clustered around, Rafiq waited beside the ancient well in the heart of Ain

Farrin, the village not far from Qasr Al-Ward where the spring, or *ain*, originated, and watched Tiffany come toward him through the grove of tamarisk trees.

His bride.

She wore a long, cream-colored silk dress embroidered with rich gold thread and topped with a gauzy silk wrap. A filmy veil covered her hair. Her hips swayed as she walked, a legacy of the high heels she wore.

Rafiq wasn't aware of his family, or the villagers who crowded around. He only had eyes for Tiffany.

Her eyes glittered beneath the draped veil. She stopped beside him in the dappled shade of an ancient olive tree, and he reached for her hands. Her fingers trembled as his fingers closed around hers.

His bride was nervous.

Tenderness flowed through Rafiq. An urge to protect her from anything that might harm her. He drew her toward him and turned to face the celebrant.

He closed his eyes as the holy words flowed over them. After placing a ring on her finger, he received one in return. They knelt, then circled the well in a train, while the village children tossed rose petals from the gardens of Qasr Al-Ward over them.

As he brushed the petals from her veil, he saw her eyes were dazed.

"Almost over," he mouthed, and his heart soared as he caught a glimpse of her smile through the spun-silk veil.

He would not let her down, he vowed. Nor would he ever abandon their daughter when she needed him most.

After the wedding festivities were over, they returned to Qasr Al-Ward. Rafiq had told Tiffany that Shafir and Megan had loaned them the ancient palace for a few days.

The knowledge that, with the exception, of a skeleton staff, they were totally alone, made her unaccountably edgy.

Rafiq was her husband.

They were married.

She was already expecting his daughter; this was not going to be the romantic honeymoon of newlyweds.

Yet as the sun sank over the distant horizon, leaving a glow of burnished gold over the desert sands, Tiffany followed Rafiq through corridors lit by torches set in wall sconces, and couldn't help being affected by the expectant air of exotic romance. It felt like a honeymoon. Blood pounded through her veins.

When he led her into a vast chamber lit by dozens of candles that illuminated a bed in the center, she balked.

"What about our marriage of convenience?"

That got his attention. He swiveled to face her. "It's not going to happen. I made that clear when I asked if you expected one. I know you, Tiffany, better than you think. I suspected you might have convinced yourself that was what you want."

"But you knew better."

The candlelight gave his skin a bronze cast. It threw warmth over the harsh features, and lit up the white pants and tunic he'd worn for their marriage. "I know what you want. You want me."

The bed behind him loomed large in the room. Tiffany could already feel that her breathing had quickened, that her body had softened. "You flatter yourself."

His mouth slanted. "Because I can never be the white knight of your dreams?"

The edge to his voice caused her to frown.

"Exactly."

"You're fooling yourself if you think you can exist

without passion. You were made to make love. I knew that the first night we were together."

Determined not to fall into his arms, she said, "I only slept with you out of gratitude."

His eyes began to glitter. "Did you?"

Her pulse accelerated and she crossed her fingers. "Yes."

"Thirty dollars worth of gratitude?"

She didn't like the way he made that sound. "Uh…"

"And this time you're sleeping with me because you're so grateful—" he stressed the word as he stalked toward her "—that I married you?"

"Of course not!"

She didn't back away as he came to a halt in front of her. "Then it must be because you know exactly how much pleasure is in store for you, hmm?"

Her stomach started to flutter. "No, Rafiq, no sex."

Not now. Not while he was in this mood, even though she knew she'd deliberately provoked him.

"It will be much more than sex." His voice deepened to a husky growl that turned knots in her stomach. "I will pleasure you, just you wait and see."

He planted his mouth on hers and her lips parted.

It didn't take long for him to elicit a response, even though Tiffany fought with herself to resist. To her utter frustration he raised his head just enough to put a space between them. "Are you suitably grateful for that?"

The high heels she wore meant her eyes were level with the sinful passion of his mouth.

"Just shut up," she said, flustered by the desire that bolted through her like a jab of electricity.

This time, when he took her in his arms, she went up on the tips of her toes, and met him halfway. All her objections had evaporated.

"You know I'll never forgive you for this, don't you?" she muttered when he lowered her to the soft satin covers.

He laughed as he slipped off her shoes. "I've been wanting to do that all day." Next he peeled off the veil and carefully eased the ivory and gold dress away from her shoulders.

He followed her down onto the bed. "You'll love every moment. That I will promise you."

When she woke the next morning it was to meet a pair of slumberous dark eyes. Embarrassment seared Tiffany. Her cheeks grew hot, her breasts, the heat spread.

Rafiq propped himself onto an elbow and started to smile as he gazed down at her. His eyes glowed. "You don't need to blush—we have done nothing to be ashamed of. We are married."

She gave an incoherent murmur.

He pushed the sheet away from her body. Tiffany snatched at the edge as it slipped away.

"Don't be shy." His hand stroked the soft flesh of her stomach. "I find it hard to believe there is a baby in here. You were so tight… You could've been a virgin."

Tiffany's flush deepened. "You're embarrassing me," she said.

"Why?" At her sharp inhalation, he said, "Let's have no pretense or secrets between us, Tiffany. I knew you were no virgin last night."

Her breath whooshed out in a frustrated sigh. "If there are to be no secrets, then you should know that the only other time we made…love—" she stumbled over the word "—I was a virgin."

Tiffany glanced up at him from beneath her eyelashes to see how he'd taken her revelation.

His face had gone curiously blank. After a moment's

pause, he said, "Ah, Tiffany, you need not worry. I did not expect to find an innocent that night we first met."

She fell silent, her lashes sweeping down against her cheeks.

"Do not sulk," he whispered, running a finger along the ridge of her nose. "I never wanted a virgin."

Her lashes lifted. She met his eyes, so close now, that a stab of desire spiked through her. "I'm not sulking! But I had hoped you'd gotten to know me better by now. That first night in Hong Kong, you thought I was scamming you—"

"I know—"

"I was in a desperate situation—"

"I know that—"

"I've repaid every cent you gave me. I've told you the truth about the baby—"

"Tiffany, Tiffany." He pulled her into his arms and rolled onto his back, tugging her over on top of his chest. "It doesn't matter whether you were a virgin or not." He lifted his head off the pillow and kissed her brow.

She opened her mouth to tell him that it did matter. That she needed him to trust her—as she'd trusted him by telling him about her parents, by confessing that her father would never be the ideal father-in-law. She needed a show of faith from him, too. And more than anything, she needed for him to believe that the baby was his. Just because she said so.

Not because of the incontrovertible results of a DNA test.

It hurt, this refusal to trust her. But he would learn that she hadn't lied to him—then he would be forced to apologize.

"Stop glowering at me." He ruffled her hair. "We will

make love. Then I will show you the desert that has always been so loved by my family."

Just as she had no doubt he intended, desire started to sing through her veins.

What did Rafiq love? Was it only sex? Would he ever love more than the attraction that burned so brightly, so wildly between them?

At that thought her heart thudded to a stop. Was this the reason she so desperately needed for him to trust her? Had she fallen in love with the husband she'd trapped into a marriage that he'd entered only from a sense of duty?

"Mom?" Tiffany pressed the telephone against her ear to overcome the hiss on the line. "How are you?"

"Holding together. I signed the final settlement papers yesterday—your father wasn't there."

Was that a wistful note she heard in her mother's voice? Tiffany fervently hoped not.

"Everything went smoothly," Linda Smith continued, "just as you said it would once we got a good lawyer."

"I'm glad." Tiffany gave a silent sigh of relief. Two months ago she'd found her mother a lawyer, and she'd gone with her to every appointment and provided moral support right up to the day before she'd left for Dhahara. With the settlement signed, at last her mother could start to put together the pieces of her life. "Have you thought any more about selling the house in Auckland and finding something cozier?"

Before Tiffany had left, her mother had still been adamant that she didn't want to move out of the house she'd shared with Taylor Smith—even though it was the best asset she owned. Tiffany had suspected her mother was clutching at straws, hoping her father would come to his senses and return.

How Linda could consider taking him back this time, when he'd physically moved out, Tiffany found hard to figure.

"No, I don't want to sell—and you'll need somewhere to stay when you come back from your holiday. Where was it you were going again?"

"Dhahara. Mom, there's something I need to tell you." Tiffany plunged on. "I'm not coming home for a while. I got married."

She held the handset away as her mother gasped, then squealed and reeled off a string of questions.

"I know it was sudden. But it was the right thing to do. His name is Rafiq…and the marriage was performed in a village near one of the family's homes. Three days ago."

This time her mother sounded more cautious than celebratory. "Three days ago? In that desert country?"

"Yes, Dhahara is a desert kingdom." Then, hoping it would reassure her mother, she added, "Rafiq is part of the royal family."

"Oh, honey, you will come visit?"

Tiffany's heart ached at the loneliness in her mom's voice. "Of course, we'll come see you. Rafiq travels a great deal—he's a banker. We'll visit soon. I'll talk to him, and let you know when."

"Tiffany…are you sure you're all right? It's such a long way away. I wish I could be there to help you."

"I'm fine. Honestly. You're better off selling the house than rushing across the world to see me."

Her mother sighed. "I don't want to move. And I feel I should be with you. I wish your father were here. He'd know what to do."

"I haven't told Dad about my marriage."

Tiffany heard her mother's intake of breath.

"But he's your father—he has a right to know."

"I will tell him, Mom." Eventually. "Right now I'm still too angry with him for walking out on you." And her father was equally stubborn—he hadn't contacted her since their stormy disagreement when he'd cut off her allowance, and told her that she'd be back soon enough with her tail between her legs.

"Tiffany, it's not your fight. With the counseling I started, I'm working on forgiving your father, and I'm starting to realize I may not have been the best wife."

"Oh, no, Mom—don't even think that! He had no reason to run around with other women. To walk out on you."

Silence hummed between them. At last her mother said, "But you need to let him know about your marriage. You're still his baby girl."

It had been a long time since she'd been his little girl. Tiffany gentled her tone. "When I'm ready—I'm not ready yet." More than anything in the world she needed time.

"Darling, are you sure you know what you're—"

"I'm expecting Rafiq's baby, Mom."

This time the silence was electric.

To break it, Tiffany said desperately, "I came to Dhahara to tell Rafiq about the baby. My little girl will need a mother *and* a father." Surely her mother, of all people, would understand that better than anyone in the world? "In time she'll need grandparents, too, so don't worry. I know I have to tell Dad the good news."

Just not now. Not while her own hurt at his countless betrayals would spill out.

"Oh, darling, you should've told me you were pregnant before you left."

Tiffany couldn't handle recriminations right now. "Mom, you had enough to cope with."

"I feel terrible. I didn't even guess—"

"You weren't supposed to."

There was a short pause as her mother absorbed that. Then she said, "I feel like I let you down."

"Nonsense," said Tiffany loyally.

"But—"

"Don't worry about me," Tiffany interrupted. "I'm fine, Mom. I needed to make this decision myself. No one else could make it for me. Not you. Not Dad. Only I can take responsibility for my actions. I went into this with my eyes wide open."

That wasn't strictly true. She'd gone in with some illusions. She hadn't expected their marriage to be so *physical*. She was terrified of losing her emerging sense of identity to the heady passion that only Rafiq had ever awoken in her.

And now he was her husband...

The man who shared her bed. Her body. His body. Every night.

At least she wasn't in love with him. Nor he with her. It was better that way. Falling for Rafiq would be insanely stupid. Tiffany was not about to let Rafiq break her heart—not even if she was pregnant with his baby.

But she couldn't share any of that with her mother. Instead she said, "Rafiq took me into the desert yesterday. Oh, Mom, it was so beautiful.... One day I will show you, too."

Then maybe her mother might understand.

Ten

Rafiq gazed down at his wife.

A heavy tide of satisfaction swept in the wake of the rush of desire. They'd made love…slept…then made love again as dawn streaked the horizon.

He should've been sated.

He wasn't.

It would be a long time before he could claim to have had enough of his wife. But he would wait for tonight before taking her again. The day was hers. He would let anticipation build through the long, hot hours. Take her to a souk to watch her touch the soft silks. For an outing in the desert to see the excited glow in her eyes. He'd take her anywhere she chose to go. It was refreshing to see his world—Dhahara—through her eyes. The want could wait.

Until tonight.

"What would you like to do today?" He walked two fingers along her arm.

She peeped at him from beneath her eyelashes in a way that caused his heart to hammer in his chest. "It's been a very busy week."

"Indeed it has been," he agreed huskily.

"Is it going to be as hot today as it was yesterday?"

"Hotter."

She pursed her lips, her expression thoughtful. Her lashes fluttered down against her cheeks. "Perhaps we could stay here."

"Perhaps we should."

A wanton warmth pooled in the pit of his belly. Rafiq could think of nothing more perfect than remaining exactly where they were—here in this bedchamber, the lacy white wooden shutters flung open to the whisper of the desert wind.

Tiffany was fitting surprisingly well into his life. His aunt Lily had taken a shine to her—probably because she was missing Zara. His brothers liked her. He was sure his father had enjoyed meeting her, too, although they had spoken only briefly the night of their engagement and at the wedding.

As for him…

He thought Tiffany was everything he'd ever wanted. Reaching out one hand, he pushed the curtain of silken hair off her face, then leaned down and pressed a kiss against her cheek. It was an impulsive gesture, done without plan. Yet she immediately turned her head and her lips clung to his in a kiss so gentle, so full of sweetness, that his chest grew tight.

He groaned softly.

He had intended to break the news of Tiffany's pregnancy to his family. To confess the real reason for their marriage. So that they knew that after the birth of the child the marriage could be dissolved. Yet somehow he'd kept putting it off. And now he couldn't very well announce she was pregnant—and in the same breath request them to keep his plan to divorce her secret from Tiffany.

In fact, Rafiq was starting to think that if the child turned out to be his, he might as well stay married to Tiffany....

Last night had only served to confirm that the nights alone would make it worth the sacrifice.

"I hadn't exactly meant to stay here—in bed—all day," she murmured breathlessly.

He reared over her and the tangled sheets fell away. "Why not?"

Tiffany glanced at his naked chest. When her gaze returned to his, her eyes glittered bright gold. "What will people say if we remain barricaded up in the bed-chamber?"

He shrugged. Who cared? "That we just got married? That I can't keep my hands off my wife?"

He matched actions to the words and ran a hand along the delicate curves of her body. She shuddered and instantly his own desire rocketed.

"Rafiq!"

"What?" He bent forward to taste her again.

She fended him off with flat palms. "We shouldn't…"

"Why not?"

Her palms softened against his shoulders, toying with the sleek muscles of his arms, moving over his shoulders, drawing him close.

"You know," she breathed, "I can't think of a single good reason anymore."

"I am pleased." Rafiq's breath mingled with hers.

Then there were no more words, only touches so sensual, so arousing, that he forgot about everything except the woman in his arms.

The first week after their wedding passed in a whirl.

It was Thursday by the time they finally returned to Katar, the capital. That evening, Tiffany crossed the threshold of the dining salon in Rafiq's home and came to an abrupt halt.

She had not yet called her mother back—or discussed the possibility of a visit with Rafiq. Her poor mother must be going nuts.

"What is it?"

Rafiq moved from where he'd been standing beside the highly polished table. As he came toward her, Tiffany took in the black trousers and loose white shirt he wore. No dark suit. Yet the casual clothes only served to heighten his raw masculinity, and the top button left undone to reveal the smooth skin of his throat underlined it.

Tiffany jerked her attention away from that taunting bit of naked skin and back to his face. "Nothing. I just remembered something I've been meaning to do." She glanced around. "Where's Lily tonight?"

"We're married—there's no longer any need for my aunt to stay with us."

"Oh."

His aunt's presence had been comforting. Without her there was suddenly a whole new tension in the air.

Before she could bolt, Rafiq pulled the high-backed chair out for her.

"Thank you." Conscious of him behind her, Tiffany sat down. He smelled of sandalwood and soap and an exotic spice she didn't recognize. Focusing on the woven table mat in front of her, she gathered her thoughts as Rafiq settled into the seat opposite her. Finally she lifted her head.

Hamal, his chef, had entered and was lighting a dozen candles arranged in a heavy wrought-iron holder on the table. The golden glow of the flame washed over Rafiq's skin, the warmth softening the harsh, handsome features. Tiffany's stomach tightened and desire, never far away, licked at her belly.

As soon as Hamal retreated, Rafiq stretched out and took her hand. "Would you like to meet me for lunch tomorrow? A date? To make up for the lack of them before our wedding?"

She flushed with pleasure. When Rafiq was in this mood, he was downright easy to like. "That would be nice."

He relaxed slightly. "I've booked a table at the best Japanese restaurant in the city."

"Japanese?" she asked, surprised.

He nodded and Tiffany couldn't help noticing how the candlelight moved lovingly across his hair, bringing a bright sheen to the rich sable. As Hamal returned to place large, white plates on the place mats before them, Rafiq released her fingers. Unexpectedly, she found herself missing his touch.

"There's a fairly large Japanese community living in Dhahara—part of the booming motor industry. You'll enjoy the food."

"I look forward to it."

"There are some upcoming events I need to discuss with you."

So, not a date. A meeting. A little of the pleasure at his invitation went out of her. "What kind of events?"

Tilting his head to one side he said, "On Saturday

night there's a banquet in aid of the children's wing at the hospital."

No harm could come from attending that. Her wariness had been misplaced. Yet images from last week's newspaper floated through her mind. Pictures of Rafiq and an adoring, beautiful woman. Lily had said that had been at the opening of the hospital's new wing. This time *she* would be at Rafiq's side.

As his wife.

Something of her fierceness must've shown on her face, because Rafiq said, "I know. I know. I should've asked you before, but it slipped my mind." The smoldering look he gave her made it clear exactly what *had* been on his mind. "I'm the guest of honor, so we can't refuse."

Tiffany pushed away the memory of the other woman and took ruthless advantage of his admission of forgetfulness. "I need to ask you something, too."

"To take you shopping for clothes to wear?"

"No. More important."

The sensual warmth evaporated as his gaze jerked back to her face, intense and penetrating. "What is it?"

She wriggled, and crumpled the white linen napkin she'd just unfolded into a ball. "I spoke to my mother a few days ago."

"Your mother?" A crease appeared between his dark brows. "Did you tell her about the wedding?"

Tiffany nodded.

"And your father? Did you get in contact with him, too?"

This time she shook her head. "I'm not ready to talk with him yet." Then she added in a rush of honesty, "I didn't invite my mother to the wedding because I didn't want her to worry about me."

"You think marrying me would concern her?"

"It was easier to present her with a fait accompli." Tiffany helped herself to what looked like meatballs and spooned a mix of eggplant, tomato and okra on the side.

"That way she could do nothing about it."

"Exactly."

"So what's the problem?" he asked slowly.

"She's worried she's not going to see me as often as she'd like. I told her we'd go visit." From the corner of her eye she saw that Rafiq had started to eat, too. "And she's worried about why I married you. I told her I'm pregnant," she added in a rush.

Tiffany took a flatbread from a basket to give herself something to do. The mundane act of breaking the bread and first dipping the bits into olive oil then dredging them in *dukka*, a fragrant mixture of roasted nuts, toasted sesame and coriander seed, steadied her.

"You're not regretting our marriage already?" Rafiq's expression was somber.

Tiffany swallowed. Was he regretting the marriage? Did he feel trapped? "What makes you think that?"

"Good to know there is no cause for concern," he purred. "Though our lovemaking is so passionate that I would find that hard to believe...even though you keep me far away from your heart."

"I'd have to be a fool to let you into my heart. You're a prince of a wealthy desert kingdom. Eligible, rich, good-looking—"

"Thank you." He set down the knife and held up a hand. "I've heard enough. It is quite clear my attributes don't match up to your list."

Her mind went blank. "What list?"

His mouth kinked, but his dark brown eyes were uncomfortably grave. "For your white knight. Your ordinary prince. You want someone ordinary. A house with a white picket fence. Two-point-four children."

Oh, God. Had she told him all about that? "You remembered!"

He inclined his head. "Everything you've ever told me."

Help. "That's not a list. Not really."

At least, it wasn't the complete list. Above all else she wanted a man who loved her more than anything in the world. A man who would never stray and would be happy with her for all of his life. That man wasn't the distant, restless, easily charmed Rafiq ibn Selim Al Dhahara.

"It's just—"

"Just a way to make sure I know I don't qualify, hmm?" He lifted a brow inviting her to agree. "A way to keep me at a distance?"

Despite her sudden loss of appetite, Tiffany tore off a piece of bread and took a bite, chewed and swallowed.

At her sudden preoccupation, he smiled. But his flat eyes held no amusement; they were cool and watchful.

"It's not you…" Her voice trailed away.

"It's you. I know." He nodded. "But I find it interesting that you're prepared to admit you do not let any man close."

"I'm not admitting anything." Frustration filled Tiffany. "Look, it's nothing like that—you're misunderstanding me." But how to explain the fear that filled her? She didn't dare relax around him—it would be too easy to be charmed. Like all the other women he'd joked found him charming.

There, she'd admitted it. To herself. He charmed her. But she'd cut her tongue out before she let him in on the secret. "Surely you can understand that better than anyone in the world?"

"*I* can?"

She nodded. "You keep women at a distance, too."

He shook his head slowly. "Not to the same extent. I've had three very serious relationships. You were a virgin when we met."

"So you do believe me?" Tiffany couldn't believe her ears.

He shrugged. "You told me you're a virgin…I should give you the benefit of the doubt. It's not like you've made a habit of lying to me."

She wanted his unconditional trust.

He wasn't ready to give it.

Deflated, Tiffany backtracked to what they'd been discussing. "You might have had three serious relationships, but you didn't marry any of those women. Even though I'm prepared to stake money on it that they would've been more suitable for the position of your princess than I could ever be."

His hand closed over hers where it lay, clenched. "None of them matter now. You are my princess. And while you let me close in our marriage bed, there's always a distance between us. And I know why."

"My father has nothing to do with this!" she said quickly.

Didn't Rafiq realize he did exactly the same thing? As passionate as he was in bed, he was remote out of it. She was starting to hate the expressionless mask he wore to close the world—and her—out.

"I think your father has everything to do with it. I'm looking forward to meeting him."

"You're not likely to meet my father—we're not speaking." Determined to put a damper on his enthusiasm, she didn't notice his intense interest. "It's only my mother I intend to visit. She sounded lonely on the phone. And she's worried about our sudden marriage. When can we go?"

Two furrows creased his brow. "Should you be flying in your condition?"

"Pregnant women fly all the time."

"Not my wife."

His possessive growl caused her to blink.

Softening his tone, he added, "Why don't you invite your mother to come visit you here? My schedule is too full to travel right now—and later may be too close to the birth."

Not a no, but not a yes, either.

A twinge of apprehension shot through her. Was he refusing to let her leave? Did he intend to keep her hostage in Dhahara till the baby was born...or longer?

The more she considered that, the more apprehensive she grew.

"If you can't come, then I'll just have to go alone." She pushed her chair back. "Now I'm tired. I'm going to bed."

Alone, Rafiq retreated to the darkened courtyard at the heart of the house. During the day the back wall opened to a wide balcony that overlooked the desert on the edge of the city. But now the courtyard retained the warmth from the hot day in the paving around the pool.

Having shed his clothes, Rafiq sank into the silken water, and fought to clear his head. There was a sense of emptiness within him at Tiffany's departure. The night of pleasure he'd anticipated had been lost. Most frustratingly he couldn't identify how everything had gone so awry in such a short space of time. He'd forced himself not to follow her. She was pregnant. She needed rest. And he had no confidence in his ability to leave her alone.

This time he didn't think making love to her would have eased the tension that had flared between them.

Reaching the far end of the pool, he hoisted himself out and sat on the pool's edge.

Moonlight streaked the water's surface with silver stripes.

Rafiq swung his feet in circles and the silver light broke up as the water rippled, changing the pattern. Like Tiffany. Every time he thought he'd worked her out, Tiffany revealed another facet.

She was far more complex than he would ever have guessed that first night when he'd written her off as a woman after as much money as she could get in the shortest space of time—even if she had to use her body to get it.

He'd been wrong about that.

So wrong...

Feet still in the water, Rafiq propped his elbows on the stone behind him that was still warm from the day's heat and leaned back to stare into the arc of the desert night sky. With the moon so bright, only the most determined stars were visible. One star sparkled brighter than the rest in its group. His gaze homed in on it. It reminded him of his wife—the one who stood out, fascinating him.

In his heart he knew Tiffany had been an innocent— even though his brain was reluctant to accept it. Because that would mean that only he could be her baby's father— that his judgment of her had been criminally wrong.

He was rarely wrong.

And Rafiq was not yet ready to concede that he'd erred in his judgment. Certainly not aloud—as Tiffany had clearly wanted him to do earlier. When the sparkle had gone out of her eyes, he'd wished he had.

Sitting up, he reached for his towel.

Nor did he want to examine too closely why he was

reluctant to admit that he'd been wrong, why it shamed him to have judged her so harshly. He, Rafiq ibn Selim Al Dhahara, who had always been ruled by numbers and logic, had lost his head, and made a spectacular error.

And it all raised another interesting question…

One only Tiffany could answer. Rafiq paused in the act of toweling his hair. If she hadn't slept with him because of money, then why had she done it? Why had she let a stranger take something so precious?

She accused him of keeping women at a distance, of being the last man she'd ever wanted to marry. So why sleep with him when there'd been little hope of seeing him again?

She wanted an ordinary man, a house with a white picket fence, and a pigeon pair. That's what she'd harked back to every time—a fairy tale. He threw the towel to one side. They both knew he was as far from her ordinary prince as it was possible to get.

Water churned angrily as he pulled his legs out of the pool and rose to his full height.

The only answer that made any kind of convoluted sense gave him no comfort at all. Tiffany had gone for a man so far removed from everything she said she wanted because deep in her heart she had no intention of loving anyone. Ever. Not even the ordinary man he'd been so knotted up inside about.

She'd let him close only because he could never be her dream man.

He had to live with that. Or make her accept him as he was, royal prince, international banker, father of her child.

And most importantly, her husband.

Eleven

The Japanese restaurant Rafiq ushered Tiffany into the next day was decorated with deceptive simplicity. Low ceilings and white papered screens set in black lacquered frames gave the space intimacy, while gold-trimmed red wall banners and bamboo shoots in large ceramic pots emblazoned with gold pagodas added touches of luxury.

Rafiq was warmly welcomed by the elderly couple who owned the restaurant, whom he introduced to Tiffany as Mei and Taeko Nakamura.

To the Nakamuras he declared, "I have brought my wife to meet you."

Taeko bowed politely in her direction yet Tiffany suspected it was Mei's black-currant eyes that missed little.

"You said nothing of a wife when we saw you two weeks ago. I suppose this is the reason why you canceled your lunch last week. But shouldn't we at least have read about your wedding in the papers?"

"It will be announced in tomorrow's paper," Rafiq promised, grinning down at the little woman, not looking the least bit chastened.

That was more than Tiffany knew. She opened her mouth to interrupt him, but Mei was already saying, "So we know a secret." And her contemplative eyes settled on Tiffany's midline. Yet, much to Tiffany's relief, she didn't ask the obvious question and led them instead to a table in a corner secluded by screens.

What surprised Tiffany was the way Rafiq's austere features had lit up with pleasure at the sight of the elderly couple, making him appear quite different from the man who only ever presented an emotionless facade.

Nor did he need to order.

Taeko brought a platter of sashimi tuna and pink salmon, and it was quickly apparent that Rafiq was a frequent visitor, though Taeko produced a menu for Tiffany's inspection.

Mei dug out a cell phone and passed it to Rafiq to admire the latest photos of her granddaughter. He made appropriate noises and asked questions about the child whose name appeared to be Keiko, revealing an intimate familiarity with the family. Tiffany couldn't prevent a pang of sadness. If only he'd shown some of this easy joy when she'd shown him the scan images of their baby...

Instead he'd been horrified by the possibility that she might actually be pregnant with his child.

"The tuna is flown in daily," Rafiq told her as Taeko brought the beef teriyaki she'd ordered. "I never eat anything else here."

"I'll stick to beef—rather than raw fish," she said lightly, not wanting to make a point about her pregnancy.

"Delicious," she declared after the first mouthful of her meal.

As she tucked in, she couldn't help wondering whether Rafiq would one day show the same interest in their child as he'd shown for Keiko.

How would she feel about that interest? Rafiq appeared reluctant for her to leave the country to visit her mother. If he grew invested in their daughter, it was possible that he would take over the decision making for her child and leave her with no say.

It was something Tiffany had not considered in any depth before.

Foolish, perhaps.

Given his opinion about her in the past, she'd never anticipated that Rafiq would want to marry her. When he'd proposed, it had been so clear that his major preoccupation was waiting for the baby to be born so that he could wiggle off the hook of paternal responsibility. She'd never contemplated that he might actually want their daughter… or be eager for input into her upbringing.

Tiffany bit her lip.

She'd wanted her daughter to one day have the right to know her father. She'd been prepared to allow some kind of visitation schedule. But she'd never intended to put her daughter within Rafiq's total control.

Breathing deeply to control her rising panic, she tried to focus on what Mei was saying to Rafiq.

"How are Shafir and Megan? You have not brought them for a while."

"They spend every spare moment at Qasr Al-Ward." Rafiq rolled his eyes to the ceiling. "The price of love."

Relief seeped through Tiffany as she watched him joking with the Nakamuras.

Rafiq was no threat to her…or her daughter. He wasn't

a monster. He was only a man. A busy man, a banker of international repute. A desert prince. With a family who were loving.

Why would he want to take over the life of the daughter he'd disputed was his? Even when the tests proved he was the father, it was unlikely that he'd have the time—or the interest—to be a hands-on father.

As the reality of the situation sank in, she started to relax.

Taeko gave a sharp bark of laughter at something Rafiq said. He replied in Japanese, his eyes crinkling, and Mei swatted his arm with the white linen napkin she held.

Rafiq was laughing, his ebony eyes gleaming with mirth.

"You speak Japanese," Tiffany blurted out.

"He speaks German and a bit of Spanish, too." Mei gave her an odd look, and Tiffany felt herself coloring. What kind of wife lacked such basic knowledge about her husband?

She'd been so caught up in her own situation, her pregnancy, her parents' problems, their hasty marriage, she'd barely bothered to learn much about her new husband.

He smiled across the table at her, and her heart leaped at the understanding in his eyes. "What languages do you speak, Tiffany?"

"English and French."

Mei glanced at him in astonishment. "You don't know? Rafiq! What have you two been talking about?"

"Important things!" Rafiq's eyes held a wicked gleam, and Taeko roared with laughter.

Tiffany's flush deepened. Rafiq knew she spoke French. He'd covered up for her. She could've kissed him for making it clear that she wasn't the only one who had been neglectful.

"We will leave the two of you alone to learn more important things about each other." Mei took her husband by the arm and steered him away.

Once the incorrigible pair had departed, Tiffany asked, "How did you meet them?"

"They came to the bank one day needing a loan against the business." His eyes grew somber.

His expression sent a chill down Tiffany's spine. She waited, knowing there must be more to the story.

"Mei had grown so upset that security had to be called to calm her. I heard the commotion, and went to see what it was about. After all, I am ultimately responsible for the safety of everyone in the building."

"What was she upset about?"

"Their granddaughter needed a bone-marrow transplant. It was a procedure that was not available in Dhahara at the time. They needed to go to America. The business was already heavily in debt because of Keiko's medical bills."

"You helped them."

"I never said that."

He didn't need to. Tiffany studied him. "That was very generous of you."

"It wasn't only me—others helped, too. Children like Keiko are the reason I'm so involved in fundraising for the hospital." He glanced away from her intense gaze. "After lunch I am taking you shopping."

"Shopping?" The sudden transition to something so inconsequential confused her. "For Keiko?"

"No, for the press conference in the morning where our marriage will be formally announced and for tomorrow night's banquet. We agreed you needed clothes. You'll need something suitable to wear."

"Press conference?" The thought of the all-too-familiar paparazzi flashlights that dogged her parents' every step filled her with horror. "Can't we just release a statement?"

He shook his head. "This is part of my duty to the people of my country."

Just thinking about a press conference made her stomach sink. Thankfully, she hadn't been photographed for years—her parents had protected her from the relentless glare of Hollywood publicity. And living in Auckland had helped. Now that anonymity would prove a blessing. It was highly unlikely that the press would connect Tiffany, née Smith, wife of Sheikh Rafiq ibn Selim Al Dhahara, with Tiffany Smith, daughter of notorious film director Taylor Smith.

But Rafiq was newsworthy.

And Tiffany knew what would happen *if* her father glimpsed the photos. He would swoop, and try and take over running her life. She already had enough doubts about her own ability to run it, so she certainly didn't need her father wading into the fray.

Laying trembling fingers on his, she murmured, "Rafiq, what if the press report who my father is?"

He closed his free hand over the top of hers. "You need to reconcile with your father. Wait—" he said when she would've interrupted him. "Not for his sake but for your own peace of mind."

Tiffany stared at him rebelliously. "That's all very well, but what do we do if anyone asks today?"

He patted her hand. "Don't worry about it, I'll take care of everything. You worry about looking like a princess. Now let's go buy clothes."

Tiffany fought the urge to tell him she didn't need any clothes. Swiftly she reviewed the contents of her luggage. The long, slim gray skirt and white shirt she'd worn the day she'd arrived would not be glamorous enough for the media baying for photos of the royal sheikh's new bride. Her classic black trousers were not feminine enough and neither of the two maxi dresses she'd packed would be formal enough. And the white dress she'd worn the day she'd met his family was far too unsophisticated for the banquet in the evening—even if it had been created by a young designer whose dresses she loved. And the long dress with gold embroidery that Rafiq had produced for the wedding was far too elaborate for a morning press conference.

It galled her to admit Rafiq was one hundred percent right. None of the clothes she'd brought with her could be described as suitable.

Finally she said, "Okay, let's go shopping."

A discreet bronze wall plaque identified the high-end fashion house Rafiq took her to as Madame Fleur's. It would not have been out of place on Rodeo Drive. The interior of beech-and-chrome cabinetry with glass shelves and black marble floor tiles gave it a sophisticated edge. The black-and-silver labels on the meager range of garments on the racks held no prices. But the cut and quality of the clothes assured Tiffany the cost would be exorbitant.

Far more than she could afford to be indebted to Rafiq at present.

"Rafiq, I don't think—"

"Don't think. Madame and I will take care of everything, won't we?" From where he'd sunk onto a black velvet couch, Rafiq cast the charming smile that Tiffany was starting to recognize at the elegant middle-aged woman whose straight black skirt and black flounced shirt shrieked "French fashion." Predictably, Madame almost swooned and hurriedly agreed.

Tiffany's mouth tightened.

"I can choose my own clothes." It annoyed her that he thought she had no taste, no sense of style.

Swooping on a rack of satin and silks, she selected a dress that wasn't quite the shade of gold or honey or amber, but a mix of all three. At the sight of the cut, she hesitated. Only a woman with supreme self-confidence would wear a dress like this.

"I was thinking of something darker, more formal," Rafiq said, rising from his position on the couch. He picked a wooden hanger off a rack and held up a black satin dress with layered flounces from the hip down. "This is perfect."

"The black dress is beautiful, so elegant," Madame said after a rapid, assessing glance at Rafiq's face.

And very expensive.

Madame was determined to make a sale.

Tiffany suppressed a growl. Did everyone do exactly as he wanted?

"This one." Stubbornly Tiffany pointed to the dress she'd picked, her momentary hesitation forgotten.

"I don't think—" Rafiq paused. Passing the black dress into Madame's waiting arms, he smiled and came toward her with long, pantherish strides. Putting his hands on her shoulders he gazed down into her eyes, his own filled with velvety admiration. "You will look beautiful in whatever you wear. I want people to see you as I do—and black suits you."

"Okay, I'll try it first," she found herself saying. A hint of spine had her adding, "But I do prefer the other dress."

He brushed his lips against her forehead. "Thank you for trying on the black."

* * *

Rafiq knew he'd made the right choice. The dress Tiffany had chosen would be too garish. Black was sedate. Black befitted the wife of a prince of Dhahara.

When the curtains parted, she reappeared looking exactly as he'd expected. Elegant. Untouchable. *Suitable*.

"Excellent." He turned to Madame. "We'll take it."

Tiffany's expression grew rebellious. "Hang on. I don't often wear black."

He approached her and stroked her cheek. Lowering his voice so only she could hear, he murmured, "You were wearing black the night I met you."

She shuddered. "And what a mistake that was."

He couldn't deny that the cheap, shiny fabric of the too-tight dress with its short skirt and tight layers had been a little tacky. But she hadn't had the benefit of his—and Madame's—discerning taste. Although he had to admit that since that night Tiffany had worn surprisingly conservative clothes.

"That was Renate's dress—not mine." She spun away, and his fingers fell to his side. "Now I'll try the other dress."

Inside the dressing-room cubicle Tiffany found that she was trembling. Not with fear but frustration…and rising fury. She put her hands over her face. How could she have chickened out like that? Why hadn't she told Rafiq she wanted to select her own dress, something *she* liked? If he wanted to choose her clothes, he should wear them!

She gave a snort of angry laughter.

All her life she'd let people run her life—make choices and decisions for her. Her father. Her teachers. Imogen. Renate.

It wasn't happening anymore.

Her hands fell away from her face, and she stared at her image in the mirror with new eyes. She was pregnant. Soon she'd be a mother. She was in charge of her own life...and her daughter's. For a couple of minutes out there she'd wimped out when she'd agreed to try on the dress Rafiq had picked—and now he thought he'd won.

He almost had.

Yanking the zipper down, she slid the black dress over her hips and stepped out of it, then hung it on a padded wooden hanger.

The cubicle door opened and Madame swayed in, holding the dress that had caused all the trouble.

"Thank you." Tiffany gave the designer a demure smile as she took the dress. Her most charming smile—she could take a leaf out of Rafiq's book. She had no intention of allowing Rafiq to step in and take over—even if he was her husband. He might be rich. He might be a sheikh. He might be a royal prince. But she wasn't going to let him strip her of the independence and self-respect she'd managed to salvage in the past few months. If she did, she might as well go back home. And tell her father that he had won: she'd come home pregnant, penniless and needing someone else to take charge of her future.

This was no longer about a dress—whatever the darned color.

It was about her...her baby...and *their* future.

Rafiq had no faith in her taste. Based on Renate's dress, she couldn't really blame him. But none of the clothes he'd seen her in since had remotely resembled that awful outfit.

As the dress slithered over her head, Tiffany hoped wildly she had not miscalculated. Too late. She couldn't fold and let Rafiq choose what she was going to wear for the rest of their lives; she had to show him that unlike all the other women he knew, he couldn't simply get what he wanted from her with a charming smile or a fake caress.

Behind her Madame eased the zipper up. Tiffany heard her gasp.

"Très magnifique."

Tiffany spun around. The mirror showed a different woman to the black-clad one who had stood in front of it only minutes ago. This woman was young and vibrant…with a touch of vulnerability and an understated earthiness.

The dress was perfect.

It was her.

For one wild moment uncertainty engulfed her. Could she let Rafiq see her like this? The whole world? She hesitated. Then her spine firmed.

She wasn't ashamed of who she was.

Before she could have any further misgivings, she pushed the cubicle door open, and stepped proudly out, her head held high.

At the sight of her, Rafiq's first reaction was a blast of pure, primal possessive desire. Tiffany was his. All his. No man was going to wrest her from him. Ordinary or otherwise. His second thought was that the color could've been created especially for her. It was hard to see where skin ended and dress began—she'd struck lucky with her impulsive choice.

Instead of looking gaudy, the shade gave her skin a honey tone and turned her hair the burnished shade of bronze.

"What do you think?" Her eyes challenged his.

He gulped.

He didn't dare tell her what he was thinking.

That way lay…

Insanity.

Trying for cool, he said, "It suits you." But he ruined the effect by glancing down at the curves that the dress hugged. Rafiq started to sweat.

"Better than the black?" At the note in her voice his gaze jerked up.

She was taunting him.

No woman dared to taunt him.

Ever.

Even if she was his wife.

His eyes narrowed to slits. This time he took his time looking her over. When he finally reached her face, her lips were parted. He knew she'd be breathing in little gasps. Against his will, his body started to harden.

"Definitely better than the black." His voice came out in a hoarse croak. Without looking away he said to Madame, "We will take this dress."

Then he smiled slowly at Tiffany. No point wasting more time arguing over clothes, not when he was in such a hurry to get home and strip his wife of every item she was wearing.

So he said softly, "Now, which outfit did you have in mind for the press conference?"

Twelve

The front door of Rafiq's home clicked shut behind them.

"Come here, wife."

At Rafiq's growl, Tiffany glanced over her shoulder… and clashed with his hot gaze. He'd barely spoken in the Mercedes-Benz on the way home. And now he expected her to fall into his arms?

"Wait a moment—"

Before she could finish, he closed in on her. Despite her intention of resisting him, desire sparked into an inferno as his lips claimed hers. His hands gripped her shoulders. She swayed back until she came up against the coolness of the plastered wall. Rafiq's body was hard and solid against her curves, and his hands softened to caress the crest of her shoulders, then moved in tantalizing circles under the weight of her hair.

He kissed her until she could barely think.

To her astonishment Tiffany felt unaccountably safe

crushed against him. When he raised his head, it sank in that they were indulging in a passionate embrace, in broad daylight, in the lobby of his home with guards on the other side of the door and his staff in the house.

The impropriety of it made her flush. Pulling back from him, from the intensity of his touch, she yanked the neckline of her dress back into place. "Rafiq, what are you thinking? Your staff could walk in on us at any moment."

"I called and dismissed the house staff. And I secured the locks on the front door and set the security system when we came in." Smug satisfaction glowed good-humoredly in his eyes. "No one is going to interrupt us."

"You planned this!" she accused.

"No, it was a spontaneous reaction to the show you put on at Madame Fleur's store."

That damned dress was still causing trouble!

Before she could put the blame where it rightly belonged, he placed the tip of his index finger against her lips. "Enough talking, I want to kiss you."

Unable to resist a wicked temptation, Tiffany slid her tongue across the pad of his fingertip. He tasted of male and the tang of salt. She licked again. Slowly. Deliberately.

This time he took her mouth with a harsh groan.

The hunger rose more swiftly this time. His lips played with hers until Tiffany gave him a gentle nip. "Kiss me properly."

She hooked her hands behind his nape and pulled his mouth down square on hers. Her hunger silenced the wisecracks, she noted with satisfaction.

The next second the world spun around her. The floor tilted and the dark blue of the walls filled her vision. Tiffany clutched at the front of his shirt. "What are you doing?"

"Taking you somewhere where we can pursue this further." His lips hovered near her ear, the soft whisper of his breath sending delicious tremors though her. "Have you ever made love in a pool?"

"You know I haven't." Excitement quaked through her. "Have you?"

"Never."

"Then we'll have to teach each other how it's done."

They made it to the edge of the pool.

Rafiq deposited her on a lounging chair before straightening and wrenching off his tie. His shirt and trousers followed, landing in a heap on the mosaic tiles. In seconds he stood naked before her.

Breathing quickly, Tiffany eyed her husband with open admiration.

Muscled shoulders sloped to a lean waist, and his stomach was flat and taut. Her fingers itched to stroke the sleek skin.

He dropped down on his knees beside her, and he touched the length of her leg where the filmy maxi dress had fallen away with reverence. "Your skin is so soft," he whispered, "I can never have enough of you."

One day he would—it was how he was made, she knew. But that day wasn't here yet.

For now, he was all hers.

And she wasn't going to let him forget it.

He kissed the inside of her thighs, his fingers slipping under the lacy edge of her panties. Tiffany's breath caught as he slid the scraps of lace down her legs. She shifted restlessly. He was touching her again, making her sigh with delight, his fingers slick against her, arousing her to fever pitch.

She threw her head back and squeezed her eyes shut,

concentrating on the sensations that he aroused. The pleasure twisted higher…tighter.

"More," she moaned, her fingers reaching for him.

Her hand found his hardness, closed around him, felt him jerk.

Then he was on the lounger beside her, pulling her up against him, spoon-fashion, curled behind her. He drew her closer, hesitated, then surged inside her.

She gasped.

He started to move, slowly at first, then quicker. His mouth closed on her neck, nipping gently, causing her to shudder at the sensitive sensation. For a moment she hung suspended in space, a place between, where she was neither herself nor his, but something between. Then she shuddered and whirled into a world of pure pleasure.

When she'd finally come back to earth, she turned to face him, and hooked her arms around his neck. Staring deeply into his eyes, she whispered, "Oh, please say we can do that again?"

Yet the next morning nothing of the playful lover of the previous night remained.

Rafiq was all business.

Tiffany wore the apricot-colored suit she'd picked out that did amazing things for her skin. She knew she looked her best.

Rafiq had barely glanced at her. All he was intent on was lecturing her. If she hadn't known better, she might have thought he was nervous.

"Nothing will be said about how we met," he reminded her as the cavalcade that they were part of turned into the road in front of the palace, the king's main residence in Katar. "Do not get drawn into the work you were doing.

As far as the public is concerned we met through a mutual university friend."

When the doors of the limousine opened, she was ready for the popping clicks of the camera. Putting on her most gracious smile, she allowed Rafiq to help her out.

The press conference started innocuously enough—with Rafiq in total command.

The announcement of their marriage was made, causing a buzz of excitement. Rafiq indulged the journalists, fielding questions, posing with Tiffany for shots, until one journalist called to Rafiq to kiss her.

Her heart thudding, Tiffany turned, raising her face to his. One arm came around her shoulders, the other around her waist and then he paused, staring down at her.

A long moment passed, then all the clicks of cameras and flashing of lights faded. It was a taut moment, full of unspoken tension.

Tiffany waited, face uplifted for the kiss that never came.

Finally, amidst her confusion, he let her go, with a hoarse mutter in Arabic that she did not understand.

Then he took her by the hand and dragged her out of the auditorium, the gaggle of royal aides scurrying in their wake.

Tiffany hurried alongside Rafiq as he strode outside, his fingers tightly holding hers. One glance at his face revealed this was not a good time to ask what she desperately wanted to know.

What had gone wrong?

***

That mysterious moment this morning had wired Rafiq. Every time he looked at Tiffany, brushed her hand, a current of electricity blasted him.

Lust, he told himself as he strode the bank's hallways.

Triggered by that damned dress yesterday...and the cataclysmic passion that had followed.

He'd never intended to kiss Tiffany in front of the media this morning—his conservative father would never tolerate such a display. Yet by Allah he'd been tempted...

He'd almost done it.

It shocked him, how near he'd come to the edge.

Where was his control? His common sense?

His hunger, regardless of the cameras, had stunned him. Never before had his private emotions threatened to spill over into a public place.

Still brooding, he turned at the tap on his shoulder. He greeted his eldest brother.

"You are not with your wife," said Khalid.

"I left her in Aunt Lily's hands—gave her a chance to meet other women here tonight."

"Father wants to run a background check on her. He says we know nothing about her—he's worried you rushed into this marriage too impulsively."

"And Shafir didn't?"

"Ah, but that was different. Father was making sure Megan was being kept under surveillance, remember?"

Rafiq couldn't stop the jab of irritation. "It's a little late for that. I know everything I need to know about my wife. We announced our marriage to the world this morning. What does Father hope to achieve?"

Khalid gave him a wry grin. "Your happiness, probably.

I will tell him to forget the idea. He should be thankful that you are married—it's what he wanted after all."

"You will be next," warned Rafiq, his good humor restored.

Aunt Lily had introduced Tiffany to a circle of women as Rafiq's new wife, and Tiffany was aware of their curiosity. She'd warded off the more nosy questions with good grace, and cautiously answered the innocuous ones.

"Your dress…is it from Madame Fleur's?" asked one woman, openly admiring it.

Tiffany smiled demurely. Though a silk wrap was draped around her shoulders, she knew even without it the dress would be perfectly respectable. It was the cut and color that made it look so revealing, not the flesh it exposed. "Yes, it is."

"Not Rafiq's usual taste," said a beautiful woman who had joined the huddle. She was clad in a floor-length black sheath similar to the dress Rafiq had wanted Tiffany to wear tonight. "My name is Shenilla."

Tiffany smiled again. "Nice to meet you, Shenilla." Aware that everyone had fallen silent, she said, "Your dress is lovely."

Shenilla smoothed her hands over her hips, the movement oddly sinuous. "Rafiq chose it for me while we were still…together."

This time the lack of enthusiasm in the slanting eyes was overt.

Uh-oh. The woman in the newspaper photo. The daughter of the wealthy benefactor. And obviously one of Rafiq's former loves. "Oh."

Two of the group hurriedly excused themselves. Tiffany said something meaningless to the woman on the other side of Shenilla—then discovered it was Dr. Farouk, the doctor she and Rafiq had visited about DNA testing. A quick glance showed no sign of Rafiq.

Thrown to the lions—or in this case the lioness.

The image brought no amusement.

A waiter appeared and murmured something in the doctor's ear.

Dr. Farouk gave Tiffany an apologetic look. "Excuse me, duty calls—one of the older women is feeling breathless. I must check on her."

Left alone with Shenilla, Tiffany considered her next move.

She had to admit to a certain curiosity. This must surely be one of the women whom Rafiq had loved—then fallen out of love with. The woman was incredibly beautiful, with a regal elegance that made it obvious why Rafiq had picked her. Of course her father's wealth would've made her a good match, too. Tiffany was instantly conscious of the differences between them. This woman's hair was restrained in a smooth knot, her slanting eyes heavily outlined with kohl.

"Rafiq grows tired of all his women."

Tiffany started to object to being referred to as one of Rafiq's women, to point out she was his wife, but the sheen of moisture coating Shenilla's eyes stopped her.

"I was so certain I would be the one he married. Two years of my life I gave him, hoping every day that he would ask me to be his wife. Instead, not long before he went off to negotiate that hotel deal in Hong Kong, he invited me and my parents out to dinner and told us that our relationship was over." Shenilla swiped her fingertips under her bottom lashes. "I'm sorry, I must be embarrassing you."

Sympathy swept Tiffany, along with another sharp, piercing unidentified emotion. Rafiq had told her that it was the pressure from his family, from the woman and her family, that drove him to break off his relationships. Shenilla had just confirmed it.

"Not at all." She touched the other woman's arm. "You will find someone."

Shenilla sniffed, then nodded. "You are kind. I hope you will not suffer the same hurt, too."

Tiffany wanted to reassure her, tell her she'd been immunized against love a long time ago…but a painful tightness in the vicinity of her heart stopped her. Rafiq was nothing like her father.

"The only comfort I can offer you is that Rafiq is reputed to be faithful while the relationship lasts. A code with him. But there is always the knowledge that one day it will end." Shenilla gave a watery smile. "Although it must be different for you, as he loved you enough to marry you."

Before Tiffany could blurt out that he didn't love her, a hand settled on her waist.

"I see you have met Shenilla." There was a dangerous note in her husband's liquid voice.

Tiffany slid him a sideways glance, and caught the edge in his examination of his former lover.

"We're admiring each other's dresses." Then she remembered Rafiq had picked out the other woman's dress, and added hurriedly, "And comparing style notes. Shenilla was saying that black is one of her favorite colors."

Shenilla shot her a grateful look.

Rafiq pulled her closer to his side. Tiffany suppressed the fierce urge to move away. Couldn't he see the pain he was causing Shenilla? Was he so insensitive? No, he wasn't obtuse. He was doing it deliberately, warning the other woman that he would stand no threat to Tiffany.

She didn't know whether to hug him or scold him for his protectiveness. For the sake of Shenilla's pride, she decided to pretend she hadn't noticed, and continued chatting about the latest fall fashions, while Rafiq vibrated with tension beside her.

A mix of emotions rattled her. She wanted to shake him. She wanted to kiss him. What on earth was wrong with her?

He tilted his head sideways, and gave her a smile. Her heart rolled over.

Oh, no. Please. Anything but that.

Falling for Rafiq was the dumbest thing she could do. Already he'd been pressured by circumstance—and by a need to legitimize their child—to marry her. She'd unwittingly caught him in exactly the kind of trap that he'd avoided so assiduously all his life.

How could he feel anything but resentment toward her?

Thirteen

The intrusive ring of her cell phone woke Tiffany several mornings later.

Rolling over, she groped with one hand for the bedside table, and the ringing stopped.

With a groan she sat up. The first thing she realized was that the morning roller-coaster ride that her stomach had been on for weeks seemed to be over. The second was that the sound of running water meant Rafiq was in the shower in the adjoining bathroom. He hadn't yet gone to work. Checking the missed call, Tiffany recognized her mother's cell phone number. She hit Redial.

What could be wrong?

"Darling, where are you staying?" Her mother's voice sounded surprisingly clear.

Tiffany tried to collect her thoughts. "What do you mean?"

"We're here. In Dhahara."

"We?"

"Your father and I."

Tiffany stomach bottomed out, and she squeezed her eyes shut in horror.

"Where?"

"At the airport. We're about to catch a cab to come and see you."

No!

She heard the glass door click as Rafiq opened it. Any moment he'd be back in the bedroom. He knew she missed her mother; he'd said she needed to reconcile with her father. Had he arranged this?

"Mom—"

"There were photos of you all over the front page of the national newspaper that we were given in the airplane. But we couldn't understand a word of the story."

Darn it.

"Why is Dad with you?"

"Tiffany, I had to tell him about your marriage—I couldn't keep it from him. He's worried about you, darling. So we decided to come and see how you were."

Not worried so much as wanting to make sure she took his advice. Tiffany sighed.

"I wish you'd let me know you were going to tell him." She would've preferred to tell him herself.

"Your new husband is a hunk." Her mother sounded downright coy as she sidestepped Tiffany's comment. "You never mentioned that."

Straining her ears for sounds of the "hunk," Tiffany ignored the subtle rebuke. "Mom, why don't you go and book in at one of the city's hotels? I'll come see you in a couple of hours. Then maybe we can arrange to spend a couple of days together. Maybe we can go on an excursion into the desert."

"But we want to see you—"

The sound of footsteps made her say hurriedly, "I've got to go—I'll call you later."

Rafiq stood in the arch that separated the bedroom from the bathroom. "Who are you going to call later?" he asked, raising a dark eyebrow.

She hesitated. "My mom. Rafiq…"

He came swiftly across the room. "Problems?"

The concern in his eyes made her feel simply awful.

"Not really. Rafiq—" she bit her lip "—my mother is here, in Dhahara."

His expression brightened. "That's good. You wanted to visit your mother, now she can set her mind at rest."

She had to ask. "Did you call my mom and set this up?"

"No!" His brows jerked together. "I don't even have her contact details, come to think of it."

He had all the resources he needed to have found her if he'd wanted to. But she couldn't doubt him. She had to trust him at his word.

"Sorry." She chewed her lip again: "My father is here, too. I asked Mom why he came, and she says he's worried about me."

"Sounds like a father. Invite them to dinner." Rafiq walked into the closet. When he came out he was wearing trousers and shrugging on a business shirt. "They can stay here—there are plenty of bedchambers."

Oh, God. "You don't understand. My father always expects me to do what he wants."

He paused in the act of buttoning his shirt and raised that expressive eyebrow. "You're a married woman now."

"In his eyes I'll always be his little girl who can't run her own life."

"You're a grown woman. You're married, and soon you'll be having a baby. You'll be a parent yourself. He can only run your life if you let him."

"You're so right," she said in wonder. She'd never thought of herself in the context of being a mother in quite that way before—or how it affected her in relation to her father.

"You don't need to love him any less—he'll always be your father."

There was something so liberating in his words. She'd fought with her father so much over her freedom that they'd isolated each other. It didn't need to be that way. She would make her own choices, make it clear to her father this was her life, her choice, but that she would always love him.

If there was no battle, there could be no hostility. And her father had made his choices, too. He'd chosen Imogen over her mother. She needed to accept that. Her mother had already taken steps to deal with that reality. Now she had to do the same.

Maybe she could salvage something of their father-daughter relationship.

"Thank you, Rafiq." She raised her face to him and accepted his kiss.

"I must go, before you tempt me to collapse beside you and spend the day in bed."

"But, Rafiq—"

"Later." He picked up a dark suit jacket and slung it over his shoulder. As he reached the bedroom door he gave her a gentle smile. "Tell your parents I am looking forward to welcoming them to our home."

It was in that moment that Tiffany realized how much she truly loved him.

* * *

Several hours later Rafiq hurried toward the grand salon in his father's palace. He nodded to the aides. The double doors were flung open. Rafiq strode forward.

"Who was it you wanted to meet—"

The king was not alone. Rafiq stopped as he recognized the man seated in the brown leather armchair across from his father.

Sir Julian Carling rose to his feet and stretched out his hand. Rafiq shook it and raised an eyebrow in the king's direction.

"What is this about?"

His father looked wearier than Rafiq had ever seen.

"My son—" He broke off.

"What is it?"

But Rafiq had a sinking feeling that he knew. He gave the hotelier a narrow-eyed glare. Sir Julian looked away first.

"I have been concerned about this woman you have married."

"We have already discussed this, Father."

"I fear that I was too hasty—I should have pursued my first instinct and had her investigated."

"Father—"

The king held up a hand. "Stop. You will listen to what Sir Julian has told me. It is scandalous."

Blood roared in Rafiq's ears as he paced the length of the room. "I am not interested in what Sir Julian has to say about my wife."

The king shook his head sadly. "I fear she will not be your wife for much longer—you will have no choice but to divorce her."

Rafiq spun around. Sir Julian must have seen the rage

in his eyes because the millionaire almost overturned his chair in his haste to stand.

"Now look here, Rafiq—"

"Rafiq!" The lash of the king's tongue called him to order.

He drew a deep, shuddering breath.

"My son, you really do need to hear what Sir Julian is going to say."

"I know what he is going to say."

The king looked shocked. "You knew this woman is a prostitute?"

"That is a lie!"

This time Julian backed away five paces.

It was the king's turn to glance uncertainly at Sir Julian. "You are sure of these facts?"

"She has hoodwinked him," Sir Julian sputtered. "He found her in a flesh club in Hong Kong."

"What do you hope to get out of this?" Rafiq demanded, advancing on the hotelier.

"Your father has agreed that my daughter will make you a perfect wife. But Elizabeth will never agree to marrying a man who already has a wife. You will need to have your marriage annulled—fraud will be reason enough."

Rafiq's anger before was nothing to the rage that consumed him now.

"I do not want your daughter—I already have a wife. And no fraud has been committed that could merit annulling the marriage."

"She lied to you."

Rafiq shook his head. "Not so."

"But Elizabeth is coming to Dhahara to meet you."

"It is a waste of her time—and mine. Nor does it have anything to do with my wife."

"I invited her—" the King broke in "—Sir Julian and I have been talking."

Rafiq knew that tone of old. "What have you been negotiating?"

His father looked guilty. "You have always been a good, loyal son—"

"Oh, no!" Reminding him of his duty would not work this time. Rafiq shook his head.

"Your wife needs to be carefully chosen—"

"I know that—I've already done so."

"Ay, me. This is about sex."

Rafiq stared at his father. "It is not about sex—at least not in the way you mean. My wife is no Mata Hari, she hasn't the loose morals Julian suggests—" in fact the shoe was well and truly on the other foot "—but I admit I cannot keep my hands off her."

The admission freed something within him. Tiffany was important to him, more important than any woman he'd ever known. He wasn't letting her go. She was his.

"This concerns me. You are in the thrall of a woman who is manipulating you. I want you to divorce her before she causes a scandal we cannot fix." The king's face could've been carved from marble.

"Why? So I can marry Elizabeth Carling?"

King Selim's eyes grew shifty. "Sir Julian has offered to make a generous marriage settlement—"

"No! I am not divorcing Tiffany. Nor am I taking another wife. My wife was a virgin the first time I took her to my bed."

The astonishment on his father's face made Rafiq curl his hands into fists at his sides.

"The information I am revealing should be sacred to my wife and me, not dragged out in such a sordid situation."

"My son, if anything happens to me, to your brothers, you will sit on the throne."

The pressure was on. His father was pulling out the big guns. "And why should I marry a woman whose father has no idea of what it means to be faithful?" He didn't even spare Sir Julian a glance. "It was not I who broke marriage vows and slept with a backstreet whore that night in Hong Kong."

Sir Julian turned puce. "You can't talk to—"

"Oh, yes, I can," Rafiq cut in. "I don't want a wife who may have slept with a thousand men because of the example that has been set by her father." He could hear the pulse thudding in his head. "My heirs will be mine alone."

Then he realized what he had said. And the irony of it hit him full force. Tiffany never stopped worrying about the impact her father's notorious affairs would have on his family. He didn't care a fig for that. Yet, even more ironic was the fact that Tiffany was pregnant—and he'd disputed her baby's paternity. And now, in the heat of the accusations, he had defended her.

Because in his heart he knew she had been true. Everything about her was pure.

Her baby was his. He no longer required a DNA test to confirm the fact.

"My wife is pregnant."

A stunned silence followed his announcement. A flash of joy lit up his father's face. "Pregnant? My first grandchild! How I wish your mother was here." Shadows replaced the joy, and King Selim glanced surreptitiously at Sir Julian.

That look told Rafiq what he had feared—that the two of them had already gone far down the road of planning his wedding to Elizabeth Carling—and if Elizabeth hadn't objected to being the second wife, both men would no doubt have let Elizabeth occupy that place.

But Rafiq only wanted one wife, and he had chosen Tiffany.

Part of his choice had embraced a decision to believe in her—there was no reason not to. His place was not here arguing with Sir Julian. His first loyalty lay with his wife—she, and their unborn baby, were now his family.

Fourteen

Tiffany wished Rafiq would come home.

She'd put a call in to his office that her parents were already here. No doubt he would expect her to make the first move to reconcile with her father.

Yet, sitting on the balcony that overlooked a stretch of desert, her father was not making it any easier.

"If you'd stayed home, Tiffany, this mess would never have happened."

Tiffany suppressed the urge to roll her eyes and point out that he was the one who had walked out.

"Taylor, Tiffany is looking forward to having the baby." The stress around her mother's eyes as she ran interference caused Tiffany to wince.

At her father's look of disbelief she only said, "I am, actually."

"This is what you want?" Her father shook his head. "To

be stuck out here on the edge of the desert, where you don't even speak the language, with a man you barely know?"

"The desert is beautiful! Look at all the colors of the setting sun. I can learn the language—and I know enough about Rafiq to know that he's a decent man."

"Decent? What does that mean?"

Anger sparked. She remembered Rafiq's distaste that first night in Le Club when Sir Julian had pulled Renate onto his lap. She thought about how Shenilla had said he only ever dated one woman at a time. "That he would never betray me by running around with other women."

Her father's face changed.

"Oh, come look at this, Taylor, isn't it interesting?"

Her father allowed himself to be distracted by her mother's peacemaking attempts and Tiffany drew an unsteady breath as they both disappeared into the house. How could she have fallen back into this confrontational relationship with her father? Hadn't Rafiq told her he could only run her life if she let him? It was time to move on.

Suddenly she wished Rafiq was beside her. He understood her—better than anyone ever had.

A wave of gratitude swept her. She'd been fortunate to find a man who suited her perfectly—yet she was far from an ideal wife. Guilt ate at her. Given any choice, Rafiq would never have married her.

She was just as guilty of boxing him into a corner as all the women he'd so smartly evaded. And one day he was going to bitterly resent her for taking away his freedom.

"Looks like your husband will be able to keep you in a style that will be easy to get accustomed to. That's quite a display." Her father's return from where he'd been inspecting an illuminated manuscript in a glass case cut into her thoughts. "But I want to see that I can leave you in this man's care."

Tiffany refrained from telling her father that Rafiq had already saved her from more scrapes than her father ever had. That she loved him. That she wanted to stay by his side for every day of her life. That the last thing her husband needed was an overzealous parent—he'd had enough of those.

The sound of voices led Rafiq to where his wife and her visitors were sitting on the balcony overlooking the desert. He loved this spot in the evenings, when the heat subsided and the desert came to life. He paused on the threshold, drinking in the sight of Tiffany.

She was perched on one of the thickly padded chairs, the center point of the family group. If he hadn't known she was pregnant, the healthy glow of her skin and the sheen of her hair would've given it away. An older woman, who had to be Linda, with salt-and-pepper hair and a kindly face sat beside her, while a thin, bearded man full of nervous energy dominated the conversation.

Rafiq strode forward. All three of them looked up.

A shadow passed over Tiffany's face, then she leaped up. "Rafiq, you're here."

She clung to him, and there was a touch of desperation in the kiss she gave him.

"What's the matter?" he asked.

She shook her head, then let go of him.

Uneasy, he waited.

She introduced her parents with a bright smile, tension evident in every line of her body. Rafiq frowned, trying to fathom what was worrying her. At first he thought her parents might be causing her strain, but he couldn't see any evidence of that. Linda appeared to be doing her best to do everything to ease the situation, while Tiffany's father clearly thought of no one other than himself.

Tiffany caught his eye. "I'd like to talk to you, Rafiq."

Her somber expression caused a dart of concern.

After excusing himself from the company, he followed her down the stairs, along the walkway lined with palms, and onto the edge of the desert beyond. "What's wrong? Are you in pain? Is it the baby?"

The helplessness that he experienced was a first. Rafiq discovered he didn't like it at all.

She shook her head. "It's nothing like that."

But she kept knotting and unknotting her fingers. The gesture didn't reassure Rafiq. "Then what is it?" he demanded. "What's the matter?"

"I've trapped you into this marriage."

His heart stood still. "What?"

"You would never have married me if I hadn't been pregnant. It's just like all those other women who tried to corner you into marriage—except this time there was a baby. You couldn't get out of it. One day you're going to resent me—even the child."

An air of dejection surrounded her.

"That's not just any child. That's my daughter you're talking about."

Tiffany hesitated, then blurted out, "You said 'my daughter.' Do you mean that? Do you believe it? Or are you just saying it to make me feel better?"

"Oh, I mean it."

"And what about being trapped?"

"I'm not trapped."

Tiffany started to shake. "I thought…" She broke off.

"What did you think?"

"I thought that you were going to hate me. That you'd one day feel that I'd tricked you."

"Oh, Tiffany. I was always going to marry you."

"To legitimize the baby—out of duty."

"Because I wanted you. Because I couldn't keep my hands off you." He stepped up beside her and wrapped his arms around her, then rested his chin on her shoulder. "I don't care what your father does in his life, I want you. And nothing, not your father, not my father, is going to keep me from having you."

From her silence he knew that she required some mental adjustment.

So he added for good measure, "If you look behind us, you'll see that your father has just taken your mother's hand. His behavior is her problem—unless they decide to get divorced."

"Do you think she'd take him back? He's a serial adulterer.... He needs to grow up."

"So I've gathered."

"Did I tell you that?"

"You didn't need to." He stroked her hair. "But don't make the mistake of confusing me with your father."

"Oh, I won't," she assured him. "You're nothing like him. My mother is in for a lot more heartache if she takes him back."

"He may have missed her. He may want to change his ways. But don't think his behavior is your responsibility."

"I thought you would think—"

"You think entirely too much!"

She didn't smile. "So who my father is won't make you think any less of me?"

He shook his head. "Just like who your father is won't make me think any more of you, either." Then he started to laugh. "I'm not being totally consistent."

"What do you mean?"

"I told Julian that I had no intention of ever marrying

his daughter because I couldn't be sure she hadn't slept around as much as he has."

She pulled out of his arms, and swiveled to face him. The waning sunlight turned the tips of her lashes to gold. "Julian? You mean Sir Julian Carling?"

He nodded.

"But you can't marry her, you're married to me."

"You noticed," he said smugly.

"Of course I noticed!"

"Good."

He leaned forward and kissed her. He took his time, and did it thoroughly, not caring that her parents might be watching.

When he'd finished, she returned to the subject like a dog with a bone. "Why was Sir Julian talking to you about marrying his daughter?"

"He wasn't talking to me about it. He was discussing it with my father," he said then laughed as she placed her hands on her hips and glared at him. "They had decided I should divorce you and marry Elizabeth Carling."

"Divorce me?" Tiffany's bravado disappeared like a deflated balloon. She looked stunned, then apprehensive.

"Don't worry. I told them that I had no intention of divorcing you—that you were pregnant with my baby. And, yes, I believe that. Just as I believe that you were a virgin that first night we made love." He also knew that this woman would never bore him. She was his forever. "Now it's my turn to make a confession."

"What is it?"

He handed her a piece of paper. "I never did intend to stay married to you after we had the tests done."

"You intended to cut and run if the baby wasn't yours?"

He nodded. "And if it was mine I intended to keep the baby here, divorce you and send you home."

"What an utterly diabolical plot!"

"I know." He pointed to the paper she held. "That contract you're holding will ensure that you will feel safe, that I will never do something like that. You only need to sign it."

She glanced at it, then flung her arms around him. "You know I told myself I was looking for someone ordinary."

"The man that you're looking for is going to be very hard to find."

"No." She released him and shook her head. "I've decided he isn't what I want. I want someone special. Someone like you. No one ordinary would ever have confessed what you did—or given me that kind of assurance in writing. I love you. That's very hard for me to say. I'm beginning to think I never intended to love anyone. But I love you because you are incredibly special."

His heart stopped at her confession. "I love you, too. You are the most important person in my whole world. You fill my world," he whispered, drawing her back into his arms. "There is only you. There will only ever be you."

* * * * *

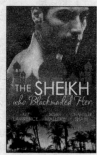